The Cross Maker

THE CROSS MAKER: BOOK 1

The Cross Maker

JACK A. TAYLOR

THE CROSS MAKER: BOOK 1
Copyright © 2019 by Jack A. Taylor

All rights reserved. Neither this publication nor any part of this publication may be reproduced or transmitted in any form or by any means, electronic or mechanical, including photocopying, recording or any information storage and retrieval system, without permission in writing from the author.

This is a work of fiction. Names, characters, places and incidents either are the product of the author's imagination or are used fictitiously, and any resemblance to actual persons, living or dead, businesses, companies, events, or locales is entirely coincidental.

ISBN: 978-1-4866-1856-9

Word Alive Press
119 De Baets Street Winnipeg, MB R2J 3R9
www.wordalivepress.ca

Cataloguing in Publication information can be obtained from Library and Archives Canada.

This book is dedicated to the generations of dreamers, starting with Jordan, Jeremiah, John, Alyssa, Anderson, Natalie, Hannah, Micah, Kylie, and Eliana.

Acknowledgements	ix
Chapter One: *Caesarea, Palestine 28 A.D.*	1
Chapter Two	12
Chapter Three	18
Chapter Four: *Caesarea to Sepphoris, Palestine 28 A.D.*	29
Chapter Five: *Nazareth, Palestine A.D. 28*	42
Chapter Six: *Sepphoris, Galilee, A.D. 29*	53
Chapter Seven: *Galilee 29 A.D.*	65
Chapter Eight: *Capernaum, Galilee 29 A.D.*	75
Chapter Nine	84
Chapter Ten: *Sepphoris, Galilee 29 A.D.*	91
Chapter Eleven: *Cana, Galilee 29 A.D.*	103
Chapter Twelve: *Nazareth, Galilee 29 A.D.*	111
Chapter Thirteen: *Galilee 29 A.D.*	118
Chapter Fourteen: *Sepphoris, Galilee 29 A.D.*	127
Chapter Fifteen	135
Chapter Sixteen: *Road to Jerusalem, Galilee 29 A.D.*	141
Chapter Seventeen: *Jericho, Palestine 29 A.D.*	148
Chapter Eighteen: *Jerusalem, Palestine 29 A.D.*	154
Chapter Nineteen: *Jerusalem, Palestine 29 A.D.*	164
Chapter Twenty: *Jerusalem, Palestine 30 A.D.*	177
Chapter Twenty-One: *Jerusalem, 30 A.D., Passover Week, Monday*	188
Chapter Twenty-Two: *Jerusalem, 30 A.D., Passover Week, Thursday*	196
Chapter Twenty-Three: *Jerusalem, 30 A.D., Passover Week, Friday*	208
Chapter Twenty-Four: *Jerusalem to Jericho, Palestine 30 A.D.*	217
Chapter Twenty-Five: *Jericho to Galilee, 30 A.D.*	223
Other Books In This Series	233
Other Books by Jack A. Taylor	235

Acknowledgements

Over the years, my greatest cheerleader has been my wife, Gayle. She sacrifices the hours that let me sit and create the characters that grow in my mind while the rest of my family members and friends wait patiently for the process to yield something they can support. Gayle always listens when I need clarity.

Bev Greenwood was leading the writer's workshop where the idea of *The Cross Maker* first surfaced. She encouraged it into life and told me clearly when I could do more. Several editors, including Bev Schellenberg, Cynthia Roy Dawn, and Evan Braun, have had their input on the manuscript.

Members of Faith Fellowship continue to be a source of encouragement and strength in my growth as a writer and a follower of Jesus. I thank God for making his own story so clear and easy to share.

Chapter One

Caesarea, Palestine 28 A.D.

The one man Caleb ben Samson wanted to see on his cross was Barabbas. For today, it looked like he might have to settle for a substitute.

The burning rays of the Mediterranean sun stretched the shadows from the masts of the Roman warships across the wharfs and warehouses of the seaport of Caesarea. Gulls drifted lazily under the cloudless sky. The aging dock and dilapidated buildings on the south side of the bay looked ready to collapse, and listless sailors tucked themselves into shelters hoping for a sea breeze to cool their brows. Offshore, the masts of international freighters listed in their mooring, their keels touching the seafloor.

Standing between the lengthening shadows, Caleb ran his calloused hand across a misshapen cross resting against a crate of olives. A steady stream of sweat had glued the back of his tunic to his skin.

Where the cross had come from was a mystery, but a blue tassel and dried apricot rested atop the crossbeam, catching his attention. The blue tassels were the identifying symbol of the zealots, a radical Jewish sect determined to drive the Romans out of Palestine. Their extremist wing included the Sicarii, a group who swore to cut the throats of any Jew found helping the Romans.

Barabbas was their leader—and the apricot was his calling card. Caleb's father had been one of his first victims.

Caleb reached for the tassel just as a tremor underfoot made him pivot. A pyramid of logs, once piled next to the warehouse, tumbled toward him in a thunderous roar. He snatched the tassel and apricot from the crossbeam, then hurdled over the first log and sprang toward the safety of a small alcove in the side of the warehouse, just wide enough to shelter him. Several of the logs hurtled off the edge of the dock.

In the aftermath, the cross lay broken on the ground.

Caleb had no doubt who was responsible for this—both the cross and the falling logs. It had to be Barabbas's henchmen. If only he could get Barabbas, the leader of the zealots, on a proper cross. He and Barabbas had played cat-and-mouse with each other throughout Palestine.

This had been a close call.

The closest call had occurred north of here, near the base of Mount Hermon. The snow-capped mountain, the highest in Palestine and the source of the Jordan River, had long been a sacred place of worship for the pagans. Caleb knew it as the fabled home of the giants who Joshua had defeated after crossing into the Promised Land.

After tracking Barabbas there, Caleb had stepped into a clever snare and ended up hanging upside-down from a tree branch. Fortunately, a young hunter had chanced upon him and cut him down. Fortunately for Caleb, anyway; Barabbas had arrived soon after and the young hunter had paid for his good deed with his life.

Caleb had then found himself a fugitive, taking temporary refuge in cities like Ephesus and Alexandria. And Barabbas had continued his murderous quests, slashing the throats of many fellow carpenters Caleb knew. It was clear now that there was no place to hide from this vigilante. It was kill or be killed.

Nothing could have focused Caleb more on his desire for revenge, not even a thousand vultures shredding the bloated corpses of a Roman legion.

You are not a ghost, Barabbas, he fumed. *My father will be avenged.*

Through squinted eyes, Caleb examined the broken cross's distorted crosscut. Then he looked down at the apricot still clutched in his hand—a calling card from Barabbas. And that blue tassel? A sign of the zealots.

The same two markers had been left at the scene of his father's murder.

Twice he had avoided Barabbas's ambushes, and now he had escaped a third time. The jagged rocks rising through the pounding surf below could easily have been Caleb's destiny if the logs had swept over him.

A crowd of curious onlookers had gathered around the pile of scattered posts, and Caleb watched them carefully. Any one of the bearded fishermen, dockworkers, or layabouts could have been the henchman responsible for the trap.

Several of the men had already begun to repile the posts. None of them even looked in his direction. Nothing seemed amiss.

Behind the dilapidated shanties jockeying for space along the wharf rose the taller public buildings of the town's new administrators. The north side of the harbor had been renovated, and its towering lighthouse guided in larger vessels. The Temple of Augustus stood at the heart of the complex, adjacent to the new palace. Even these majestic structures were nothing compared to those at the Alexandrian harbor which had drawn his awe. That city's great lighthouse of Pharos, with its temple and library, was considered one of the seven wonders of the world.

King Herod's architectural feats in Caesarea also paled next to the magnificent monuments of Ephesus: the Temple of Diana, the great agora markets, the gymnasiums and public baths, the palatial homes of the rich, and the theatres and libraries and arenas… Ephesus was a place of infinite learning and pleasure.

Caleb's three-month stay in Ephesus had been overwhelming.

Now Caesarea. How had Barabbas known he was here?

In the distance, he noticed that a Roman aqueduct neared completion. Closer at hand, a few hundred yards away, a fisherman was gutting his catch under a tarp. Three sailors were playing knucklebones under that same shade, exchanging ribald jokes.

A cacophony of sounds washed over Caleb: the barking of dogs, the laughter of sailors, and women hawking incense and their services as temple prostitutes. People spoke dozens of languages, bargaining for food, drink, and pleasure. Wild music erupted from different taverns and Caleb's stomach rumbled in hunger.

None of these noises captured his attention long; it was the sounds of bygone memories that plagued him. The endless weeping of his leprous mother, the berating scorn of a drunken father, the unending laugh of a murderous zealot… and silence from the heavens as he'd pleaded for the Almighty to help him exact revenge.

He looked around impatiently. Where was Barabbas, that God-forsaken alley rat?

A rumpled burlap tarp, sheltered by a dozen barrels of salted tilapia, shifted nearby as if touched by a breeze. It would be the perfect place for his attackers to hide. Before he could act, a sparrow took flight from a perch next to him. Caleb's jaw tightened and his shoulder muscles knotted.

The more encounters Caleb had with Barabbas, the more he wished he had just stayed in his hometown of Nazareth.

A dozen strides to his right, a small horsewhip hung from the ancient Phoenician relic known as Straton's Tower, and Caleb snatched it up. The whip was the sort used by herders to move livestock on and off the ships.

Caleb backed away from the tower and returned to the shaded entry of the warehouse. He grasped the handle of his carpenter's knife, twisting it. He knew Barabbas favored a razor-edged dagger; with only his own small blade in hand Caleb needed whatever other weapon he could find.

A giant of a Persian suddenly rounded the corner of the building and stopped, his ankles rattling with chains. His firm but protruding belly hung over his loincloth. His thick jowls jiggled as he rotated his neck. The man's piercing dark eyes missed nothing. He carried a crate of bananas on one shoulder and a crate of coconuts on the other. Rivulets of sweat streamed from his bald head and down his neck.

"Why can't they send me an apprentice who cares?" Caleb asked him, nodding toward the broken crossbeam still lying on the wharf.

"Master, I warned you," the Persian said. "Chasin' the devil in this hell is not like catchin' fish. Using yourself as bait is not my kind of game. All that boy cares about is getting his dagger into your neck. And ol' Barabbas is going to get the rest of your family before he's done."

"Nabonidus, you've served me well, but you talk endlessly like a child. Finish this load and I'll free you. Now, run. I have work to do."

Caleb turned his back on the slave and focused again on the misshapen cross. What Nabonidus had said was accurate—no one near him was safe. Barabbas was a shifting shadow, sometimes ahead and sometimes behind.

Bile rose at the back of his throat. He sensed that Barabbas was close, that it was Caleb's turn to make a move. He would use their own misshapen cross as a weapon against them.

He took his anger out on the knee-high section of broken cross, grasping the rough beam with his calloused hands. He tugged at the base, wedged into a gap in the wharf, and nothing happened. For a moment, he considered getting Nabonidus to do it, but his pride was strong. Instead he set his foot against the warehouse wall and pulled harder. A sliver pushed deep into his palm, and his fingers sprang open as if releasing a hot coal. A guttural howl seethed in his throat.

He snatched at the sliver with his teeth, but he only succeeded in breaking off the splinter at the surface of his skin. Snatching his carpenter's knife, he cut around the splinter and drew blood. He freed most of the offending wood and eased it out.

Still in pain, Caleb turned his attention back to the remnants of the broken cross lying among the timbers. He set the cross on the wharf, its notched side down, and used his sandaled feet to stomp the beams apart. All the while he sucked at his wound, the bitter saltiness of iron puncturing his senses. The taste and smell of blood always brought to mind a gallery of terrifying faces—faces frozen to bodies fastened to crosses he had built. Young faces and old faces. Angry, defiant faces. Fearful faces. No matter how far he ran, those faces chased him.

One face was still missing.

He shook his head to clear the images and worked again to staunch the bleeding. Caleb looked for something to cover his wound, but there wasn't a scrap of material in sight.

The comforting aroma of fresh-cut timber pulled him into the warehouse, where Nabonidus had gone. Inside, Caleb pried off the top of a crate and he beheld a sunset of colors nestled within, beautiful fabric designed to enslave the eyes. The cool, smooth material felt like it would melt away under his touch. It was the most delicate thing he had ever handled.

Carefully, he chose a foot-long section of crimson cloth and ripped it. Binding his wound tightly with the strip of cloth, he replaced the rest back in the crate. He then pounded the lid back in place and stepped back outside the building.

The fishermen on the dock still seemed preoccupied with their tasks, and a few wharf rats sat chatting on one of the unpiled logs. A wealthy businessman leaned out of the litter he was riding in and yelled at the four Ethiopian slaves who carried him.

No one looked in Caleb's direction for more than a moment.

Caleb shouldered the horizontal beam of the broken cross and set out to find the zealots who he assumed had helped Barabbas. He knew the neighborhood well. Near the butcher's shop, a row of buttercups drooped in the shadows. Red anemones arched over with their petals resting facedown on the parched soil.

He turned up the lane of the weavers, which was home to hundreds of zealot sympathizers.

Rats always find their gutter, he thought. *Is it foolish to come here alone?*

As he moved into the lane, he realized that he was perspiring more than usual—and it was more than the humidity in the air. The stares of loiterers told him something else was afoot.

Behind him, a trio of boys stopped their play and began to follow Caleb. He'd seen their style of walk before. They stepped deliberately, prancing on their toes like nervous horses.

Sure enough, among the fringed tassels at the bottom of the boys' vests were clear blue cords. These were zealots.

As one of the three boys bent to retrieve something hidden in the folds of his vest, Caleb saw the unmistakable glint of steel.

Up ahead, a blind man with a snowy mane pasted to a skull with sunken cheeks sat with his hand out, begging for alms. The raggedy blanket covering the beggar would have been more suitable for wrapping fish. His long, dangling beard waggling as he called out in a shrill voice. Caleb only offered him a grunt in return.

Caleb noticed the old man's walking stick tucked in close to his side, right beside a papyrus scroll. It was a strange sign. A blind man with a scroll? Was this friend or foe? Things were not as they appeared.

Caleb stopped and looked toward the shadowed archway ahead. He sensed a presence there without seeing it, almost as if a feather had brushed against his neck. The alley was narrow and there was no retreat; the three zealots now carrying their daggers openly ensured that.

He tamed his breathing, slowed his pulse, and atuned his vision. He moved his hand away from the knife hidden in his carpenter's belt. The crossbeam shifted slightly on his shoulder, and he intentionally stumbled, as though about to fall under his burden.

As he regained his balance, he casually checked the position of his pursuers. The zealots were forty strides behind, closing ranks and moving fast.

"Caleb, carpenter of Nazareth, you betray us with your blood," one of them called.

The challenge sounded a little too shrill. Perhaps quavering. A warrior without experience. A boy trying to show bravery he didn't have.

Two strides short of the archway, Caleb swung the beam of lumber as if wielding an axe. He aimed chest-high and connected with the ambusher he knew was hidden in shadow. The dagger dropped, as did the unsuccessful attacker. Caleb hit him again with the beam.

The tunic of the fallen boy, as well as his shoulder-length hair, looked familiar. A smudge of blood on his cheeks didn't offer much camouflage. Caleb had seen him just the day before, begging to be his apprentice. He'd accepted the offer, but only after enduring considerable begging from the lad.

"Remember whose apprentice you are next time Barabbas comes calling," Caleb murmured, his feet fixed to the cobblestones.

Ignoring the dagger on the ground, Caleb instead clenched the beam. The weapon had worked against one zealot, and it could work again. As he shifted the beam, another sliver dug deep into his skin. The fiery pain driving into his palm would have to wait.

In his peripheral vision, he watched the three zealots keep coming. Caleb pivoted to face them. They weren't even old enough to grow facial hair. Their legs were thin and their walk had changed to an uncertain shuffle. They seemed to be in a trance they couldn't escape, like little boys who had dared each other to enter a haunted house.

Only the one who had taunted him earlier seemed to register surprise when Caleb screamed and took a run at them. Their raised daggers didn't stop the crossbeam from crashing into their knees and bowling them over. Caleb smashed their skulls onto the cobblestones before they had a chance to recover.

The life went out of their eyes, just like so many others he had seen hanging on his crosses. It was usually a merciful grace before the birds arrived.

A rag filled with dried apricots lay on the ground near one of the attackers.

Caleb smiled. "I know you're nearby," he called out, wondering if Barabbas himself was within earshot.

He snatched the rag and ate his fill.

That night, after scouting the market, Caleb sat with a group of Grecian traders while a fire held off the cool Mediterranean breezes. A dozen clay lamps spouted illumination from strategically placed porticoes on three of the four walls. Only one wall remained cloaked in darkness. A small courtyard fountain featuring a statue of Apollo gurgled near the porch entrance. The smell of roasted mutton was a refreshing change from fish, and the wine was diluted but satisfying.

The weary men cheered him on as he entertained them with his flute and then embellished upon his conquest earlier in the day. Caleb relished the attention. He unwrapped the soft stretch of cloth and showed the wounds on his hands as evidence.

"Silk!" announced one of the merchants. "Chinese silk. Smuggled past Armenia. Plenty of bribes for this rag."

"By the gods, Ca–leeb," shouted a stout, bearded drunkard named Hermes. "You know the harbor district is nothing but alleys and streets filled with smugglers, thieves, swindlers, and zealots. You're just begging to get your throat slit."

"It's Barabbas or me," Caleb said. "Besides, I know that half these swindlers and smugglers are your brothers, Hermes. Probably half the zealots, too. Tell me, where do you hide him?"

"Ca–leeb. You know I hide him with your sister. I would hide him with your mother if I knew where she was."

"She's gone to a place Barabbas could never dream of."

"Good. Then may Barabbas warm your sister enough to give you seven nephews to plague each day of the week. Come home with me. My daughter Portius begs me every night to bring you for her. Why waste your good looks on lesser women?"

The flames fluttered as a newcomer stepped out of the shadows.

"So you've switched from carpenter to bounty hunter, have you?" asked the man, clearly a Roman. The firelight revealed his red cloak over a bronze breastplate. A white plumed Imperial helmet cradled his hip, showing his importance. His off-duty stance was casual. No greaves or armor protected his legs, and his shoulder belt was empty. The short sword was visible on his waist belt.

Caleb recognized his voice, even though shadows still hid the Roman's face. The warmth inside him, brought on by fire and wine, evaporated.

"What brings out the mighty Sestus on a night like this?" Caleb asked. "Has the great Pontius Pilate run out of dancing girls and wine for his centurion?"

Sestus stepped into the light. "Unlike you, I still have the strength for many women in my life. I am now a legate, commanding a whole legion. Tonight I came to breathe in the sea breeze, but this place hardly compares to Alexandria, Athens, Gaul, or even Sepphoris."

The soldier withdrew his short sword and waved it at the others around the fire. They scrambled into the shadows.

"Take your lamps!" Sestus ordered, and within moments seven lamps had disappeared.

Caleb shifted to a more comfortable stool. "So you remember me?"

"Oh yes, I remember. The carpenter from Nazareth. The one I trained to build crosses. The one who disappeared into the night. The one who let a woman get the better of him."

Sestus rested his foot on the back of a marble lion crouching in the center of the courtyard. Shadows flickered across his clean-shaven face and close-cropped hair.

"You promised me peace through the power of the cross," Caleb said. "All I saw was tragedy becoming as common as dust."

He stroked his beard and then pulled at his shoulder-length hair. He poked at the fire with the toe of his sandal, nudging a small log into the flame.

"And you promised me a thousand crosses," Sestus said. "Or did you forget about that when you set off to exact your own revenge?"

Caleb picked up a stick and stirred the embers. "I only want peace."

"And are the four zealots you crushed today signs of this peace? Are you any closer to avenging your father's death as you search for Barabbas?" Sestus picked up an abandoned clay jug and greedily swallowed the contents.

"Your armies have had no more success than I have. What brings you back to this pit of hell?" Caleb felt the breeze off the water, like a dark spirit passing. He shivered. "I thought you were travelling from Damascus to Rome."

Sestus hurled the clay mug against a wall, his aim extinguishing a lamp. Its shattered pieces exploded around the darkened room.

"Apparently, service is no longer enough," Sestus remarked. "The senators follow bloodlines, connections, bribes, and advocates. They sit on their pillows sucking hummingbird tongues, goose livers, and sows' udders, waiting for some gift that will promote their own fortune."

"So why are you here?"

Sestus turned his head and surveyed the courtyard. He spoke through gritted teeth. "My success depends on bringing peace to two more cities—Sepphoris and Jerusalem. I only know of one solution strong enough to eliminate these zealots and messiahs. The power of the cross. I need a cross maker I can trust."

Caleb swiveled on the stool so his back was to Sestus. A moment later, he turned back again. "I have no interest in building crosses for zealots who show their patriotism by smashing your statues and disrupting your drunken orgies."

"We will leave that sort of rabble to others." Sestus took his foot off the lion and backed toward a table with food on it. "They are like buzzing bees, annoying us. We will hunt the Sicarii, the dagger men who killed your father." Sestus dipped his forefinger into a bowl of honey, licked it, then set his hand on the hilt of his sword. "We will clear the country of bandits who steal the life from your tradesmen. We will chase the warriors who shoot their arrows into the heart of Rome."

"Why me?" Caleb stood and dabbled his hand in the waist-high fountain. "Apart from the crosses you think I owe you."

"I've been assigned to be the new legate for the governor in Judea and Galilee. A new Messiah has emerged there and Herod Antipas and Pilate are wary." Sestus let go of his sword and dipped his finger into the honey bowl again. "I only heard today that this latest Messiah was also a carpenter in Nazareth. A friend of yours, I believe. You called him Yeshi."

Sestus turned from the table and stepped closer, positioning himself almost nose to nose with Caleb. His eyes stared into Caleb's, and he refused to blink.

Caleb felt the hairs on his neck stand up. "I see you still have a memory for details. I haven't been in contact with Yeshi for years." Caleb stepped back, turned away, and sank onto his stool. "He has gone his way and I have gone mine."

"But you know him. His family. You can reach him if necessary." Sestus sat on a log next to Caleb. "You can persuade him to keep our crosses to a minimum."

Caleb pulled back. "What are you hearing now?"

Sestus's eyes were hidden by shadows. His body, however, leaned forward, eager for news. "This friend of yours is gathering followers in Galilee. Some speak of small wonders he's doing—healing the lame, curing lepers, changing water to wine. Is he capable of raising the people against us?"

"We all worked in Sepphoris for you without any trouble. What makes you think things have changed?" Caleb stood and stepped across the small enclosure. "He is a man who loves his God. He is a man of prayer. He is faithful to the teaching of his faith. He is no trouble for you or anyone else."

Sestus paced the shadowed side of the room, rubbing the back of his neck as he slowly rotated his shoulders.

Caleb reached into the fountain and cupped the cool water with both hands. He washed the food and dust from his face. His teeth were clenched. His jaw tight. The tension between them was thick, but he wasn't going to run from Sestus any longer.

The centurion reached out his hand. "I am here for you."

"Why? What good am I to you now?"

Sestus's face came into focus like a phantom taking form. The centurion stepped closer again. "You never finished your training, but I can see that you have not forgotten what you learned. Your father remains unavenged and your friend needs protection from authorities who might misunderstand his actions. You will come with me and work again for peace in this land."

"And if I don't?"

Sestus patted his sword. "Roman justice is always accomplished, one way or another."

A pan flute sounded clearly below as mourners in a funeral march howled their grief.

Caleb's resistance melted away like the last snows of spring. "You know I only want to use my skills for peace. Yeshi must be spared."

He picked up a clay jug and scooped up water from the fountain. He poured it out on the fire. Smoke stung his eyes and brought on tears. The hiss and crackles intensified the darkness as the flames faltered.

"I want Barabbas on one of your crosses."

"So do I." The moon crested the nearby hills and Caleb stared into it. "So do I."

Sestus stepped toward the courtyard entrance. "I see that in your encounter today with the zealots. Ask yourself, will the peace you seek last only for today, or do you want to gain skills which will help you win the kind of peace that lasts?"

"Even Rome can't do that in this God-forsaken land."

"Come and see. We leave tomorrow."

And with that, Sestus was gone.

Moments later, the silence was broken.

"Pssst."

Caleb waited as Hermes's large shadow separated itself from the darkness.

"He knows you were here," Caleb said, stretching his arm toward the alcoves on the wall behind him. "You fooled no one with your disappearing act. Your two lamps still burn as a witness."

Hermes snatched up his two lamps and shuffled up to Caleb. "Don't let that puppet of Rome get you killed in some foolish quest."

"You know the only quest I have is for Barabbas."

"Ca–leeb, leave this foolishness. My cousin is taking his ship to Alexandria tomorrow. I can get you on it." Hermes hoisted his meaty arms above his shoulders. "Six months in Alexandria brought you peace. It soothed your soul. Remember the library, the fountains, the markets."

Caleb turned away. "What good did all that do me now?"

"If you serve these Romans, you know that your father won't be the last carpenter of Nazareth to pay the price. The zealots' daggers are sharp and swift." Hermes moved to the exit, then extended an open hand toward Caleb. "Ca–leeb. Save yourself. When the rooster crows. Be here. When the cows are being loaded, then come to the ship. I will hide you."

Chapter Two

Caleb hunkered down behind the barrels of salted tilapia, peeking out from under the same burlap sacking the young zealots had hidden under the day before to spy on him. The faintest glow showed along the horizon as two dozen ships slipped into place to take advantage of the high tide. Semaphores were raised as signals for new arrivals.

Dockmen held torches to light the way for workers and slaves grunting and struggling with boxes and barrels of assorted goods. An untiring drum beat out a rhythm designed to keep the men moving, along with the free use of horsewhips. Barrels of salted tilapia were rolled toward an Egyptian grain ship.

A herd of lowing cattle added to the chaos of shouting merchants, weigh scale operators, tradesmen, sailors, and passengers vying for position along the wharf. The tide of humanity flowed around a group of Nubian slaves chained to a post.

Caleb spotted Hermes, slipped out from under the burlap, and moved toward the warehouse doorway, his attention intercepted by a huddle of young maids from Britannia. They were scantily dressed and pressing together to keep warm. An Egyptian and Roman were in heated debate about the worth of the girls.

As he turned away, a flock of seagulls dove into the fray as a fish merchant began unloading his wares. Deckhands swung a pulley and canvas filled with marble slabs. Caleb was nearly hit by it as it swung around.

He stepped back into the path of the cattle, the smell of dung now joining the aroma of sea air, body odors, spices, grain dust, and freshly tanned wool.

An iron grip closed on his bicep and Caleb turned.

"I see you've lost your way already," Sestus growled.

Caleb glared into the man's steely eyes. "Not at all. I'm here to bid farewell to a friend. He owes me dates and figs in trade for a job."

Sestus kept the lock on Caleb's arm and nudged him toward the warehouse. The centurion was three inches taller and much heavier than the carpenter. It was like being cornered by a bull.

A cage of screeching black- and white-faced Colobus monkeys from Africa was pushed into their path and Sestus steered Caleb around it. A cage of peacocks required another detour. Next, they stopped near a pyramid of barrels filled with Palestinian olives destined for Greece. Woven reed baskets of nuts and fruits were also piled high nearby.

A wildcat's howl sounded behind him and Caleb twirled like a top. A cage full of young boys was being pushed up against the warehouse. An emaciated blond child, howling, looked right at him and Caleb's soul stirred. The distinctive smell of feces and urine arose from the cage. Horror stories of Roman lust filled his mind as he turned to Sestus.

"Surely you can spare the boys. Cages? What else can they endure?"

Sestus pulled him away. "Those who understand all the pleasures of Rome are coming here. The merchants are providing what is wanted." Sestus moved Caleb away from the cage. "Don't worry. They were purchased honestly. Your chief priest and his council members have been here to protest. It will all be done quietly."

Caleb fell to his knees and emptied his stomach. Where was the Almighty and his judgment? It was no wonder a man had to reap his own justice.

A plump baker wheeled his cart of bread rolls past and Sestus reached out and grabbed two without offering to reimburse the man. The merchant gave him a disgusted look, but without further protest he kept moving toward his paying customers.

Sestus pressed a roll into Caleb's hand and pulled him to his feet. "You'd better eat. It'll be a while before we stop. And change that rag on your hand. It's soaked in blood and will keep you from healing. It marks you for death."

Caleb discarded the crimson silk rag and purchased a small white cloth from a merchant willing to part with his wares for some immediate profit.

The maids from Britannia were sold and sent on with their new owner. The Nubians were prodded across a plank toward a waiting vessel. Sacks, barrels, baskets, and crates changed hands in the universal circle of trade, the backs of broken men always ready for another load.

A Roman galley pulled into place at the dock as slaves below deck banked their oars, maneuvering the large ship. Wide planks dropped and a cohort of troops began to unload. Their hobnailed boots beat a steady rhythm on the wharf as they marched off.

Sestus gazed ahead, unwavering as a dozen stallions were being led off the ship. Caleb winced under Sestus's vice grip. He tried to pull away to ease the pressure, and Sestus relaxed. Deckhands, legionnaires, fishermen, and wharf rats all began to turn toward the stallions.

"They're from Beth Togarmah," said Sestus, wiping his brow. "Bred for war by the Armenians."

The giant Arabian stallions, black, grey, and white, were blindfolded to keep them calm. Haltered to keep them guided. Muscles rippling. Hoofs unsteady as they felt their way forward. The horses were calmed by the voice of their handlers speaking through the chaos. Any of them could have been the pride of charioteers riding in the Roman circus.

Sestus pointed. "There, the bay and the black! The last two. Our mounts for today. They'll get checked, and within the hour we ride. The power of your crosses will finally rise to bring peace to this house of rebels."

From across the wharf, Hermes angled his way toward Caleb. The merchant stopped a foot away.

"So this is the way you treat your customers. Refusing to deliver what I want." Hermes pushed a finger into Caleb's face. "You will not get what you want either. I won't be doing business here for another three months. You take risks when you let me down."

"Move on, you blasphemous Greek," Sestus growled. "This is my carpenter. Find another."

Hermes lowered his chin and spun away without a word.

Caleb quivered from neck to torso. Hermes knew more about Barabbas then he was willing to admit, and now the veiled threat was clear. By siding with the Romans, Caleb may have invited a zealot dagger for his own throat.

The daylight was generous as Caleb and Sestus began their march toward the stables. Along the way, Sestus grabbed handfuls of dried apricots, dates, nuts, and figs from vendors and merchants. Caleb reluctantly accepted his share of the confiscated goods.

At the stables, a legionnaire handed the centurion a plump wineskin and Sestus drank deeply before wiping his mouth with the back of his hand and handing the flask to Caleb.

"Drink now, carpenter. The dust from this ride will make you wish you had stayed in Nazareth."

As Caleb drank his fill, he watched a load of felled trees being piled onto a large cart. The pounding in his temple intensified: the length of those cuts was familiar.

"For your crosses," Sestus said. "There's been another zealot attack in Galilee. We start in Sepphoris and then head to Jerusalem. The zealots will soon know that Sestus Aurelius is back."

Sestus walked away, leaving Caleb to groom the horses. The soft whinnying of the huge beasts and the familiar smell of soiled hay brought its own comfort. The peace of the stables was a welcoming change from the chaos of the docks. That peace came with the loss of his own freedom, though. Caleb felt chains rewrapping themselves around his soul.

Twenty minutes after he was finished grooming the horses, a messenger hurried in the door. Caleb had burrowed himself into a large bundle of hay, and he watched the young boy search through the stalls. Finally, the lad stopped and called, "Carpenter. I bring a message."

Caleb emerged quietly behind the boy and enjoyed seeing the startled expression on the boy's face.

When the lad had recovered, he delivered his message. "Sestus Aurelius wishes to tell you that the governor has instructed him to stay another day or two. He will call you at the warehouse when he is ready to go. You are supposed to look around and see what you can learn."

Caleb grabbed the lad's arm before he could run off. "What does he mean by that?"

The boy pulled away. "How am I supposed to know?"

Caleb hurried to the docks, but Hermes's ship was gone.

I guess Alexandria isn't an option anymore, he thought.

Where chaos had reigned before dawn, now there was only the common noise of a city at work. A flock of pelicans sliced through the skies.

As he scanned the few ships still in port, Caleb heard the tapping of a stick behind him. It was the old blind man he had seen in the alley with the zealots. Did the old man know what he'd done to those boys?

"Old man!" Caleb spoke up. "I'm here. Where do you want to go?"

"Only where you go, oh carpenter of Sestus."

"How do you know me?"

Caleb stepped up onto a log near the warehouse to gain some space between them. The old man scuffled up right next to him.

"I am the eyes of Rome in this city," the blind man whispered. "I saw you take on those zealots. I saw you ready to make a deal with the devil."

Caleb felt for his carpenter's knife. It was missing. "If the devils possess you, old goat, then go prophesy at the shrine of Pan. Leave me alone. And return my knife."

The blind man smiled. "You are not as alert as you think, are you? I was sent to keep you alive for Sestus."

A knife flashed in the beggar's hand and Caleb recognized it as his own.

"Give me the knife!" Caleb demanded.

"Take it!"

Caleb reached for it, and suddenly it vanished; the blind man's empty hand remained. Caleb grabbed for the old man and instantly found himself spun around with the knife at his throat.

"Things are not as they appear, carpenter."

"I hope for your sake that this is true." Caleb stopped struggling. "What do I have to do?"

"As part of your training, you will learn to listen to my stick. It will signal what is happening around you." The old man held out the knife so Caleb could take it.

Retrieving the knife, Caleb stepped down and backed away. "I don't need any more training. I've had enough. These hands have tasted enough death for one lifetime. The Almighty can find other hands to do his work."

The old man furrowed his eyebrows. "This Almighty you speak of, do you believe he fights only for the Jews? Is he someone the Romans will have to conquer like the gods of other nations? Is he someone I will have to contend with in our training?"

Caleb stepped toward the man, whose hands moved warily in front of him like a wrestler getting ready to grapple.

A passion rose in Caleb which he hadn't felt in years. "The Almighty cannot be conquered," he said. "He is not a god to be betrayed and angered. He claims to be the Creator of all things. His temple is open to the people of all nations, but his followers do not always let others into their place of worship."

"What must we do to silence these zealots who rise against us?" the old goat asked. "Will there be peace if we take their lives, or do we have to take their temple and their land as well?"

Caleb paused, weighing his loyalties. "Peace won't be easy if you take the land or the temple. Rome has the power and the zealots have the passion. Perhaps one day the power and the passion will meet on a cross or in a tomb."

"Carpenter!" the old man responded. "Are you by chance a prophet or only a philosopher?"

"I am only a carpenter."

The man's stick tapped four times in quick succession. "The silk rag you tore to bind your wound, it was meant for a senator's wife in Rome. The apprentice you tried to train, he is the nephew of the fig vendor—a zealot spy. The Persian slave you freed, he is already chained and on his way to the arena in Ephesus. The horse you were meant to ride was a trap… an ambush was set up outside the city gates for the men riding the bay and the black. Others have been sent to die for you. Listen to me and you may live."

The humidity suddenly increased. It was like wearing a wool blanket under a scorching sun at noonday. Even the gulls had vacated the skies.

How did this blind man know all this? The very walls seemed to have ears.

"Who are you?" Caleb asked.

"Underneath the burlap where you were hiding this morning is a sea rat. He is your next test from Sestus. Keep your senses alert. If you are going to work for the death of others, you must first ensure life for yourself. Beware the Gates of Hades."

With that, the blind man pulled his head rag a little lower and tapped his way off into an alley.

Caleb scanned the cross-shaped masts bobbing in the waves—almost mocking him, reminding him he couldn't escape his calling as a cross maker.

The tide was out and the moored ships would be going nowhere for the day. His own soul bobbed under the pressure of what to do. To run or to stay? Both options involved death.

The inland hills of Judea beckoned, hills currently hiding zealots like Barabbas who would one day rest on his crosses.

His left pinky began to twitch. His destiny would be decided by this next test.

Chapter Three

The burlap was still in its place, now surrounded by mounds of fishing net. A few sailors were back to playing dice. Others slept in the entrances of various shops and warehouses. No one seemed interested in a carpenter with a white rag on his hand.

Caleb hadn't washed his feet in days, and the grit between Caleb's toes irritated him. His whole body was covered in days of sweat, dust, and smoke. The humidity was oppressive, even hours before noon, and his scalp itched. He didn't doubt that lice had found a new home there. He smelled of fish and sheep and cow and half a dozen other odors he couldn't even identify.

The tension in his chest was suffocating. His lower back pulsated and the wound in his hand seemed to throb more.

He stepped up to the burlap, his steps slow and casual, the pace of a man bored and shiftless, and quickly threw it back. A sea rat, no older than ten, lay curled up there, fast asleep. His dark curls marked him as a local.

Caleb spotted a horsewhip on the ground and picked it up, standing over the boy. He debated whether the test before him was to strangle the young zealot in his sleep or to prod him awake to see what adventure might come.

I have enough blood on my hands, he thought, noting the red stain on the white cloth covering his hand.

Using the end of the whip, Caleb poked the boy's ribs. The sea rat rolled away and sprang to his feet, a dagger firmly in his right hand and a look of death in his dark eyes.

"Take a step and I'll stick you like a pig," the boy taunted. "Come on. Are you a thief or just stupid? I have nothing."

Caleb broke out laughing. He was just a boy, a full foot shorter than himself. *This is my test from Sestus?*

The boy was clearly offended at the laughter and began to swing his dagger. Caleb ignored the feeble threat.

"Have you eaten anything today?" Caleb asked. "You look so thin the gulls could carry you away."

"I don't take handouts."

"I don't give handouts. I've got a day with nothing to do. If you give me a tour, I'll feed you."

They quickly negotiated the price—a handful of dates, another of figs, and a single dried apricot if possible. The dagger and horsewhip were set aside.

"What language do you want the tour in?" the boy asked. "I can speak Phoenician, Latin, Hebrew, Aramaic, Greek, and a little Egyptian."

"I was hoping for Persian, but I'll settle for Aramaic. It's the language of my birth."

"So are you a Roman pig or a Jewish goat? Where were you born? You talk like a Galilean."

Caleb fended off the intended insult. "Are we going to get your food, or would you rather stand here starving?"

The boy knew the shortcut to get to the food merchants, where a date vendor was generous to the boy. Caleb was sure he saw a conspiratorial glance between the two. He was eager to move on.

"Where to first?" Caleb asked.

The boy looked around. "I will take you to the Gates of Hades."

Caleb heard the words of the blind man echoing inside him: *Beware the Gates of Hades.* He looked toward the distant cliff, which he knew housed the giant cave purported to be the entrance and exit for the devil and all his demons. A flock of vultures hovered overhead its rocky outcroppings.

"Why there?" Caleb asked.

"It is the house of all pleasures, with any god you choose. Pan is the best."

"What does Pan offer a stranger like me?"

"Women and goats from paradise. Even fresh maids from Britannia are now here to serve your pleasure. The baths are a house of celebration in themselves. You will be denied nothing."

As Caleb stared at the British maidens, someone grabbed him from behind and threw him to the ground. As he fell, he twisted and lashed out with his legs, taking down his attacker with him.

The wind was knocked out of him and he gasped as one attacker grabbed his beard and jerked his head back while another planted a knee firmly on his back.

He fought to regain his mind as a piercing whistle broke through the fog. In a moment, someone reached inside his tunic, searching for a hidden bag of coins. He rolled onto his arm and brought back his elbow into the man's jaw. He heard the sickening crack of bone, and then the weight on him rolled off. The attacker let loose a profanity-laced tirade.

Caleb twisted onto his back and witnessed the sea rat who'd been guiding him around thrashing a trio of young thugs. One of the ruffians lay dazed on the ground while the other two held their arms over their heads as a thin cedar branch rained down relentlessly over them.

Joining the fray, Caleb tackled a target and brought him down. The sea rat then knocked the thug senseless. The remaining attacker assessed the situation and abandoned his comrades.

A cheer rose from the crowd that had gathered to watch the altercation. In response, the sea rat lifted his weapon into the air and waved at the onlookers.

In full sight of everyone, he reached into the tunic of the unconscious attacker and withdrew a small bag of coins. The crowd cheered again.

"Come," he said to Caleb.

Caleb followed, then turned in a complete circle, observing the potential hiding spots from which he could be ambushed again. Was this the extent of his test? To rein in his lust and desire? To fight off a few thugs?

"There is no place as defiled as this wall of caves and shrines," Caleb said. "These maidens are distractions for the benefit of thugs."

"But isn't the sight of fresh maidens worth the beating?" the sea rat asked. "I have money. Choose a woman."

"What do you understand about fresh maidens? You're too young for such knowledge. The moment I chose a woman or goat, you would steal everything I have. Now finish my tour."

The boy shrugged and headed toward the marketplace. He nodded at several vendors and gave significant space to those who eyed him warily.

They eventually arrived at the waterfront warehouse which Caleb knew well.

Caleb scanned the breadth of the harbor with all the new construction underway. "What do you think Herod is trying to do here?"

"That fox is trying to reshape our city into Rome or Athens as a way to please the emperor," the boy said. "If you're the kind to blush at every statue and temple prostitute, I'll take you elsewhere."

Caleb turned slowly, taking in the sights. No one seemed interested in his passing except the old blind man, who was enjoying the cool ocean breeze at the edge of the wharf.

"I hear the sister of Barabbas has married into a family here," Caleb said. "Do you know where she lives?"

"What do you care?" the sea rat asked.

"Barabbas murdered my father."

The slightest smile creased the face of his young guide, and his chest expanded. No doubt he was just another zealot. Caleb determined to watch his back, especially as they turned deeper into the warrens of the city's marketplace.

"Follow me," the guide directed.

The lad walked confidently ahead, swinging his stick in front of him. The fact that he had battled on Caleb's behalf meant nothing now; Caleb had been his mark and the boy wasn't going to share his target with anyone else.

The change in quality of people's clothing was the first giveaway that they'd crossed an invisible boundary. Caleb had seen the same telling clue in the back alleys of cities in many countries.

His pulse quickened as he noticed the eyes of the women and children following him. He was a stranger and potential danger. There were no old men, and the young men crouched like wolves ready to spring. The smoke from cooking fires irritated his eyes, and it seemed to him they had been deliberately set for that purpose. His left hand closed instinctively on his carpenter's knife.

As they walked down a dark alley, Caleb saw a slight movement in his guide's right hand. Caleb backed up quickly, without a word, and almost made it out before three young thugs rushed into the darkness to grab him. Three others stepped out of nearby doorways, completing the ambush.

He delivered a kick to the left knee of the closest assailant and the thug buckled to the ground. But he couldn't run fast enough, and his arm was twisted and jerked behind his back. He brought his elbow back and smashed it into the face of his opponent, who screamed and released his hold. Another thug moved in close enough to take Caleb's punch to the jaw. He was knocked out cold.

By the time Caleb heard the slapping sandals of the other three assailants, he was away and off into safer parts of the city. He had carefully watched the twists and turns the young guide had taken him through and knew exactly how to escape. Fifteen minutes later, he was bent over, panting on the docks.

The old blind man was nowhere in sight. A palate of crossbeams rested where he had stood just minutes before.

As dusk approached, Caleb strolled calmly past a familiar vendor who was closing up his stand for the evening.

"Some dates, if you will," Caleb said, putting out his hand. "And perhaps a suggestion on where a stranger can spend the night without perishing."

The vendor wrapped up a handful of dates in some palm leaf and waited for payment. He smiled when Caleb handed him the coin.

"So the young guide couldn't hook his fish this time?" the vendor asked.

Caleb smiled back. "He did hook the fish—at a price to the other fishermen. Now, a room, if you please. I see the streets may not always be this friendly."

The vendor finished closing up his cart and walked with Caleb to a modest-looking inn a few blocks from the dock.

"This one is usually safe for Romans," the vendor said. "If you stay in all night."

"But I'm no Roman."

"I can see that from your face. But you travel with Romans, and apart from your long hair you dress like a Roman, walk like a Roman, and smell like a Roman. How do you expect to be identified around here? Do you seriously want to die young?"

"I can take care of myself," Caleb replied. "Things aren't always as they appear."

He almost laughed out loud. *I'm starting to sound like that old blind goat.*

The vendor walked away into the darkness and Caleb entered through the inn's sturdy cedar door. Inside, a large Briton brandished a sword and pointed it right at his throat.

"Declare yourself!" the Briton commanded.

"Caleb ben Samson, carpenter of Nazareth and confidante of Sestus Aurelius, the senior centurion in Jerusalem and legate of Judea, newly appointed."

The Briton examined Caleb a few moments before lowering his sword. "What business do you have in Caesarea?"

"The legate is receiving his orders from the procurator," Caleb answered. "And I am waiting until we move on."

The Briton moved aside and waved his sword in a downward arc. Caleb followed the movement and next approached a smiling Hebrew with a beard that reached halfway down his chest. The man's blue-patterned robes looked Persian in their weave and quality. His silky red turban, perhaps Indian. A large green emerald had been fixed to the middle of the turban. His gaze examined Caleb quickly.

"Ah, fresh from Alexandria I see," the Hebrew said. "You are safe in this place. Business has never been so good since we hired the Briton."

Caleb stepped up to the table. "Who are you to know my travel schedule?"

The Hebrew chuckled as he twirled a large ruby ring on his index finger. "It is my business to know the world's business. Thank you for choosing this fine house of rest."

"I would thank the date vendor, if I were you."

"No need." The innkeeper took the coins Caleb offered. "He is my brother."

"I would warn your guests about the wharf rats who crawl around the docks and lure newcomers into dark alleys to rob them."

"The wharf rats are my nephews," the innkeeper replied. He stepped out from behind the table and moved toward a hallway door. "As long as you are here, you are safe."

Caleb followed the innkeeper the few steps to a curtained alcove, where the Hebrew bowed.

"For you, the baths for the inn are free," the man said. "Please take advantage of our offer. You may want to avoid the public baths. Some of our noble patriots spent yesterday smashing the more erotic Greek statues. There is mixed bathing now, and while the internationals love it the practice is not easily tolerated yet. Things are a little tense right now."

The complimentary baths and massage were heaven-sent, and the clean straw pallet he was given would be a welcome relief after the more rustic sleeping quarters he'd had during the past week. The flickering lamp light made the room warm and inviting. He stretched out and prepared to rest.

A soft knocking on the outside wall got his attention, and suddenly the curtain moved aside to reveal a young Greek maiden. She looked like a goddess. As she slipped into the room, her long blond hair flowed over her shoulders. She held a tray heaped with quail, fruit, and a selection of seafoods.

Without hesitation, she set the tray down and removed her outer robe.

"Your meal, my lord."

As if by magic, she produced two clay mugs and a bottle filled with wine. It wasn't the food or wine that got Caleb's attention, though, as the Grecian dropped to her knees and poured the wine; the whole time, her eyes never left Caleb's. He felt the hook in his loins as she moved closer with her gift. The hot flush on his face and body made him glad for the dim lighting.

It took every ounce of self-control to convince her that he wasn't in need of her services, or of anyone else's.

23

That night, he was plagued by the images of sea rats, rogue zealots, Sestus, Barabbas, and the Grecian girl. The bottle of wine proved to be the perfect tonic, though, and troubled sleep finally swallowed him a few hours before dawn.

The new day arrived with a rooster's crow. It had been years since Caleb had imbibed so much and his head throbbed. He washed himself and left the inn without waiting for a morning tray to be delivered. The dinner tray still sat untouched.

He stumbled through the streets and narrowly avoided a pail of slops being emptied out of an upstairs window. A vendor satisfied his thirst with a cup of wine while another offered papaya and mango and oranges. Caleb ate as if he was breaking a weeklong fast.

Deciding to explore more of the city in a safer way, Caleb kept his sightlines clear and ensured that he attached himself to trustworthy groups moving through the market. At times he drew long looks, but he refused to be intimidated.

In a moment of weakness, he stopped near the Rock of Gods by the so-called Gates of Hades. The large cavern in the middle of the cliff face was surrounded by smaller caves, giving off a mystique to the dozens of shrines that formed this heart of worship for every pagan deity in the city. Setting up shop here was an economic windfall for merchants, priests, and sex traffickers. It was a dream destination of sailors and men from many parts of the world.

Sure enough, as the lad had told him, the maids from Britannia were on full display near the statue of Pan. The large crowd of men there proved that this form of worship was profitable.

Caleb left quickly. The lure of these temptations were the most powerful he had ever felt.

God, have mercy.

The sandy shores and grassy parkland near Caesarea provided a perfect refuge and Caleb took note of the sea and songbirds that nested on the outer edges of the port. He hiked for some time and took pleasure in flushing out quail and partridge. With a sling, he could knock enough of them out of the sky to feed a whole cohort of Romans. He only took enough for a meal, then roasted the three birds on the hills overlooking the sea.

In the late afternoon, he watched a slaver, accompanied by six mercenaries, prod six chained gladiators onto a ship bound for Ephesus. He then decided to hike down to the dock to see if Nabonidus might be there. The old goat had told him his slave was bound for Ephesus, after all. Surely the Persian was free and on his way to his family by now.

Nabonidus was not among the group. The gladiators included two Africans, a Briton, a Gaul, a German, and a Parthian. All were six or seven inches taller than Caleb and rippling pillars of muscle. They spent most of the day in the hot sun carrying heavy sacks aboard the ship.

Caleb approached a dockworker. "What are they loading?"

The dockworker pulled him away from the mob of merchants and slaves. "They carry Egyptian sand to soak up their own blood in the arenas at Ephesus. In the carrying, they grow stronger for the fight ahead. At night they train in the new amphitheater. Today, they live. Next week, they die."

Caleb shuddered as he considered the fate of the gladiators. If the blind man had been right, Nabonidus was already on a ship to perhaps face these very same trained killers.

That night, before the moon rose, he lay out on the beach and watched the constellations dance across the black velvet canvas above. Shooting stars gave witness to the war in the heavens. He remembered the childhood stories his mother had told him about angelic forces who had fought for the Almighty. Caleb was tempted for a moment to plead with the Almighty for intervention in his own situation. He shuddered, shook his head, and moved on.

On his second day without Sestus, Caleb left notice at the procurator's quarters that he was available at the dockside inn whenever the senior centurion was ready.

It was while resting in the shadow of some crates that Caleb came to overhear a conversation.

"We need to warn Barabbas again," said the date vendor Caleb had spoken to the previous day. The man was speaking to the dockmaster.

"Are you talking about the centurion?" the dockmaster asked.

"Yes," the vendor said, almost in a whisper. "He almost stopped us before. It's taken a long time to get this supply route clear. The Romans are hungry for that Chinese silk, and we have to keep them happy. The nobles want the powders, to lace their wines with intoxicants and cures."

"Don't worry. The centurions in Tiberius and Sepphoris are happy with our current arrangements. Sestus Aurelius is on his way to Jerusalem. He won't last long. If the zealots don't get him, we'll see him transferred again."

Caleb could feel a smile creep across his face in the shadows. The Almighty had blessed him by putting him in the right place at the right time. He busied himself arranging the transport of a small shipload of crossbeams.

That night, he wandered the docks and wrestled with his temptation to sail away. The almost full moon cast its shimmery light onto the ships bobbing at anchor. The water sparkled as if wooing him. Once again, he saw the old blind man sitting quietly near the warehouse.

Just prior to dawn on the third day, Caleb was awoken to the sound of an elephant's trumpet. The chaos of ships loading and unloading was the same every morning before dawn, and every night the dogs barked at all who passed. The cargo kept changing, but the smell was much the same.

Caleb felt the fury build inside him. Things had changed during his time in Ephesus and Alexandria and he had learned to love independence and freedom, doing what he wanted when he wanted. Waiting for Sestus was pointless. Twice he began discussions with merchants to see if they might be headed to Sepphoris, and twice he backed out. Sestus was the key to avenging his father's murder.

Two more days passed before a messenger came with news that Caleb should prepare to leave at dawn. He went for a final walk along the wharf, the swirling darkness on the horizon looking like the dust cloud of a numberless army charging down on the land of his birth. Soul-piercing thoughts shackled his mind to fear and he had to force himself to focus on a hunting kingfisher diving into the shallows.

Oh to be free as a bird.

He heard a tapping sound behind him but refused to turn. The smell of ash and cheap wine fought the salty aroma of the sea.

But his inattention didn't stop the blind man from speaking.

"The Persian slave is fighting his new masters," the old man said. "His time is almost up. The Grecian goddess you spurned was bribed to poison your wine. I switched the flasks before she entered your room. Otherwise you would never have woken from your sleep."

The faint tap of the man's cane against Caleb's ankle almost made him turn. He tried to refocus on the kingfisher.

"She has returned to the Gates of Hades. The zealots know that you and the Roman avoided their ambush. They will try again. Ominous winds are blowing for your Jewish Messiah. Things are not as they appear."

The tapping sound faded away, along with the smell.

If Yeshi is the Messiah, he can take care of himself, Caleb thought. *There's one thing I need to do.*

He took a deep breath, but it failed to relieve the tension that gripped his shoulders and neck. He pulled out his flute and tried to soothe himself with the eerie strains of a long forgotten love song: "Love is as easy to keep as a rainbow, as easy to stop as a river. Rebekah, how did everything go so wrong? Where are you now?"

The night passed slowly. When deep thunder sounded above, Caleb instinctively rolled against a wall and curled up into a fetal position. Cold sweat soaked him.

But no logs came, no ambush from Barabbas. The thunder rolled over and over.

He uncurled himself and chuckled to himself. *Will I now act like a child every time the sky gets angry?*

Caleb gave up hoping to sleep and went to the stables where he could scrub himself down. He then went out for one last walk. The city never slept. Sailors and ladies were still in the taverns. Ships were already slipping into moorage. The merchants were beginning to claim the streets.

Sestus was already mounted and waiting when Caleb arrived slightly before dawn. A contingent of legionnaires milled about with torches as they prepared horses and equipment for travel. The pungent odor of dung and horse and fires and sea air was a strong stimulant this early in the morning.

Sestus motioned him over next to the head of his stallion.

"I see you are alive and well," Sestus remarked while adjusting the saddle bags filled with his belongings.

"I am. I was almost ready to sail away."

"What kept you? You know I can capture Barabbas without you."

"I need to go home." Caleb scooped up a jug of water from a horse trough and poured it over his face and hands.

"We have new horses," Sestus said as he bridled an impressive white stallion. "Someone tried to set us up. Or did you know that?" He threw on the saddle bags. "You will take the black."

Caleb motioned for the stable boy to bring his horse. "I want the Persian slave set free."

"He's already on his way." Sestus patted his mount and shuffled a few things between the saddle bags. Then he stared hard at Caleb. "How do you know about the Persian?"

Caleb stared back, then took his mount and caressed its neck and shoulder. "I freed him. I'll serve you without question if you release him from the arena."

"He is only a slave." Sestus mounted and turned to survey his surroundings. "Gaining his freedom isn't worth what it will cost you."

Caleb mounted and rode up beside Sestus. "You may take his cost from my wages, but release him. He has served me well."

Sestus urged his horse forward. "If you serve me well, I will consider your request. Perhaps I can hold him back from the arena for now." He drew his sword and waved it around. "We will follow our plan, but we'll have to hurry. The others will leave in a few days and we'll catch them near Jerusalem. When we get to Sepphoris, we will cut your hair."

Caleb patted his Arabian and scanned the horizon. "When we get to Sepphoris, I will give you a reason not to cut it."

Sestus smiled and moved his mount onto the main road. "When you finish your training, not even Barabbas will see you coming. And if he does, he won't be able to stop you."

Chapter Four

Caesarea to Sepphoris, Palestine 28 A.D.

The distant hills bobbed up and down as Caleb settled into the ride. The motion reminded him of his recent trip from Alexandria. A faint queasiness slid its way up his throat. He swallowed hard.

Mount Hermon's snowy cap glistened in the first rays of morning sunshine. The shrines at the Rock of Gods and Gates of Hades were empty at this early hour, with only a few ravens and starlings flying in and out of the groves. Above, an eagle drifted lazily on a thermal high. By the seaport, a parade of merchants and craftsman accompanied carts, donkeys, and oxen for another day of labor.

Four hours of riding brought them to a caravansary and stable. A lunch of dates, figs, and goat cheese quieted the grumbles in Caleb's stomach. As Caleb ate, Sestus unrolled a map and discussed the terrain with another centurion who rested under the shade of an olive.

A Persian slave brought them a wineskin of fresh drink. The man reminded Caleb of a smaller version of Nabonidus, only one dressed in a tent-like tunic. He had the same bald head and thick jowls, the same easy manner and work ethic.

Another Ethiopian slave fed pigeons which were housed in a dozen cages stacked three high and four wide. The whir of wings drew Caleb's attention, and he noticed that one of the cages was marked by small blue tassels.

"Peace to you," Caleb called to the Ethiopian.

"And peace to you," the slave replied.

"You have the finest pigeons. Do the blue tassels mean these are already purchased?"

The slave stared hard at Caleb and then looked over at Sestus and the other centurion, both of whom were still poring over their map.

"These birds will pay for the sins of the zealots in Jerusalem," the Ethiopian man said. With that, he moved quickly back into the stables.

A short time later, Caleb and Sestus were given fresh mounts.

"These pigeons will be going to Jerusalem for zealot sacrifices," Caleb remarked to Sestus once the man finished going over the map. "If we follow them, we could intercept a courier who might tell us where Barabbas is."

Sestus glanced at the pigeons and then examined his horse. "Our assignment is Sepphoris. Someone else can worry about Barabbas and the zealots in Jerusalem. We don't even know if Barabbas is near."

Caleb stepped closer and spoke softly. "I nearly met his sister in Caesarea. A young zealot took me right into the hornet's nest. I had six of the young dagger men on me. I fought them all. Kicking, elbowing, punching."

Sestus chuckled. "Those boys weren't dagger men. Sounds like bear cubs playing to me."

"I felt more alive than ever," Caleb whispered. "I tell you, Barabbas is close. He knows I'm closing in on him."

"There's still hope that you may be more than a carpenter, but don't be arrogant," Sestus cautioned. "Those zealots were little more than children."

Tension gripped Caleb's soul as images of his futile attempts to please his own father washed through his mind. The time when he'd built his first wall and his father had ripped it out. The time he'd finished a crib for a neighbor, only to have his father crush it with an axe. The time he'd first gone with Yeshi to find work at Sepphoris. And each time, he'd heard the same words: "You're so worthless. You are nothing. What do you think you'll ever accomplish?"

Sestus wasn't his father, though.

"I'm ready for any zealot," Caleb said, looking toward the centurion riding easily on his white stallion.

Sestus shrugged and patted his sword. "Once you learn to ride, swing a sword, and throw a javelin, you may be ready for the next level. Don't forget, Barabbas and his followers are experienced in killing. You are nothing to them."

In order to redeem himself, Caleb shared the conversation he'd overheard between the date vendor and the dockmaster in Caesarea.

Sestus shrugged and set his jaw.

"They say you're standing in the way of their silk trade," Caleb said. "They're planning to eliminate you."

"They've already tried. You're not telling me anything I don't already know."

Caleb swung up onto his fresh mount and turned it around as if to wait for the caravan that was following them. His fists clenched.

I am not nothing. I know things.

In his mind, he conjured the image of the blind man who had recruited him for training as a young man. The invisible chain around his neck was quickly suffocating him.

He stopped his mount from following Sestus.

"Is this the tantrum of a child I see?" mocked Sestus. "Or the pouting of a woman who didn't get her way?"

Caleb pivoted on his mount and dug in his heels. The stallion jerked forward and almost broadsided Sestus. One second the centurion was in front of Caleb's charging warhorse, and the next second he was behind it. By the time Caleb turned, he found himself facing Sestus's drawn sword.

"You've got the anger of Mount Vesuvius, carpenter," Sestus said, smiling as he swung his sword menacingly. "I can see that woman got to you."

Caleb reined in the stallion. "What woman?"

"Certainly not the Greek goddess at the inn who tried to poison you with her body and her stew. Definitely not the Egyptian masseuse who waited to strangle you at the public baths. Not even the mother of the three zealots whom you left childless. There's really only one option, isn't there?"

Caleb felt the heat in his neck and cheeks. "How do you know about her?"

Sestus sheathed his sword and took hold of the reins of Caleb's horse. "Ever since your encounter with your little mistress, you've treated all women as if they were striking cobras. The guilt and shame are in your eyes. Your manhood is shackled and your anger is out of control. You dance with death in ways you don't even know." Sestus pranced his horse around Caleb. "I have faith that your manhood is not completely lost. Work with me."

The secret was broken and Caleb felt his spirit wilt like a sheaf of barley flattened by a hail storm. His neck no longer had the strength to hold his head and he felt himself droop.

"Don't worry," Sestus said. "Titius will watch out for you until you get eyes of your own."

Caleb's brows furrowed. "Who is Titius?"

Sestus laughed. "Titius is the old blind goat you met in Caesarea. He'll be playing the part of someone else in Sepphoris. Don't worry. You may not see him, but he'll see you."

"What else am I facing in Sepphoris?"

"Much has changed since we last walked in Sepphoris." Sestus reached into his saddle bag, pulled out some dates, and rode close enough to hand them to Caleb. "Pontius Pilate and Herod Antipas are both concerned about the rise of Barabbas and the new Messiah. The Sicarii, those dagger men, have broadened their impact beyond Galilee since we've been gone. It seems Yeshua ben Yuseph has collected a following of fishermen, tax collectors, philosophers, and possibly zealots to support his cause. Yet no one is sure what his cause might be." Sestus stopped his mount and let Caleb ride on. "Those hills ahead may not be filled with your friends any longer."

Caleb turned his horse around. "You know he's only a harmless carpenter. He loves his God, and the people respect those who are devout."

Sestus's horse plodded on as he worked his way around a broken-down oxcart in the middle of the road. "Galilee births messiahs like rabbits birth offspring. You are aware of the cost incurred when Judas rose up in revolt against the census of Quirinius. He ransacked the armory at Sepphoris and we had to destroy and rebuild the city. I'm sure you still remember all the crosses that had to be built. Your father may have invited the dagger of Barabbas when he built some of them. Even if Yeshua is a good Messiah he may have to be stopped."

As they rode, a field of wildflowers appeared on the right. Caleb drew a deep breath. The Almighty had dropped a rainbow masterpiece right into the pit of hell.

"Are you sure you have the right man?" Caleb asked.

Sestus nodded. "Yes. I told the procurator that my own counsel had grown up as a carpenter with Yeshua ben Yuseph, that you were like a brother to the man, and that you could influence him if there were any further problems."

Caleb watched a pair of swans glide gracefully onto a nearby pond. "You require too much of me. Yeshi is like a brother. When Barabbas killed my father and leprosy took my mother, Yeshi's family gave me back my life. I cannot be asked to betray him."

Sestus smiled. "I do not ask you to betray your brother. I only ask that you keep your ears open and that you do your job well when the time comes." The centurion pointed toward the distant hills. "The zealots are alive here and we may have more work than we think. You may not think Yeshi is anything special, but our informants tell us that the people are coming to believe that Yeshi is the Messiah who has come to free them from Roman rule."

"It seems to me that this Messiah everyone is chasing isn't the friend I once knew."

Sestus stopped to give his horse a drink. "As Titius the blind will tell you, things aren't all as they appear to be."

The stop was short and then the journey continued. The ride through the rolling countryside became slower as more pilgrims began to clog up the road.

"Passover," Sestus observed as they were forced to walk the horses. "This is a blood-soaked ritual." He spit and shook his head. "Pilate wants me in Jerusalem as soon as possible, yet he thought this was the worst possible time for a change in command."

Even before Caleb heard their feeble cries, he saw a small group of women huddled off to the side of the road.

"Unclean, unclean," the beggars called to them. "Alms for the poor, alms for the poor."

Images of his own mother filled his mind: pieces of her leprosy-marred flesh slowly disappearing, her helplessness as his dad furiously fought neighbors from forcing her into isolation, her weeping as his dad refused to let her beg.

Caleb's volcanic anger surged up again. Where was the righteousness and justice of the Almighty? What great sin had the women of this land committed?

He looked away from the group and focused instead on the plumed helmet of the centurion riding in front of him.

It was past noon on the second day before the riders reached the gates of Sepphoris. The southern entrance had been fitted with a towering arch of stone. The top of the city's amphitheater was visible from here, along with a section of the marketplace. Row after row of buildings had risen since Caleb had last climbed to this hilltop city.

Sepphoris was indeed a crown jewel, even though Herod Antipas had moved his royal quarters to newer buildings at Tiberius on the Lake. The initial zealot threat had been thwarted and the forts Herod had built were proving effective as a deterrent against Parthians and zealots.

The urge to return home was strong, and Caleb and Sestus had just passed through the gate when Caleb could resist no longer. He looked across the valley at the hill where his hometown of Nazareth sat baking in the afternoon sun.

"I need to go home for a few days before we get started," Caleb said.

Sestus dismounted in order to lead his horse through the crowded streets. "You'll have time in between assignments."

Caleb also dismounted. "If you give me time now, I'll ask for fewer days away later."

"Leave the horse," Sestus said as he reached to take the reins from Caleb. "Three days. Now go. And when you come back, tell me everything you learn about your friend, Yeshi."

Caleb was gone before Sestus could change his mind.

Memories flooded over Caleb as he walked confidently toward Nazareth, including the days of exploring caves and groves and ravines with Yeshi after chores were done. He remembered the joys of exploring the woods and finding the perfect tree for a carpenter's project that would prove his worth in the world.

Most of the travelers he met along the road to Nazareth were strangers from distant lands—Persians, Armenians, Egyptians, Romans, and Gauls. Each had their own cart of wares meant to entice. The merchants called out to him, but he waved them off.

Caleb eventually decided to take a shortcut off the road to see if his favorite mushroom patch was still offering its harvest. As he roamed the forest, he saw in his mind's eye the image of Yeshi searching tree by tree for the perfect wood for a project. He saw him praying and singing the psalms. He saw him running and celebrating the creation all around.

The foliage brought immediate relief from the heat. Caleb stretched himself out on the ground and breathed in the scents of a living forest untouched by carpenters and woodsmen. The songbirds sang a lively symphony of joy. The bustle of the city seemed utterly far away.

He pulled out his flute and tried to recall again the early songs of Nazareth where life had been full of hope and peace. Songs that brought dancing and mourning, that grieved lost love and celebrated new love, that haunted the soul and filled the heart.

When the warning cries of a raven joined those of other birds, he dismissed the clench in his gut. It was probably warning of nothing worse than a stray dog. When the tide of calls rose more loudly, though, he began thinking of more dangerous terrors… lions and bears and wolves.

While putting his flute back into his pack, he noticed five men slowly walking toward him. They wore leather vests despite the heat and two shoulder hunter's bows. Caleb breathed a sigh of relief as he stepped out from behind the oak he had been resting against and called out to welcome them.

The five men immediately pulled daggers and halted, eyes scanning the brush.

Caleb put up his hands and smiled. "Easy. I'm alone. Just going home. To Nazareth."

He turned to walk back the way he had come, but the five ran up to him and surrounded him. They were close to Caleb's own age. Three were heavier built, and the other two were slight. Tight curls. Angry eyes. Full beards. Four blue cords wound through the tassels on their vests.

A large ox of a man shoved a dried apricot into his own mouth and chewed. A warning light went off in Caleb's mind. These were Barabbas's men.

"What brings you here?" growled the apricot-chewer. "Have you no work in Sepphoris? Have the Roman dogs unleashed your chain?"

"I don't work in Sepphoris and I have no chains," Caleb said.

Two of the men visibly relaxed, but the ox stepped forward just inches from Caleb's face, and grunted. Another man reached out and took away his carpenter's knife. Yet another grabbed his pack, removing his flute and breaking it.

"Swear allegiance to Barabbas and to the Almighty," the ox said.

Caleb hesitated a second too long, and fists began pummeling his face and body. An avalanche of fire consumed him as he was kicked to the back and to the ribs. His hand closed on a branch for support, but a foot stomped his fingers. Hard. A rock dug into his hip. All sunlight vanished as he slammed his eyes shut. The body odor of unwashed men suffocated him.

The crushing weight of the five men prompted an image of his father mocking him after he'd been trapped under the first tree he'd chopped down.

"You are worthless. You are nothing. You'll never accomplish anything worthwhile."

He attempted to shield his face as a dagger reached his throat. Searing pain along his neck and chin left him breathless. He felt life and hope and strength draining away.

Finally, the shadows shifted and the attackers stepped back. A rumble of words sounded through the storm of brokenness. Several voices penetrated the darkness.

A branch was dropped across his back. "If you live, the scar will be a witness to all. You have the warning mark of Barabbas."

A sandal stomped down on his hand. "If you continue to serve the Romans, the next time won't be just a warning."

The wind caressed his face. "In the darkest caves, we will find you. In the highest cliffs, we will find you. Spread the word, carpenter from Nazareth. If you try to escape, we'll find you. Your village has been marked."

Another world and time flooded Caleb's mind, a time when his dreams had gone so horribly wrong. He and Yeshi were sixteen. Young men exploring their worlds. Eager. Ambitious. Still believing that love could change it all, even with a dad like Caleb's.

The two young men had explored the river gorges along the Jordan and now headed toward Sepphoris for one last adventure. Hearing the sound of chopping, they moved toward it knowing that Caleb's dad might be just ahead wielding an axe. He didn't relish the encounter. Still, Yeshi pushed him on.

Caleb twice dismissed the prickly feeling along his neck as he and Yeshi entered the last stretch of forest. Twice he ignored the warning chatter of the birds. When he saw Yeshi duck behind a gnarled old olive tree, he followed suit. He peeked around the rough bark, the oxygen disappearing from his lungs. Horses, six of them sheathed in dark leather armor, were speeding up the hill through the trees. Their stealthy riders lay flattened on the backs of their mounts, swords and spears at the ready. There was no question they were moving straight toward the sound of the chopping.

Filtered sunlight refracted off the death squad. A mirage? Shadows? Imagination? Were these warriors real? Caleb could accept anything, but the reality was that his dad was somewhere nearby, so busy chopping down a tree that he wasn't listening for the sound of raiders.

And now he might pay for it.

Yeshi waved his arm and slithered uphill on his elbows and knees. Caleb followed, peeking around an oak to see the warriors position themselves below the hilltop garrison of Sepphoris. They tied their horses and disappeared into the underbrush. If the leather-clad guerrilla squad succeeded, the Romans' desperate attempt to rebuild this frontline fortress would fail. And then all the Nazareth carpenters would lose their jobs and security. The region would be thrown back into conflict.

Caleb crouched low behind his tree, pulled a slingshot out of his carpenter's pouch, and reached down to scoop up a stone. He wasn't going to let these intruders invade his neighborhood without consequences.

Somewhere ahead of them, the chopping continued.

Chop. Chop. Chop.

Thud.

Silence.

"Doesn't your father work in this forest?" Yeshi whispered.

"Yes. He's just been promoted as chief carpenter for the Roman centurion."

Yeshi frowned. "May the Almighty bless us!"

Something was wrong. "Do you think that's my father?" Caleb asked.

Yeshi stepped out from behind cover and sprinted up the hill, and Caleb worked hard to keep up. Shadows flitted across a clearing ahead.

An arrow twanged and embedded itself into an old cypress less than six strides away. Yeshi rolled behind an adjacent bush and then melted into the ground cover. Caleb slowly lowered himself even further to the earth, feeling an icy shiver run right down to his feet. If they were seen, it would mean certain death.

That just couldn't be my father, he thought. Chopping a tree. *Alone. Unguarded, with the death warriors headed his way.*

Caleb couldn't stop worrying. Surely, as the centurion's chief carpenter, his father would have a couple of legionnaires to protect him.

He listened hard for the sound of an axe, but there was only silence.

"Who do you think they are?" Yeshi whispered.

Caleb reached for a stone to put in his sling. "Sicarii!"

Yeshi reached out to stop him. "Didn't the Romans chase them off?"

"Look at the horses," Caleb said. "Romans don't use leather like that, and Romans don't use those kind of arrows either."

Yeshi stood up and raised his hands as if to pray. "Then why are they here?"

"Remember the zealots, Judas and Zadok? Didn't they ransack Sepphoris, take the Roman arsenal, and go after Herod? Haven't their sons become a terror to the Romans? Didn't the Romans just lose two legions to the Germans a year ago? Maybe these Sicarii, these dagger men, think Rome is vulnerable again."

"What could they hope to do with so few men?" Yeshi asked.

Suddenly, Caleb had a different thought. "The warriors… could they be here for you? Could the Parthians be on the move again?"

"What are you talking about?"

"Do you suppose your Parthian friends are coming to check on their king?"

Yeshi lowered his hands. "I'm not their king. The Romans defeated the Parthians here when my own father was young. Keep silent for a moment before you draw attention to us."

Caleb gained courage, stood up, and looked around the trunk of the olive tree. Seeing nothing, he spoke louder. "I heard my father whispering to my mother last night…"

Yeshi made a sound of disgust. "Sometimes stories grow in the darkness."

"My father said he heard about the Parthians and you, and he heard it directly from your father while they worked."

Yeshi stared toward the area where they'd heard the chopping. "I don't see how any of this has to do with me."

"My father says that when you were still living in Bethlehem, the Parthians came to pay homage to you. He says they were a thousand strong on horseback, that a dozen magi from the royal courts of Persia rode on camels and laid their treasures at your feet. All of Jerusalem trembled, and Herod himself took revenge on Bethlehem."

Yeshi took a cautious step forward. "I was less than two when we moved to Egypt."

Caleb would not let it go. "But you know these things to be true?"

"I'm just glad to live in Nazareth," Yeshi said with a sigh. "We'd better get back quickly, before we're seen."

"What about my father?"

"Your father?"

Caleb took a couple of steps toward the upper forest. "That was my father we heard chopping." He swallowed hard.

Yeshi frowned. "Are you sure?"

"No. But I have to find out."

Yeshi looked around, almost as though he could see through the forest. "Don't you fear the Sicarii?"

Forgetting that he'd been groveling on the forest floor a moment ago, Caleb raised a fist. "Of course not! For fifteen years I've heard stories of the kings who fought for and gave us this land. I was not born to hide forever."

"None of the kings were carpenters, like us."

"David was a shepherd. All he had was a sling and a stone."

As Caleb turned to go up the hill, he felt a gentle tug on his waist belt.

"First sit. Eat, wait," Yeshi encouraged. "They will be gone soon."

Caleb knelt and strained to see through the maze of trees. His mind struggled to explain what was happening.

"Yeshi, would you ever join a revolt against the Romans?"

"What makes you ask?"

Caleb stretched his sling. "Ten years ago, my uncle was killed by the Romans with that group led by Judas from Gamla, up in their fortress on the Golan Heights. Zadok convinced him they would change the world. James and Simon, the sons of Judas, came by my home yesterday and told me I would soon be ready to fight. Do you think I'm ready?"

"Do you feel ready?"

Caleb didn't know how to answer that question.

As they approached his father's worksite, they heard no sound of horse or axe. They heard no sounds at all. Even the birds were silent.

The young carpenters stepped onto a beaten pathway, with Yeshi moving in front of his friend. After a short walk, he turned and held his hand against Caleb's chest. "Stop!"

Caleb had been looking so hard for the fallen tree where his father had been working that he missed the scene of carnage. He followed the direction of Yeshi's extended hand and discovered his father's body, empty eyes staring up into the sky, glazed. They'd never see anything ever again. Two javelins were still embedded in the body, an axe still lay embedded in the tree.

Caleb felt his friend's strong arms around him as he wept and screamed without care about Parthians, zealots, and Romans. Anger urged him to chase down the marauders, but his friend held him still and gradually the volcanic fury inside him became numb.

A few minutes later, they heard approaching footsteps on the pathway. Fearing the worst, Caleb slumped into the clods of mud at his feet and waited for the inevitable.

When he opened his eyes, a grim Roman centurion towered over him.

"Galileans! Rise." The man's voice was as hard and sharp as the sword which glinted in his hand. "You must help me bury the dead lying by the city gates. The gods have made their choices. The zealot murderers have vanished like the clouds. Choose now: a shovel and live, or take your lot with the rest."

The next hours of the afternoon were a blur of muck and the stench of death. Caleb had never seen the gore of human slaughter before. His mind felt like it was being swallowed by quicksand. Fog blocked out all rational thought.

Why? Why? Why?

Carpenters, soldiers, the young, the old, even women who had only come to cook… they all lay dead. Murdered by Sicarii who didn't even know them.

The fourteen graves were shallow, and located in a clearing among the trees, two stone throws away from the city they had come to serve.

The centurion and Yeshi collected the dead and dragged them to where Caleb dug.

Why? Why? Why? Caleb asked himself again. *I should be home…*

When the centurion finished the job by covering the bodies with a few inches of earth, he said, "We should burn the carcasses to keep them from being dug up by wild dogs. Cover them with branches until I can send a cohort to do things properly."

Caleb numbed himself as he pulled his own father's axe out of the tree where it had been embedded. He mindlessly removed branches as Yeshi hauled them to the centurion.

They gathered again over the makeshift memorial as the centurion addressed the young men. "The zealots are only proving how wise Emperor Augustus is when he dictates that we build fortresses everywhere until they are conquered. The peace of Rome gives us time to grow stronger. Sepphoris will yet rise as a mighty fortress for Rome. Now, be gone, lads, before the demons of the night swallow you whole."

Caleb and Yeshi didn't need a second warning. Caleb picked up the axe then jogged with Yeshi down the hill. The sun had almost set.

They felt drained, both from physical exhaustion and lack of water. Despite the shock of death, they obediently set their feet on a straight path back to Nazareth.

"We need to do something to stop these assassins," asserted Caleb. "I need revenge."

"What do you have in mind?"

"Yeshi, let's stay here tonight and ambush them in case they come back." He whacked the trunk of a pistachio tree with his father's axe. "By this mark, I swear vengeance on my father's murderer. Only his death will give me peace again."

Yeshi pulled Caleb along the path. "Think, Caleb. What about our mothers? They will worry. And who will share the news about your father? When Caleb stumbled and fell in the darkness, the axe spinning off into the darkness, Yeshi grabbed his wrist and hoisted him back to his feet."

"I suppose you're right. It's too dark out here, and I'm in big trouble." He looked around in the darkness. "I've lost the axe."

Yeshi dropped to his knees to search for it, and Caleb waited. But Yeshi wasn't looking for the axe; he was praying. His words rose eerily into the darkness. "Blessed are you, O King of the universe, for you made the moon to rule the night. You are a father to the fatherless. Give light to our path, O God."

As if on cue, the full moon crested the Galilean hills and lit the pathway before them.

Caleb was stunned. "How did you do that?"

He watched Yeshi rise and lift his hands toward the moon. "My father taught me well."

With that, Yeshi began walking toward Nazareth. Caleb spotted the axe lying on the ground only a few feet away, then picked it up and followed, filled with a strange certainty that somehow things would turn out all right.

Chapter Five

Nazareth, Palestine A.D. 28

The wild dog's whine was distinctive. A pup. Caleb felt it licking at the wound in his neck. His senses heightened as he felt the animal nip at his ear. He grasped for the branch still under his crushed fingers. Was the rest of the pack nearby, watching? Waiting for the pup to make a kill so they could all feed?

I'm not going to be dinner for some wild dog, he thought.

He let loose a primal yell and jammed his elbow into the pup's jaw, bowling the animal over. He rolled himself up to a sitting position, the pain in his neck and ribs excruciating, as he watched the pup run off into the darkening forest, yipping all the way.

Caleb stumbled up and hoped his feet remembered the way to Nazareth. Somewhere nearby, the pack of wild dogs barked excitedly. It wouldn't be long before they converged on the bloody patch where the zealots had left him for dead.

If the pack was hungry, they might track him down as an easy meal.

Twice he tripped and stumbled. The first time he instinctively used his crushed hand to brace his fall. Never had he been so crippled by the fire which ripped at him inside and out. Never had he been so terrorized at the thought of what might happen if he didn't keep moving.

The second fall left him empty of strength. He was ready to give up. Then, from the shadows up ahead, came the sound of singing. Singing like an angel, beckoning him home.

He set his mind on the sound and stumbled on.

Caleb arrived in Nazareth after dark and was welcomed by the usual chorus of village dogs. Their barks would keep the wild pack at bay.

An old man with a cane met him at the gate and called for his identification.

"Samuel, it's me, Caleb ben Samson, carpenter of Nazareth."

"What is your business?" the gatekeeper inquired.

"I've been wounded by Sicarii. I need help from the family of Yuseph and Miriam, who took me in as a child."

"They have gone to Passover in Jerusalem," Samuel responded. "There are few of us left here."

The torchlight thrust in Caleb's face blinded him and he sank to his knees. He heard the old man yelling for help.

Caleb awoke on a reed mat and noted three or four people hovering over him in the flickering torchlight. The warmth on his neck was intense and only softened by the pain everywhere else.

"Almighty God, spare me," he whispered.

He sipped from a cup of wine he'd been offered and embraced the darkness, falling asleep quickly.

Sestus sent a messenger in the morning requesting Caleb come to Sepphoris. Caleb acknowledged the messenger, but couldn't lift his head off the tunic which served as a pillow. He couldn't even lift his arm. His groans covered up any words he tried to formulate and the messenger soon withdrew.

When Sestus came in person, he examined the wounds and walked back out without a word.

He knows I'm nothing, Caleb thought. *He warned me. I didn't listen. He thinks I deserve this.*

A week passed like a never-ending tunnel, with flashes of consciousness and pain mixed with moments of sweet nothingness. The faces of the Sicarii mixed with the faces of wild dogs, the daggers rising, the nipping and nibbling of dogs chewing him. Razor sharp pain over and over. Fire burning his body. Then light, and the scent of Jasmine.

Yeshi's sister, Rebekah, gently applied damp cloths to the scrapes and bruises on Caleb's face.

"Oh, Caleb," she groaned. "Why you? I came as quickly as I could from my aunt's in Cana. Abba and Mama will be here soon. Just get some sleep and feel better."

The pain from his broken hand, ribs, slit neck, and pummeled face left him longing for the darkness which came when Rebekah gave him a drugged wine. Through it, as he fought fever and wrestled with consciousness, Caleb could hear snatches of conversation. The old man who owned this house was furious.

"The Roman dogs won't even send a guard here," the man was saying. "These Sicarii will kill every carpenter. I say we stop going to Sepphoris."

Caleb pondered this. *Refuse the Romans and die. Obey the Romans and die.*

Rebekah's singing was the only gift to break through the unending pain. For Caleb, she was the voice of hope in a hopeless situation. He longed for her songs each time he felt a cool cloth or sipped spoonfuls of broth and water. He hardly even noticed when she shaved away his beard and cut short his hair in order to keep the wound clear and clean. Her fingers worked magic as they massaged his back and neck and limbs.

"His eyes were swollen purple and yellow," Rebekah said, reporting to someone else in the room with them. "See how they've faded to black? I've closed the gashes across his right cheek and neck with fine stitching." Caleb felt the lightest touch along his neck. "See how the scabs are holding and healing? The blood clots matting his hair have all been washed away. His chest was covered with cuts and bruises. They too are healing. Mother, how can men be so evil?"

For Caleb, the darkness descended again, but not so strongly. And not for so long.

Somehow a group of men had managed to carry him on his mat to a new location. The light felt nearer here. Warmer. The scent of jasmine was deeper. The voice of the angel stronger. He willed himself toward the light, stretching to reach the angel.

When he opened his eyes, he saw her. Dark, gentle eyes. Dove-like. Pools of compassion. Willing him to hope. Pouring out strength.

Her words purred into his ears. "Open your eyes, Caleb. You're here, Caleb. I'm here, Rebekah. We've waited three weeks for this day. Wake up, Caleb."

His lips formed a single word: "Yeshi."

The angel disappeared again, and the jasmine scent with her, but her words reverberated off the walls. "Yeshi might be back in Capernaum. I'll send a messenger to get him."

While Rebekah was gone, her mother Miriam took over.

"Things have changed here, Caleb," Miriam said as she laid a cool cloth over his forehead. "Last year, Yeshi tried to speak to the people in the synagogue. He said some things the people didn't like. They tried to push him over a cliff."

A soft sob escaped her lips and was quickly stifled. Caleb felt droplets of tears on his ear and Miriam quickly wiped them up.

Caleb worked to push himself up onto his elbows, but the pain shooting through his back, ribs, and arms forced him to lay back down.

"People love Yeshi," Caleb mumbled.

"We all had to leave for a while," Miriam said. "I hope he can come back here without trouble. He may only be able to see you a short time."

While he waited for Yeshi, Caleb's mind filled with the joyful face of his friend, always smiling, raising his eyes heavenward, and thanking the Almighty. He imagined Yeshi dancing in a pile of wood shavings. Yeshi carving a doll for his sister. Yeshi caught up in unseen conversations with someone just out of sight. While so much of this world seemed dark, Yeshi brought him peace.

But now, his peace came from two places: Yeshi's boyhood face and the voice of the angel who hovered over him.

Caleb tried to force his arms and legs to respond to the signals from his mind.

"Move!" he shouted to himself.

This time they did—enough to give him courage.

He forced his eyes open, just a slit, and scanned the room in which he lay. It was small and shadowed, with white-washed lime plaster hardened over sun-dried bricks. The roof was flat and he heard the scrabble of chickens and a goat up above him. He had helped his father work on many such homes, but he had no specific memory of this one.

As a beginning carpenter, he had been tasked with cramming the limestone chips in between the bricks. As he'd gotten older, he had waterproofed the homes with lime plaster. Once he'd even been allowed to put the bricks in place. He still felt the pain as his father later laughed at his work and smashed out his bricks to form a window.

With great effort, he moved his fingers around the rough edges of the mat of woven rushes underneath him. The smell of an old cooking fire lingered in the air.

He grasped the edge of his tunic and wondered about his modesty before the women who had cared for him. The simple tunic he wore covered him, but surely when nature called it had been soiled. And then what? Who had changed him? Surely not the angel. His face burned at the thought.

Determined not to face another moment of embarrassment, he pushed himself hard to roll onto his side. As he did, he felt firm hands grip his shoulder and help him to sit up.

"Caleb, I'm here," a familiar, strong male voice said. "Praise the Almighty who gives you the strength and life. Stretch out your hand and be well."

Caleb eased onto his back again and looked up into the eyes of his friend. Strong eyes.

"I tried," he said to the full-grown Yeshi.

He forced his hand out and it popped out from under the blanket with ease. He watched his fingers in fascination as they curled and uncurled.

Yeshi smiled. "How good is the Almighty."

"How? What? Did you really heal me?"

"How can I serve you?"

Caleb could think of only one thing. "Out! Take me out."

Yeshi's strong arms cradled him and then lifted him off the reed mat. Caleb felt no pain from his ribs. A deep chuckle sounded from Yeshi's throat.

Caleb tried to struggle but failed. "What's so funny?"

"You're as eager as Noah's dove to find your place of rest. Know this: the Almighty has created just the place to renew your strength."

Caleb craned his neck and looked toward the door. "Where am I? My home is a palace, not a hovel." He picked up a stick and swung it around like a scepter. "What did you do with my hand?"

Again, Yeshi chuckled. "I see that you have continued to dream of Sepphoris. There's no other palace around. You have rested on my mat for three weeks now. It's all the palace you have. You've been well-cared for by my neighbors and sisters, but you'll have to get back to work if you hope to have a palace of your own."

Caleb reached over and squeezed Yeshi's bicep. "I don't remember you being so strong," he whispered. "What have you been doing?"

Yeshi moved Caleb carefully toward the door and called for his sister. Rebekah opened the door and Caleb got his first clear, pain-free glance at his angel. A waterfall of long, dark locks cascaded over her shining olive cheeks. A smile, as bright as the sunshine, grew on her face.

As Caleb was squeezed through the doorway and emerged into the fresh air, the young angel broke away. She flung her arms in the air as her bare feet beat an energetic cadence into the dirt. She threw her head back and spun in circles, giggling with glee.

It wasn't long before Miriam's calm, motherly voice intervened. "Rebekah, there are men present. You are more than a girl now. Show your joy, but mind yourself."

Caleb couldn't keep his eyes off Rebekah.

Yeshi lowered Caleb onto a crude bench. Then Yeshi, Miriam, and Rebekah huddled together.

"Food!" Miriam said, stepping back. "Rebekah, come! Your brother and father need to prepare for work again. Food doesn't appear by itself."

Miriam hustled Rebekah away and Caleb tried to distract himself. Yeshi stood, a sun-bronzed statue looking calmly toward the horizon. His brow was furrowed, his head cocked as if listening. Something had changed in the years Caleb and Yeshi had been apart. Confidence? Assurance? Determination?

Caleb looked out over the hedge at the surrounding village. Nazareth's numerous crude homes were huddled within a fence of thorn. It was all so familiar, yet it made no sense that he had been brought to Yeshi's home.

Awnings of woven goat hair shielded a few old men from the sun outside the home. Was that Samuel and Aaron? A young mother hauled a basket of wet laundry up to the rooftop to dry. Two young children tormented a dog with sticks and laughed when it yelped. A butcher shielded his eyes from the glaring sun with a freshly slaughtered chicken.

The scent of baking bread caught Caleb's attention and he rotated himself toward the small baking kiln across the courtyard.

"Blessed be the Almighty for our daily bread," Caleb said.

Yeshi walked over and slapped Caleb's knee. "Amen. I think you are getting it, my friend. The Almighty is to be blessed for everything."

Yeshi stayed a day and then was gone. Caleb remained in the village through another rotation of moon phases, gaining strength and hope. Eventually the scabs fell away and only the scar testifying to the wrath of Barabbas remained.

Every day, over and over, Caleb traced the mark of the scar on the right side of his neck and chin. He reminded himself of his blessings to at last be in a place of peace. Every day he worked his hand to test its strength—by chopping wood, carving, and slinging stones.

One day, when his legs got stronger, he trekked out to the old pistachio tree where he had chopped his mark as a young man to avenge his father's death. He carried a hatchet, and once he found the tree he hacked out a chunk to make the mark even more pronounced.

"Upon this mark I swear my vengeance on Barabbas," he announced to himself.

In his times alone, he thought back on Rebekah, cleaning, feeding, and singing as he lay helpless. He could almost re-experience the sensation of her gentle touch on his scar when he'd pretended to sleep.

But as hard as he tried to find excuses to be with Rebekah, it seemed Miriam found excuses to keep her away: "She is promised... She has chores... She needs to visit her cousin."

One other memory betrayed him, however, and kept him from pushing harder for time with Rebekah. In his early days, he had visited a winemaker and found himself too fond of the varieties on offer. The daughter of that winemaker, Sophia, had been a living embodiment of joy and celebration. She had danced without restraint and drew him into her world of wonder. They had both been drunk when they'd lost their innocence.

She had refused to see him again, and he hadn't known why. He remembered seeing her later at a friend's wedding. He'd noticed two blue cords tied amongst the tassels on her vest, which he now knew to be the secret sign by which the zealots identified each other.

As the memory worked its way out, he finally understood the cause of his rejection.

Sleep ceased to be an ally the night when Yeshi's younger brother James tried to shake Caleb awake from a dream.

"Caleb, Caleb, Caleb," James had whispered. "Who's Sophia? Why are you calling for her?"

The visions were worse and even more soul-gripping in his daydreams, and through them he began to fantasize about what might have happened if the relationship had turned out differently. Only now Rebekah's face blurred in with his experiences, and he heard echoes of his father: *You're worthless. You're nothing. You'll never amount to anything.* He was beginning to believe it.

Twice Sestus sent messengers to inquire of his health, and twice Caleb informed him that he was no longer able to make crosses. He flexed the right hand, which had been healed by Yeshi.

It's not just Barabbas who needs to face the justice of God, Caleb thought. *My hands have also been defiled by blood.*

The rabbi at the synagogue had been very convincing about the need for the people to take a different road to peace. "Swords need to be beat into plowshares," he had said. "Forgiveness needs to be given."

One night around the fire, a young Greek merchant shared about how the world had improved under the Romans.

"It's time to embrace our pleasures," said the merchant. "The time for revenge is finished. Justice can't be found in looking back. Nothing can be changed."

And then there was Rebekah, his angel. Who could focus on a faraway zealot when she was here?

What if I got married and had a family? he wondered. *Would my sons turn out better than me? How would I support them?*

Two weeks before Rosh Hashanah and the Feast of Trumpets, marking the new year, a messenger burst into the small square of the village and yelled out his news.

"The curse of the Sicarii has fallen on Nazareth! The curse has fallen on us! Five carpenters are dead!"

Caleb quickly joined a group of neighbors, and it soon evolved into a howling mob. They gathered around the messenger and learned that the five carpenters had been ambushed on their way home from working in Sepphoris. Their throats had been slit.

Shrieks sounded as the men's names were announced.

The messenger, a fellow carpenter, had discovered the dead men at the side of the road when he'd stepped out to relieve himself in some bushes. Caleb was encouraged to hear that Yeshi's father, Yuseph, and his four sons had been spared. The dagger men had sworn that they would destroy anyone who assisted the Romans, but no one had expected this.

Caleb traced the dagger scar on his neck. He had paid the price for this village. He was sure that Barabbas's men had assured him the mark on his neck would mean the rest of his village would be spared.

Liars. Murderers.

Nazareth had already been marked and should not have been marked again.

Two of the slain carpenters had been circumcised the same year as Caleb. They had learned together and played together. One had been an uncle, and another a neighbor.

Caleb felt like Barabbas had reached out and cut him again.

The widows of the slain woodsmiths, along with the other village women, wailed long into the night, the keening stretching across Galilee.

For safety, Miriam and her family moved down to Capernaum for a time. Yuseph relocated to Sepphoris to avoid any potential attack. Caleb remained in Nazareth, seething.

Barabbas must pay for this.

Caleb began to share with others his encounters in beating zealots. As his status grew, so did his stories. The villagers of Nazareth urged him not to leave the village until justice had been done, but Caleb was ready when Sestus's messenger came calling, telling him that Barabbas still ran free.

Caleb prepared his horse, packed his few possessions, and followed the messenger back to Sepphoris. Much of the forest had been cut, and the city was easy to see from a distance. While climbing the hill, he tried to figure out where the attack on his dad had taken place.

It was a relief to reach the gates safely.

As he looked back toward Nazareth, he came to terms with many of the doubts that had haunted him.

My father tried to provide for us and protect us, he thought. *He kept Mom at home when most people sent lepers away. How can I have the energy to avenge my father and still be angry at him? I swear before the God of heaven that I will not hold on to my father's sins against me.*

Before entering the city, he asked the messenger to wait a moment and then turned back toward the forest where he had been attacked by the zealots. He swore an oath to himself as he rubbed the scar along his neck.

In the name of the Almighty, I swear my allegiance to Sestus until we catch Barabbas and bring him to justice. I know the centurion is trying to prepare me for my fight, and I will endure whatever I must to succeed.

Caleb turned away from the landscape below him and entered the city. The crush of crowds around the agora marketplace was an indication that the place had indeed grown. He dismounted and walked his horse out of respect for the people.

The messenger ignored the crowd and led Caleb straight to the fortress.

Sestus met Caleb at the door, holding out a uniform for Caleb to put on. He waited patiently as the carpenter struggled to fit the Roman gear into place.

"Good to see you on your feet," Sestus said. "I need you to hear something from a centurion who's been staying in Capernaum."

Sestus led the way into an inner room brightly lit from lamps and colored-glass windows. Babylonian carpets hung from the walls without windows. Gold and silver chalices full of wine waited for them on various tables with plates of pomegranates, dates, nuts, goat cheese, and boiled quail eggs.

None of these delicacies were offered to Caleb.

"Your Messiah is centered in Galilee," Sestus said, laying his hand on Caleb's shoulder. "Because there is new rebel activity in Sepphoris, we will delay our ride to Jerusalem. Grow your beard and hide your scar. You'll serve as more than a carpenter for me."

Sestus was joined by a cohort commander who stared at the curious uniform that had been given to Caleb to mark him as a Roman of rank, not as someone in the military. Its purple trim indicated nobility while its crimson belt indicated his position of influence. The commander noted the line of the dagger across Caleb's neck, and then he turned to wait for his superior to give him permission to speak.

When the signal was given, the man began. "I speak on behalf of a centurion who has served us many years. He has been tasked with Capernaum, where he loves the people. Out of his own resources, he even built them a synagogue. He is held in wide esteem and honor in this community."

The commander hesitated, his gaze reverential.

"Speak on," Sestus said.

"I thank you for honoring me as I tell you the story of what happened. This centurion, a good man, saw that his favorite servant became sick. He was paralyzed and dying, so the centurion begged the community to find the best healing possible, whatever the cost."

"What happened?" Caleb asked before he noticed Sestus was signaling him for silence.

"The centurion sent servants to Yeshua Ha Meshiach to summon him," the commander continued. "When he came, the centurion told Yeshua that he didn't deserve to have him under his roof and that all he needed to do was say the word and it would happen. Yeshua proclaimed that this man had more faith than all the Hebrews in the country."

Sestus paced and then turned. "So what happened to the servant?"

"He was healed immediately, as soon as the word was given. So many followers are coming from the areas around the lake. The man calmed an entire storm with just a word. He fed many, many people with few supplies." The commander took a stride toward Sestus. "I would say that if the Jews want a Messiah, they should have someone like this."

Sestus began to pace again, as he often did when deep in thought. "Are there other confirmations of these miracle workings? Caleb, have you witnessed any of this when you were younger? Is your friend trained in magic?"

"I only knew him as a normal young man." Caleb's hand tingled and he stretched out his fingers. "He was good, obedient to his parents. They would go to the festivals and follow the laws. They helped me find my way."

"I hear from Pilate that he heals people," Sestus said. "That he gives sight to the blind, healing to the lame, and even hearing to the deaf." He stepped up close to Caleb. "What do you say?"

Caleb stood his ground. "Those are the signs of the Messiah. I can only say that though Yeshi met with me, my scars remain. If he is on a pilgrimage to Jerusalem, we should meet with him as soon as we can. He needs to know the trouble he's in if people keep up these expectations."

The commander looked toward the exit as if looking for someone. "They say he exorcises demons from people."

Caleb hesitated. "I think we better make sure he's on our side."

Chapter Six

Sepphoris, Galilee, A.D. 29

The weeks eroded like sand before a windstorm as Caleb put himself under the mentorship of Sestus. He knew he needed to be at his best if he was to ever face Barabbas again. He grew in his understanding of the different networks used by the zealots, smugglers, and international traders on their way through the city and surrounding countryside.

His training fell into a rhythm. The mornings started early and focused on carpentry projects around the city at buildings set aside for the Roman military. His ear was open to the talk of soldiers as he worked quietly among them. The talk was free as they passed the time in boredom. At noon, he then reported anything of interest to Sestus.

One day the centurion took Caleb on a walking tour of the agora and the business district.

"Trust no one," Sestus said. "Keep your eyes open. And watch the weaver's shop and the wench who lives there."

In the afternoons, Caleb was placed under the tutelage of a Latin instructor. When the soldiers were bent on conspiracy, they often reverted to their Latin tongue, and none of them would suspect that the carpenter could understand them.

Before he was freed for supper, Caleb practiced his Latin on Sestus and then was given riding lessons at full gallop. Most of the carpenters in Nazareth could sit on the animals, but being able to control a galloping warhorse was a skill to set warriors apart. Just staying on the horse most days was a major lesson and minor victory.

A month into Caleb's training, Sestus commanded him to march with the new recruits.

"I need you to be with us at the point of battle," Sestus said to the seventy men before him, swinging his cape over his shoulder and setting his foot on a stool. "I want justice to be swift, and I don't want to have to come back here with prisoners who die on the march. Also, there may not be enough horses to spare for you. I won't carry you like a child."

Right behind Caleb stood a dozen centurions with whips. In front stood six veterans, hardened by years of training.

A horn sounded and the group began to run, at a pace of twenty miles in five hours. Caleb stumbled often and felt the whip when he slowed. The rest stops were brief and his sandaled feet blistered. Still he ran. Day after day.

His feet were treated each night for a week with baths and massages. The food was plentiful, but sleep was short.

Then the training regimen changed to include running, swimming, jumping, and then more marching. Twelve legionnaires had been eliminated from the exercises. Another ten dropped out with the introduction of heavy packs for marching.

Caleb grew envious of the legionnaires who were given double-weighted wooden swords to practice their fighting techniques. He had nothing.

Sure, march me into battle and then leave me defenseless, he thought resentfully. *How am I supposed to fight without a weapon?*

He had agreed to train so he could get Barabbas, not to serve Rome as fodder.

Two months into his training, Sestus and six other centurions assembled a cohort of five hundred fifty legionnaires and marched them for three days along the roads of Galilee. The coordinated thud of so many hobnailed military sandals pounding the ground was a fearsome sound. Mothers gathered their children close. Men cleared the path and tried to calm their skittish donkeys and oxen. Young men melted away into the forest.

On the fourth day, Caleb was outfitted in full fighting regalia and pushed into line with the other recruits. He took his sword and spear and shield without question.

So they finally trust me. I'll show them even carpenters can fight.

The recruits were pushed to the front of the cohort as the march began, and this time they were joined by a hundred cavalry and hundreds more archers.

The centurions rode their stallions in full battle dress, their scarlet capes flapping in the breeze. The cavalry riders, upon warhorses sheathed in armor, divided up and added the sound of hoofbeats to the sandals. A dozen Roman war chariots were pulled behind the mass of legionnaires, who raised their shields high. Veterans beat their shields and chanted.

It didn't take long before Caleb realized this was no longer a drill, and that there was no escaping the battle ahead. The rush of adrenaline energized him. When the veterans took up positions behind him, and the cavalry filled in both flanks, he saw that the newcomers would clearly be the first to face the fire ahead. Caleb waited in the fourth row of marchers and could see that their enemy was no more than a huddled mass of ill-equipped rioters supported by a few men on horseback.

With a horrific yell from the veterans, the cohort began to run as a perfectly timed unit—right at the heart of the mob. The frontrunners held their shields before them, the outside rows held them to the side, and the soldiers in the middle held them above. This was known as the turtle maneuver and provided maximum protection. The ground seemed to shake beneath them.

Arrows rained down on the rioters, and then the roman frontrunners unleashed their spears and swords. Caleb hurled his spear as the others did and kept running, trying not to stumble over the bodies already strewn on the ground. The veterans applied killing strokes to the wounded without losing step.

When the resistance was gone, Sestus called for the company to halt, and the mass of warriors stopped instantly. The cavalry continued to chase down rioters who had escaped, impaling them on javelins or trampling them beneath their horses. Two of the chariots then went out into the field of dead, searching for booty, weapons, or wounded who still needed to be put out of their misery. There wasn't much work to do on this occasion, and no crosses were needed after the skirmish.

When the legionnaires were dismissed to retrieve their weapons, Caleb noticed that many of the dead looked like farmers, tradesmen, and villagers unaware of what it meant to defy Rome. Some were clearly zealots.

He wandered almost aimlessly, examining the victims' facial expressions and trying to determine their ages. The look of surprise frozen into a death mask on the face of a young boy of about ten caught his attention. He looked a lot like Yeshi's younger brother, James, and a baby chick was still nestled in a fold of the boy's tunic. A killing stroke to the boy's neck had set his head at an odd angle, but Caleb realized that a javelin in the boy's leg had taken him down first. As Caleb retrieved the javelin, he noticed that it was his own. Without regard for his dignity, Caleb fell to his knees and vomited.

A sharp jab caught him right in the side and flattened him. A moment later, strong hands were grabbing him by the collar and belt and lifting him to his feet. Caleb saw the javelin that had inflicted the pain, and realized it had come from one of the veterans. No veteran would tolerate such weakness.

His humiliation increased when he was dragged before the commander to explain himself. Caleb then appealed to Sestus, but when the centurion rode up and heard the charges his disappointment was clear.

"I expected more by now, carpenter," Sestus said. "You will never be a match for Barabbas. We'll have to train you differently."

Caleb was granted a leave from further slaughter, and he decided to return to Sepphoris, which would be a welcome refuge from the demands of the legionnaires.

Still, Caleb wondered what Sestus had planned for him next.

Most of the carpenters of Sepphoris began to skip workdays as harvest time arrived for the wheat and barley. A few early winter rains had begun to cool the air and make outside work more miserable.

Once a week, while most of the Hebrew workers stayed away from the worksite to honor the Almighty's command for sabbath rest, Caleb wandered the city. On his third Sabbath in Sepphoris, he chanced to find the weaver's shop which Sestus had brought to his attention.

Now, where's the wench I'm supposed to find? he asked himself. *And why do I have to watch out for her?*

The fountain nearby eased his troubled thoughts as he watched it gurgle up from the mouth of a fish. Images of what the illusive wench might look like played with his mind. A hag in rags, no doubt.

He knew that a Greek merchant had originally installed a nude marble replica of the goddess Diana as the centerpiece of this fountain, but a Hebrew carpenter had used his hammer to shatter it. That carpenter had in turn been pierced by a Roman javelin, and still he had hammered at the image until his blood filled the pool. It had taken days to clean away the red stain. Other carpenters had refused to work for months until they received assurance that the erotic Greek statues wouldn't be put on public display.

Loitering in the nearby stalls, Caleb purchased a few dried dates, figs, and raisins being sold by an Arab merchant. A city like Sepphoris refused to shut down because of the worship days of one group or another. Some were always willing to work to earn their daily wage; someone was always in need of provision.

Caleb felt hunger pangs and set out for a familiar shop: his favorite bakery. The large purni oven was a wonder, and the oven burned wood, not just charcoal. It was lined with stones instead of clay. A baking sheet had been placed over an opening above the fire and the thick dough rested and browned in the heated sanctuary.

Caleb looked over the unleavened flat loaves, and even the thin wafers, but a thick loaf was even more amazing than the breads made for the temple rituals, and there were so many varieties. Different flours combined with different fruit and vegetable juices to produce a gourmet menu of tastes which he was determined to sample every week.

After making his selection, the baker prompted Caleb to pick up his purchase from the merchant at the corner table. There, he found three loaves instead of two.

"I only purchased two," Caleb said.

"Perhaps the Almighty is providing for you," the merchant replied.

Caleb stared at the man's familiar, hawk-like nose and cropped beard. The brown Arab shawl hugging his skull draped over the reed basket of coins and shadowed his face. His bony fingers snatched the payment Caleb offered and then pushed the loaves toward him.

"I won't take what isn't mine," Caleb stated.

"A worthy man, no doubt." The merchant reached under a folded carpet and withdrew a small parchment. "The Sicarii are closer than you think. One day you will need this. Hide it well until that time. This is not Caesarea."

Caleb watched the man's thin frame slide off the stool and then hobble out the back entrance of the bakery.

A shudder ran deep to his liver. That had been none other than Titius, the blind old goat.

The parchment fit easily into the sleeve of Caleb's tunic and he kept it hidden there until he reached home, where by candlelight he examined the writing while chewing on the fresh bread.

> Beware the spider and the fly.
> Test all before you taste.
> The rebel heart beats deeply under the most beautiful faces.

None of it made sense, but Caleb knew the messenger, and he knew the message had to be taken seriously.

If he could only figure it out.

Free of the legionnaire battle-training, Caleb spent his days around the city performing carpentry jobs for the military, all the while listening for any signs of subversion. Titius continued to pass him an extra loaf of bread at the bakery from time to time, but the messages accompanying the loaves included few details of significance. He stored each of the manuscripts for Sestus.

On the fifth Sabbath, Caleb was soaking his feet in a fountain nor far from the amphitheater. The fountain sported a statue of a magnificent horse spouting water from its mouth. Some orator could be heard faintly above the chaotic chatter of the marketplace, whose smells included exotic spices and perfumes from India, Persia, and Arabia. Sparkling stalls of gems and jewels caught the sunlight, their merchants guarded by heavily armed protectors.

He felt lonely this way and pondered a visit to Yeshi's family in Nazareth. Hanukkah was near, and no great conspiracies had unfolded, although he had heard much complaining among the troops about the lack of action. The men were restless.

On this day, Caleb sensed the woman before he saw her. Perhaps it was her shadow. Perhaps her perfume was different than the other women who tested the resolve of the soldiers. Whatever the reason, he closed his eyes and breathed deeply with pleasure.

"I've seen you pass by the weaver's," the woman said.

"Many times," he replied without opening his eyes.

She moved beside him, put her hand gently on his shoulder, and stepped into the fountain. Her hand shivered as her feet touched the icy water. She gasped, and he turned to examine her face. She wore her braided hair fastened to the top of her head. Her curve-hugging stola was like nothing Caleb had ever seen; her ankle-length, long-sleeved tunic, dyed crimson, shimmered in the sun. She hoisted it discreetly just below the knee as she soaked her feet.

"I see it pleases you," she purred. "I made it myself with linen and silk. Right now it's the finest dress in all of Sepphoris. The style of the wealthy is white, but I don't want to look like everyone else."

"To what do I owe this pleasure?" Caleb asked, fascinated.

"My own pleasure."

Caleb looked into her eyes and felt himself drawn in like a fish on a line.

"I had to show this to someone I could trust," she continued. "To stand before a woman-starved soldier in this outpost would be both stupid and dangerous. But the material is so light, I sometimes feel like I'm wearing nothing at all."

Caleb smiled as she turned slowly so he could get a full sense of her creation and the way it accented her womanhood. The dress was translucent without being transparent. It pulled his eyes to all the right places.

"So, you assume I'm not women-starved like the others," he said, his internal stirrings testing her assessment.

"I'm counting on it," she teased. "But I'm also counting on the self-control you're learning with the centurion. We will begin meeting every Sabbath to learn the next steps of our mission, and I need you to play the man."

"And what does that mean?"

"First, you must know my name. I am Deborah."

Caleb tried to keep focused on her eyes, which were watching him intently. He looked back at the fountain. "I assume you already know who I am. But what else must I do to 'play the man'?"

"You must make it seem as though you are interested in me so I'll have an excuse not to be courted by these hungry barbarians. This will give us reason to stroll the markets and talk. Sestus has hired other girls to play the harlot, to loosen the lips of visitors and soldiers alike. I only have to run the weaver's shop, sell goods, explore the minds of my fellow merchants… and spend my Sabbaths with you." She cocked her head slightly and smiled. "I trust you have resigned yourself to this as well?"

Caleb wasn't sure what to say. Admitting that he had resigned himself to the assignment might indicate that his genuine interest would never be considered true. Saying he wasn't resigned to the assignment might create a misunderstanding about his willingness to be with her.

Without a word, he rose to his feet and put out his hand for her to take. He saw her hesitate, so he stepped out of the fountain and reached for her again. She waded to the edge and stepped out to be with him. They both put on their sandals and stood face to face.

"So how do we begin this courtship?" he asked.

She smiled and released the pin that held up her hair. She ran her fingers through the braids so they were loose around her shoulders.

"We shall go for a walk and be seen." Deborah tilted her head back, closed her eyes, and smiled. "You shall feed me grapes at the marketplace and I shall laugh at your wit and wisdom. We shall walk near the fortress and listen to the soldiers. Then you will see my father so that he knows not to put a knife between your ribs when you're near me."

Caleb stared at her. Was she serious?

Deborah lowered her chin, looked across the market and started walking. He followed.

Five minutes later, she tugged hard at his arm. "Slow down. Why do you have to walk so fast? No one will think we're lovers if I'm constantly chasing you."

The rest of their time together that day was a little more strained than Caleb had hoped. He couldn't seem to think of anything to talk about. He didn't have to worry that she noticed his awkwardness, since she carried the conversation without much effort from him.

Only once did he venture to say very much, after she asked him what he wanted to do with his life—more than anything else.

"I want to create a trophy of wood that will always be remembered for the peace it symbolizes," he replied.

Deborah stopped in front of two legionnaires and pulled Caleb into an embrace. She tugged playfully at his beard. "I can give you bigger dreams than that."

When they neared the fortress, she reached up and ran her fingers through his short, cropped hair. "Tell me, my mighty carpenter, what are the greatest fears of carpenters?"

Caleb didn't hesitate. "I assume we fear death like everyone else."

Deborah ran her finger along Caleb's scar. "I see you bear the mark of Barabbas. Perhaps you have already faced your fear of death."

"I'm not sure anyone fully faces it."

Deborah took her hand down from his head. "I hope you are prepared to face death. If not, you will soon learn. My father will teach you."

Two months passed before Caleb met with Sestus and explained his first impressions of Deborah's father. The centurion and carpenter sat by a small stream and watched a stallion as it munched the grass after a hard workout. A covey of pigeons cooed in the trees nearby. The sun was nearing the horizon and the faintest red tinted the clouds above. Patches of snow still survived on the crest of nearby hills.

"So what goes with Deborah?" Sestus asked after Caleb had debriefed him on the soldiers' talk.

"She is a mystery still," Caleb answered. "The first time we met, she dressed herself like a queen and tempted me like a woman whose passion is waiting to be unlocked. I bit hard and she teased me with how we would be a make-believe couple to both protect her and get the Romans talking."

"You have won her heart then?"

"Not at all. We walked through the city for hours and she warned me that I must meet her father so he didn't put a knife between my ribs." Caleb pulled out his own carpenter's knife and feigned a stabbing motion into his side. "I can count the words I spoke on two hands. I wasn't sure what I was facing. She was right to warn me."

"So you met her father, Eustace?"

"Eustace? I met Hercules! Deborah told me I had to give a coded knock, and I did. Nothing could have prepared me for what I met—a giant! He must have been my size plus a half. His head was as round and smooth as the stones in that stream." Caleb pointed to two large boulders at the far bank of the stream. "He had fire in his eyes, and if there be dragons still then surely the ferocity was there in his teeth. The few that there were."

Sestus lay back on the ground in helpless laughter. It was the first time Caleb had heard the centurion laugh.

"And if that were not enough, the beast grabbed me by the throat before I had made introductions," Caleb went on. "He hurled me into his cave and slammed the door. The darkness and foul stench of the place convinced me I was on the menu for dinner."

"Continue," Sestus said between gasps of laughter. "Did the beast eat you then?"

"Not at all. It was as though I was a mouse with a cat. He growled at me, boxed my ears, and tossed me around the room. I was sure Deborah had set me up for death."

Sestus stopped laughing. "So, what then?"

"The beast began to scream at me that I was a Parthian. He tore off my tunic and threw me against the walls. The blood began to flow and I felt terror like I've never felt before."

"So you confess that you were a coward."

Caleb stood and looked him in the eye. "I was a coward for the length of a rooster's crow. When terror numbed my heart, I fought to live. I saw the beast reach for a club and I rushed at him, hitting him at the knees with my shoulders." Caleb made a swinging motion with an imaginary club. "He was off-balance and toppled like a tree. Before he could get off the floor, I had taken the club and knocked him in the head."

Sestus put his hand on Caleb's shoulder. "A good contest. Did you kill him then?"

"Not at all. The beast lay on the floor laughing, just like you were laughing. And then I heard Deborah laughing." Caleb ran his fingers down the back of his head, then down along his beard toward the scar on his neck. "Here I was, a meek, naked, bleeding carpenter standing over Hercules with a club, as if I was about to dispense with him. My self-control had been lost and these two thought it hilarious."

Sestus smiled. "So you passed the demon's test. That woman can destroy the best of men. You wonder why no man is with her. What did she do?"

Caleb blushed. "She walked around me, staring at me in the same manner I had stared at her dress. Then she ordered the beast to get me bathed and to find me a new tunic for dinner."

"Was this your first bath then?"

"My first private bath and my first Roman feast."

"What did she feed you?"

"A fowl called a chicken. And its egg. There was also quail, venison, sheep's tail, veal, salted perch, pistachios, almonds, pomegranates, yogurt, raisin cakes, wheat loaves, and the finest date wine."

"She mocks us with her indulgence," Sestus said. "Do not trust a woman who pleads to your stomach with so many foods in one meal."

"I only watched to make sure it wasn't poisoned. And then I ate as much as I could. Even cross makers can enjoy the foods of the wealthy when it's offered."

Sestus turned and called for his horse, and the majestic stallion came at once. He mounted and looked down on Caleb.

Before extending his hand for a lift, the centurion asked one more question. "Were there further pleasures to be had?"

Caleb was surprised at the question and he answered honestly. "If further pleasures were intended, I denied them all. As soon as the feast was over, I left for my own mat."

Sestus withdrew his hand as Caleb reached for it. "I will see you back at Sepphoris. There is a further test this night that you must endure. Watch the forest and tread carefully. Trust no one. There is treachery about in Sepphoris. Move swiftly. May the gods be with you."

With that, the horse and rider galloped away.

Caleb felt a renewed terror reach for him as he looked around. No significant landmarks drew his attention. He began to walk after Sestus.

He longed for the safety of Nazareth. The gentle laughter and conversation as ancient stories were told over and over again. Stories of the first parents who had lost their garden paradise after being deceived by a serpent, stories of the righteous eight who had survived a worldwide deluge of water that rose above the highest mountaintops, stories of faithful Abram who fathered a promised son at one hundred years of age, and stories of mighty kings like David and Solomon, and prophets like Elijah and Jeremiah. Stories of bold and brash heroes to make any boy long for the days of old, the days before the zealots and the Romans.

As Caleb considered his position, his throat tightened.

I've never seen this place before, he realized, looking around. The terrain was unfamiliar, no matter how long he surveyed it. *Maybe I'll go back the way we came. But which way did we come?*

He had been confused several times during the ride, as Sestus had seemed to ride in circles, in and out of forests and up and down through valleys. After a few hours, Caleb had stopped paying attention.

The sun vanished and no moon appeared. The stars, however, were out, and in this blackness they were too numerous to count.

The wary carpenter attempted to remember the words of Sestus. Something about a further test tonight to be endured. Something about trusting no one, about being wary of the forest, about moving swiftly.

The hills surrounding him offered no geographical markers. His only hope was above—the stars. As he looked up, though, he realized that his hope lay even above the stars. He needed the Creator of those stars.

A night like this would invite a song in Nazareth, but not in this place of testing. If Sestus was right, his testing may have already begun. If he'd brought his flute, he would have played it, but his instincts told him not to give away any evidence of his presence. No sound, no movement.

Thoughts of Yeshi came to mind and he wondered what his friend would do in this situation.

The answer came quickly.

He knelt beside an old oak tree and raised his arms. Quietly he prayed, "Blessed be Almighty God, King of the universe, who has made the stars to guide us. Blessed be Almighty God, King of the universe, who has given us strength to live and not to die. Blessed be Almighty God, King of the universe, who has given us courage and strength and hope for this night."

Having said his prayers, he wondered what to do next. The thought came to him that he should climb the oak tree and wait. This went against everything he had learned from Sestus, and he almost dismissed the thought. The problem was that the idea had come directly after his prayers. If there was one thing he had learned from Yeshi, it was to pay attention to what one heard right after one's prayers.

He climbed the tree without further debate, feeling his way branch by branch, inch by inch, until the tree began to sway from his weight. From this vantage, he could see the distant lights of village fires burning. No lights from Sepphoris were visible in any direction.

As he rested his back against the trunk, he looked up and again studied the stars. Two weeks before, Sestus had forced him to spend two nights with an old merchant sailor who had come to town. The sailor had talked endlessly, pointing out the star patterns and explaining how to find one's way. Caleb wished he had studied harder and remembered more of what the merchant sailor had explained. His head spun from all he saw.

As he prepared himself to descend, the noise of movement caught his ear.

Probably a deer, he told himself. Still, he recalled the words of Sestus and waited, remaining as still as he could.

The sounds grew louder and more frequent. Footsteps treading over leaves, carefully and quickly. Caleb froze against the trunk.

He heard whispers too quiet to understand. Then movement again. Away from the tree. Into the forest.

Was this still a trap? Would it be better to shinny down the tree and run, or stay and wait for the sun? Waiting for the sun could mean that whoever was looking for him would find his prey a whole lot easier.

Caleb looked up and tried to see past the stars.

Chapter Seven

Galilee 29 A.D.

Dawn seemed like an eternity away from Caleb's treetop perch. The constellations continued their march from horizon to horizon without a whisper from the Almighty. An icy breeze bit through his tunic like teeth bent on gnawing off his grip on the trembling branch. The worst of winter was past, but he had come dressed only for a day excursion.

At first light, his feet found the footholds to take him down to the lowest limb. Caleb felt his heart beat faster as he neared the ground. His breathing rate increased and every movement or sound focused his concentration. Sweat trickled down his spine despite the chill. Cramps knotted deep into his back and legs.

There hadn't been any sound or movement in the past several hours, so cautious optimism began to take over.

Maybe the test is over. Maybe I can get down without being seen.

The six feet to the ground felt like twenty. As a boy, he had climbed hundreds of trees. As a carpenter, he had scaled hundreds more. But this was different. Any bush could hide an arrow or a dagger.

He rubbed the scar on his neck. *Barabbas isn't going to get me twice.*

Caleb perched on the tree's lowest limb for what seemed like an hour. Daylight was rapidly chasing away the shadows and he knew courage would soon demand he take the risk of making the leap to the ground.

I'm going to prove myself worthy to Sestus. He might track me down and destroy me, or he might find me and reward me.

When he did make the leap, he hit the ground and rolled just as Sestus had taught him. He scrambled into a crouch and headed for the brush at the edge of the forest. There he knelt and waited for another long stretch of time. He listened and watched the stirring of a few birds, a rabbit, a jackal on the trail of the rabbit, and a deer heavy with fawn.

Seeing that the wildlife were relaxed, he made his break. He ran toward the east, half-expecting an arrow or javelin to cut him down in midflight. He dashed from cover to cover through the brushland, holding his breath until safely hidden again.

Despite not having water or food, he continued without slowing for several hours. He jogged through a grove of olives, an orchard of apples, a copse of junipers and pistachio, and then rested briefly under the thorny umbrella of a huge acacia. When he resumed his run, the landscape rose and fell like waves under his feet.

Caleb skirted several villages he didn't recognize and ducked for cover when farmers and workmen emerged from the gates destined for places unknown. Twice he stopped at streams to scoop up water in his hands like the alert warriors of Gideon had done in this same land uncounted years before.

By scouting the path of the sun, he estimated that it was after midday when he emerged onto the top of a hill which overlooked a vast expanse of water. A survey of the lake gave him time to catch his breath. Overhead, a few white clouds and birds drifted by.

Had he been running away from something, or toward something?

Several fishing villages dotted the shoreline. Plastered homes were surrounded by nets and fishing gear. Small shops and shelters seemed designed to accommodate travelers, worshippers, and hopeful merchants. Dozens of small boats were moored at the water's edge and a few men mended their nets.

Off to the left, a cluster of buildings revealed a Greek tavern, an Ephesian market stall, a Roman trading post, a horse barn, and a local fish vendor. Even farther left lay a sprawling synagogue.

He headed right.

By the time Caleb reached the last rolling hill above the settlement, he was so hungry that he believed he could eat anything. Fortune smiled upon him as a young girl waved from the stoop of a nearby home. He took it as an invitation to come closer.

As he stepped toward her, he looked down at his feet and tunic.

Goodness, I look like a boar fresh from wallowing in the dust pit. Blessed be the Almighty for calling our people to feed the stranger.

He covered the last two hundred yards to where a woman and young man had taken their place by the girl.

"Welcome, stranger," called the woman. She bound her mantle tight and tied up the girdle that held it closed.

"Your welcome is received with gratitude," Caleb replied.

"Have you come far?" the woman asked. Her broad shoulders and bronzed face gave evidence to her strength in adversity. Her smile seemed genuine. A faded embroidered shawl across her streaked raven hair suggested former glory long since lost to time.

Caleb looked into her dark compassionate eyes. "From Nazareth. I've been on the road since dawn. Where might I be?"

The little girl giggled and the young man smiled.

"You are a strange traveler," said the woman. "Traveling through the heat of the day and not knowing where you are going?"

"It is an unusual task that forces me to your doorstep," Caleb said, feeling the rasp in his throat.

The young man stepped in front of the woman and young girl. Perhaps they were his mother and sister? He raised his fists, showing off his large biceps. He expanded his chest as if he meant business, but his squinting eyes and pursed lips took the edge off. His unkempt beard struggled to assert itself along his square chin.

"Do you bring us trouble?" the young man asked. "Our welcome is removed if you do."

"Simon!" rebuked the woman. "It is not the way of Capernaum to lash out at those who have shown us no harm. Alert your father that we have a guest. Bring the sardines." She turned and picked up a large clay soup pot. "My boy, it's too bad your bride is away helping her sister give birth. I could use her help."

"We should have stayed in Bethsaida," Simon said as he turned his back to Caleb.

Caleb stood awkwardly as Simon walked away and left his mother and sister behind.

Next, the woman turned to her young daughter. "Elizabeth! Bring more water. There are hands and feet to wash, and the lentil and fish soup will feed more than just the family today."

She stepped briefly into the shade of her home but emerged again a moment later with a full wineskin.

Caleb accepted the offered wine and followed his hostess into her courtyard. He waited patiently as water was poured and the girl washed his feet. Afterward, she dried them with the edge of her tunic. Although she smiled, she remained silent throughout her task, pushing back her shoulder-length braids. When she was done, she slipped away behind a canvas lean-to.

The mother proceeded to set fresh dough in her small clay oven. She set the soup over another open fire.

"My name is Ana, servant of the Lord God Almighty," she said once the meal was underway. "By what name does your mother call you?"

The tired carpenter responded without hesitation. "Although my mother be dead, she once called me Caleb."

"May the Lord have mercy on your mother and those who grieve her," Ana said. "So Caleb, what brings you to the shore of Galilee on a day like today? Have you come to work on the new city named after the emperor?"

Before Caleb could respond, her burly husband barged into the courtyard, a strong odor of fish surrounding him. He carried a reed basket filled with sardines, and he dumped these sardines into the soup pot without ceremony. Only then did he acknowledge his guest.

"Shalom. Isaac, fisher of Galilee," he announced. "Whose mouth has the Almighty asked me to feed on this day of his?"

"Shalom. Caleb, carpenter of Nazareth. Honored to receive what the Almighty has prepared through you."

Isaac broke into a deep-hearted chuckle. "A carpenter? Does the Almighty send me answers before I can ask for them?"

This guy sounded a lot like Yeshi, Caleb decided. But what did the Almighty have to do with his arrival here? He gave the fisherman an inquisitive look.

"Only last night, I noticed the sides of my boat had worn down beyond my ability to repair," Isaac explained. "I told my brother that my family may have to borrow some fish from him until God could find a way to solve the problem. And now here you are."

Caleb winced. "Sir, I have never repaired a boat before, but I am a worker of wood and I would be happy to help you in return for your hospitality."

Isaac leaned back and lifted his feet as his daughter set about the task of washing them. She ignored her brother, who also lifted his feet.

"We will talk after we eat," Ana said.

As they gathered together, Isaac offered the blessing. "Blessed are you, Lord God Almighty, King of the universe, for you have opened the ground and sea to fill our bellies on this day. Amen."

Isaac grabbed several chunks of freshly baked flatbread and used one to scoop up the broth of fish and lentils that came to him in a large clay bowl. He ate as if he hadn't eaten in days. Caleb soon followed his example.

When the bread and soup were done, and the pot empty, Isaac wiped his mouth with the back of his hand and announced, "Now we will hear the story of Caleb, the carpenter. The Almighty has opened the hills and produced a carpenter on the very day we needed one. Tell us the tales of Nazareth and of how the Almighty brought you to our home."

Caleb found it easy to share his stories, and even to embellish them. Isaac and Simon frequently doubled over with laughter and then tried to share their own versions of similar happenings.

In the late afternoon, the trio wandered down to the shoreline so Caleb could take his first look at the boat. The vessel was almost thirty feet long, eight feet wide, and about four feet deep. It was fairly flat-bottomed so it could be brought close to shore. Cedar planks had been joined together to form its core. Caleb recognized its pegged mortise and tenon joints and was surprised by how few nails had been used. A few other types of wood showed where previous repairs had been done.

Caleb smiled to himself as he examined the hull and knocked on specific boards to check for rot. The fishermen wandered around behind him like lost puppies reacting to his every "hmmm." Fishing nets lay strewn about on racks. It seemed to Caleb that those nets were going to be sitting for a while.

"Is it serious then?" Isaac asked.

"Serious enough."

Simon watched him carefully. "What do you need me to get for you?"

"I'll need four good cedar planks to replace these boards here." He indicated a section at the bow on the right side. "The rocks have had their say against this hull. You don't want to be feeding the fish unexpectedly during the next storm."

Simon spouted off his bravado. "Storm? You can hardly imagine the storms we've survived on this lake. My brother Andrew and I have scooped more water out of this barge than sits in most lakes around here."

"I'm sure you have," Caleb said. "You sure wouldn't get me out on this thing. I've been learning to ride a Roman horse, and that's enough to make me ill."

Isaac jumped on that remark. "Are you telling me that you've never been out for a sail on the lake? And with this place, right in your backyard? In exchange for your services, we'll take you out and give you everything we catch in our first three casts. We'll even prepare it for you so you can take it back to that Roman market of yours. It's about time you got some good tilapia in the bellies of those city folk."

Caleb didn't barter with him; he was just glad to be safe and well fed.

The clouds overhead were dark and boisterous as the evening arrived. The swell on the water picked up and small whitecaps began to rise from the brisk wind. Caleb began to feel queasy.

Isaac slapped him across the shoulder blades. "Okay, carpenter. Tell me then, where do we find these cedar planks?"

Caleb explained the process of finding a good cedar tree, cutting it down, and preparing the timbers.

Isaac held up his hands and furrowed his brow. "Whoa, whoa, whoa. All that just to fix this?"

Caleb scanned the fishing boat in drydock and then looked out at the choppy waters. "I would want to be sure if I was you."

"We could be off the sea for several Sabbaths," Isaac said, throwing up his arms in frustration. "Are you stalling to eat me out of house and home? Did the Almighty send you to teach us how to fast or just to empty our cupboards? I don't suppose you even have an axe or tools to prepare this tree."

Caleb realized the obvious: fishermen didn't necessarily have the tools of a carpenter. It would take four or five hours to walk from Capernaum to Nazareth. Gathering tools, locating good trees to cut, working the wood… Perhaps it would be three or four days of hard work.

"I'll go back to Nazareth and borrow some," Caleb said. "The best tools are at Sepphoris, but I don't dare go back there."

Isaac stopped for a few moments and looked up into the hills toward Nazareth. "With treachery looking for you, son, you can't go alone. We'll fish hard tonight with the sons of Zebedee, and then they can join you for the trip. It's been a long time since any of us have left this place." He patted his belly and smiled. "Perhaps they will get a taste for goat cheese and lamb's tail. But I can only spare them a week."

"It's enough," Caleb said.

The evening meal was fried tilapia with more of that delicious baked bread. They also enjoyed a seasoned stew of chickpeas and lentils mixed with onions, garlic, and leeks.

As soon as Elizabeth picked up the crude wooden plates and pottery bowls for washing, the men stood and stretched. Isaac pointed at a tarp tied from the edge of the basalt block house and pegged into the ground at a forty-five degree angle.

"Your mat's inside," Isaac said. "We'll be out early, but we'll let you sleep. You've come a long way and it'll be a long way back."

Caleb spent a fitful night despite reliving his run from invisible pursuers the night before. He was anticipating the prospect of walking back into the realm of this hidden threat he didn't understand. The night was cooler than he was used to and the breeze found its way through the tarp. The mantle he'd been given wasn't quite enough to keep him warm. Still, he had rest and safety.

Caleb's eyes opened at the break of dawn and he smelled fish. Raw fish. He raised himself on one elbow, turned toward the opening of the tarp, and saw a basket of fresh tilapia waiting for him there, still wet. The breeze blew across them and into his face.

Give me woodchips and sawdust any day, he thought. *How do they live with this stench?*

He crawled out of his den and searched for the others. Ana was crouched over an open fire with several tilapia suspended on sticks over a bed of coals.

She turned at his approach. "Shalom. Peace to the servant of God and thanks to the Almighty for his provision of rest."

"Shalom," Caleb responded, taking up an axe and chopping more wood for the fire.

Ana straightened up and smoothed her mantle. She stepped gracefully around discarded fishing gear in the courtyard and checked on the baking bread.

"The men are determined to bring in one more catch," she said over her shoulder. "They've already taken their breakfast. Isaac says you should be on the road when the sun crests over the hills. That won't be long."

Caleb ate the simple gruel that was given to him along with the fish and bread. By the time he was finished, he could hear voices come up from the beach. He expressed his appreciation to Ana and set the bowl down near the others which had been left for washing.

Elizabeth appeared as he stood on the beach later, waiting for the fishermen to return.

"You're not like him, you know," the girl said.

Caleb uncrossed his arms and looked at the dark eyed girl. "Like who?"

"Yeshua ben Yuseph," she answered. "He laughs more and tells stories even I can understand. He's always calm and peaceful. He healed Simon's mother-in-law here last year."

"You know Yeshua?" Caleb asked, taking a step back. He examined Elizabeth closely. "I thought I was the only carpenter you knew. Why didn't your father get him to fix your boat?"

"He's not that kind of a carpenter here."

"So you left the hard work for me?"

"You know, he did something even more amazing than healing an old woman…"

Caleb watched a fisherman struggling to hoist up his net so it could dry. "What did Yeshua do that was so amazing?"

"He healed Anthony," Elizabeth said. She was staring at a palatial home a short distance away, smiling as if she had caught a prize fish on her hook. "Yeshua was in Cana and Anthony was on his mat in that house. His father works for Herod, but Yeshua still healed him. Yeshua is the voice of God to us. Who are you?"

Caleb knelt on one knee in front of her. "Yeshua and I were friends when we were young. We worked as carpenters together, although we have different destinies now. He knows his and I'm still searching for mine. When I find my purpose, the Almighty will give me the same peace Yeshua has."

"Be safe," she said. "And be careful of those Sicarii. They've taken plenty of sleep from us with their raids on our villages. Now go with the Almighty. Be strong and courageous."

Caleb was astounded at the girl's bold words. She stood like a statue despite the cool breeze ruffling her thin wrap. Her arms were crossed and her jaw was set.

"What makes you worry so much, little dove?" Caleb asked.

She looked up at him with clear almond eyes. "I have no worries. Only this morning a lone Roman rider was silhouetted against the sky on this hill. I marched right up to him to see what he wanted."

The breeze sent a shiver up Caleb's back. "And what did he want?"

"He searches for the Parthians, for the Sicarii, for strangers. He rides here often. Parthians used to burn our villages if we didn't help them. Romans burned them if we did. We were caught between. Now the Sicarii threaten to slash our throats if we don't rise up against the Romans. They disguise themselves as Parthians to make us afraid."

"What did he ask of you?"

"The Roman wanted to know if there are any strangers among us. I told him no. There are no strangers among us. This is the truth." She looked up at him, took his hand, and gave it a brief squeeze. "You are no stranger here."

You don't know who I am, girl.

He released her hand and crouched down, examining the beach for round stones. "Why would the Parthians come here when they were defeated by Rome so long ago?"

He stood up and skipped one of the stones across the water. *Five.*

"My father told me that many of the people we now call Parthians are really descendants from the original tribes of Israel. The true Parthians have moved away." Elizabeth stepped out of the shallow water and shook her feet. "Those who raid us are our former brothers searching for their homeland. They're ruthless because they feel they have no choice. The enemy is too strong."

"Capernaum is a busy little place," Caleb said.

"There's another group, trying to find a way to bring Chinese silk past the Romans."

"Are they zealots?"

"No!"

"Do you know of any zealots in this area? Have you heard of Barabbas?" His next stone sank after three skips.

"I've only met one zealot, and he followed after Yeshua Ha Meshiach with my brothers."

"It seems the whole world is following after Yeshua."

Elizabeth's glistening eyes betrayed her enthusiasm. "They have been on many journeys with him. They say that he turned water into wine at a marriage feast in Cana. He says many great things about the Almighty, but not everyone understands him." She began to walk toward home. "Many of the girls know that no one has been promised to him."

"Perhaps he has another mission," Caleb said, following her.

Elizabeth shrugged her shoulders and walked over to where her mother was rinsing more pots.

Caleb looked back up toward the hills. *Am I fighting my own people and keeping them from regaining their homeland? What am I doing for Sestus?*

Peering down the shore, he saw a band of fishermen stepping out of their boats, including Isaac and Simon. The burly father remained with the boats while his son and three others approached Caleb. On the way, the muscular Simon wrapped a tunic around himself. The trio of newcomers with him were similar to the boy in build and dress; they all wore tattered brown shoulder capes that partially covered knee-length tunics, along with sandals whose straps wrapped loosely above their ankles.

Simon called out the introductions. "Caleb, boat-builder of Nazareth, meet the fishers of Capernaum. My brother Andrew is my little helper." Little Andrew rewarded him with a punch to the shoulder. Simon laughed, brushing him away. "Pesky flies. One of these days I'll have to squash them all."

The others playfully pulled the brothers apart.

"Meet the other half of the team," Simon said. "Brothers as well. James and John."

"I'm James," said the tallest of the group. He had a weathered face from years of sun and wind, and the crinkles on his forehead spoke of deep thought and worry. His bushy eyebrows and well-developed beard distracted from his bulbous nose and prominent chin. "May the Almighty bless you, Caleb."

The other man, John, had a bare, youthful face. His wide mouth and sparkling eyes seemed to invite Caleb into his world. "Shalom, Nazarene. We salute you in hopes of the coming Messiah."

Simon elbowed the young man in the ribs, and then all four jostled with each other.

After a moment, they turned their faces inland toward the trail Caleb had descended the day before. The pathway wound up to the top of the basalt hills surrounding the lake.

As they set off, the quartet of fishermen from Capernaum quickly outpaced Caleb, and in their joking they gave Caleb the impression that they didn't have a care in the world.

He kept his eye fixed on the road ahead and kept his ear tuned for hoofbeats.

Chapter Eight

Capernaum, Galilee 29 A.D.

"So, my brother was telling us this morning about all the tales you told around the fire last night," Andrew said. "I was sorry to have been on an errand with the Zebedees."

"Sitting around a fire brings out the hero in all of us," Caleb replied as he reached the top of the path. "I'm a simple Jewish carpenter who too often finds himself in the wrong place, doing what I would rather not do."

James put an arm out in front of Caleb. "Why should we trust you? You seem so Roman, so much more than a simple Jewish carpenter. Look at the tunic you wear."

Caleb turned his back to James and stood overlooking the vista of Galilee. He drank in the shimmering expanse of water. In the distance, the rich farmland of the Jordan Valley spoke of abundance, and the forested hills of Gilead spoke of security and peace. Three towns of the Decapolis poked up from the greenery, and small spires of smoke gave evidence of people going about their daily life.

"A man is always more than he appears to be," Caleb said. "Just like a land is always more than it appears to be."

"It's a beautiful land," James said. "Speak to me again about Sepphoris. This place sounds like they are bringing Rome to Galilee. Roman baths and markets, with all you can imagine. Women dressed in silk and soldiers ready to crucify anyone who breaks the peace. What is this world that's rising?"

Caleb adjusted the fisher's mantle given to him by Isaac. He looked identical to the others, who had already turned away from the lake and continued on toward the forests.

"The Romans are trying to protect this land from the zealot raiders," Caleb said. "They're only sharing the wealth of the world with us."

He bent over and picked up a stone, then threw it dead center against the trunk of an oak tree fifty feet off the road.

"Nice shot," encouraged John from behind. All four of the men failed in their several attempts to duplicate Caleb's feat.

"I know nothing about zealot raiders," James said. "The zealots have left us alone for years now. It's the Sicarii we fear, those radicals who would cut our throats if we refuse to rebel against the Romans."

"The Sicarii are zealots, Barabbas the worst. I bear his scar on my neck." Caleb smoothed out his beard to show where his scar remained, and he allowed Andrew to run his forefinger along the line. "I wear the shackles of Rome. I'm not sure who to fear any longer."

Andrew ran ahead a few steps and leaped into the air. "Surely the Messiah will be coming soon. We have all dreamed of this day. The prophet Daniel points to our day, you know." He walked quickly backward, ten paces ahead, urging Caleb and the others to walk faster. "God never forgets his people. We will celebrate Purim soon, to remind ourselves of Esther's great victory. The signs all point to the time of our deliverance."

Caleb looked back at the three fishermen now walking faster right behind him. He jogged a few steps toward Andrew. "Are you involved with the Baptizer, or with the Essenes in Qumran?"

"Sure, I used to follow the Baptizer," Andrew replied. "What do you know about the Messiah?"

"I know you've met Yeshua. Some people think he could be the Messiah. I have a hard time believing it." Caleb picked up another stone and hit an olive tree well off the road. "He and I used to compete to see who could make the best tables and chairs and toys for our sisters. There are many stories whispered about him." A jack rabbit scurried across the road and Caleb reached for another rock. "Yeshua was born in Bethlehem, not in our village. Your sister told me that he has visited you here."

Andrew pointed back toward his home. "He's amazed us with his words and actions. Surely, he must be the one."

"None of us in Nazareth have noticed anything special. Yeshua was welcomed by the Parthians as their king, but he's denied being their king to me." Caleb glanced up at the cloudless sky and slipped off his fisher's mantle. He was already feeling sticky in the heat. "Perhaps Yeshua didn't tell you that he fled with his family to Egypt to escape the wrath of Herod. But now he is in Nazareth. A nobody. I know our deliverer will be born in Bethlehem, so the issue of whether he could be the Messiah isn't yet settled in my mind."

"What would it take to settle it?" Andrew asked.

Caleb walked stride for stride with Andrew. "Yeshua is rugged and strong and understands the ways of God. He's always questioning the ones learned in Scripture." Andrew nodded in agreement so Caleb continued. "I've heard others say there's much talk in Jerusalem about the Messiah. The country blazes with rumor, but I've been too busy trying to live to pay very much attention."

The other three travelers bunched in close to listen in.

"We ourselves have been with him and heard his teachings," Simon spoke up. "We await the day when he calls us to follow. He is the Son of David who will bring in the kingdom of God."

Caleb stopped. "If you're right, then Yeshua must be warned that the Romans are watching him. You must tell him when you see him. The Romans won't allow their peace and pleasure to be destroyed—"

"But what will they do to keep their peace and gain their pleasure?" Andrew asked.

"They'll do almost anything to keep peace. I've seen the Romans crucify people and slice open the back of a man with their cat o' nine tails. It's a horrifying experience, and it reminds us all to mind what we do."

"We are only fishermen," Simon said. "The only thing we need from the Romans is their absence."

"And their mercy," John added. "All of us in this land need mercy when times are so unsettled."

"The Romans have no mercy on the Sicarii," Caleb said. "They have no patience with insurrection and treachery. They erect fortresses everywhere and bring their soldiers to build and guard what they've gained." He turned and faced the four. "They're constantly playing political games with their comrades, trying to advance ahead of each other. The one who wins tries to destroy the one who loses. It's a harsh and violent world they build to keep the peace."

"So why are you a part of it?" James asked. "Why are you helping them?"

"Barabbas killed my father. I'm looking for justice." Caleb began walking again. "The centurion I serve is my pathway to avenge my father."

Simon put a hand on Caleb's shoulder, stopping him. "Enough talk of Roman power. Our power comes from the Almighty."

"And what of Roman pleasures?" Andrew. asked

Caleb nodded. "Their pleasures are tempting for men far from home. They love their baths, feasts, and women in fancy clothing. They love their fighting, their building, and their ornaments. They love their stories, politics, and sports."

"What about their gods?" John asked.

"Their worship is very confusing to me. They have so many gods, and none of them seem to have the ability to accomplish what the Almighty does without effort. It's a world that cannot last."

"Tell us again," Simon spoke up. "Will the Messiah bring fish to all of us then? There's nothing like fishing to bring both peace and pleasure."

John gave Simon a playful punch to the shoulder. "Perhaps you will be the Messiah. You've caught more fish than anyone I know."

Simon pumped his fist into the air. "I'm a champion of fishers. Fish without number. Praise be to the Almighty, King of the universe, who has filled my nets with fish. Amen. I've caught twenty-two different kinds of fish in Galilee."

Caleb raised his arm in unison with Simon. "You truly are the champion of fishers. Has the Almighty blessed you with an appetite for all those kinds?"

"There are clean and unclean fish both living together," Simon replied. "I would petition the Almighty to sort the clean and unclean to make this work easier."

Without warning, the sound of hoofbeats began to reverberate in their ears. They sprinted toward a grove of trees several hundred yards off the roadway, throwing themselves on the ground and attempting to blend into the underbrush.

A Roman rider in full battle gear galloped into sight and almost immediately yanked on his reins and halted his horse.

"Reveal yourself or die!" the Roman shouted.

To reinforce his words, he moved his horse steadily in their direction. Within a minute, three other horsemen had joined him with their javelins at the ready.

As the fishermen stepped out of their hiding place, one of the horsemen trotted through the grove to look for others who might still be hiding. When no one else was found, the group of mounted Romans crowded their horses in close, trapping the fishermen.

The sound of hundreds of hobnailed sandals echoed in the trees, and soon a cohort of legionnaires came into sight, marching down the road. Caleb started choking on the dust.

Five hundred warriors seems excessive, he thought. *There's nothing out here.*

One of the scouts extended his javelin up to Simon's chest. "Speak. What is your business?"

"We are fishermen from Capernaum," Simon said. "Galileans all, looking for cedar to repair our boat."

Seeming satisfied, the scout signaled for the horses to back off a step. He then prodded each of the fishermen with the butt end of his javelin.

"We seek Barabbas," the scout said. "He was seen in Tiberius. Have you seen him?"

Simon continued on as the spokesmen. "We have not been near Tiberius. Neither have we seen Barabbas."

The scout nodded and turned toward the soldiers he was escorting. When the legionnaires had passed, the group of riders galloped after them and disappeared from view.

"Let's stay off the road." Caleb angled away from the main thoroughfare. "If the Sicarii are nearby, we don't want to be discovered. Stay quiet."

"Why should we be quiet?" Simon asked. "We haven't done anything."

Caleb moved into a stand of pistachio trees and then proceeded past them into a grove of olives. When they were out of sight of the road, he stopped and faced the four fishermen.

"James, I told you that Barabbas killed my father, that I was working with the centurion to get my revenge."

James furrowed his brow. "Yes, I remember."

"Well, there's more to the story." Caleb felt pressure as the group took steps closer to him. "I'm enduring a test from that centurion, so I know he'll be doing all he can to find me. If one of those scouts recognized me, you can be sure it won't be long before we get more company."

"You're not going to get us crucified, are you?" Simon snarled.

"No one innocent gets crucified," Caleb said. "We need to stay off that main road and be careful. There's no use having people think we might be guilty of something."

"Show us the way," Simon said. "But hurry. It would kill my dad to send us for a few cedar planks and then hear we were locked in a Roman prison."

Three hours later, the travelers stopped by a small stream for a drink. Sporadic trees and a few hills covered in dense forest had provided them cover, yet they also gave their journey a sense of risk and adventure. Almond trees in bloom and a citrus harvest ready for the taking added a tantalizing aroma to the air.

Simon scooped up a handful of water and looked back on the forest they had emerged from. "Are you sure we're not lost? It feels like we're going through one set of trees after another. Give me the open waters any day. In the storm, at least you can see where you want to go… and you can see if you're getting closer."

Caleb leaned against a small oak at the edge of the stream. "We're not lost. You'll have to trust me on this."

He grabbed hold of a limb and swung himself up, then shinnied up the tree until he neared the top. From there, he looked around and noted the landmarks.

"We'll be in Nazareth in just a few hours," he called down. "Then you can meet the king of the Parthians. He and his father can show you all the tools we'll need to repair your boat. Next to me, they're the best craftsmen in Galilee."

"What kinds of tools do you think we'll need?" Andrew asked.

Caleb stretched his arms. "We'll need more than an axe. We'll need a plane, an adze, an auger, rulers, a chisel, a drill, a hammer, and whatever else we can find. We don't want your boat to sink when we rebuild it."

James got to his feet. "Let's keep moving. I'm getting stiff."

Some time later, Caleb spotted a leopard slinking through the brush. None of the others saw it, fortunately. As they pressed on, however, other wildlife appeared.

"What's that?" John called, pointing toward a mulberry tree.

Caleb spotted a quail darting behind the tree. He laughed. "Nothing that will hurt you. The only things that might get you are lions and bears, and leopards, but they'll be running from us long before we're running from them. Just keep your eye open for Romans."

The sounds of hammering and shouting filtered through the forest and the fishermen ducked behind some trees. When Caleb kept right on walking toward the sound, the rest stepped out behind him. On the crest of a rolling hill rested a large row of pylons being set in the ground on a shallow grade.

"Aqueducts for Sepphoris," Caleb announced, glad to be back in familiar territory. "I've heard some of these aqueducts can be as long as forty or fifty miles, if the water is that far away." He pointed out some of the men scrambling on top of the structure. "Some of their engineers are as good as ours, but our carpenters are still better when it comes to wood. Some of these trees have special grains and twists which are hard to work with."

As the young men passed an olive grove, they noticed a group of young women standing in the middle of it, stretching sticks up into the branches and smacking the berries.

"Andrew," Simon called. "Now there's a sight for you. If Capernaum doesn't give you your fill of fisher-maidens, you can always cast your net in these waters. I'm sure the right word, and the right price, will settle things quick."

"Why are they smashing the trees like that?" John asked. "It can't be just for our entertainment."

Caleb suppressed a smirk. "You should escape the sea once in a while, fisherman. This is how they make oil for your lamp. The women use sticks to knock down the olives. This is hard on the tree, though, and it will refuse to bear olives the year after its beating. But it's a forgiving tree, and the following year it will give its fruit again. It takes about fourteen years for a tree to become fully mature, and then it produces about twenty gallons every second year."

"It's a wonder these things survive in the hard dirt," James said as he tried to scrape up some of the topsoil.

"Where nothing else lives, they bring life," Caleb said.

"The trees look old," Simon observed. "After so many beatings, I imagine the wood is only good for building with."

"Actually, these trees last for centuries, bearing crop after crop after crop," Caleb assured him. "They're eternal, always giving and forgiving. Like the Almighty himself. Blessed be the Almighty, King of the universe, who has given us the olive tree to remind us of himself."

"Amen," the others echoed.

The sounds of clip-clopping echoed through the trees and cemented them in place. When the source of the noise came into view, the group could hardly keep from laughing. A donkey, protesting all the way, was being lashed by a huge mountain of a man trying with all his might to not fall off the rebellious beast.

The rider was on them before the four fishermen seemed motivated to move. A dozen yards away, the mountain of flesh hurled himself off the donkey with a curse and stumbled. When he regained his balance, he rose to his full height and became a tower of terror.

"Run!" he bellowed.

James and Andrew sprinted left and John and Simon dashed right, but Caleb knew who this man was and held his ground.

"Eustace, I see you're joining the Roman cavalry," Caleb said. "What gives you reason to run from that dictatorial wench in linen?"

Eustace extended a hand toward Caleb and suddenly broke out into laughter. "Oh ho… dictatorial wench in linen… oh, that is good. And did you see those fish catchers run? Like honey-stealing school boys being chased by a swarm of bees."

Caleb looked over Eustace's shoulder at his friends, who were now circling back around in an attack posture.

"I told them about how you thrashed me when I came to court Deborah," Caleb said. "I also told them how I beat you in return. How is that daughter of yours?"

The ogre released a broken-toothed grin. "She sent me to tell you to run. Sestus has just learned from a Roman patrol that you're still alive and on the way home. He's sending a patrol to bring you back after you evaded his last search force. So run! I have told you."

Having delivered the warning, Eustace turned and looked for his donkey. He glared at the fishermen, who parted to let him pass through.

The four friends slowly joined Caleb again and asked about the strange confrontation.

"Who was that?" John inquired.

"Surely not the mountain of terror you told us about," Andrew scoffed. "He seemed to be some ogre working for your protection. Are you a follower of the Almighty still?"

Caleb raised his hands to stop the questioning. "He's the brute I told you about. You can see that I've tamed the beast. The wench I told you about sent him to warn me that the Roman centurion is about to pursue me and take me back to Sepphoris for unknown trials. You remain with me at your peril."

Simon turned toward the others. "What should we do?"

Andrew stepped toward Caleb. "You know this place better than we do, Caleb. What would you suggest?"

"Nazareth is over that hill," Caleb answered, pointing ahead. "Tell the gatekeeper that you are friends of Yeshua and Yuseph and let him know of the trouble with your boat. Tell him I sent you and that you need four cedar planks about the length and a half of Simon. The carpenters there can help you. They may even take some time to come to Capernaum and fit the boards themselves. They're kind-hearted people and you won't soon forget them once you've met."

"But where will you run?" John asked.

"I'm supposed to endure a trial," Caleb said, the words of Sestus still clear in his mind. He turned to watch Eustace disappear into a grove of cedars. "If I live, I'll not need to run. Please greet Yeshua and Yuseph and Miriam for me." He grabbed Andrew's forearm. "And Andrew, do not stake your claim with Rebekah if she's there. She is promised to another."

Simon took hold of Caleb's arm. "Our father told us not to leave you. We can fight with you if the Roman comes."

"Considering the way you all ran?" Caleb laughed. "The centurion could kill us all without effort. No, it's better that you get to Nazareth quickly without me."

Andrew stepped away from Caleb's grip. "Will you come to see us when your trial is done?"

Suddenly Caleb stiffened and the others followed his gaze. A small dust cloud appeared on the horizon, and he knew that the Roman centurion and his cavalry were on the way.

"Listen," Andrew said. "Let's use the women in the olive grove as a distraction. We'll give them our outer coats and then get away while the Romans go after them."

"They'll never do it," James said. "It's too dangerous. They're women."

"We'll give them the rest of our provisions and wild honey," Andrew replied. "And I'll promise my gratitude."

Simon and John agreed to this plan, and they were already running by the time James grabbed Caleb's coat, raised his hand in farewell, and sped to catch up.

Caleb watched the four fishermen run off toward the olive grove to give their mantles to the young maidens there. As he watched, the women looked toward the road where Andrew pointed, and after a brief time of persuasion they donned the gear.

Caleb ran east, the girls went west, and his new friends set off to the south.

Before the Romans veered off the road toward the mantled runners, Caleb was watching securely from a tree perch in the forest. He could see six horsemen with javelins already drawn.

God Almighty, please spare these girls. Hold back the hand of the Romans.

Chapter Nine

Just as the lead horseman came within striking distance of the disguised olive pickers, the girls threw off their mantles. Two of the girls threw themselves on the ground while the other three crouched with their arms over their heads.

The effect was immediate. All six members of the cavalry halted their chargers and held their javelins frozen in strike position. Two of the riders spun their horses around in search of their intended prey while the others surrounded the women.

Caleb leaned a little tighter against the trunk of the tree and held his breath. Two of the legionnaires dismounted and stood in the midst of the cowering women.

When the Romans finished questioning the girls, they mounted their horses and turned southeast toward Nazareth.

Good. They're looking for me. Praise you, Almighty, for delivering the girls.

Caleb watched the five girls slowly get to their feet and gather into a tight circle. Several hugged each other. Perhaps in tears, they watched the retreating riders, then picked up the fisherman mantles and collected their baskets of olives to head home.

What now? Wait outside Nazareth until the Romans left again? Connect with Simon, Andrew, James, and John and head back to Capernaum? Go into hiding and work out something with Yeshi to keep the village safe? Maybe head back to Sepphoris? He could hide at Deborah's. Sestus wouldn't suspect Caleb was back in Sepphoris hiding right under his nose.

It was nightfall before he dared to crawl close enough to attempt to enter Sepphoris. In his early years as a carpenter, he'd enjoyed finding gaps in the walls to sneak through. It was more difficult now. The forest had been cut back further from the walls, and the breaches where he'd once gained access had been closed up. Even the sentry towers seemed higher and at more regular intervals than he remembered. Sepphoris was truly becoming a fortress.

As he walked slowly along the wall, he found the market entrance open with several cartloads of goods still making their way into the city. Evening shadows provided some cover as he waited, but the gates would close soon. He made his way up among the carts and slipped in close to a spice merchant. The sentry at the gate was screaming at the vendors who were moving too casually; he unsheathed his sword and swatted at a donkey laboring under its load. The owner began to protest and while the legionnaire was preoccupied Caleb slipped in behind him.

Caleb's stomach growled as he made his way quickly through the streets and alleys toward Deborah's. He reached for his nose when stepping over a generous portion of slops sitting under the open window of a boarding house. The stench of the city hit him strongly after several days away from it. Sepphoris needed a good rain to clean it out. The gutters were foul.

His coded knock on the door wasn't answered the first two times. Had Deborah and Eustace abandoned this place? He walked around the side of the building and looked for light in the windows.

He tried knocking a third time, with a little more energy, and then moved back into the darkness in case the noise attracted unwanted attention.

Finally the door opened a few inches.

"The stench of death is great," the voice said from the door.

Caleb called back, "But the hope of life is greater still."

The door swung open and Eustace stood silhouetted in the pale light of a candelabra. Caleb ducked around him and entered, coming to stand next to Deborah, who held the light.

"So the runaway has come back," she said before turning on her heel and heading away without further greeting.

"Sestus set for me a trial of death," Caleb announced, following her inside. "I've been outrunning my pursuers for days."

Deborah finally stopped when they reached the dining room. "There are more than two hundred cities and towns in Galilee and you have to come here."

"It's the only place I could think of to hide from Sestus."

"Did you ever notice that when he's not riding or pacing, he's in a perpetual march?" Deborah moved to the door and pushed it firmly shut. "I haven't decided whether he looks good or whether he just dresses good. He's got those sharp eyes that pierce into you. And that eagle beak of a nose on his long face, and those twitching eyebrows when he's deciding whether he believes you or not." Deborah brushed a moth off the Persian tapestry hanging on the wall. "He almost scares me some days. What do you think of him?"

Caleb stood his ground and looked her in the eyes. "Who, Sestus?"

"Yes, Sestus! Who else are you running from?" Deborah waved her hand in front of her nose. "Why did you have to wear that tunic stinking of fish?"

"It's the only one I had."

Deborah moved across the tiled floor and picked up a small clay lamp. She lit the wick and waved it around in the space. "Eustace will get you some stew, but first you need a bath. I'll find you another tunic."

An hour later, after soaking himself in a scented bath in Deborah's private room, Caleb emerged wearing a special tunic selected by Deborah.

The scent of freshly heated stew filled his nostrils.

"Blessed be the Almighty, King of the universe, who has filled my nostrils with the aroma of heaven before I die," he prayed. "Blessed be he for preparing this stew for my belly."

Deborah harrumphed at his blessing. "Do not mistake Eustace for the Almighty. He's strong, but not that strong. The stew is provided by our mercy, but Sestus will have little mercy if he finds you hiding here without his consent. He's hiding the truth from you and you're his blind puppet."

Caleb began stuffing his mouth with the bread and stew. When he was done, he looked up hopefully for a second serving, but Eustace snatched the bowl and left without another word.

Deborah walked around Caleb and massaged his neck and shoulders. Her touch was hypnotic. So was her voice.

"How did you like my bath?" she asked. "No more public bathing with the masses. I can share it with whomever I choose."

"It's a good idea," Caleb said, sighing, "although it will be difficult and expensive to get the impact of the hot and cold waters of the public rooms. And how will one catch up on the latest gossip?"

"It's not gossip I'm looking for in my private bath," she purred.

As he nestled back into her massage, he breathed in her scent more fully. He felt his muscles relax as her hands moved softly across his brow, down his cheeks, and along his scar. She played with his beard—and then a death grip closed off his windpipe. Blackness wasn't long in coming.

When Caleb's eyes opened, he knew immediately he wasn't in heaven. The smell was wrong.

"You're still not ready," sounded a deep voice.

Sestus.

Caleb allowed himself to adjust to his surroundings. It was cool. Musty. Damp. Confined. His throat hurt badly.

"Where am I?" he rasped.

"Dungeon," Sestus uttered. "Unless you think this is Deborah's bath room."

Caleb felt the restraints on his ankles and wrists. Where was this conversation going? His throat hurt too much to talk anyway. His eyes adjusted to the dim light cast by a distant flickering torch. He saw nothing except the centurion seated on a stool in the corner.

"Never let your guard down," Sestus began. "Never let beauty fool you. Never assume you are safe." The man stood up and began to pace. "Never let the look in a man's eye dissuade you from the task you have to do. Don't you ever betray me."

The centurion walked out and the torch went dark.

For days.

The pain around his throat was intense, and not just because he'd been strangled. He thirsted. Deeply. He could hear, and almost feel, the rats skittering across the floor. Numerous times he jumped to save his toes from their bites, only to feel the chains tear the flesh from his ankles. Bugs rustled through his hair and beard, but the chain around his neck kept him from shaking them off. He kept his lips tight even though his growling stomach tempted him to crunch them down.

By the time Sestus returned, Caleb would have done anything to be released. He couldn't stop his whimper. Through cracked lips, he whispered his pleas: *I will never betray you. I'd rather die than stay here another day.*

Two legionnaires were given the task of freeing him from his shackles and then stripping him of his stinking garment. He was dragged naked out of the dungeon and hauled up to the fortress entrance. A grizzled wisp of a man proceeded to dump a bucket of water on him. Three times this watering happened, and still he couldn't move.

Soldiers walked by Caleb, prodding him with the end of their javelins. The humiliation didn't kickstart his adrenalin and he lay as he was, wishing he were dead, yet fearing he might get his wish.

Sestus finally stood over him and Caleb realized Deborah had been right. The centurion really could pierce a person with those eyes.

The centurion spoke without betraying any emotion in his voice. "I'm bringing the woman Miriam and the girl Rebekah here in a very short time. If this is the pride you wish to show them, then lay in your filth."

With that, the centurion walked away.

Caleb used the words as motivation to roll onto his side. He ignored the ongoing jabs of javelins and willed himself up onto his hands and knees. He steadied himself against the legionnaires' gentle kicks. With no dignity at all, he crawled to a wall and pulled himself erect.

He winced as the old man threw another flask of water on him. Then a soldier draped a mantle over him and he wrapped it tight, staggering back into the soldiers' quarters.

There Sestus sat, chewing on a cluster of grapes, examining his ring. "Carpenter! There may be some hope for you yet."

Caleb felt two strong soldiers grab him by the shoulders and force him to walk. They took him down a tiled hallway and into a bath room. Without ceremony, they threw him into the pool of warm water. He felt so weak that he didn't resist sinking into it. He was too exhausted to fear.

Eventually he floated to the surface, then turned his face up and breathed deep.

Strong arms grabbed him once again, then dragged him out of the pool and across the frescoed floors. Once more he was dumped into water, but this time frigid. The shock seemed to jumpstart his heart and he found the strength to kick himself to the surface. He heard the faint sound of applause and looked up to see Sestus clapping.

"You will live," the centurion pronounced. "Get dressed, eat, and I will see later."

Again, he was gone.

Caleb noticed a young boy holding out a towel and tunic at the edge of the pool. It took a few minutes, but Caleb eventually hauled himself out and flopped onto the floor where the boy began to dry him. The image of young boys being held in cages for Roman pleasure played back in his mind. Caleb grabbed the towel and successfully shooed the boy away.

The same boy was waiting when he stumbled out of the pool area some time later. He took Caleb's hand and pulled him down the street into a room where food had been set out: roasted pigeons with their eggs, goat cheese, dates, figs, sardines, wine, grapes, and a bowl of stew. Caleb felt ready to vomit even as he felt his mouth water.

He knew he needed to eat for strength, but now his trust was gone. Nothing was as it seemed anymore.

Sestus stepped through a hidden doorway and watched him for a minute. Caleb eyed him but said nothing.

"You are right to hesitate," said the Roman. "The stew is poisoned."

Caleb swiped the bowl from off the table and knocked it onto the floor. "Pig slop."

Sestus walked closer. "You are worthier than I imagined. Hiding from my men, escaping my women, avoiding my search party, sending decoys to Nazareth to set a false trail, penetrating our security perimeters around Sepphoris…"

Caleb waited without moving.

"I lost six more men last week to the Sicarii," Sestus continued. "I have been tracking them through the villages of Galilee. They will pay, but not before you have shaped new crosses for me."

Caleb set his foot on a stool and rested his forearms on his knee. "And what will give me the strength or will to shape these crosses?"

"The lives of your friends in Capernaum and Nazareth." Sestus walked past a small fountain to the window and looked outside. "Your crosses today will spare their lives tomorrow. But of course, it is your choice."

Caleb sat on the stool. "I won't build crosses to crucify my countrymen."

Sestus moved an embroidered drapery across the window. "It is your countrymen who are trying to kill you."

"And why would they do that?"

"Because you are helping to build Rome. They will kill anyone who helps our cause." Sestus pulled out a knife and scraped at his fingernails. "They have the blood of your Judas in their veins. You only live because I hunt these dagger men." He took a step toward Caleb and held up the knife. "Remember, your father's death still isn't avenged and your village Messiah is becoming more of a threat all the time."

"I will not build crosses to crucify my neighbors."

"Then build them to save your family. Neither Barabbas nor I will suffer if you sit in your village and rot." Sestus moved toward the door. "You have already been marked as a friend of Rome. It doesn't matter whether a Sicarii dagger or Roman javelin takes a life. It's their lives or yours. The dungeon is still hungry for your blood."

Caleb watched the door swing shut behind the centurion.

Just watch me, centurion. We'll see whose blood is claimed. The sword, the cross, and the dungeon will always be hungry. Their appetites will never be satisfied. I'm just getting started.

Chapter Ten

Sepphoris, Galilee 29 A.D.

Two days later, Caleb selected the six trees he would harvest to build his crosses. He transferred the anger he felt toward Sestus into each swing of the axe. He removed the limbs and then rolled the logs into a row, ready to be hauled. He convinced a merchant to lend his horse in exchange for a new wagon wheel.

The carpenter was shaping his second tree outside his workshop when Sestus stopped by to check on his progress. The centurion held the reins of his warhorse, but Caleb continued as if the centurion wasn't peering over his shoulder. He finished squaring off the trunk and started cutting and chiseling out a notch.

Finally, Sestus spoke up. "It's time to find those zealots. Another band raided near Nazareth last night." He swung up onto his stallion. "I have a tracker following them now. It won't be long until we return. I just hope they don't visit your friends in Capernaum."

Caleb let the words sink in as he set down his chisel and picked up his plane. Was that a threat? What was Sestus trying to prove? Had he taken the fishermen hostage now?

Caleb skimmed the surface of the log to smooth down the roughest spots.

"Are you trying to make a soft bed for these criminals?" Sestus mocked. "These are murderers. Remember the terror of the cross. I will stretch them out to send a message clear enough for everyone to see that plundering the lands under Roman protection isn't a worthy pursuit."

Caleb spat on the ground and threw down his chisel. "What do you want from me?" he yelled. "I'm not your slave. I've been doing this for months and you haven't gotten me one step closer to Barabbas." He picked up a plane and ran it across the notch. "Why don't you do your job and let me do mine?"

"Maybe you don't really want to hurt anyone," Sestus answered as he dismounted. "Impaling these raiders won't keep them alive long enough. I want them to suffer."

Caleb stopped his plane in mid-stroke and brushed aside the shavings. He took several deep breaths to calm himself.

"There's a difference between justice and mockery," Caleb said. "People will tolerate justice, however cruel. Mockery will only deepen their resistance. My only desire is to create trophies of wood that will bring peace."

Sestus rammed an elbow into Caleb's ribs. "Is that justice or mockery?"

Caleb doubled over and gasped for breath. He took several steps away from Sestus. "What do you want from me?"

Sestus remounted his horse.

"Do not ever betray me," the centurion spoke in a low voice. "Our message of peace will be the terror of the cross. Finish this work and then I'll tell you what I want from you."

Caleb set the plane aside. Why was he making this cross so smooth? The cross was designed as an instrument of torture, a deterrent for murderers and invaders trying to destroy the peaceful way of life for Yeshi's family and others in Nazareth.

The sweat poured off his brow and down his back as he hacked out the joint for another cross piece. It would be easier to just impale those sentenced to death on a single pole, or to a tree already in place.

Why do the Romans waste so much good wood? he asked himself. *Why smear this good grain with so much blood?*

That evening, as Caleb left the public baths and headed for his quarters near the fortress, Deborah walked across his line of vision. He averted his eyes, unsure if she noticed him. She turned in his direction and he increased his pace away from her. Caleb rounded the last corner toward his room and entered an alley where Eustace blocked his path, arms folded. Deborah blocked the way out of the alley behind him.

"A word," Deborah said.

"Not a chance."

"I understand you've never felt the break of your arm before," Deborah replied calmly, as if she were discussing the weather.

"Neither do I wish to."

"I see how that Roman treats you as if you were a slave. You deserve better, but you won't get it—not under his hand. I'm wealthy enough. Allow me to keep you comfortable for the nights as you work."

Caleb eyed her shrewdly. "And what is the price this time from the one who betrayed me?"

The wench in linen eyed him carefully. "Only that you fill my ears with the gossip you hear around the fortresses."

"And why don't you fill your own ears with gossip? You have your way with men." Caleb looked straight into her eyes. "You beguile and destroy them at will. You capture them like jewels and discard them like refuse. They are helpless around you."

Deborah smiled coyly. "Sestus has forbidden me to be near his men any longer. He says I play too rough with these legionnaires, who are barely more than boys." She stepped closer and gently ran her finger along his scar. "You are much more than a boy, aren't you?"

Caleb pushed her hand away. "You know I'll never trust you again. Why don't you just move on?"

Eustace snarled like a wolf and Deborah smiled, backing away.

"Daddy's unhappy," she said, putting an arm on her father's arm. "Think about what you want. Think about how the centurion treats you. We are both at his mercy. Give me a chance to give you what you deserve."

Images of Deborah filled Caleb's mind. Deborah in her finest clothes, images of her smiling and laughing, images of her strutting with her hair down.

And then the words of Titius floated up like a specter: *"Beware the spider and the fly. Test all before you taste. The rebel heart beats deeply under the most beautiful faces."*

Pieces of disjointed conversations, warnings, and events fell suddenly into place for Caleb. Sestus and Titius knew something about this girl. They had put him and her together for a reason. He just had to discover what that reason was—before someone killed him.

Caleb took Deborah's hand. "It would be too suspicious for me to move into your quarters. Resume your Sabbath strolls with me at the fountain after the noonday meal. You can tell me what you know, and I'll tell you what I know."

Deborah pulled her hand away and stepped back. "How do I know you aren't playing me for a fool again?"

Caleb smiled. "I see we understand each other perfectly."

He avoided Deborah and enjoyed peace for three Sabbaths, as Sestus and his hunters were away. He avoided making any trips to the fountain, despite his words to Deborah, and determined that he wouldn't easily fall under her control. In the meantime, he continued to accept parchments from Titius at the bakery the morning after every Sabbath.

The agora market and its craftsmen were continuing to transform and expand. There was now linen from Egypt; silver, iron, and lead from Tarshish; slaves and bronze from Greece; horses and mules from Armenia; ivory and ebony from Africa; agates, corals, and rubies from Edom; wheat, honey, oil, and millet from Judea; wine and wool from Damascus; lambs, rams, and goats from Arabia; dyed textiles and carpets from Assyria and Media; spices and fruits and vegetables and fish and poultry… and almost anything the imagination could dream up. He quietly got to know many of the vendors and set up contacts for future news.

Halfway through the fourth week, he heard the sound of a trumpet call. Was it a warning? War? Zealots attacking? Barabbas?

No one ran into hiding, though. As the garrison scrambled into formation, Caleb rushed to discover the cause of alarm.

A herald rode in on horseback, shouting, "The king is coming. The king is coming."

The streets quickly filled around Caleb and he felt pressure from behind as more and more bodies pushed into the causeway. Hundreds of cavalrymen in full battle gear trotted in through the gate on horses decked out in fine blue linens with golden tassels.

"Make way for the king! Make way for Antipas, King of the Jews!"

A quartet of black warhorses dragged an opulent gilded carriage draped in purple linens into the covered entrance of the fortress. Legionnaires marched steadily into place until there was no space left in the plaza. Trumpets sounded and shouts of celebration erupted from the troops. Then officers dismissed the soldiers and the honor guard melted back to their barracks.

When Caleb and the others in the crowd saw that the attraction was past, they slowly dispersed, returning to their former tasks. They had paid their homage and no more was expected this night.

Caleb headed toward the baths to see what news he could discover.

Three large pools sat under a twenty-foot-high dome. Flickering light bounced off the blue and white tile fixed above and below. Dozens of bathers soaked in the pools, lounged in conversation on the decks, or took advantage of the massage tables along the walls. The ever-present small boys hustled to deliver towels to anyone who beckoned.

As he took his place in the bathing chambers, Caleb tuned his ear to the conversations around him.

"I would never empower that man, Antipatros, as king," said one bather as he reclined against the edge of the hot pool. "He is the Tetrarch of Galilee and Perea, yes. He was confirmed by Emperor Augustus on the wishes of his father, yes. He was educated in Rome, yes. He bows his head at the temple in Jerusalem at Passover and Succoth, yes. But the man is a fox. This marriage of his to the daughter of an Arab is a sham. He must be watched."

The speaker's companion glanced in Caleb's direction, so Caleb looked away to examine the light reflecting off the ceiling tiles. He still heard the man's warning.

"Guard your tongue, Phalon. There are ears in these walls ready to take your words where you do not want them. The crosses of the centurion are hungry for prey. Guard your lips."

The picture of the unmade crosses stood out clearly in Caleb's mind. The six long stipes waited to be planted upright in the ground. The shorter patibulum, or crossbeams, were stacked neatly beside the stipes, waiting to be attached in place for the corpse of the next victim of Sestus's revenge. Surely they weren't meant to be used on idle gossipers, such as these simple men. Surely the terror of the cross didn't need to be felt by everyone.

Caleb replayed the conversation from the baths over and over in his mind as he lay to rest that evening. The man had been shaking. He had actually been afraid that Sestus might put him on a cross. Since when did innocent men have to watch their words and hide away just to talk with their friends?

The power of the cross was stronger than Caleb had anticipated, and it was impacting the wrong targets.

Barabbas should be the one shaking in fear, he thought. *Barabbas should be the one hiding away.*

Two weeks later, Sestus returned to the city with eight zealots stumbling naked behind his horses at the end of long ropes. Barabbas was not among them. Two of the prisoners had short scruffy beards, but the rest were still clean-shaven, too young to show their manhood. The ropes were tied around the necks, their hands bound behind their backs. The five corpses dragged behind the final horses gave proof that there had been no second chances for those who stumbled or fell.

Caleb watched as Sestus turned his prisoners over to the control of the city's senior centurion. The prisoners were then made to kneel before the seated master of the court. Two magistrates stood to read the charges against the accused. The zealots were given a short chance to defend themselves, but Caleb couldn't hear their pleas. Whatever was said, it wasn't enough. The sentence of death was imposed. Caleb knew that once a man had been sentenced to death, all manner of torture was permitted against them to extract information. He didn't want to be nearby to hear their screams.

The eight were then dragged away, likely to the same dungeon where Caleb himself had been imprisoned.

He was about to turn away from the spectacle when he felt a steel grip on both his elbows. Before turning to look, he knew it was Eustance.

"I was sure we had an agreement," Deborah said, stepping in front of him.

"I've been busy."

Deborah helped escort Caleb into a shadowed alcove. "With Sestus back, you will be getting busier still. He'll need more crosses. He'll demand more of you. You'll be his slave again." She prodded his chin with her finger. "If we're going to survive in this city, we need to work together. Intrigue is everywhere. We need to collect and sell information, to protect us if the power in this city shifts. Don't make this harder than it needs to be."

Caleb remained quiet, and finally Deborah nodded at Eustace to release his grip. The carpenter didn't bother looking behind him at the human-crushing machine.

"I'll work with anyone who treats me with dignity and respect," Caleb said. "I think I've been close enough to death now that you can't threaten me."

Deborah stared at him, unblinking. "One day someone you care about is going to be on those crosses you make, and then you'll have to rethink everything you believe." She looked toward the market square and took a deep breath. "When I was thirteen, my brother was stretched out and left to die for three days. The Romans nailed his feet and hands, then ignored him. I had to stand there and fight off the birds so they wouldn't peck at his eyes." Deborah hung her head. "I had to endure the tongue of the Romans and their advances on my womanhood. I have not forgotten. Neither has my father."

"Sestus isn't like other centurions," Caleb defended. "Those he kills are finished justly and quickly."

"Hunters have a strange taste for blood. They begin honorably, but soon they have a reputation to uphold. Sestus may be different for now, but not for long."

As sunlight touched the distant hills and the evening shadows lengthened, Caleb relaxed somewhat. "You live like a mouse waiting for revenge in a village of cats. I may not be your friend, but I'm not your enemy yet. Do not push me in that direction."

"Don't let the centurion deceive you," Deborah said. "Those he brings back are merely scouting parties for the silk traders who feed Rome. Yes, they are Sicarii, and yes, they act out their manhood in inappropriate ways, but the true danger is much closer. Don't be blinded by what Sestus teaches you."

Caleb took a step toward the agora and stopped when Eustace blocked his way.

"I saw the Sicarii kill my father," Caleb said. "They're more than scouts for the silk traders."

Deborah held out her hands as if pleading. "I know you chase Barabbas. He too has a story. His father and brothers died fighting the Romans. He's the only one left to care for his mother. He just wants a safe place to raise his children."

Caleb felt the growl from deep within. "If I can help it, he will never have children."

Deborah ran her fingers across her abdomen and turned away. "You may be too late. Meet me at the fountain this Sabbath. I'll come alone."

He took a step after her. "Whatever happens, don't let that murderer near you."

"Are you trying to tell me that you do care?"

Her smile was too inviting. Caleb turned away and saw Sestus moving in his direction with two men in carpenter's aprons close behind. Deborah quickly faded into a group next to a nearby stall.

"Carpenter!" Sestus announced. "I need two more crosses by morning. You shall work all night if necessary. Fortune is yours: you are now my chief carpenter. I'm assigning you two assistants."

Caleb pulled his shoulders back and looked into Sestus's steely grey eyes. He took a deep breath.

"Centurion, do you still hunt justly, or do you hunt to maintain your reputation?" Caleb asked. "The last zealots seemed not much more than boys. Where do you find your quarry? In our villages or theirs?"

Sestus slapped him so hard across the face that his lip split and began to bleed. "These boys were outside your village lying in wait for your neighbors," Sestus barked. "I have warned you for the last time. Build your crosses."

Caleb assigned the task of making the crosses to his new assistants. He showed them the samples he had previously cut and left them to find their tools and finish the task. Their blood would be on their own heads if they failed to produce crosses for Sestus.

The next day, he was in a forest near Cana when he heard a voice singing like a lark. He moved like a shadow through the grove of wild olives and nestled in close behind a gnarly trunk. Several large trees blocked his view, but he could hear the voice clearly. The woman's songs were of love for the Almighty, for his creation, and for a man. Some were psalms from Scripture and others were unknown to Caleb.

He stepped out from his shelter and saw a maiden alone, her dainty hands waving a sturdy cane pole, gently hitting at the tree's branches while singing toward the heavens. She was slender and tall, her long dark hair flowing from a scarf fitted loosely around her head.

His heart was mesmerized. She was the woman of any man's dreams. He took two steps toward her, then stopped.

I can't scare her, he realized. *How do I show myself? Shall I call out to warn her? Do I just walk out as if I happened to be here?*

He stepped back behind a tree, at first not knowing what to say.

"Shalom, my friend," he ventured.

The singing stopped. "Who goes there? And what is your business?"

Caleb took three steps out from behind the tree and planted his feet. "I am Caleb, a carpenter from Nazareth. I come looking for wood for my craft."

"What happened to your lip?" The woman's eyes examined his face closely.

He touched the split lip where Sestus had slapped him. "I made someone unhappy."

"A woman?"

"No, a Roman."

She focused on him and then lifted her cane pole and held it in front of her. She adjusted her scarf, tugged at her mantle, and took a step backward.

Finally, she broke the impasse. "What delays you from your task of finding wood?"

He stepped slowly forward, watching to see if she would back away again. She stayed where she was.

"I heard the voice of a lark and my heart had to find the source," he said. "I promise you, on the graves of Naphtali and Zebulon, that I mean you no harm."

"You are a Galilean then?"

"I was born and raised in these hills. And what is your lineage?"

"We are of Judah, recently arrived from Bethlehem. My father is the rabbi in the synagogue of Cana. I am Hannah."

Caleb gestured widely. "Does your father understand the danger from Parthians in the woods up here?"

"Are you also a Parthian?"

"Of course not! The only good Parthian is a dead Parthian."

The maiden dropped her pole to the ground. "If you are not a Parthian, then am I still in danger?" she teased.

"Not at all," Caleb said as he stopped ten feet away from Hannah. "I just wanted to make sure your father understood the ways of protecting you in these woods."

Hannah picked up her clay pot and began to retrieve the olive berries she had dislodged through beating the olive branches.

"My father knows some good Parthians," she said. "When he was younger, they came to bring gifts to a young child in our village. They said this child was a king." She adjusted the pot and picked up another handful of berries. "Only Herod became angry and killed many babies out of revenge. My father says it was a sad time, but it wasn't the Parthians who created the sadness."

Caleb felt a constriction in his throat. "I know the child of which you speak. He is like a brother to me."

The girl straightened, her dark eyes glistening. "You know this child? You know the Jewish king? He is here?"

"He also works as a carpenter. He is very religious and follows the Law of Moses carefully."

"This is good," she replied. "My father told me that if he ever found that child, he would speak to the family about a marriage. I heard that the family went to Egypt and disappeared." Hannah came close enough to grab Caleb's wrist and squeeze it. "Now perhaps my father's dream can come true. You must come with me and tell my father all about this carpenter from Nazareth. Hurry, you can find your wood later."

Caleb felt like an anchor had been attached to his feet. *I meet an incredible girl and all she wants to do is find Yeshi? Why does he always get what he wants? Am I the only Hebrew meant to be alone?*

Hannah's chatter was pleasant, even if it was non-stop. "The Messiah will bring us all peace again… The whole earth will be filled with the glory of the Almighty… Our land will be the envy of the world."

Caleb carried her basket of olives the two miles to her home in Cana. Her spontaneity and joy along the way were unquenchable. *She's like Rebekah. Birds, flowers, clouds. She notices and celebrates everything. Why do I end up in these situations with women who are unavailable?*

Hannah guided him to a large stone block home with a generous property filled with gardens and blossoming fruit trees. Several young men were busy turning the soil in an overgrown vegetable garden. The diggers watched the girl as Caleb and Hannah approached the front entrance.

Hannah walked in without hesitation. "Father, we're home," she called. She then instructed Caleb where to lay the olives.

Her father called from outside, and Hannah led her charge out another door. Caleb saw quickly that Hannah's father was a man who satisfied himself often with good food and wine. The generous specimen of humanity waddled as he crossed the courtyard to welcome his daughter and her guest.

"I am Ezekiel," he said. "I'm much less ecstatic than my namesake, but the Almighty has blessed me anyway. I have a wife named Sarah, and this angel is Hannah. My studies in Jerusalem are done and I have been assigned to Cana. Are you from Cana?"

"No," Caleb admitted regretfully. "I am from Nazareth."

Caleb and Ezekiel grasped each other's forearms in greeting.

"I am Caleb, a carpenter."

Hannah was dismissed to prepare the food, but she soon returned to wash their feet. Her touch was magical, and Caleb suddenly wanted to resign his trade and move to this town.

When the task of hospitality was finished, and the towel and bowl put away, Ezekiel began probing Caleb about his family background. The two men soon found their common ground.

"Tell Daddy about the Messiah in your village," Hannah prompted at one point. Her mischievous smile was captivating. "The one born in Bethlehem."

Once Ezekiel heard that Caleb knew Yuseph, Miriam, and their son Yeshi, he told his story with enthusiasm. "There has never been such a day in my life as that day in Bethlehem. A young family had sheltered in a home near mine. I had met them first at the temple in Jerusalem when they'd gone to circumcise their son. An old prophet named Simeon and prophetess named Ana spoke wonders about this child."

The old man hoisted himself out of his chair and waddled around the room as his memories rolled on.

"Months later, our town was filled with dozens of camels. This was unusual for us. We had more sheep than we could count. But camels? Most of us in the neighborhood gathered to watch the camel riders take expensive gifts into the house and proclaim the child a king. I found out they were part of a huge Parthian trading caravan. A bright star had led them all the way from their homeland."

Ezekiel described the escape of the family, the slaughter of Herod on the infants of the village, and his own joy at finding out his wife was pregnant.

"From the day my Hannah was born, I have been trying to find this boy," Ezekiel finished. "Perhaps God has ordained a match for my girl with this Messiah."

How was it that Yeshi could still beat Caleb in competitions, even when he wasn't around? What was wrong with him?

I wonder if my dad was right? Caleb thought. *I'm worthless.*

He sat through the meal as Hannah served them. The meal was simple, with dates, stewed apples, figs, goat cheese, crackers, pomegranates, olives, and quail eggs.

As the meal came to a close, Hannah changed the course of the conversation. "If you're wondering about my mom, she's off helping my older sister with her new baby. Another girl. It seems the woman in our lineage give birth only to girls. There may no longer be enough men in Israel for us."

Caleb cleared his throat and examined Hannah's finely sculptured nose and chin. "I'm sure there's a few around if you keep looking. I've met some great unmarried fishermen down in Capernaum."

Hannah rose to clear the plates. "That's all I need. A house stinking of fish every day."

She left the room and Caleb turned toward Ezekiel.

"Do you understand why we are in the olive business, my son?" Ezekiel asked as he rolled an olive gently between his fingers. "The olive provides oil for cooking and lighting. It is food, it is ointment, it is used in sacrifices, and it is used in anointings. Everyone from slaves to kings depend on it. It is the lifeblood of our nation."

"Without lifeblood, a nation can't survive." Caleb bit into an olive and savored the briny taste. "Maybe if the Romans discover your secret for making the best olive, they'll suck the lifeblood right out of this place and send it all to Rome."

"We learned the technique from the Romans. We immerse the olives in lye, and then in brine to reduce the bitterness. This has increased the demand in markets everywhere."

Ezekiel appeared to accept the chance encounter of Caleb and Hannah and give it no further thought, regardless of how much Caleb complemented and expressed delight in the girl.

When Hannah returned to light candles, Caleb arose and bid his farewell. Darkness had settled across the land and he already regretted staying so long. He left wondering why Ezekiel hadn't offered lodging and hospitality.

As Caleb found the pathway and made his way into the darkest section of the woods, he heard the distinct rustling of bushes.

Chapter Eleven

Cana, Galilee 29 A.D.

He rolled under a patch of shrubbery and lay breathless, controlling his heartbeat and listening. For ten minutes he remained still, taking short, shallow breaths. He curled up into a fetal position, hoping the cloudy skies would keep the moon from exposing him.

Hearing a thud by the roadside hedges, fifteen feet away, nearly made him stand and run. Instead he stopped breathing and listened.

Again, he heard the thud, just inches away. It was a javelin hitting the ground. As he listened, someone picked it up and threw it a few feet further on. Again... and then again.

"Probably a rabbit," a man muttered.

"Sounded too heavy for a rabbit," someone else whispered. "Maybe a fox. Anyway, whatever it was, it's gone."

"We don't need one of Sestus's spies finding out about us now that we're so close," the first voice said. "We need to get rid of him. I don't know who we can trust anymore."

"Then let's finish this and get back. My daughter's almost finished the negotiations with the merchants."

"Who can we trust?"

"We have twelve confirmed. Three centurions are with us. Blastus is my first contact."

"How will we do this?"

An owl hooted in the distance, a haunting sound.

"Philip says he can secure two cohorts of legionnaires for the diversion. We have five of the Sicarii as well. The payment is confirmed. We must regain control of the Chinese silk trade."

"What's our best target?"

"Nazareth. It's close to Sepphoris and will strike at the heart. A lot of the carpenters working on the fortress are from there. Nazarenes are considered worthless, so we can do what we need without getting the rest of the country overly riled up."

"Didn't Barabbas already target the carpenters there?"

"Exactly! And what have the Romans done in response? Nothing."

Caleb wanted to rise up and fight, but his gut, neck, and shoulder muscles knotted. He didn't dare move.

He was glad he remained still when he heard a third voice enter the conversation: "What about that cross maker your daughter is seeing?"

"She's got him under control. Don't worry about him."

So that low voice had belonged to Eustace! Sestus had once told Caleb that when clandestine meetings took place, a watchman would be left behind to look out for hidden spies. The key was to outwait the watchman.

He settled himself for a long cool wait in the damp earth.

By regulating his breathing, he counted out an hour of time. The stillness magnified the night noises tenfold—the scratching of a mouse, the call of a wolf, the padded feet of a fox. One of the men relieved himself at the base of a nearby tree and the smell of urine created an urging in his own bladder. Shooting stars frequently hurtled across the constellations above. Still he stayed.

Caleb was about to finally move again when he heard hoofbeats on the roadway from Cana.

"Nothing on the road," stated the rider.

"Nothing here," said a watchman across the road. "I think we're safe."

"Climb up," the rider ordered. "I'll take you home."

In minutes, the hoofbeats faded away.

Twenty minutes later, Caleb slowly and cautiously unrolled himself. His back, neck, and joints all hurt and dampness had seeped through his clothing. He finally rose to his feet and rotated his wrists and ankles for relief.

He began quietly moving through the bushes parallel to the road. He wasn't going to take any chances walking out in the open, getting caught, and failing to get this news to Sestus. Anyone who would target Nazareth was an enemy now.

Caleb crouched in the woods opposite the fortress guardhouse, watching the sentry. He needed to identify himself to someone loyal to Sestus without raising an alarm. The recent meeting he'd overheard had proven there was a conspiracy against Sestus, but even Caleb didn't know all of those involved. Who could he trust? He hadn't signed up to die for Sestus. All he had ever wanted was Barabbas.

He decided the most inconspicuous way to enter was to come into the city with the carpenters as they arrived for work. He moved further away into the trees, out of sight of the sentries.

All I ever do is wait.

The first group of carpenters arrived within the hour. Fifteen minutes later, he stepped out onto the road and knelt down. His plan was simple. Carpenters always travelled in groups to avoid attack, so he needed to join this trio of men. But joining the men would arouse their suspicion.

He removed his right sandal and broke the strap, then sat down on the road and looked as though he was trying to repair it. In this way, the next group of carpenters might assume he had been with the group ahead of them. They might consider him safe.

The ruse worked. Five carpenters from Nazareth soon appeared on the road, and Caleb recognized them.

"Micah!" Caleb hailed. "Praise the Almighty. Do you have a tailor's needle and thread to restore a broken sandal strap?"

"Caleb!" The tall, bearded carpenter gave a jovial shout of recognition. "Is that you? Shalom. I thought you were staying in Sepphoris. You could have travelled with us instead of with those worthless friends who abandoned you. Here, walk with us. There's good thread at the home where we're working."

Barefoot, Caleb walked in through the gate with the others and made his way with them to their construction site: a centurion's quarters with fine mosaic tile floors. A slave took his sandal and left to get it repaired. Even the carpenters had some privileges here.

Micah stayed with Caleb as the other four began to prepare for the workday.

"Isn't this the palace you want for your wife one day?" Micah teased. "The home of Blastus Seguntus, senior centurion. He commands a thousand men. Not one of them can say no to his command."

Caleb felt a shiver down his spine. Blastus was the same name whispered in the forest earlier.

How could a Roman of this stature be in league with the Parthians? he asked himself.

"Look at the size of this sundial in the atrium," Micah said. He walked Caleb to a carved marble table with a marked face and upright triangulated piece of iron attached to its center. "When we work inside and can't see the sun's position in the sky, we look at the shadow on the face of this sculpture and know when to work and when to rest."

Caleb ran his finger along the perfectly rounded edges of the table. "This must complicate life so much. My life is easy. When Sestus says work, I work."

By the time his sandal was repaired, he had heard plenty to tell Sestus.

At dawn, Caleb left the home of Blastus Seguntus and worked his way through the agora. He paused when he saw Hannah, basket in hand, at the spice vendor. Without hesitation, he walked up and examined the cloves of garlic in the space next to her. How had she gotten here so early?

"Hannah, welcome to the city," he said.

Hannah looked up and responded as though this were an everyday occurrence. "So you really do live here? I've come in search of the carpenter from Nazareth you spoke about."

"I'm a carpenter from Nazareth, and I'm at your service."

She took one of his hands in hers. "These hands are covered in blood. My father would never accept the service of someone who traffics in death."

Caleb jerked his hands away and looked at his scarred and calloused palms.

No, I cannot be condemned for chasing Barabbas. He turned and walked away, completely forgetting his original mission. *I am not worthless. I know God refused to allow David to build his temple because of blood on his hands, but this work is different. Where is the justice of the Almighty? Where is the love of the Almighty? Who is left to avenge my father?*

His anger at Hannah's rejection only drove him to work harder. He chopped down twice as many trees as he needed and delimbed them quickly. He requisitioned the legionnaire's carthorse and by nightfall he had hauled ten logs into the open square beside his workshop.

Caleb was untying the last of the logs when he noticed Sestus approaching quickly over the cobblestones.

"Come with me," the centurion demanded as he pulled the carpenter through an arch of stone into an underground passage. Trickling water could be heard in the darkness below.

Caleb hunched his shoulders, the coolness of the stone pressing through his tunic. They had to crouch even further as they walked deeper into the tunnel. The centurion appeared calm, but continued pulling him along until all sunlight had disappeared.

A break in the stone walls appeared and the two men stepped into a room paneled with embroidered Babylonian carpets. Caleb caught his breath and waited as Sestus paced back and forth across the room.

Finally, the man looked him in the eye. "You would never betray me, would you, Caleb?"

"Never!"

Sestus continued to examine him, then nodded with affirmation. "There is conspiracy in Sepphoris. I don't know who and I don't know how and I don't know why, but I know it as surely as I stand here."

Caleb caught his breath and sank down onto a stool. "There is conspiracy. And I can tell you who and I can tell you how. I cannot tell you why."

Sestus's face flushed. "You knew about this conspiracy, didn't tell me, and then declare even now that you would never betray me?"

"I only discovered this last night near Cana. I was on my way back when I heard the conspirators on the side of the road."

"Tell me what you know! What is wrong with you? Are you worthless as a soldier and as a spy?" He clenched his fists and towered over Caleb. "If you ever hear news, you find a way to tell me without excuse. I'm training you to be more than a carpenter."

Caleb stepped back against the wall. Terrified, he could feel the effect of Sestus's barrage in his bowels.

"The conspirators spoke of the senior centurion, Blastus Seguntus, and two other centurions." Caleb stepped away from the wall and also began to pace. "They spoke of a raid on Nazareth to humiliate you. They spoke of two cohorts of Parthians being recruited to serve as a diversion." He rubbed his beard, trying hard to remember. "And some Sicarii. They spoke of getting control of the silk trade."

"Who are the plotters? Who seeks my life?"

Caleb pushed the words out of his mouth. "Eustace, and perhaps Deborah. I don't know the others. At least one lives in Cana."

Sestus turned on Caleb like a tiger. "Why did you go to Cana?"

"I was in the forest selecting trees for the crosses when I met a young maiden harvesting olives. She asked me to speak of carpentry with her father, and I went with her."

The centurion's eyes were burrowing into him and the air in the room seemed sparse.

Caleb's throat was tightening, so he spit out the words quickly. "I ate with them and left late. On my way home, I heard the conspirators in the forest and hid to be sure I was safe."

"Did anyone discover you?"

Without waiting for a reply, Sestus moved to the small entranceway and scanned for eavesdroppers. A few breaths later, he sprinted across the room and opened an interior door. He took a brief step into the hallway before returning.

"Did anyone discover you?" he repeated.

"No. They came looking for me, poking the bushes with javelins, but I lay still, just as you taught me." Caleb got to his feet and moved to a small bowl of water. He washed his hands and face. "Afterward I waited until the watchman had been collected. I arrived back in the city with the first carpenters this morning."

Sestus smiled. "You have done well, my son. You truly are more than a carpenter. You shall be rewarded in time, but first I have another assignment for you."

"Whatever you ask." Caleb wiped his face with the sleeve of his tunic. His eyes wanted to close in sleep, but he doubted he would have time for that. "What would you like?"

"Run to Nazareth and warn those you love," the centurion ordered. "Find them a safe place to stay. Then go to Cana. Live there and get to know everyone. Stay close to this rabbi. Woo his daughter. Do what you must to find out the truth. I'll take care of things here."

"I will go tomorrow."

"No, tonight!" Sestus hissed. "There is no time to waste."

The carpenter stepped through the gates to leave Sepphoris as the legionnaires prepared to shut the city for the night. Caleb held a loose sack of clothing in anticipation of being away for several days.

His feet were sure on the path in the dim moonlight. He felt no temptation to take a shortcut through the forest where the wild dogs lived. Not that night.

The village dogs were barking long before he got close to the gates of Nazareth. Yuseph and several others were awaiting his arrival by the time he stepped up to beg admittance.

"Yuseph," Caleb called. "I come late with news. May I enter? I haven't slept in days."

Caleb accepted his welcome and moved through the opened gate. He sagged down onto a mat inside the courtyard where Miriam stood in a doorway, wondering if Rebekah was home.

"Our home is your home," Yuseph announced. "Only eat with me before you tell your news."

Caleb tucked his elbows against his ribs and raised his open hands. "I will eat quickly, because the news is urgent."

Yuseph turned to Miriam. "Please, some food for our guest. The Almighty has burdened him with a great task. He needs strength for the journey." He turned back to Caleb. "Yeshi is on another pilgrimage to Jerusalem with questions for the rabbis. James, Joseph, Judas, and Simon are all working in the family business. The girls are preparing for the fulfillment of their betrothals."

Caleb felt a tightening in his gut. That meant Rebekah was gone.

Miriam emerged with a bowl of heated stew and some leftover bread. Caleb thanked her and let her know that he was well.

They ate quickly and Caleb shared the suggestion from Sestus that, because of possible trouble in the area, the family should find another place to hide for a short time.

Yuseph pondered the news. "But what of the others here?"

"No one else can know. There is trouble, but the trouble could be worse if people think something strange is happening. The things I've told you are in complete confidence. The lives of many depend on this."

"Then we shall stay and trust the Almighty," Yuseph said.

"Yuseph, I know you have the heart of a lion, but the centurion insisted. The threat is real. I heard it myself."

Yuseph stirred the glowing embers of the dying fire. "You have done well, Caleb, to deliver the message so quickly."

"For the sake of Miriam and the others," Caleb said, standing. "You must show wisdom and courage and move them while you can."

"May the Almighty bless you for your care," Miriam said.

Yuseph nodded. "We will do all that God tells us."

"So be it." Caleb sighed. "Now, I must leave at first light to complete the rest of my mission."

"Go with God! And Caleb, please remember who you are. I will pray for your safety."

"I need those prayers more than you know."

They doused the fire and Caleb soon stretched out to sleep. As he was drifting to sleep, though, he felt a strong grip latch onto his shoulder.

Chapter Twelve

Nazareth, Galilee 29 A.D.

Caleb instinctively rolled through the intense darkness and moved into a crouch position, his arms out. He fought to remember where he was. Pale moonlight filtered through an open window and Caleb saw the outline of a man near where he had lain.

"Caleb," the man whispered. "Shalom. It is Benjamin, the watchman."

"What are you doing here?" Caleb asked.

"Horsemen have come. They hide in the darkness nearby, and I need you to go out and see who they are. I will wake Yuseph and the others."

Caleb slipped through a small break in the fence behind the latrine, his instincts sharpened by Sestus's persistent training. He waited there, letting his eyes and ears adjust to the darkness around him.

More dogs began to bark and he heard voices in nearby homes. After making a short dash into the treeline, he waited again to see if there had been any response from the shadows. When nothing moved, he inched his way along the edge of the forest until he could get a better look at the main gate.

Along the thorny hedge, he saw movement at the edge of a clearing. He froze.

A horse! Two. No, three.

Across the way, two swiftly moving shadows crossed a patch of moonlight, moving in his direction. Torches were being lit in the village and the dogs were active. Whoever these visitors were, they weren't going to surprise anyone tonight.

Who dared to attack his own people? His home? Especially while everyone slept! Anger surged inside him. Were they Parthians? Romans? A combination of the two? Someone was definitely up to no good.

I'm just glad I didn't have to tangle with them alone, he thought.

Caleb slipped back through the trees and fence. He walked back to the shelter as if he had been visiting the latrine.

Yuseph appeared with a torch. "Are these dogs barking at you?"

Caleb weighed what to say. "There were three men outside the gate. They had horses. I don't know who they were or what they wanted, but they're gone now."

"How do you know there were three?"

"I should say I only saw three," Caleb answered. "I think we're safe now, but I think you should post an extra watchman in the future. There are strange things happening in this area. It's just confirmation of what I told you earlier."

"We shall trust the Almighty."

"And I will move on to complete my mission. Remain in peace with God."

The two men exchanged embraces, and then Caleb collected his things and slipped out through the fence again.

The moonlight was strong enough to give him good visibility as he crossed fields and skirted the main roadways on his way to Cana.

As dawn broke and workers, merchants, and travelers began their trek to the fields and distant places of business, Caleb walked along the road with purpose. The greetings of "Shalom" sounded and he returned salutations to all he met.

By the time he sauntered through the main gate of Cana the market stalls were humming with busyness.

Sestus had told him to get close to the rabbi, to woo his daughter, to do anything to blend in and find out more news about the hidden conspirators in this town. He was ready to do what he had to do to finish this conspiracy.

I wouldn't be surprised if Barabbas was mixed up in the middle of all this. Justice is coming.

By mid-morning, he was feeling conspicuous standing near the gate. He meandered to a well and drew some water for himself. The market stalls were close by, so he spent time examining the fruit and purchased some grapes, pomegranates, dates, and figs. He ate these in leisure, sitting in the shadows with his back against the synagogue.

There he fell asleep until he was nudged awake.

The speed at which Caleb sprang to his feet surprised him. The carpenter stood staring at the wide-mouthed rabbi whose cane was angled inches from Caleb's ribs. He immediately recognized Ezekiel.

"I sense you are more than a carpenter, young man. I thought my daughter told me she saw you in Sepphoris just yesterday morning."

"I was there," Caleb said honestly. "I've come looking for work and wisdom, and I thought perhaps you could help me with both."

"And what makes you think I can help you?" Ezekiel asked as he heaved his shoulder against the synagogue door and pushed it open.

"You are a learned man. There aren't many learned men in these parts. We have soldiers and merchants and carpenters, but not many teachers."

"What do you know of the Torah?"

"I know that it came from Moses."

"It's a start," the rabbi grunted. "Pull up a stool. We will study in the morning and you shall work for me in the afternoons. I have a spare room you can sleep in. You may take your meals with us, but there is one thing I ask."

"What's that?"

"Treat my daughter as a sister. Her mother and I have another we wish to pledge her to."

"The moment I cannot honor your wish will be the moment I disappear from your sight," Caleb promised. He bowed his head and received Ezekiel's blessing.

The days and weeks passed quickly. Caleb knew he could soak up information quickly, without much effort, and he gained it in the synagogue and on the streets after dinner. He spent as little time as possible around Hannah to avoid temptation.

One day, as he worked on a sandal strap that needed repair, she came to hover over him.

"Do you find me distasteful?" she asked.

Caleb kept his eyes on the sandal, his hands pushing at the needle and thread. *Do I tell her that the man she looks for has been in this very place, changing water to wine and healing the son of Herod's officer from Capernaum?*

"Do you find me so unsuitable for companionship that I'm not even worth a word?" she pressed.

Caleb finally relented. "You are a fine woman and I have promised your father that you'll be only a sister to me. If I linger in your presence, I may not have the strength to keep my promise."

"A sister? This is how you treat your sister?"

Caleb secured his strap and put the sandal on his foot. "I ignore my sisters. I don't know what to do with them."

He was out the door before any further words could be said.

That evening, Caleb merged himself with the crowd making their way to the market for last-minute purchases prior to Sabbath.

When he rounded a corner, he came face to face with his aunt, the woman who had taken in his two sisters a year before his mother had succumbed to the ravages of leprosy. He recognized her from his childhood days when she'd lived close in Nazareth. She'd told him many biblical stories which had inflamed his imagination, about kings and giants and heroes of this land.

Her lengthy nose cast a shadow over her jutting chin, and her bushy eyebrows sat like caterpillars above droopy eyelids. She moved like a ship in a storm-tossed sea, and her short, bulky legs only added to that impression. Every step she took threatened to tip her over to one side or the other.

The woman showed no sign of recognition, so Caleb skirted out of her way and then turned back to follow her. He had never known where his sisters stayed, and he hoped she would lead him to them. Perhaps they could sit down over a meal and see what the Almighty had done for them.

At the outer limits of Cana, the woman entered one of the humbled homes. Its limestone covering had chipped away in places and a loose window covering swayed in the breeze. Two broken crates lay next to the crude wooden doorframe. Weeds sprouted through every crevice along the house and from what had once been a vegetable garden.

What a hovel. My poor sisters.

Caleb examined the peeling whitewash and chipped limestone and thought about how easy it would be to fix. The sounds of laughter coming from within made him wistful for the company of family. The smoke swirling up through an opening in the roof made him long for a place to call home.

As darkness closed in, he rested in a nearby alcove, wondering if perhaps one of his sisters would show herself. He noticed a stealthy figure working its way along the side of the home's courtyard. The man, for he was sure it was a man, towered more than six and a half feet and was capped with a smooth boulder of a head. It could only be one person. Eustace!

The newcomer knocked and was admitted into the home next to his aunt's. Caleb walked calmly across the courtyard and planted himself on the ground near a window, listening.

"They've taken my daughter!" Eustace proclaimed.

"We have no choice but to attack tomorrow night," a sharp-pitched voice stated.

"That's too soon," a deeper voice replied. "The men are still on their way."

"How long then?" the first voice asked.

"Two weeks," the second responded.

"Can we count on Blastus to take out the centurion and the cross maker?"

"What about my daughter?" Eustace asked.

"She knew the chance she was taking. Especially working so close with the Romans."

When the voices inside lowered to a whisper, Caleb raised himself to try and hear better.

At that moment, the door to his aunt's home opened and his sister emerged. He looked quickly in her direction. Her hawk-like face swung in his direction and her head cocked. Her eyes strained and her mouth opened.

The sudden scream that broke the stillness, however, did not come from her.

Caleb scrambled up as his sister turned and raced back into the house, closing the door. Just then, the neighbor's door opened and Eustace poked his large head out and saw him.

Caleb ran down the alley as fast as he could go, but his strap loosened and his sandal fell off. He hesitated to grab it, then decided he didn't have time. He dodged through another courtyard and over a low wall.

As he crouched behind the barrier, Caleb saw seven men scattering across the various courtyards. He wanted to sneak away, but barking dogs would give him away. Instead he kept running, not even slowing down when a thorn pierced his heel.

He spent half an hour perched in a nearby tree and working out the thorn imbedded in his heel. The barking dogs had quieted and the seven figures seemed to have returned indoors.

Caleb saw Eustace walking through a lane. As Caleb watched, the man moved into a shadowed alcove and led out a stallion. He looked over his shoulder, mounted the beast, and galloped away.

When all was calm again, Caleb shinnied down the tree and began his long and painful walk back to Sepphoris. He didn't dare return to Ezekiel's home in case his sister had recognized him. He didn't want to put his own family or Ezekiel and Hannah at risk. He had accomplished what he'd come to do.

Halfway home, Caleb realized he had to get some sleep. He curled up in a small ravine under a crude footbridge and fell into a deep slumber.

Some time later, the heavy rumble of thunder woke him with a start. The steady drip of water let him know the rains had come.

But was it thunder? The rumbling reverberated wrongly; it was dull and rolling from one end of the bridge to the other.

Caleb poked his head out from under the bridge and watched as a team of oxen, pulling a heavy cart, disappeared up the road toward Sepphoris. He then looked down at his unsandaled foot and considered his options. He removed the lone sandal and cast it aside. Within a minute, he was running through the muddy track and calling after the driver. The man heard, stopped, and Caleb joined him atop the rig under a makeshift leather canopy.

"Shalom," the driver said to him. "I'm Zechariah. Tile maker. From Sidon. Going to Sepphoris."

Caleb set a foot up onto the wagon wheel. "Caleb. Carpenter. Nazareth. Also going to Sepphoris."

The driver pointed toward the seat beside him. "You are welcome. What brings you out in this weather?"

"I was walking to Sepphoris and took shelter from the storm."

"It may be faster to walk than wait for the oxen, but you're welcome to ride as long as you wish. I have another cape under the tarp which will keep the rain off."

Caleb rummaged under the tarp, donned the cape, and settled in for a back-jarring ride.

It was midday when the cart finally groaned and creaked past the sentry and through the gate. Caleb watched as the senior centurion, Blastus, stood under a covered porch, scanning the new arrivals. Caleb kept the canvas over his head and averted his eyes.

Caleb heard a shout and in his peripheral vision noticed Blastus pointing at his cart—he was alerting a legionnaire, who proceeded to halt the oxen. Another soldier stepped to the side of the cart and lifted the leather covering that kept the baskets of mosaic tiles dry.

Caleb wrapped the cape tighter around himself and hunched low. He watched the cart driver try to cover up his merchandise once it had been inspected.

Finally, they were cleared and Caleb abandoned his new companion.

An hour later, he saw Blastus Seguntus striding across the plaza toward a table where Eustace sat. The centurion stopped next to the big man, and it only lasted a minute; to the untrained eye, it would have appeared to be a chance encounter between strangers. But Caleb saw the parchment Eustace left behind when he got up to leave, and he saw Blastus pick it up and conceal it in his tunic.

Despite being covered in mud and smelling like an unwashed street urchin, Caleb sprinted to the fortress. A legionnaire stepped in his way as he neared the steps, but he declared himself on a mission for Sestus and the guard let him pass.

Moments after sorting out how he would present his news, Caleb stood in a room with the centurion. There had been no greeting. Only expectation.

"What news?" Sestus demanded.

"Eustace again. He met someone in Cana and told them that you have his daughter. Their plan is set to be put into motion two weeks from now, and a short time ago he passed Blastus Seguntus a message. The centurion is now in the baths."

"Well done!" Sestus clapped the palms of his hands together. He paced the room and inquired. "What is the plan?"

"I don't know," Caleb admitted. "I was discovered while I was hiding in Cana and I ran for my life. I hid in a tree, then came immediately to inform you."

"We must hide you until this conspiracy is ended. No one must know that I'm aware of this plot." Sestus moved to the door and signaled for a servant to come in. "Caleb, go with my servant. Wash yourself, change, and then I'll send a covered cart to Capernaum to pick up fish. You can hide with your friends there until I call for you. I'll need more crosses when you return."

Chapter Thirteen

Galilee 29 A.D.

Caleb endured the bumpy cart ride through the rutted track to Capernaum. It was even more uncomfortable than riding the tilemaker's oxcart. Sestus had carefully instructed him not to emerge from under the canvas no matter what happened, and toward midday the space became stifling hot and breathing was a challenge. Still he stayed.

Hoofbeats and voices sounded outside, but no one halted the transport. He could smell the faint aroma of wine soaked into the wood of the cart, and it lulled him.

He began to dream of the late summer days he'd spent with a winemaker in Nazareth. His two sisters had always been the ones to fetch the water from the village well. Caleb's daily chore had been to collect sour milk, yogurt, and cheese from the shepherds. Exploring the rocky crevices sheltering the herds was a bonus. He had imagined himself as David fleeing from Saul, as Samson laying ambushes for the Philistines, and as Judas of Gamla spying on the Romans.

One summer day, while exploring the land, he had heard a woman's voice and crouched low to hide in the shrubbery. He'd crawled on his belly toward the melody of a young woman's laughter, the distinctive smell of fermented grapes tickling his nostrils. The woman had stood next to a fire alongside a grizzled outdoorsman stirring a bubbling vat. She chatted away with him, dancing around a trough of pulpy fruit in her knee-length purple-stained tunic. They were winemakers!

Caleb had been afraid of a beating from his father for being late returning home, so he left behind the hypnotic song and dance.

It took three more clandestine visits before he revealed his presence to the pair as casually as he could. The man then gave him his first taste outside the libations offered at feasts. From then on, Caleb had determined to become good friends with this winemaker and his daughter, Sophia, even though she was several years older than him.

The man's winepress had been hewn from the rock, with vats nestled all around it. The majority of the winemaker's crop was destined for traders, merchants, and soldiers who stopped by to fill their wineskins with special Galilean nectar. The *yayin*, or new wine, was poured into large amphorae for storage in a series of underground caves. The *tirosh*, or mature wine, was poured into wineskins and offered to travelers.

At first, Caleb had just watched the master at work. The process of fermentation was fascinating. He marveled as different spices were added to the batches of tantalizing liquid. Even honey, lime, herbs, pepper, and seawater was added to the mixes.

When the master winemaker had begun rubbing wood resin against the sides of the press, Caleb had gotten hooked. The familiar aroma had lured him to come close and finally have a taste. And when a merchant stopped by one day with glass bottles shipped all the way from Rome, Caleb had become determined to add the skill of winemaking to his repertoire.

As the memory faded, Caleb noticed his parched throat. He knocked against the side of the jostling cart, in hopes of drawing attention to his plight. The driver ignored him. A long time seemed to pass before the cart came to rest in a shady place. A few moments later, the driver inserted a clay jar underneath the covering where Caleb lay. The water in the jar was lukewarm and his stomach churned for sweet-tasting wine. He forced himself to quell the queasiness inside and stay silent.

As the cart rocked, he curled his knees into his chest and thought back to Elizabeth in Capernuam, who he hoped to soon see again. Did she miss him?

Everywhere I go, there's a woman, he thought. *Elizabeth in Capernaum, Hannah in Cana, Deborah in Sepphoris, and Rebekah in Nazareth.*

Maybe it was more than the wine that had made Sophia dance for him so long ago. Maybe she really had cared!

It would be good to see Isaac, John, James, Simon, and Andrew again. This time Caleb determined to learn to fish. The life of crossmaking had almost gotten him killed. He was ready for something new.

As he lay pondering his next steps, the wagon lurched to a halt. The cart hadn't descended any significant hills, so he knew they couldn't have arrived at the lake yet. Perhaps he would have to walk the last part of the journey.

He could hear voices nearby, but they seemed to be Roman voices, not Galilean.

Suddenly the canvas was ripped away and the bright light of the sun hit him with blinding force. Someone grabbed him by the arm and pulled him out of the cart and dropped him onto the ground. Instinctively, he covered his head.

That's when he heard familiar laughter. Sestus was nearby, standing with two other centurions and several legionnaires. The wagon had brought him to a crevice in the hills, a rock canyon. No one looked at him as he lay on the ground.

When he dared, Caleb rolled onto his side and slowly used the cartwheel to pull himself up.

"Welcome, carpenter," Sestus called. "You have almost passed your final test. If you had lifted the canvas, you would have been shot with a dozen arrows." He pointed at several archers storing their bows in an empty crate along the edge of the canyon. "No outsiders may know of this place. I have one more thing for you to accomplish before sundown. Come with me."

Caleb demanded life from his wobbling legs as he moved to keep up with the centurion. He noticed the huge contrast between his own stained tunic and the impressive battle dress and headpiece worn by Sestus. Caleb staggered uncertainly while Sestus moved with confidence and without apology.

As the pair rounded a corner, Caleb was startled to discover Deborah stretched out and tied to a crossbeam. Her clothing had been torn away and she was at the mercy of the sun.

What was going on? Sestus must be out of his mind. This was a woman.

Caleb looked away, but Sestus turned on him in anger.

"Is this the daughter of Eustace who worked to betray me?" Sestus yelled. "Is this the woman who humiliated you and stared at your naked body? Is this the one who mocks Rome and is prepared to sacrifice your family at Nazareth for the sport of the Sicarii?"

Caleb didn't answer. *All I care about is Barabbas. I don't make crosses for women.*

When Sestus grabbed him by the neck and pushed him toward the girl, he tried to focus on her eyes. He didn't know whether he saw terror or defiance.

Sestus turned to a legionnaire. "Bring the hammer and nails!"

Caleb shuddered as Sestus took the hammer and nails from the legionnaire and then turned to Caleb.

"Take them!"

Caleb stared at the tools of death: two large iron spikes and a heavy wooden mallet.

"Take them!" Sestus roared again. "This is your terror if you ever betray me. Prove your loyalty."

The carpenter reached out his hand and wrapped his fingers around the familiar wood of the hammer. It was heavy.

As Sestus steered him toward Deborah's right hand, the woman gasped. She pulled against the legionnaires holding her in place.

The centurion forced him to his knees.

"The Sicarii must pay for their crimes," Sestus said firmly. "Why do you think we chase Barabbas near Sepphoris? One reason: this is his lover. He can't resist her. She will have his children. In fact, she carries one now."

Caleb stared at Deborah. This time, defiance flared like fire in her eyes. "It could have been yours, carpenter, if you knew how to be a man." She spat in his face.

"These monsters must not be allowed to kill our mothers and our sisters," Sestus hissed into his ear. "They must not be allowed to steal our nation, nor to betray our leaders. Now fasten the traitor in place so she may pay for the Sicarii. Strike terror into the heart of Barabbas."

Caleb dropped the hammer in horror, but the centurion's grip on his neck intensified so strongly that he reached for it again. He had never actually seen someone nailed while still alive, and he felt like he would vomit. His eyes glazed over with tears, but still he knelt in place holding the hammer and nails.

The others began to yell, repeating the crimes of the Sicarii in detail. Caleb found himself lost in the images being painted, yet none motivated him.

Finally, a legionnaire held back his head and poured wine down his throat. In that instant, he remembered Sophia again. The winemaker's daughter.

The woman who had turned out to be a zealot. The woman who had held his head in her lap and poured wine down his throat. The woman who had betrayed his innocence.

When he had first met the long-haired beauty with her deep olive complexion, he had thought her rather plain. The wine had somehow changed things. It had freed her to dance hypnotically and suggestively. Her dark eyes had pulled at him to taste of the fruit she offered. It was like a game, arousing strange sensation in his body, sensation that whirlpooled with fear and curiosity.

Despite feeling repulsion at images of his father out of control and under the influence, the more Caleb had sipped, the less resistance he'd offered.

He had never learned to trust in the same way again. Sophia had stolen his innocence that night, and the beating from his father the next morning had left lasting scars.

When Caleb had attempted to initiate closer contact with Sophia the following week, in a sober state, she had openly mocked him.

"I don't have time for boys," she'd taunted as she whistled for an older zealot to join her. "This is the boy who tried to rape me."

The older zealot had picked up a stick and beat Caleb across the back and legs. Paralyzing pain had raced through every nerve ending as he covered his head and endured the lashing. He had been so humiliated that he'd backed away, never to return again.

The welts had lasted for weeks. The memories had lasted longer.

The woman on the cross today was no longer the woman who had walked through the markets and fountains with him. She was no longer the one who had fed him stew when he was famished and who had allowed him to clean up in her own private bath. She was the one who had controlled him through her father. She was the one who had lulled him into trust and then strangled him and turned him over to Sestus for torture. She was the one who had tried to lure him into turning against Sestus, losing his only chance to get Barabbas.

No, this was a seductress working to betray everyone he loved to the Sicarii. She was probably a Sicarii herself.

In anger, he placed the iron spike against her palm and swung the hammer over and over as her screams rent the air. He moved to her other hand and fastened it in place, too. Then he retched and retched until he had nothing left.

Through the night, Caleb heard Deborah's cries for mercy. The patrons of death, in their scarlet capes, rested in their tents and took turns through the night tormenting her further, pulling all the information they could from her tortured lips.

Caleb twisted on his mat. *What have I done? No one deserves this fate. There will be no redemption for me now.*

The soldiers refused to break her legs to hasten her death. In fact, they delayed a whole day before even erecting the cross so she could suffocate. Caleb numbed himself to her cries to keep from going insane. By the end, only desperate gasps escaped her parched lips.

It took two days for the condemned woman to breathe her last.

His only distraction had been found through Sestus, who took him out for further equestrian training. The centurion also taught him special javelin thrusts to be used in warfare.

As Caleb began the third day of practice, Sestus waved him over. "The vain wench is gone. Not once did she plead her innocence. All she cared was that we kept the birds from her eyes." He took the javelin from Caleb's hand. "And we were merciful. We kept the birds away. When she served me, she served me well."

Sestus himself pulled the nails from her hands and offered the bloody trophies to Caleb.

"Good luck charms," Sestus said. "The soldiers fight for them."

Caleb turned away without taking them. "I don't care."

"Then you are finally ready to embrace life as it is," Sestus called after him.

He heard the centurion give orders for the legionnaires to wrap up the body in canvas and dump it into the same cart that had brought him to this place of nightmares.

He walked into the strangely silent woods. For some reason, in this part of the country even the birds had no song to sing. Rabbits and jackals and foxes and deer had vacated the land.

Life had left.

Hours later, as he rambled along the cart trails and pathways, Caleb heard the sound of hoofbeats approaching from behind. He didn't try to get out of the way. But the hoofbeats stopped inches behind him and he could feel the breath of a warhorse on his head.

The voice of Sestus sounded in his ear. "My father once came to this place when he was a legionnaire."

Caleb turned and spoke out of the numbness of his soul. "What was your father really like?"

A look of longing rose up in the centurion's eyes. He seemed to gaze past the dusty hills and half-built stone walls of a new fortress being constructed in the distance.

"Away."

"What do you mean, away?" Caleb asked.

"He was always off fighting in foreign countries, or else explaining his campaigns to the Senate." Caleb began walking again and Sestus took up his pace with the horse close behind.

"What was he like at home?"

"Distant, busy, angry."

"Was he always that way?"

"No," said Sestus. "When we entertained the senators, the generals, the noblemen… he would come alive. He was strong, in control, a man to be respected and adored. He was a great storyteller."

"You must have loved his stories."

"I only heard them when he told them to others." Sestus patted the nose of his stallion. "I hid with the servant boys so I could get close to him." The centurion patted his sword and looked back toward the legionnaires following at a distance. "Enough of this. We need to get on with it."

"And what must we get on with?"

"Our fathers are gone," Sestus said. "We are the men who must fight and win the day. We are the men who must prove ourselves. We are the men who must survive though all the world seeks to betray us."

Caleb stopped again. "Why did she have to die? And why did you bring her here to crucify her?"

"Traitors must die or we will die. Crucifying her alive is the way to let her bear witness to the pain that will come to those who betray us." Sestus rubbed the back of his neck. "We brought her to the quarry to prevent outrage from Jewish observers. Your people will create more trouble over her exposed body than her crimes."

"What will happen to the others in the conspiracy?"

"True Romans cannot be crucified. When we catch the next group of Sicarii, we'll crucify the rebels and behead the Roman traitors as the dying watch from their crosses. Then we'll bury them together and destroy any dignity and honor they've gained."

A fawn tiptoed unsteadily at the edge of the forest and nuzzled its mother. The doe, ears flickering, stood still and seemed unafraid of the two soldiers of destruction who talked about death so freely.

"Does it always have to be so cruel?" Caleb asked.

"It is the way of Rome. The strong will rule. The weak will die." Sestus scanned the forest on both sides of the road, gesturing with his right hand as he spoke. "Just as we defeated the Parthians, so we will defeat the Sicarii. Many of these dagger men are sons of those we killed."

"Why do you still fight the shadows of the Parthians?"

"In my father's time, under Crassus, the Parthians defeated more than seven legions of Roman soldiers. Twenty thousand of our soldiers were killed. Ten thousand were captured. Ten thousand disappeared without a trace. It was the worst defeat in the history of our nation. My uncle was among the dead."

So that's why he's so focused on the Parthians, Caleb thought. "But you kill zealot and extremist alike. Even those who know nothing of the Parthians."

"Surely your father must have told you how the Parthians took this land, sent Herod scrambling to Masada, and then installed Antigonus as the king of the Jews. We sacrificed to regain this land and to give you the peace you now enjoy." Sestus stopped in the middle of the road and reached for Caleb's elbow. "Surely you know the history of your own land and why we must always be on guard. If we prove weak to small enemies, we will once again have to face bigger forces."

"All I've ever wanted to do was create wooden trophies of peace." He had a hard time believing that the way of Rome was the only road to peace.

"First let me give you something to sustain you," Sestus conceded. He walked back to the stallion and dug into a woven bag tied to the horse. He withdrew from it two foot-long tan stalks. "Sugar cane! Newly imported from distant lands. It is sweet juicy wood of some kind. Rome has everything you can imagine."

Caleb nodded in thanks. "What will you bring to Sepphoris that is purely of Rome?"

Sestus raised his right arm and flexed his shoulder. "Battle wounds," he said, grimacing. "To understand Rome, you must know the story of Rome, the story every boy learns at the knees of some slave whom Rome has conquered."

Caleb peeled back the cane and nibbled at the tender inner pulp. "Does this mean you will be my slave teacher?"

"It means that you're still a boy. Now let me tell you what you need to know." He took a nibble at his own sugar cane. "For eight hundred years, Rome has been at war, fighting and conquering. We followed in the pathway of the Greeks, who spread their language and culture." Sestus threw his shredded cane stick into the bushes. "We brought our government, art, literature, architecture, religion, and language. We built aqueducts, roadways, palaces, and great public arenas where people of all races and social classes could be entertained. The endless routine and boredom of life was eliminated through variety and emotion. Before, merchants couldn't travel freely to supply our thirst for new tastes and fantasies. By securing the lands around us, we made the roads safe. Our perimeters were always under attack by others trying to expand or migrate, and our leaders rose and fell. Each new leader meant new wars to prove who was strong and who was weak—"

"So that is all I need to know…"

Sestus ignored the interruption. "When Rome was first founded, its leaders invited all the undesirables to come and grow the city. But there were no women, so the Romans had to steal women from others."

"So this tradition of imposing your will on women arose at the beginning?"

Sestus raised his fist and struck hard at Caleb, but Caleb instinctively rolled away from the punch and raised his hands in self-defense. Sestus came at him like a bull and Caleb sidestepped the charge, punching the centurion in the side of the head as he passed. The soldier stumbled to his knees and then sprang back up and reached for his sword.

To Caleb's surprise, Sestus began to laugh.

Caleb stepped back. *What's wrong with this man? He's out of his mind.*

Sestus raised his sword and his arms above his head. "I have succeeded!" he yelled at the skies. "Caleb is more than a carpenter."

Chapter Fourteen

Sepphoris, Galilee 29 A.D.

Less than a week later, Caleb heard talk among the legionnaires about the conspiracy by Blastus Seguntus, his partner Eustace, and the others. Deborah's body had been found in the fountain by the agora. The message to the traitors was clear.

Another carpenter told Caleb that Blastus had been ambushed outside his home and then sent to Rome in chains, along with two other centurions. Eustace and a dozen others were held in the dungeon until the next Sicarii were captured. Then Sestus kept his word and beheaded the lot of them, one after another, as the crucified looked on. All were buried in a large pit near the east gate of the city.

Caleb avoided the executions and huddled in the barracks where Sestus had given him a space to lay his mat. His body succumbed to constant shivers and even three blankets didn't provide the warmth he needed. His dreams were haunted by empty eyes and screaming mouths. Grotesque faces swam across his vision. Deborah, Eustace, his father, Sophia.

Never Barabbas.

When he woke sweating and wanting to scream, he clenched his jaw and fists.

Two days after the executions, Caleb heard the distinct tapping of a stick in the hallway. The rhythm was familiar. He dug his fingernail into his palm, and enough pain pulsated to ensure he wasn't dreaming.

He rolled off his mat and scooted into a shadowed corner of the room. He wrapped his arms around his knees and pressed his back to the wall.

The tapping stopped. No one came through the doorway.

He waited until his legs cramped and then pulled himself upright. The smell of fresh bread filled his nostrils. Three loaves lay on his mat, along with a scroll. Not once had he seen anyone enter or leave.

But he knew.

Titius.

He gnawed on a paprika and basil raisin loaf while examining the parchment that had been left for him. Its message was cryptic, as expected:

> The spider has been squashed.
> Your time for training has risen like an eagle on the wind.
> The apricot feeder is within your reach.

Titius wasn't at the bakery when Caleb arrived there, but a sign was posted above the door: *"Gone to the baths."*

In the baths, Caleb dipped into the warm water of the tepidarium. No one came near him, so he dunked quickly in and out of the frigidarium. No one came there, either.

He tired of waiting and stopped for a massage. Firm hands kneaded his stiff shoulders. Strong fingers worked down his spine. An elbow prodded a knotted muscle in his back and he started to relax.

"I could break your neck," a voice whispered into his ear.

Caleb swung hard with his elbow, but it was grabbed and wrenched behind his back. The pain was too intense to try anything else.

"Who are you?" Caleb said, trying to turn his head to see who had ambushed him.

The pressure on his arm eased. "I'm your trainer. Lesson one: never relax your awareness of who's around you."

Caleb knew, though. It was Titius again.

When the fingers of the masseuse stopped, he slowly turned to find a small boy standing five feet away with a towel.

Two hours later, he heard the stick tapping again. This time he moved toward the sound and discovered a gardener slowly pouring water on the garden by the barracks. He was using the stick to squash locust invaders. A large headscarf hid the gardener's face, but Caleb knew the cadence of the tapping.

"Titius, I'm here," Caleb said. "I'm ready."

The old man turned, revealing himself. "So we begin."

In the coming weeks, Caleb trained in self-protective maneuvers both with weapons and without. Titius continually pushed the carpenter to his limits. He learned the art of disguise, and his body filled out as he ran and fought and built his crosses. He became an expert horseman and could soon hit a moving target with a javelin at full gallop. By paying attention to his breathing, he could run to Nazareth and back without stopping, and even submerge himself in water for almost three minutes.

Two months into the training, during an intense wrestling match, the trainer submitted to Caleb's hold for the first time. Caleb refused to release Titius.

"The master has been mastered," Caleb said in triumph.

Titius relaxed under Caleb's lock. "Why do you treat Sestus as you do?" He breathed and exhaled slowly. "You try so hard to please him. It seems like he's become a father to you."

Caleb released the slightest pressure on Titius, and in a moment he was facedown with his own arms pinned back.

"Never lose focus," Titius snarled. "You will never be the master if you do."

Sestus watched the training sessions several times a week. During a session in which Caleb was being trained on how to disarm a warrior with a dagger, Sestus vented his anger.

"Titius, he's fighting Barabbas, not a child."

Sestus then stepped in between the combatants and urged Titius to attack him. When Titius thrust the dagger toward Sestus's ribs, the centurion stepped in close to his attacker, blocked the stabbing motion, and drove his forearm up into Titius's jaw. Titius went down and didn't move.

"Move inside the attack and don't give him a second chance," Sestus said to Caleb. "Barabbas isn't going to give you mercy."

Sestus crouched down and briefly felt along Titius's throat. Satisfied, he stood again and moved to pick up a wineskin of water. He dumped the contents on the downed man.

Sestus motioned to two legionnaires to care for the groaning trainer. "Get him help." He then turned to Caleb. "I'm heading to Caesarea again to see the governor. Don't draw attention to yourself while I'm away."

Once Sestus had disappeared down the road, Caleb ran most of the way to Cana.

Near the market, he noticed his two sisters arguing with a salesman about the price of a live hen. Without warning, he stepped between them and gave them side hugs. His oldest sister, Ruth, and his youngest sister, Naomi, both dropped their baskets and enveloped him with squeals of delight.

Caleb took over the bartering and selected two black hens. The salesman handed over the purchases. One of the chickens pecked at Caleb as he stuffed it in a basket, so he broke its neck.

"Caleb!" Naomi protested. "We needed that hen for eggs."

"Now it's for your dinner," Caleb replied. "Come, I'll get you another one. Let's enjoy our feast and share our news. Has anything interesting been happening around her lately?"

After the meal, Caleb headed to the home of Rabbi Ezekiel, where the door was answered by a stunning middle-aged woman who had both the beauty of Hannah and the wise eyes of the rabbi. Her raven hair streamed over her shoulder without shame. Her crimson tunic and amber shawl set her apart from the drab colors worn by the other villagers.

"You seek the rabbi?" she asked with a welcoming smile.

Caleb looked past the woman into the home. "I am Caleb. Perhaps the rabbi told you about me. I also know Hannah."

"I'm Phoebe, the rabbi's wife. Hannah is visiting relatives, if you wish to see her. Ezekiel is at the synagogue."

I can see where Hannah gets her beauty. How does a rabbi like Ezekiel become so blessed? May the Almighty give me such blessing.

The synagogue entrance was open and Ezekiel was kneeling in prayer before a scroll of the Torah. The vellum manuscript was perched on its own waist-high table. Caleb slipped in and settled on a stool to wait.

Without turning, Ezekiel spoke up. "So you have returned. Did you find your peace?"

"If there is peace in this land, it's as elusive as an eagle," Caleb said. "The zealots slither like snakes out of every hole in these hills and there aren't enough crosses to pin them all. Yeshua has more and more people speaking his name as the Messiah, and the Romans are becoming more anxious. I'm doing things I never dreamed possible." Caleb stepped backwards toward the door. "I am lost."

Ezekiel rose and moved toward Caleb and gently grasped his wrist. "The Almighty sees your heart. He knows your pain."

"The Almighty is blind toward me!" Caleb muttered, defeated. He turned and hammered his fist against the doorframe.

"Our home is open," the rabbi said. "After you've spent your time walking the streets, please join us for the evening meal."

He turned and knelt again before his scroll.

Caleb ignored merchant and citizen alike as he shouldered his way through the crowded streets of Cana. As he reached the high point of the village, he noticed an eagle circling effortlessly far above, riding the thermals. The volcano inside him that had been building since his crucifixion of Deborah spilled over as he raised his fist and vented at the heavens.

"Why am I so unfit to receive mercy? Why is there no love left for me? Why does my father's curse rest on me?"

He didn't notice the terrified eyes of those who slunk away from his vitriol.

Caleb ignored the rabbi's invitation and slept under an old cypress tree that night. His stomach was rumbling by the time morning arrived, so he stopped by to see if Phoebe would still offer hospitality. She did, in the form of cheeses, olives, figs, dates, unleavened bread, and grapes. Caleb consumed the meal and then noticed that a pile of wood lay unchopped; he hoisted his axe and began to reduce the pile to kindling.

That night was spent back under the cypress, cursing at the stars. In his dreams, memories of his father flooded his mind. Sweat soaked his tunic. Embers smoldered in the eyes of the one person he fought to please, and once again he heard those mocking words: "You will never amount to anything, boy. Why do you think your mother is cursed with leprosy?"

Caleb saw the little boy in his vision cringe and back away from the raging carpenter.

"She left you to watch your brother and you let him fall from the tree," his father had ranted after throwing a stick at him. "She loved that child and now the Almighty has cursed her because of you."

He had hurled another stick at Caleb's head. The one blessing of his dad's drunkenness had been the poor aim that came with it. But the cursing continued.

"The Almighty always demands his due. You should have been the one in that tree."

The full moon scaled the heavens and Caleb crawled up into the upper limbs of the cedar. It would be so easy to just let go. The haunting death faces would all be gone. The tests of Sestus would be no more. The temptations pulling at him, from the women he could never have, would disappear. This tree could be his own cross, his own place to face the Almighty and pay for what he had done.

He eased himself out on a branch and felt it bend under his weight.

Ezekiel's voice sounded from below. "Caleb, the Almighty brings us light once again."

His dark thoughts averted, Caleb hugged the branch in a death grip, even as the branch continued to bend and creak.

A hand grabbed his ankle. "I see the Almighty wants you to find a better foothold in life. Let me help you find the place. This next branch is much firmer."

Caleb gripped his perch even tighter. "How did you get up here?"

"May the wonders of the Almighty never cease," Ezekiel said. "I may be big in girth, but I've always kept my limbs strong. Is that not funny to you?"

Caleb yielded a little to the downward pull and allowed his foot to find purchase on a lower branch. "I'm not sure why I would find it funny."

"Surely you see the play on words. Strong limbs… my limbs and the trees'?"

"Oh."

Within minutes, the pair reached the ground again. Sweat glued Caleb's tunic to his back, making it impossible to peel the garment off when he reached the rabbi's home.

He ignored the urge to wash and be clean.

I don't deserve it, he told himself.

Sleep came easily once he settled into the straw mattress.

Most of the morning had passed before he walked back down the streets of Cana toward the synagogue. He needed answers.

Caleb paced back and forth across the floor as Ezekiel watched and waited.

"You are as restless as a lion in a cage, Caleb," the rabbi said after a while. "I watched you chopping wood yesterday, and it was as if you wanted to drive the axe through the heart of the earth. I see that today you want to wear a trench deep enough to lose yourself in. What does the Almighty bring to your mind that troubles you so much?"

Caleb trudged toward the open doorway of the worship center. "There is a fire in my heart that burns me, and everyone who's near me." Caleb turned and then sat near the rabbi's feet. "It's consuming me day and night."

"What feeds the fire?"

Silence took over as Caleb clenched his jaw and furrowed his brow. "Death. Fear. Betrayal. Disappointment."

"Who feeds the fire?"

Caleb got to this feet again and paced some more. When he was ready, he faced the rabbi. "I do. I've always blamed my father, Sestus, the zealots, the women in my life…"

"Perhaps if you didn't feed the fire, there would be no fire consuming you."

If there were no fire in me, I could never pursue Barabbas. If there were no fire, I could never work hard enough to please Sestus.

He paced right out the door and down the street.

Of course, if there were no fire, perhaps I wouldn't have to pursue Barabbas or please Sestus.

For two days, Caleb sensed that something might be different. He felt a pull to return to Sepphoris and he walked with joy as he encountered the flowers, birds, wildlife, and even people who passed him on the road. He re-engaged in his carpentry work with a new spirit and focused on making flutes and playing music. The timbers for his crosses lay unshaped.

Just before Passover, Sestus returned from Caesarea and announced that it was time for them to move to Jerusalem. Sestus had been given the responsibility to bring peace to both Sepphoris and Jerusalem. With Sepphorus subdued, the capital was next.

Sestus sat thoughtfully on his horse, riding next to Caleb as they left the stables in Sepphoris.

Caleb reached into his carpenter's pack and withdrew the head covering used in his trade to keep the dust and shavings out of his hair. He draped it briefly over his head, then removed it, carefully folding it up into a small square. He set it down on the flute which had been his latest project.

"What is this ritual of carpenters where you fold your headpiece beside your project?" Sestus asked.

Caleb removed his headpiece and folded it upon the neck of his horse so Sestus could see it. "It's the sign that we are finished the work, and that we are satisfied."

Sestus moved his horse closer to examine the folded cloth. "Why do you never fold your headpiece beside the crosses you make for me?"

Caleb unfolded the cloth and fashioned it back into place on his head. "It seems that the work of building crosses will never be done. I'm never finished and I'm never satisfied."

"One day soon you will have Barabbas. Then you can fold your headpiece and be finished."

They had reached the halfway point of their trip when Sestus asked Caleb about the challenges he had faced when Sestus had abandoned him in the forest. The two men were negotiating a narrow ledge in a steep ravine and they walked, leading their horses.

"Before I tell you anything," Caleb said, "why have you worked so hard to kill me?"

Sestus stepped around a boulder jutting out from the cliff face. "I have never tried to test you beyond your limits. From the first day until now, I've been preparing you to face Barabbas."

Caleb rode around the same boulder, but he had to work harder at encouraging his mount when one of its hooves slipped toward the drop-off.

"What was that test all about anyway?" Caleb asked. "Tell me that my fear wasn't for nothing."

Sestus began riding up a trail away from the ravine. "Perhaps your fear was founded and perhaps it was not. I sent twelve women and six men to help you find your manhood or to lose it. I believed you could survive."

Caleb settled into a steady ride as the trail opened up into a meadow. Travelers could be seen moving on the road at the far side of the clearing.

"How were these men and women going to help me find my manhood?"

Sestus smiled. "The women were offered two handfuls of gold if they could seduce you. The men were offered two handfuls of gold if they could kill you. I wasn't surprised that none of them were successful." Sestus pointed at the road ahead. "We'll go that way."

Caleb slowed his horse. "You play with my life as if this were all a game."

Sestus ignored the comment. "Where did you hide during that week?"

"Capernaum."

"Every road and every pathway was watched," Sestus asserted. "No one saw you pass that way."

"I hid at the top of a tree until everyone had passed. I prayed to the Almighty and he watched over me. God is great."

"You had better hope so," Sestus said. "Barabbas grows stronger every day, and Titius warns of an ambush. Stay alert."

Caleb nudged his mount along the road.

Perhaps Barabbas isn't the only one growing stronger every day.

Chapter Fifteen

Caleb and Sestus pushed their horses hard and stopped every two hours at the Roman stables to choose fresh mounts. There was pleasure in feeling their muscular shoulders and in sifting his fingers through their coarse manes. He chose a dappled mare while Sestus chose a white stallion. Some men were so predictable.

"We'll continue riding hard," Sestus said. "You'll need the other horse to share the load. We'll switch horses every twenty leagues."

Caleb wrapped the reins of a chestnut thoroughbred around his wooden saddle horn and coaxed his spare horse to come in tight behind the mare. The saddle was solid, and although this Roman invention was hard on the spine, its attached stirrups doubled a rider's stability at high speeds.

Caleb pointed at the small caravan of travelers bunching up and turning toward the east.

"Almost all the pilgrims will be crossing the Jordan and heading down to Jerusalem on the far side," Caleb pointed out. "They want to keep themselves uncontaminated from the Samaritans."

Sestus mounted his horse and turned south. "We'll go this way. Straight and fast. Less traffic. Less trouble."

The first village they travelled through was called Nain, where several hundred celebrants were gathered in the market. Caleb could hear shrill ululations of celebration before they actually arrived. As Sestus pulled up to watch, several women danced in the middle of the loose circle of humanity.

"Let me talk to them," Caleb offered. "It looks like mostly women, and I think you might frighten them."

Sestus chuckled and took the reins of Caleb's extra horse as the carpenter trotted his steed up to the group and dismounted.

Before a sundial could register the hour's passing, he was back with the centurion.

"Yeshua was here a few weeks ago," Caleb reported. "The widow in the center of that group says her son was dead and that Yeshua raised him. The young man next to her is the son." He moved his steed a few steps closer to Sestus. "All the people confirm it. They're saying that God has raised up a great prophet among us."

"What are we facing?" Sestus asked, rubbing the back of his neck. "Is this Messiah of yours good, or is he someone we need to stop before things spiral out of control?"

"He is good," Caleb affirmed.

"Did you know that Herod Antipas has beheaded the cousin of Yeshua for speaking out against his marriage?" Sestus prodded. "There may be a reason this new Messiah is rousing up the crowds. Perhaps he's creating the appearance of miracles to kindle people's emotion."

"I know the man well. Some things he does seem like magic, but how do you stop storms with a word? How do you make blind people see? How do you make leprosy disappear? My mother died of leprosy. I know only death removes it."

Sestus scanned the road ahead. "He lived in your village. Why didn't he take the leprosy from your mother if he's such a healer?"

Caleb hung his head. "I ask that same question many nights. He never did anything special in our village." His hand twinged and he looked at his restored limb, remembering Yeshi's touch. He clenched and unclenched his fist without pain.

"Where is he now?"

"They say that he and his followers departed for either Capernaum or Jerusalem."

Sestus motioned to Caleb. "Who is this man we're following? Like you, he must be more than a carpenter. What's hidden in the mother's milk of Nazareth? You are all different."

Caleb laughed at the mental image of nursing mothers. "It is the blessing of the Almighty. Nothing else."

The pair of riders took one last look at the crowd, which was continuing to draw newcomers, and then turned to ride.

After a hard journey of several hours, they bypassed Samaria on Mount Gerizim and came to the town of Sychar, nestled between Mount Gerizim and Mount Ebal.

The carpenter and centurion stopped to water their horses at a well and again noticed a large group of people celebrating.

"I thought all celebration was confined to the temple in Jerusalem," Sestus said. "What is happening to these people?"

"They're Samaritans, so they don't celebrate in Jerusalem. They worship on this mountain. I'll ask the elders by the gate while you water the horses."

Caleb dismounted, handed the reins of his horse to Sestus, and walked directly to the huddle of men engaged in passionate discussion.

The horses were ready to ride again by the time Caleb returned.

"Don't tell me," said Sestus. "The Messiah was here."

"Yes, they definitely met with Yeshua. They say he's not only a great prophet, but that he is also the savior of the world."

"So we Romans conquer and change the name of the city from Sychar to Flavius Neapolis, but we don't change the hearts of the people?" Sestus shook his head. "What else did Yeshua do here?"

Caleb reached out and took the reins of his mount. "He met with a woman and told her about her life as if he knew her."

"That's it? And for that the people hold a celebration?" Sestus adjusted the bags tied to his saddle, then offered a handful of dates and apricots to Caleb.

"Sestus!" Caleb exclaimed. "They see Yeshua as a holy one. Jews don't talk to Samaritans, and they certainly don't drink from the cups of Samaritans." He pointed out a group of men and a group of women standing a stone's throw away from each other. "The men don't talk with the women in public settings. The rabbis don't associate with people who have impure reputations. Yeshua did all of those things and accepted these people."

Sestus mounted his horse and pulled the reins hard to face toward the main gathering of people.

"You're right! This is bigger than we thought," Sestus said, staring at the Samaritans. "If he can unite all these groups, we could be in really big trouble. He could declare himself king of the Jews and cause a major revolt. This could be worse than the Parthians or the zealots."

"I don't think that's what he is doing," Caleb cautioned. "I know the man. He doesn't have an evil bone in his body. He just likes to help everyone."

Sestus turned to his companion. "I believe it's been eight years since you've spent real time with this 'brother' of yours. A lot can happen in eight years."

Caleb clenched his fist.

You can't even imagine, he thought. *With Yeshi, a lot can happen in eight days.*

Sestus turned his horse away from the town. "When the prophet who announces your coming is beheaded at the height of your popularity, it can create strange reactions. Especially when that prophet is your cousin." Sestus drew his sword and swung it overhead. "Rome has survived this long only by chopping off the heads of the cobras before they strike."

"Sestus, you survive because you are calm. If you see snakes where there are no snakes, you may be bitten by the snake that's really there." Caleb stretched out his hand and pointed at an ancient well site. "This place of Shechem has been the source of much trouble for our people. Our father Jacob gave this land to the descendants of his favored son, Joseph. Joseph was a powerful ruler in Egypt and his bones are buried in this soil as a testimony that the Almighty keeps his promises. These people think the Almighty is arising to keep his promise of salvation through Yeshua."

Sestus frowned. "I think the place must be cursed. What is so good about such a place?"

"This is where our father Abram first stopped. Here is where the Almighty met with him and promised the land to us. Here is where the first altar was built and the first worship was given. Here is where our father Jacob bought a field for a hundred pieces of silver. It is truly the birthplace of our people, not a place of evil."

"Then it's another place we have to watch," Sestus muttered.

Even if you watch, it doesn't mean you'll see. These people can act almost as invisibly as the Almighty.

The centurion and carpenter dismounted near a small pool of water to let their horses drink. Sestus kept his eye on the small groups of people huddled around the area and Caleb searched through the horse's packs for morsels to chew on.

When they mounted again, Caleb initiated the conversation. "Tell me more about the birthplace of your people. What makes Rome so great?"

"It's a long and violent story. But if your ears can bear it, listen."

Caleb pointed ahead. "The ride will be longer than the story. Speak on."

"Five hundred years ago, the Republic was established. Four hundred years ago, we had to retake our city from the Gauls after they took Rome."

"So you understand defeat," Caleb said.

Sestus ignored the comment and urged his steed toward a group of carts being pulled by oxen. He demanded the right of inspection and searched the load. Soon after, he returned with a handful of figs, dried apricots, and pastries. He handed a share to Caleb and continued the conversation as if he'd never left.

"Three hundred years ago our people came under the threat of Carthage. The merciless Hannibal invaded Italy itself."

Caleb stared hard at the dried apricots in his hand. *I wonder if those are zealot supply carts. We should have checked to see if they were hiding pigeons for sacrifices.*

He pivoted in his saddle to look for the Ethiopian slave he had seen in Caesarea. He saw no sign of the man, and neither did he see any caged pigeons. He glanced at Sestus, remembering the centurion's rebuke from the last time Caleb brought up the pigeons. He turned his attention back to the road.

Sestus continued, unaware. "We engaged his army to delay him while our main forces gathered. While he plundered our fields and villages to supply his troops, we plundered his capital, which had been left unprotected."

"So you proved your power and achieved your peace?" Caleb looked back. The carts had pulled off the road behind them. Why were they pulling off so early in the afternoon?

"It actually took many years for our generals to quench this wildfire. When we were done, Sicily, Hispania, and Africa were all ours." Sestus raised his arm toward the sky. "But the wars were still not over. The Macedonians and Seleucids had to be brought under control. Many grew rich off the booty of war and Rome suffered from the greed of those who sent us out to conquer. The wars between the classes continued."

"You Romans are worse than brothers who hate each other," Caleb said while watching the carts move into the shadows of the adjacent forest. "How did you establish peace anywhere?"

"The winners always impaled the losers' heads. That was the way. The generals brought peace with the sword and javelin, just like I bring peace through the cross."

"So how did we get to where we are now?"

"After the assassination of Julius Caesar, Antony and Octavius defeated Caesar's assassins in the battle of Philippi. Antony married Cleopatra of Egypt and more war broke out."

Caleb sighed. "I'm sure I've heard this part. What does it have to do with us?"

Sestus dug his heels into his mount and charged another caravan of donkeys and oxcarts up ahead. Caleb worked hard to catch up.

Sestus slowed to a canter and concluded his history lesson. "Octavian destroyed the Egyptian forces and Antony and Cleopatra died by their own hand. My father fought as a legionnaire in Octavian's army and was there to see him crowned Augustus Caesar."

"So now you're the one charged with bringing the glory of your people to our land?"

"Now I'm here in the tradition of Rome," Sestus said. "The Parthians will be our next threat and we must prepare to beat them back and fortify ourselves to preserve the glory of our empire." Sestus reined his mount and turned toward the forest. "Instead I'm left to swat at zealots, bandits, and hidden Messiahs. Where is the glory?"

Caleb held up a dried apricot. "Perhaps it's closer than you think."

Chapter Sixteen

Road to Jerusalem, Galilee 29 A.D.

Sestus glanced at the apricot in Caleb's hand and then back at the carts pulling into the forest far behind them.

"Do you think only Barabbas eats apricots? Not everyone is a zealot, even though it may seem like it." Sestus pointed his sword at a break in the forest. "By now you may be thinking I ignored the importance of those carts. But I've been fighting zealots for years, and they are predictable. They choose the same distractions, the same areas for ambush, the same bands of attackers… the zealots will come at full charge through that opening. There will be at least six of them." He pulled out an extra sword and handed it to Caleb. "Your training is about to be tested. If we go now, we can avoid the ambush and put some distance between us. Don't fall behind."

Just as Sestus had predicted, seven horsemen galloped out of the clearing with bows, javelins, and swords at the ready.

"Faster," Sestus called over his shoulder as Caleb struggled to keep up. "Head for the ravine on the left."

The two men raced for their lives, eventually reaching the trail to the left of the ravine. Caleb glanced back and saw the zealot riders still several hundred yards behind them. He looked back ahead, ducking tree branches that had grown low over the trail.

"Stay low," Sestus called. "And release the extra horses."

Caleb untied the reins of the Chestnut, then watched as the Chestnut and Sestus's grey ran behind them. As he watched, though, he was swept out of the saddle by a tree limb. He hurdled into the trunk of a cedar and fell onto a pile of boulders. Pain flared in his ribs as the spare horses thundered by.

He crawled behind the tree and waited for their pursuers to pass. Frantically, he looked around for the sword Sestus had given him, but it was nowhere to be seen.

When the sound of the horses had faded into the forest, Caleb used the cedar trunk to hoist himself to his feet. The silence all around was eerie. He took a step toward the trail and slipped on a patch of moss. As he stumbled, an arrow whizzed overhead and embedded itself in the cedar. He dove behind the tree and scanned the trail.

Nothing.

The archer obviously knew where he was, though. There would be an ambush. The zealots would try to flush him out and move him into a trap.

He stayed put, even though it meant inviting another arrow. Caleb held his breath and darted ten steps toward another cedar. A silent swish passed overhead and thudded into the base of a juniper tree.

You're either a poor shot or you're playing a game, he thought.

When Caleb slipped around the huge gnarled base of a sycamore, a javelin bounced off a rock two feet in front of him. He extended his arm out, as though to reach for it, then ducked as another arrow stuck into an exposed root.

He peered into the forest and saw the archer, hiding behind a fallen log. Caleb crawled into the underbrush and worked his way around so that he crossed the trail and could come up behind his attacker. The huge bearded warrior was peering around an olive tree, scanning the spot where Caleb had been hiding. And he was eating an apricot.

Could it be Barabbas himself?

The ambusher's left hand swung a dagger in loose circles, and his bow rested against the tree. No javelin was in sight.

Caleb pried a small sharp stone loose from its soil, then collected two larger rocks.

Titius, all that training comes down to this, Caleb thought to himself. *I know I should run and hide, but that's not who I am anymore.*

He threw the stone hard, right at the zealot's hand. The missile struck and the man dropped his dagger. Before he could turn, Caleb threw a larger rock, and it bounced off the attacker's shoulder. The third rock glanced off an elbow.

The man vanished in the brush.

Caleb reached behind him for his carpenter's knife. He flexed his fingers and listened. From Titius's training, Caleb was sure the man would come up from behind. But he didn't have his bow this time.

He decided to go vertical, scaling a sycamore and laying low on a hidden limb. While there, he heard the call of a nearby warbler, and then a lark's response several hundred yards away. He frowned. It seemed so out of place.

Caleb focused on the brush near where the warbler had sounded, and there he saw a slight movement among the trees—a shadow, slithering slowly from behind a log.

Come and fight like a man, Caleb thought, keeping his eye on his foe.

He hurled a stone just beyond where the zealot lay, and with the other hand he launched himself off the branch. He landed on both feet and ran toward the man. By the time the zealot had gotten onto his feet, Caleb kicked him in the side of the knee and elbowed him across the jaw.

The man stumbled and then lashed out with his dagger. Caleb avoided the slash and hit back with a thick mulberry branch across the side of the zealot's head.

The man spun and Caleb almost gasped as he recognized his foe. At last, he had come face to face with Barabbas himself.

Barabbas grabbed the branch and wrenched it out of Caleb's grip. The madman had dark, angry eyes and a droplet of blood flowed down from a gash on Barabbas's temple into his curly black beard. His arms bulged with muscle and his black leather vest only emphasized his solid physique. He brandished a dagger in one hand and a branch in the other.

His eyes opened in recognition.

"You have my mark already," Barabbas said, lowering the branch. "Why do you tempt fate again? You're the one who killed Deborah."

Caleb kept his eye on the dagger. "You killed my father and my friends."

"We are both men of death. We should combine our power against the Romans and not waste it on each other."

The lark sounded and Barabbas turned slightly toward the source. In that moment, Caleb charged in close. As Barabbas plunged his dagger toward Caleb's ribs, the carpenter blocked the zealot's arm and brought his own fist up under the man's chin. Barabbas wrapped Caleb in a bear hug, but Caleb used his momentum to bowl over the larger man. As soon as the two men hit the ground, Caleb began to punch Barabbas as hard as he could.

In seconds, Barabbas grabbed Caleb by the hair and yanked him sideways. Caleb brought his elbow back against Barabbas's ear and pushed himself away from the tangle. He escaped an elbow to the head, bounced up, and jumped over a log to create space.

The sound of hoofbeats alerted Caleb to Sestus, coming in fast with a raised javelin.

Barabbas faked a charge and then raced into the forest. Caleb let him go.

Sestus pulled Caleb up on the horse behind him.

"I took down two," Sestus yelled, "but the other two are behind me. One's missing. Why didn't you take down Barabbas while you had the chance?"

Caleb had no reply as Sestus rode.

They galloped through the forest until they reached the main road near a pool of water. There, Caleb slid off the back of the horse and collapsed to the ground. Sestus scooped up a flask of water and threw it into the carpenter's face.

"You trained for this, Caleb. Get up and have some water. We need to get to safety."

Rather than risk being ambushed by bandits, the pair pulled off the road and camped overnight in a ravine. Two other families on a pilgrimage to Jerusalem joined them as the sun dropped from the sky.

Caleb sat alertly, watching the ravine's entrance, but quiet settled over the campfires that night.

"Tell me about the Yeshua you knew," Sestus prodded. "I saw him only as a carpenter. It's strange to hear what others are saying."

Caleb stretched out by the fire. "I remember the first day we walked to Sepphoris as young carpenters. A donkey brayed as we left our homes, and Yeshi took a moment to walk across the courtyard and scratched behind the charcoal mare's ears. 'Caleb!' he said, 'Why do you think the Almighty put a cross like this on every donkey's back? Do you suppose it's a sign?'"

"What did you say?"

"I glanced at the donkey's back as if seeing the cross for the first time. 'Every donkey has that marking,' I said. 'I suppose the first donkey had the cross and so every donkey since has that same mark. Come! Let's go. Sepphoris waits.'"

"Was this the day we met?" Sestus asked.

"No, years before. Let me paint you a picture. The blue sky over the Galilean hills was a canopy of peace. Only a few white clouds nestled like lambs along the crest of the hills toward the Great Sea. The Passover pilgrimage was still weeks away. Adventure was in our blood. Sepphoris was calling."

"It's almost as if you are painting my own story."

"Ah, but it's mine. A sprinkle of light rains passed and the smell of earth emerged from the clouds and left everything fresh and alive. The barley and flax fields waved gently in the breeze. They called to the harvesters to be ready. In our last days before the responsibilities of manhood, we skipped stones, entertained each other with the stories of ancient biblical heroes who walked these trails, and challenged each other to identify the trees that were vital to our craft."

Sestus grabbed a stick and knelt by the fire, prodding it into a stronger flame. "So you have always understood the trees?"

"That day, I felt cheated. It was almost as if Yeshi was schooled in the heart of the forest. How was I supposed to remember that the algum from Lebanon, used in Solomon's temple, was also the Grecian juniper? At least I knew that a dozen men could lay head to foot to mark its height. I told him to ask me another."

"I'm sure you did better after that." Sestus rose up and strolled twenty feet to retrieve a few chunks of wood Caleb had chopped earlier. "What happened next?"

"Yeshi glanced at the orchards cascading down the nearby hills and took up my challenge. He said, 'This tree is related to the peach and was used in the lampstands in the Tabernacle. What kind of tree is it?'"

"Did you guess it?"

"I did. 'The Almond,' I answered. Aaron's rod sprouted almonds to show the authority of the Almighty, and the blossoms of the almond were carved into the lampstands. So I proved myself, and Yeshi slapped my back in celebration. 'You have studied the Torah well, my friend,' he said. 'What hopes do you have to leave your mark in this world?'"

Sestus spread his palms over the fire to warm them. "Is this the hope you've been telling me about all these years? You want to make a symbol of peace?"

"Yes! I wanted then to create a trophy of wood to serve as a symbol of peace in our world. I still want that." Caleb rose up and moved to his mat. "I'm tired of trouble everywhere."

Sestus stretched, threw dirt on the embers of the fire, and moved away to stare into the darkness. "We are born into trouble. What did your Messiah say back then?"

Caleb lay back with his head on his interlocked hands. "'The Almighty can help you find your way,' Yeshi told me. 'Just like he will help me to create peace in the world.'"

"It looks like neither of you have made your peace yet," Sestus noted. "We had best sleep. We ride early."

In his restless dreams that night, Caleb relived the rest of that day long ago. By the end of the forty-minute journey, the lads had been able to tell that Sepphoris was near. In the meantime, they had covered the identification of the red sandalwood, used by Solomon for his temple pillars, the chestnut tree used by Jacob in the breeding of his flocks, the cyprus used by Noah in the building of his ark, the sycamore fig, and two dozen other varieties in the area.

Yeshi had stopped at the foot of the hill rising toward Sepphoris. "Caleb, a moment to thank God, if you please."

"Whatever for?"

Yeshi had spread his arms wide and pointed out the trees surrounding them. "When we were at home, we mourned the loss of trees in our land. Now we see they are still plentiful. Blessed be our God, King of the universe, who causes trees to come out of his earth."

"Amen," Caleb had replied as the sound of chopping echoed down the hill. He'd pivoted to look up toward the Roman project. "Not for long. If Rome has its way, these trees will all be part of their fortress within the year. And if Herod Antipas has his way, this city will be as big as Rome."

The two boys had picked up their pace as they reached the halfway point up the hill.

It had been Yeshi who first spotted the woodsman ahead. "It's your father!"

Caleb had hesitated, as there was only one clear trail to the settlement above. "I probably should have told him we were coming. My father doesn't like surprises, especially when he thinks my mother has been left alone."

The boys had stepped into the axeman's line of vision and it hadn't taken long for the sound of chopping to stop. The powerfully built Hebrew man stared at them.

"Shalom," Yeshi called, waving. "Peace be upon you."

"And to you," came Caleb's father's gruff reply. "What are you two zealots doing out here?"

Caleb stepped forward. "We come looking for work to assist our families."

His father had stooped to snap the limb off a fallen acacia tree. He swung it fiercely in front of him.

"Go home," the man had growled. "You're not going to assist your families in this god-forsaken place. Come back when you're men. Your mothers need you still. Go home before the Parthians skewer you like pigeons. I'll bring you back here when you're ready."

Caleb had felt his cheeks burn as he turned to face Yeshi and saw the empathy in his friend's deep, dark eyes.

"Let's get out of here," Caleb had whispered. "Some days I wish he were the one getting skewered like a pigeon."

Yeshi had tugged at Caleb's elbow as they descended the hill. "Let's cut through the woods and get out of sight. I need to find some chazaret and mushrooms for the Passover."

"That wild lettuce is so bitter," Caleb said. "I'd rather eat the sweet Roman lettuce."

"Just come with me. Maybe you'll find some radishes. You always like those."

Within moments, the boys had gotten lost in the cool peace of a world sheltered from the glaring sun and drying mud. The distant sound of chopping had seemed so far away.

It was always at this point in the memory when terror swallowed Caleb. Sicarii had chased him through the woods with javelins, determined to skewer him to a tree.

He was still thrashing when Sestus shook him awake.

"Awake!" the centurion said. "Night terrors have no mercy. We need to ride and be free of this place."

Chapter Seventeen

Jericho, Palestine 29 A.D.

The two other families camping with them were still in their tents when Caleb and Sestus departed, leading their horses down the path and then galloping away down the main road.

The pair soon descended toward Jericho. As they approached the ancient city, Sestus pointed toward a high tower.

"Jericho is one of the oldest inhabited cities in the world," he said, "and it shows its history in the endurance and hardiness of its people. Keep your eyes open."

Centurion and carpenter reined up their horses to spy out the activity around them.

A group of Arab merchants were huddled in intense discussion beside a dozen camels kneeling under crates of dates and other wares. Women with water jars on their heads strolled majestically from the town well into narrow alleyways. Children with sticks feigned swordplay. A tax collector harangued a merchant with a loaded donkey.

"I don't see anything unusual," Caleb said.

"Then Titius is a poor trainer. Note the woman by the third palm to the right of the gate. See how she rests the jar on her shoulder? She is not a woman beneath that robe. No woman would carry a water jar that way."

Caleb noted the hooded figure and then saw a similar figure leaning against a different palm nearby. "I see she has a twin."

Sestus grunted. "Get down. I'll find us new horses and find out why they wait."

Caleb slipped off the horse and gained his balance quickly as Sestus moved on. He watched the centurion ride close to the figures and draw their attention. Caleb quick-stepped to shelter behind a gold litter carried by four Persians.

I wonder where Nabonidus has ended up, he thought, thinking back on his former slave. *Sestus better have saved him from the gladiator pit.*

A Greek merchant inside the litter screamed down curses on the world around him. "My cousin in Alexandria will tear your heart out if you think this is a good deal. Is every alley and street in this city filled with smugglers, thieves, swindlers, and zealots?"

Caleb watched a young Egyptian man scramble out of the halted litter as the curses continued to rain down. When the curtain parted, Caleb found himself staring into the surprised face of the merchant Hermes.

It can't be, Caleb thought.

Quick as a cobra, Caleb's hand snaked up to hold the curtain open and look inside.

"Hermes?"

Hermes switched from curses to blessings faster than a scorpion's sting. "Caleeb, is that you, my enlightened friend, my supreme musician, the heartbreaker of my daughter Portius?"

Caleb shook his head, trying to clear away the exotic image of Portius's belly-dancing during his last visit.

"You know, she would never have been happy with a scoundrel like me," Caleb said.

The man motioned Caleb to enter the litter. "Oh, what of it? What is a little heartbreak for a girl like her? She married an Egyptian and is happy as a crocodile."

Caleb stepped up into the lowered litter and sat across from the stout, bearded merchant.

"What brings a fox like you to Jericho?" Caleb asked. "I don't suppose you have Barabbas coming by for more of your merchandise?"

"Barabbas!" Hermes exclaimed. "He's no longer interested in my merchandise. I offered him your sister and he turned me down. He said he would wait until you found a wife. Then he would take her instead."

Caleb watched Hermes rock back and forth in laughter at his own joke. The laughter stopped as quickly as it had begun.

"Where do you want to ride? I have another hour in this litter fit for a king."

"I need to pass through the city gates without being seen," Caleb said. "There are spies near the palm trees… spies who may be zealots."

"So you still work for that worthless Roman?" Hermes parted the curtains and looked toward the palms. "If you come back with me to Alexandria, my cousin is still looking for a carpenter. He tells me there is no one finer than you. He will pay well."

Caleb waited until Hermes let the curtain fall back in place. "I'm sure he will pay well—only you will be the one to benefit. Take me into the city and I'll not tell the Roman that you're involved in smuggling the Chinese silk."

Hermes squinted at Caleb and smiled. "Ca–leeb, you drive a hard bargain with your friends. Very well, but just inside the gates. Barabbas would not be pleased to know I was betraying his family."

The merchant called for the Persians to pick up the litter and begin moving it again quickly into the market. Caleb bounced along and laughed at the jiggling jowls of the man across from him.

Once they were into the city, the litter slowed again and Caleb slipped out into the busy market inside the walls of Jericho.

I wonder if this is how the spies of Joshua got into this city the first time.

Caleb found Sestus at a tax collector's booth. He and the collector were shouting at each other, drawing a crowd. Caleb slipped into the shadows behind the booth of a nearby Persian carpet dealer.

The "twins" from earlier had joined the crowd, Caleb noticed, although they no longer carried their water jars.

Sestus pulled out his sword and waved it above the head of the tax collector. He continued shouting, but he backed away in the direction of the two men in disguise. As Caleb observed the scene, he noticed two legionnaires moving in the same direction. Suddenly, when Sestus was two steps from the disguised men, he spun toward them. Before they could get away, the legionnaires closed in and grabbed them.

In seconds, the disguises were removed, exposing two bearded Sicarii. Another two dozen legionnaires pounded their hobnailed sandals into the fray, dispersing the crowd. The prisoners were chained and taken away.

The uproar was immediate, but Sestus slipped away as the mob split into factions and began fighting each other.

Caleb followed the centurion down an alley and met him near the city wall.

"What now?" Caleb asked. "Are you expecting me to make crosses right here, right now?"

"You'll have time for that in Jerusalem. These men can wait until we get there. It's always important to send a strong message. Barabbas will hear it."

"I don't think Barabbas will hear any message right now."

Sestus wanted to check out some of the key towns around Jerusalem, and Caleb had no choice but to go along. They secured fresh horses from the Roman military stables.

The carpenter had never been in the saddle so long, and he felt the discomfort. He nibbled on the delicious local dates and mingled with merchants as Sestus stopped by to see other tax collectors, centurions, and legionnaires assigned to the region.

After the worst of the noonday heat had passed, Sestus took the reins of his horses in hand and began to walk up the final hill toward Jerusalem.

"The system is designed to cause revolt," the centurion said as Caleb trotted up beside him. "The people are taxed so heavily by cheats, and we do nothing to relieve them of the burden. As always, it is the rich and the powerful who grow richer and stronger on the backs of the honest. There's so much to do in this land."

So now someone notices! Caleb thought bitterly. *Hard work has no reward here. The people are fleeced of every denarius so the Roman elite can live in their gold and ivory palaces.*

Caleb pointed toward the city. "There are others along this road who aren't tax collectors. They're just as willing to grow richer and stronger through their own methods. We should find them and take them with us."

"We don't need others."

Caleb felt the intense heat of the sun-drenched rocky surfaces all around. His wineskin was almost depleted of water, and there were still several miles to travel before nightfall.

They were halfway up the long ascent before Sestus pulled his horses off the road and into a shady alcove in the rockface they'd been skirting. He sat on a boulder and seemed to lose awareness of what still needed to be done. The young Roman pulled a piece of parchment from his bag and made notes on it. He was so absorbed in his work that he hardly glanced up at the group of about twenty merchants who were encouraging their donkey carts up the hill behind them.

Five minutes later, both Caleb and Sestus were startled by loud shouts and screams of terror. Without hesitation, Sestus mounted his horse, grabbed a javelin and sword, and galloped up the road. Caleb jumped on the other horse and had nearly caught up before he realized he had brought neither sword nor javelin.

It didn't take long before a donkey ran by Caleb, with two elderly merchants in tunics chasing it on foot. The full-bearded one, looking as though he weighed little more than a skeleton, held onto a pouch of coins with one hand and a tattered headpiece in the other. The other, his beard short-cropped, carried a lamb and yelled, "Thieves! They're killing us!"

Caleb rounded a bend and a scene of disarray lay before him. Merchant carts had been twisted into each other and donkeys were tangled together. Bandits had ripped off canvas tarps and threw merchandise off to the side of the road.

In the midst of the fray, Sestus was fighting off five bandits who swung short swords at him.

Caleb dismounted and moved quickly toward the carts, his only weapon a long knife intended for cutting reeds. He slashed through the donkey reins to set the animals free, wondering how he found himself in these messes.

A bandit nearby saw what he'd done and called for backup. Before long, two other thieves were scrambling down the hill toward him.

Okay, Titius, I hope I've learned everything I need to know.

"Come, or all will be lost," he yelled toward the merchants cowering against the road bank. "We must fight together. Grab rocks, sticks, anything. We'll rush them as one."

Several of the younger merchants seemed energized by Caleb's leadership and grabbed whatever they could find. Two even approached with donkey whips in hand.

When the charge was sounded and the screaming merchants made a united effort toward the cargo, the bandits looked up from their looting, grabbed a few bundles, and started running toward the embankment.

Sestus broke off his battle with the last two swordsmen and charged into the group of fleeing bandits. His sword chopped into the necks of two bandits and his horse charged over a third. The other three scattered up the steep incline beside the road. Sestus hurled his javelin and skewered one of the men through the back.

Caleb watched the display in awe. The centurion was a madman of destruction, but at least he was on their side.

Out of eleven bandits, only four escaped. The other seven lay dying on the road. Sestus motioned for one of the merchants to offload his merchandise and put the bodies onto the cart instead.

One of the bodies belonged to one of the merchants, and a great wail went up. Some of the men freely beat on the bodies of the bandits, and Sestus didn't intervene.

The grey-bearded elder knelt at Sestus's feet and wept, holding up the pouch of coins to the centurion. "We owe you our lives," he said.

Sestus took the pouch of coins. "I accept your gift and I return it to you as a reward for your courage in helping keep the road safe. Buy your sacrifices in Jerusalem and worship the Almighty, who has spared you this day."

Caleb stood back, stunned, as the merchants all knelt before the centurion and touched their foreheads to his extended hand.

Why does this man need my crosses if he can sway these people with his wisdom? he wondered. *What has happened to him?*

As the merchants collected the remnant of their supplies, Caleb took the time to check in with the centurion and retrieve the abandoned horses. Caleb tied the reins of the three horses to the closest cart, then saw Sestus pacing back and forth along the side of the road.

"Crosses," Sestus murmured. "I'll need more crosses. Crosses. Lots of crosses."

Caleb knew that soon his crosses would be erected high in yet another city. He would have to look for some good trees closer to Jerusalem. But when would this end? He was too tired to keep doing this.

Several other merchant caravans had stopped at the scene by the time the caravan was disentangled and reloaded. Caleb was sent out front to scout for any other bandits and Sestus rode alongside the death cart to guard the rear.

As the group approached Jerusalem, a chant of psalms began to sound from the Hebrew merchants. Caleb lost himself in the moment. A shiver went down his back and he felt like he was starting to breathe a whole new kind of air.

The evening sun shone off the temple buildings, blinding in its glory. The group stopped as one and stared. Caleb noted the large military fortress at the eastern end of the great wall on the northeastern side of the city, close to the Temple Mount to ensure peace.

The chant of the psalms ceased and silence reigned.

It was Sestus riding to the head of the column that broke the spell. "We're almost there," he called out. "Keep moving. We've got crosses to make."

Chapter Eighteen

Jerusalem, Palestine 29 A.D.

The crush of traffic was almost suffocating as the group neared the main gates. The recitation of psalms drifted over them, creating a cacophony with the different groups following the chants of different leaders.

Caleb was glad to be on horseback above the fray so he could maintain perspective on what was happening around him. It was one such glance that allowed him to see a trickle of blood flowing from a long slash on the centurion's leg. Sestus seemed unaware of his wound.

"Sestus!" Caleb called.

The centurion kept urging his mount through the crowd, leaving Caleb and the group in his wake.

The merchants were soon left behind in the throng and Caleb tried to coax the donkey that was pulling the death cart. The groans and cries of the few bandits who still hadn't died ensured a parting of the crowd.

Caleb was surprised when several boulders bounced off the cart. One struck him on the shoulder and almost dislodged him from the horse. Another struck the donkey, causing it to bray and pull sideways.

Five Pharisees strode up to Caleb. They looked almost identical with the black prayer shawls flowing down from the peak of their heads, over their shoulders, and down to their ankles. Their black inner garments draped right down to their heels, topped by black-striped tunics fringed with wide tassels. Their sandals were of the finest leather.

The tallest of the five pious men pointed at the cart. The ruby and gold ring on his forefinger sparkled as he glanced around. His large, split-in-the-center grey-and-black beard waggled as he spoke.

"How dare you defile the sanctuary of the Almighty. Turn around and leave. Now!"

The identically dressed puppets beside him nodded for emphasis. Then, as if on cue, they all bent low and began praying in loud voices to the Almighty.

Others stepped in front of the quintet of Pharisees and formed a solid barrier. They took up the chant of their religious leaders.

"Go, take your dead. Go, take your dead. Go, take your dead."

When the blockade of chanting protestors refused to move, Sestus made his way back to Caleb.

"Take the cart back to the valley until evening," Sestus shouted above the throng. "I'll send a contingent from the Antonia fortress. Then we'll take these bandits to their fate."

Caleb pointed at the wound on the centurion's leg. "Care for your wound, and I'll wait outside until you return."

The four imposing towers of the Antonia fortress held several sentries who watched as they approached. Two dozen legionnaires rushed out to welcome their new commander.

When Caleb turned, he watched the steady stream of humanity surging into the city as far as the eye could see. Turning against this force would take all the strength he could draw out of his horse.

The breeze carried the smell of coagulated blood, adding it to the odors of donkey, humanity, spices, and sacrificial smoke. Caleb looked into the cart and his stomach lurched at the sight of blood gurgling out of the mouth of a dying bandit.

God, spare me.

Energized, Caleb's first effort was to move his cargo to the perimeter of the roadway in order to limit the people pushing against his cart. Shouts flowed over his ears like a tidal wave.

"Go, take your dead. Go, take your dead."

Another rock hit Caleb in the back. He pulled hard at the cart, but the donkey wouldn't budge.

His next effort was to appeal to a stout young man leaning against the wall. His simple brown tunic marked him as neither wealthy nor poor. Probably a tradesman like Caleb himself.

"In the name of the Almighty, will you help me?"

The young man looked around, realized that Caleb was appealing to him. He turned away.

Caleb released the donkey and stepped up to him again. "I appeal to you, by the mercy of the Almighty, to help me take this death cart out of the holy city."

The young man examined the cart, then looked at all the pilgrims surging up the hill toward the temple.

"And what in the name of the Almighty is this act of mercy worth to you?" the man asked.

Caleb reached into the fold of his tunic. He considered his options, then withdrew the pouch coins. "There are three denarii. It's all I have."

The man's fleshy hand snatched the small leather bag and opened it. "Fine. Stand back."

The man was very effective. He simply yelled, "Make way for the dead! Make way for the dead!" and the crowd somehow opened up.

Partway down the hill, Caleb passed the gaggle of merchants who Sestus had rescued, and the men heaped on him their praise and appreciation. Caleb waved with one hand and clung hard to the donkey's mane with the other.

Where were you all before I lost my three denarii?

When Caleb reached the lower levels of the city, he forced the donkey to move off the road and into a small patch of green near a cemetery. There were fewer groans now; most of the bandits had died from blood loss. He studied the youngest of the bandits, who looked like he slept. His neck was bent at a strange angle.

What a waste, Caleb thought, his heart fluttering. *What would your mother think of you now? What would my own mother think of me if she saw me now? Almighty God, spare me.*

Caleb was still in the cemetery when the sun kissed the top of the hills and the last pilgrims straggled toward the soon-closing gates. A cohort of legionnaires marched in formation down the hill, making way for the three horse-drawn carts which followed them.

Sestus rode last in the procession.

"Climb up!" the centurion called. "The men will take care of the bandits. You've done enough for one day. Come and eat."

Caleb followed Sestus into a large open room where wooden dishes had been set out on a table. Roast mutton, plates of vegetables, quail, and a thick porridge awaited them. The feast, and the break from constantly moving, felt like a touch of heaven to the weary carpenter. He was saddle-sore and bone-tired. If all he had to do was sit in a shop from now on, he would be satisfied that the Almighty had given him a good life.

Even if that means making a few crosses for the Romans. And one for Barabbas.

In the morning, a legionnaire prodded him awake. "Sestus Aurelius, commander of Jerusalem, herald of the Emperor, calls you to do his work," the messenger proclaimed. "Wash and follow me."

A Nubian slave poured warm water into a basin and Caleb, groggy as he was, crawled off his mat and scooped the water over his head. He stripped off his tunic and poured the contents of the basin down his body.

The slave handed him a perfumed towel and he dried himself off.

"Praise the Almighty for a basin and a towel in the hand of his servant," Caleb intoned. "Praise our God for his generous supply of water to satisfy our thirst and keep us clean."

Caleb danced around the room singing a psalm of David. As he passed the Nubian, staring at him, he wrapped the towel around the servant's neck and invited him to join the dance. The Nubian bowed his head, backed away, and turned to retrieve a fresh tunic.

When Caleb was given a short-sleeved fresh tunic and scarlet mantle, he put on the clothing without question. The sandals wrapping around his ankles were of higher quality than any he'd worn before.

He leaned back against the room's strong wooden table as another slave handed him a flask of cool water and a platter of dates, figs, cheese, and grapes. He ate the lot like a famished beggar while a legionnaire waited for him just inside the door.

When all was consumed, Caleb fell into step with the patient legionnaire. The pair emerged from the fortress complex to walk the crowded cobblestone streets.

Caleb felt a sharp elbow in his ribs, winced, and turned to spot a large man pushing through the crowd away from him. As Caleb turned back, he felt another jab in his ribs. He grabbed at the sharp pain and stopped to catch his breath—just as another elbow jostled him.

By the fifth or sixth elbow, Caleb understood. The scarlet mantle was drawing the subtle ire of the pilgrims. He was wearing the color of Rome, thereby identifying himself with the occupiers. As such, he was not much higher than a tax collector.

I've got to get some Hebrew clothing, he decided. *Quick.*

The aroma of baking bread rose powerfully as they walked into an open square.

"Soldier," he called. "A moment to visit the bakery."

The legionnaire joined Caleb at the bakery where flat bread, just like Miriam used to make, was being piled up on a counter. The young woman inside the door took his order and filled a woven basket with three fresh loaves.

Caleb shared a loaf with the legionnaire.

"By the gods," exclaimed the Roman soldier. "Diana herself has sprinkled this offering with the nectar of nirvana."

The look on the legionnaire's face was so filled with pleasure that Caleb felt good about his action. He wolfed down the second loaf and was halfway through the third when he saw a blind beggar sitting just out of the way of the passing mob.

"Alms for the poor," the beggar called out. "Alms for the poor."

The beggar's head was bowed under a scruffy brown tunic, his hands outstretched. A lengthy beard quivered at the end of his bony chin. His dirty feet were bare and calloused.

Caleb walked over to him and placed the last half loaf in his hand. "All I have is fresh bread. Today the Almighty has given us his bread. Blessed be he who rules over us with justice and mercy."

"Amen," the beggar chimed in. "May God meet you when you have no one else to turn to."

"Amen. May he meet us all, and may we recognize him when he does." *And may he recognize us when he comes.*

Caleb turned to go.

"Carpenter!"

Looking over his shoulder, he saw the beggar standing near an alley and holding up the half loaf.

"How do you know who I am?" Caleb asked.

The beggar lowered the bread and lifted his voice. "The hand on the blade is not far from the heart of a friend." He tapped his walking stick rhythmically. "Search for truth where you think it can't be found."

With a quick step, he was gone.

Realizing the beggar had been none other than Titius, Caleb rushed toward the alley but found no sign of the man among the flow of people crushing each other through the passageway.

The legionnaire grabbed his arm. "Come, we have delayed enough. Your shop awaits."

"What is your name?" Caleb asked the soldier. "And where were you born?"

"I am Portius Lunas Magnamus." He took out his sword and raised it above his head. "My father is a dealer in pearls and gold and silver. Although we are from Neapolis, my father is curator of the games in Ephesus."

Caleb stopped in his tracks. Ephesus? That was where Nabonidus had gone. *Oh, God, spare my servant.*

"Carpenter, come!" Portius called.

Caleb stepped up onto a pile of discarded building stones at the edge of the road and surveyed the crowd. He needed to find Sestus. Titius had said, "The hand on the blade is not far from the heart of a friend." That seemed to mean that Sestus was in danger.

He ran a few steps and jumped up onto the lid of a barrel of salted fish. If Sestus went down, Caleb would never get his revenge on Barabbas—and he'd never save Nabonidus either.

Caleb followed Portius into the dark interior of a wood and stone structure, one of many such structures pasted side by side and row after row. The carpenter stepped past the legionnaire and nearly stumbled over a stack of logs piled a few feet inside the entranceway. He instinctively dove toward the wall. No logs tumbled after him.

"Carpenter?" Portius called. "What in the name of Jupiter are you doing? Is it a snake? A scorpion?"

"No, Portius, I'm just careless."

Although for a moment, Caleb had been sure Barabbas had set another trap for him.

The legionnaire nodded at the logs as he lit a series of lamps. "The commander needs them all. He will be here at the end of the day to tell you more."

With that, he turned and left.

The shop was fully equipped. Caleb examined the teeth on the saw, the edge on the plane, the weight of the hammers, the angle of the chisels, the length of the rulers, and he rearranged the other tools into an order he preferred. He would need them all to build more crosses.

He removed the scarlet wrap and his tunic, slipped on a short working tunic and carpenter's apron, and began his task.

Caleb had barely chosen his first log when movement at the door caught his attention.

A young woman, her hair in dark ringlets and jewelry in lavish display, stood with her hands on her hips, looking not at all pleased. Her brow furrowed and her lips pouted. She seemed startled to see him.

May the Almighty bless me with such beauty. That isn't the tunic of a modest maiden.

Warmth rushed up his neck as he reached for his scarlet wrap and covered himself. She hardly seemed to notice.

"Where is Eli?" she asked, stepping back from the doorway as if examining the street to make sure she had entered the right place.

Caleb stood up. "I know nothing of Eli. I've only just arrived this moment."

The visitor took a bold step inside. She moved to a cupboard, opened it, and found it empty. "Who are you?"

"I am Caleb, a carpenter from Nazareth," he answered. "I work for the new commander of Jerusalem."

"What did they do with Eli?" She seemed to almost dance her way closer. She stared into Caleb's eyes. "Where did you send him?"

Caleb stood his ground, overcome by her scent. Was this another trap?

"You can't just take over someone else's shop," she said.

"I still do not know this Eli. Who are you that you come here looking for him?"

"I am Suzanna," she said. "I came seeking wisdom from a friend."

Her movements were mesmerizing and he fought against staring at her inappropriately. Instead he turned away and looked at the stack of logs filling the space.

"And who is Eli, this friend of yours?" he asked.

She was close and her words were like breezes across his ear. The scent of apple blossoms wafted by.

"He is a teacher from Cana who has found the Messiah," she said. "Each day he teaches me more."

"And who is this Messiah?"

"He is our king. Now, I must go and find Eli." She turned, surveying the pile of logs, the carpenter bench, and Caleb's discarded tunic. "The Passover is here. The king is coming soon."

Suzanna was already out the door when Caleb called for her to wait. There was no response, however, He moved quickly to the doorway, but she was gone.

She hadn't felt like a trap, but neither had Deborah. He needed to focus on work.

For three days, Caleb shaped logs into crosses and explored the local shops for his dietary needs. The shopkeepers were friendly and not offended at all that he had taken over Eli's shop. Caleb especially enjoyed the baker and the vendor who sold tender chunks of lamb on a skewer. They easily shared the humor of the streets and were quick to accept him into the neighborhood.

The sun was fading away for the start of Caleb's first Sabbath in Jerusalem before he laid down the plane he was using.

I'm in Jerusalem, he reminded himself. *Here, I have to rest and worship.*

The hypnotic chanting from the streets and distinctive shuffling of thousands of pilgrim feet vibrated as Sabbath preparations were finalized. The heart of the city beats as if it lived.

Caleb began to realize how enormous the task of overseeing the security of the Judean capital was for Sestus. These people moved as if controlled by an outside force.

The next morning, having taken his breakfast with Sestus in the Antonia fortress, Caleb asked permission to climb the tower. It was granted.

"You'll be met by an engineer who is also a centurion," Sestus instructed. "I've told him to expect you."

Caleb saw several commanding figures waiting near the bottom of the stairs, but only one paid him any attention.

"Cato is my name," the man announced with a nod. "I have served in Alexandria, Carthage, Germania, Gaul, Britannicus, and in Rome itself." He pointed up the stairs. "Rarely have I seen a sight like this one."

The Roman appeared to be in his late fifties, and fit. He had no trouble climbing the winding staircase and was eager to instruct Caleb on the marvels of the city spread out below them.

Upon reaching the top of the tower, Cato waited for several minutes as Caleb adjusted himself to the height and panoramic view. The temple itself was blinding, the sun reflecting off the white marble and gold exterior. As much as Caleb tried to fix his eyes on it, the pain in his eyes discouraged him. The sound of music and chanting floated up from below. Again, he felt the pulsating life of the temple. He trembled and looked down at his shaking hands. What was happening to him in this place?

At first Caleb hesitated to approach the waist-high barriers around him. When he did follow the example of the Roman and move closer to the edge, he saw the mass of humanity pouring through the streets and alleys below.

"Herod accomplished his goal," Cato said, pointing at the temple. "He knew above all else that he must keep the people happy, that he must find a way to pull them together." He bent over the wall as though to get closer to the life below. "There are now more than one million souls pressing in on the new temple grounds."

Along with the pilgrims who had come to worship, there were donkeys carrying merchandise, lambs and oxen being herded into holding pens for sacrifice, slaves and servants and craftsmen, and the legions of soldiers tasked with overseeing order.

"Do you see what Herod did to build this plaza?" the centurion asked. He pointed to the perimeter walls around the Temple. "Herod built a large box around the mountain you once called Moriah. You can step almost five hundred paces one way and three hundred paces the other within the walls. I've taken this walk many times on duty. The walls are five paces thick and we could drive a chariot in there if we wanted."

Caleb was fascinated by the engineering involved. The massive stones had been fitted with precision, and large pools of water spread out for cleansing.

"This is the place where our Father Abraham tried to sacrifice his son, Isaac," Caleb said, glancing down. "This is the place where our King David stopped a plague with his sacrifice. It is a place of great action."

He moved to the corner of the tower and tried to mentally calculate the size of the foundation stones under the Temple Mount.

"How did Herod get those stones set up around the mountain?" Caleb asked.

"I only know that he brought in great engineers," replied Cato. "I was told that one of the foundation stones weighs four hundred tons. I walked around the bottom of these walls two days ago. The inward slope of the walls is a masterpiece of architecture. The walls are as tall as twenty houses and every stone is precisely fitted so that not even a piece of papyrus can be slipped between them. This reminds me of the great stones I saw in the pyramids of Egypt."

Cato stepped back from the wall and watched a pair of eagles drift high overhead.

"All the gods and kings want to create something bigger than themselves," he continued. "Ten thousand men worked on this site to create the temple. Herod would only allow specially trained priests to work on the Sacred Sanctuary inside."

"I was told that Herod's workmen have been building this site for more than forty-five years," Caleb said. "What else can they still do?"

Cato pointed at a large overpass near the royal portico. "Do you see that arch? More than a thousand tons of rock are suspended over it. In order to build it, the engineers built a hill and dragged the rocks on top. When everything was locked in place by weight, they removed the hill underneath."

"Those columns are a wonder of the world," Caleb remarked, indicating a construction site where three Hebrew were standing around a column in progress.

"There are one hundred and sixty two columns so far. Money is exchanged here from all over the world, a result of the Jews purchasing their special temple coinage. The city is filled with so much wealth, I think it must rival Rome."

Cato nudged Caleb's shoulder and pointed toward a group of youth running around in circles. Nearby, a group of six men stood at a table shouting with a merchant. Cages of birds were stacked on the other side.

"That's the Court of the Gentiles," Cato said. "As you know, none of us non-Jews are permitted inside. We must remain where the animals are kept, where the money is exchanged. It's more like a market than a place of worship center." He chuckled. "At least it's not as bad as it used to be."

Caleb's eyes fixed on the centurion's face. "What do you mean?"

"Two years ago at Passover, the one many think is their Messiah took up some whips and chased away all the merchants and moneychangers. I was called in to try to settle the angry mob outside the walls, but of course we couldn't step into the structure. They have their own guards for internal problems."

Caleb glanced down at the uniformed men standing erect next to the columns nearest the entrance to the inner court. Meanwhile, Cato turned away from the scene below and crossed his arms over his chest.

Caleb moved away from the parapet. "I can tell you that I wouldn't want to be on the wrong side of so many worshippers. I think I need to go down there and get a look at the temple from inside those walls."

"Just make sure you wash yourself," Cato warned as they began to descend the stairs of the tower. "You've been near death and you've eaten with Gentiles. And if the zealots hear what you've been up to, you wouldn't last a minute in that crowd. A knife would cut the life out of you and not one person would mourn."

"Perhaps I will first spend some time in the baths," Caleb agreed.

"Someday I'll show you the tunnels and waterways that flow into this city," Cato called over his shoulder. "I hear that Sestus needs you to build more crosses. Do your job well and ours will be easier."

Chapter Nineteen

Jerusalem, Palestine 29 A.D.

Six months into his time in Jerusalem, Caleb's cross-building services were rarely needed anymore. After Sestus crucified the first dozen zealots, the residents seemed to understand the need for cooperation. Most of the troublemakers moved away from the capital and Sestus started travelling to other cities in Judea.

Caleb was glad to be able to go back to creating specialty furniture for the centurions and royal family members who frequented his shop. He hid away the extra money and spent time expanding his repertoire of flute songs.

When Sestus was in town, he would send a legionnaire to the shop to see if Caleb needed anything. Or he would send an order for some item of furniture for his residence.

On the first day of the week, right after Sabbath was over, Suzanna would stop by the shop to update Caleb on what she was learning from Eli about the teachings of the Almighty. She urged Caleb to play his flute, and when he did she would dance freely around the room. She often plopped herself down on a stool afterward and took five or ten minutes to watch him carve or whittle. Why did she keep coming? When Suzanna finished her update, she would get up off the stool and walk out the door. She never said goodbye.

Titius limped in every few days and Caleb listened to reports of life on the streets. He began to see a mental picture of the joyful baker singing psalms as he worked, the moody weaver cursing and celebrating the failures and successes on his loom, the quick-fingered Armenian slave in the market who skimmed a few pieces of dried fruit from customers after the purchase had already been weighed.

One conversation tapped into Caleb's soul in an unexpected way. The day after the Feast of Tabernacles, he was busy on a new dining table for Caiaphas, the high priest. He'd hardly been able to take part in any of the festivities, but the pulse of the city vibrated into his shop through the chanting and conversations of celebration. It filtered into his senses through the smells of seasoned roast lamb, incense, and sweaty animals and travelers.

Soon after the final evening sacrifice, Titius appeared like a phantom. Caleb saw his faint shadow and looked up to see his former trainer leaning on his carpenter's table.

"So you must have news," Caleb noted. "This isn't your usual time for visiting."

Titius ignored the comment. "What do you really know about Yeshua?"

Caleb set down the hammer and chisel. "What do you mean? He was my friend. He's a good man, a carpenter, and now a teacher."

Titius stepped closer and warmed his hands over the fire. "He thinks he is more than that. I listened to him. He says he's the one who satisfies the thirsts of your people. He says he's the light of the cosmos. He says he's the presence of God in the temple."

Is Yeshi trying to get himself killed? Caleb asked himself. *Whatever's happened to him? Surely this is all a misunderstanding.*

Caleb stared hard at Titius. "That would be blasphemy."

Titius straightened up. "Exactly what your Pharisees and priests thought. They tried to stone him to death."

Caleb grabbed his outer wrap and threw it over his shoulders. "Is he okay? I need to go to him."

"Oh, he's okay. Put away your wrap. He vanished in the crowd and no one can find him. I think your own authorities will finish off this Messiah before the Romans deal with him." Titius limped back toward the doorway. "All I know is that he's more than he appears to be."

Caleb ran to the temple, but only a few hundred people lingered there. None of them included Yeshua or his close followers. For days, a great hush had settled over the streets as the rains poured down, washing the streets of all the dirt and evidence of pilgrims come and gone.

The tapping of Titius's cane always warned the carpenter of an impending visit, so when Titius adjusted his disguises Caleb was sometimes surprised. But he was rarely surprised at the responses he gained from his questions.

"Where do you sleep at night?" Caleb asked.

"Wherever I can," Titius answered evasively.

"What do you learn out on the streets?"

"Whatever I need to know."

"How do you get what you need?"

"However I can."

"Why do you speak in mysteries?"

"Because I can."

"When did you get into spying for the Romans?"

Titius stopped nibbling on a date and examined the pit. "My story is my story."

The old man's bony fingers then flicked the pit into a corner across the room. Those same fingers poked and prodded a mound of dried apricots on the carpenter's table.

"Barabbas is active near here again," Titius added. "He thought you were hunting him."

Caleb looked up from the bowl he was chiseling out. "Is he here, in Jerusalem? Does Sestus know?"

"Barabbas moves like a shadow. He'll find you if he pleases. I see his zealots moving through the streets." Titius pulled a covering up over his head and stood in the doorway. "I hope you continue your training. You may not see me again, though, and I'll soon be gone to Rome."

After Titius's warning, Caleb started roaming the streets for himself. He utilized his own disguises, trying them out on unfamiliar vendors and then on ones he was acquainted with. He was amazed at how much a person could learn simply by sitting in one place and not moving.

He noticed that the division of classes was even more pronounced in Jerusalem than in some of the other cities he'd been in. The few thousand members of the upper class—the temple priests, the aristocracy, and the Sadducees—were surrounded by luxury, pomp, and comfort. While others walked, the upper class was carried in litters, hoisted by slaves. While others shopped for their own meals, the upper class issued orders for satin and linen. While others sidestepped the slops flowing from open sewer drains, the upper class kept their jeweled sandals clean and dry.

The tens of thousands of middle class consisted of merchants, traders, masons, sculptors, metal and woodworkers, clothdyers, Pharisees, sages, teachers, and scribes. The hundred thousand lower class laborers—slaves, stone carriers, weavers, beggars, lepers, the blind, and the lame—filled in the rest of the mass of humanity surging through the streets and alleys of the capital.

Jerusalem was also unique in its ethnic diversity, which was more pronounced than in places like Nazareth or Sepphoris. Religious seekers, international traders, merchants, and food vendors integrated into the rich Jewish cultural life. With this mix came many languages, including Latin, Greek, Syrian, Aramaic, and Hebrew.

Two days after Titius had slipped away, and one hour before the Sabbath started, Caleb heard the sound of pigeons in the back of a weaver's shop. He was leaning against the exterior wall, watching the bakery across the lane. Nothing suspicious was happening, but the birds reminded him of the blue-tasseled pigeons under the care of the Ethiopian slave in the caravansary outside Caesarea.

The start of Sabbath meant he couldn't stay, but he came to an important conclusion for himself: *Follow the pigeons, find the zealots.*

He arrived home just as the Sabbath candles were being lit, signaling the start of the sacred night.

As he ruminated over his findings, he realized that the zealots' spiritual fervor might be their undoing. They recognized that killing was sinful and collected their sacrificial animals in advance to secure their atonement.

The zealots must be planning something big if they need more pigeons, Caleb thought. *Maybe they're just getting ready for the Day of Atonement.*

Caleb was tuning up a flute the morning after the Day of Atonement when Suzanna stepped in, out of the drizzle, and into the coolness of his shop. She wore a scarlet tunic with a white shawl. A light blue scarf nestled around her neck and thin leather sandals graced her feet. Sparkling raindrops slipped down her olive cheeks and off the tips of her raven hair.

She stood boldly a few feet away, then slowly turned. He couldn't keep his gaze off her and felt the heat rising along his neck and cheeks.

"Do you see me like other men see me?" Suzanna asked. She stepped away and leaned against the carpenter's table. "Please forgive me."

Caleb washed his hands in the basin. "What is there to forgive?"

Suzanna pushed herself away from the table and walked over to a cupboard. She took out a cup, grabbed the ladle sitting in the pot hanging over the fire, and poured herself some tea. She wrapped her hands around it.

"I presumed on our friendship. Eli told me it wasn't appropriate for me to dress as I did and to dance as I do in front of you." She took a sip of the hot brew.

"I promise you that my intentions were not to disgrace or shame you. I'm the one who has lived a life of shame, even worse than I imagined."

The heat rose in him again. Caleb moved to the pot and ladled his own cup of tea. "I too went to the Temple for the Atonement. I too seek your forgiveness for failing to warn you of the weaknesses of men. I wasn't a true friend."

Suzanna held her cup in both hands and moved closer to him, examining his face again.

"Caleb, look at me," she said. "No man has ever before asked for my forgiveness."

Caleb looked into her dark eyes as tears flowed. He reached up and wiped them away. More flowed. Silence was the only gift he could offer.

The autumn rains were steady and the trickles of water had found their way in through the back of his shop. Caleb lifted his creations up off the floor onto the tables, then ensured that his tools were properly hung in place. The shavings had been swept up and the baskets of curios and flutes were hanging from the rafters.

"Caleb," Suzanna began. "Last time I was passing, I heard you playing the flute."

"I was just testing one of my new ones," Caleb rushed to explain, feeling his face flush. "I was actually thinking of you when I played."

"I felt like my spirit was held captive by the music," Suzanna whispered. She stepped reverently toward the table and picked up the slender instrument.

"Would you like to learn to play?" Caleb stepped up beside her and positioned her fingers over the proper holes in the wood.

She trembled at his touch. "First, I'd like you to play me another song." She let go of the flute and walked the few feet to ladle another cup of tea.

"What kind of song?"

"A song of love."

Caleb hesitated and then pulled down a basket containing other flutes. He selected one of polished olive wood and set his fingers over the holes. "I haven't played a song like that in many years."

"Who did you play it for?"

Caleb smiled. "I played it for a girl named Rebekah. She was the sister of my friend Yeshi, and she was an angel."

"Where did this angel live?"

Was that a tinge of jealousy in her voice, Caleb wondered?

"She lived in Nazareth with the rest of us carpenters." Caleb positioned himself to get a better view of her eyes. "When my father was killed by the Sicarii, I fell into darkness and she coaxed me back to the light. When I was attacked and my neck was slit by dagger men, she was there for me again. She and her brother Yeshi."

Suzanna set her cup down on the table and picked up another flute. She looked coyly over her shoulder at Caleb. "So which part of this girl made you think she was an angel?"

Caleb cocked his head. "Whatever do you mean?" He raised the flute to his lips. "She cared for me several times over three years. She spoke softly to me when I needed it, and other times strongly. She was never unkind or inappropriate. Her mother made sure of that."

"So how did she like your love song?" Suzanna replaced the flute, picked up her tea, and settled herself on a stool.

"She was captivated, of course." He tried to chuckle, but it caught in his throat. "Her mother kept her busy after that and sent her away often."

Suzanna finished her tea and moved to the washing bowl to clean it. "So you haven't given your heart to another woman since?"

What can I say? he asked himself. *Did I give my heart to Deborah and Hannah?*

Caleb gathered his flutes and replaced the basket on its shelf. "I've had no time. The centurion keeps me tethered as if I were his own slave. Some days I long for those times when I could talk with Rebekah's brother."

"This brother of this angel you speak of." Suzanna picked up a rag and began to dust the shelving in the cupboard. "Did you say his name was Yeshi, and that he was a carpenter from Nazareth?"

"Yes, this Yeshi was my friend. He walked the hills of Galilee with me. He taught me how to love wood like no other carpenter. He was a good son and a good brother. It was a sad day when he moved away from us."

"He sounds so much like Yeshua Ha Meshiach, the one who took me from darkness into light. He's the one who released me from my shackles and let me feel free to love again in the way God designed. He's the one who Eli took me to when I had nowhere else to go."

"They are the same man," Caleb affirmed. "And yes, that sounds like my friend Yeshi all right. The girls all loved him when we were young."

"It's not like that," Suzanna said. "Yes, he has eyes that draw you in and make you feel like you're the treasured daughter of a king. He has a touch that's gentle as a dove's feather. But there's something about the way he prays and talks with God. It's as if he were talking to his own father."

Caleb stopped Suzanna in her scrubbing and eased the rag from hand. "Tell me what you know. It's been so long since I've seen him."

"It's been so amazing. I've watched him heal lepers through his touch. He's opened the eyes of the blind. He's freed those who were shackled by demons. He healed a woman who had been bleeding for twelve years… she even touched him and he refused to act as if she were unclean." Suzanna reached into the cupboard, removed two cups, and took them to the washbasin. "He even raised the dead through his touch. With just a word, he sometimes changes everything. That's what happened with me."

"So he's become a magician," Caleb said. "He captures the minds and hearts of his countrymen. He makes the Romans nervous."

Suzanna stepped away from the table toward Caleb. "You should hear him speak. He teaches with authority. He shuts the mouths of the Pharisees and teachers of the law. He speaks of God's kingdom as if it were here with him. I've heard him talk about things so simply that even I can understand them—of seeds that grow in the ground and die, of pearls hidden in a field, of lost sheep that are found, of wedding banquets and new wine that bursts the old wineskins."

Caleb moved to the back of the shop, picked up a crossbeam out of a pool of rainwater, and propped it up against the wall. "You sound like you have become his follower."

"If only I could follow him," she said, adjusting her white shawl around her shoulders. "It would be a dream come true. It seems that the whole world is following him."

She grabbed a straw broom and swept the water toward the entrance.

"Many of the women I once worked beside have gone to be with him. Even tax collectors have left their money stalls to learn from him." Suzanna laid aside the broom and lifted her prayer shawl over her head. "He speaks in ways that make people think he's claiming to be God himself. Some at the temple this last feast even tried to stone him for blasphemy."

Caleb removed his carpenter's apron and kicked a chunk of wood under the table. "He sounds like a dangerous man to be around."

Suzanna moved to the doorway and smiled back at Caleb. "Only if you're afraid to love. Now, next time, play me that song you play for angels."

After that day, Suzanna dropped by the shop more and more often. She wanted flute lessons after all, and still wondered if he knew other songs to play. She sometimes discovered special treats at the market and asked for his thoughts on recent events or sayings she had heard from the Messiah.

I don't even care why she comes, he thought. *She almost makes me forget about Sestus and Barabbas.*

The Feast of Dedication, in the month of Kislev, brought an extra array of bright lights and festive celebrations. Caleb enjoyed watching Suzanna light a new candle on the nine-branched candelabrum for Hanukah each of the eight days of the holiday.

On the last day, Suzanna dropped by the shop and begged Caleb to walk with her in the blanket of virgin snow settling over the streets and hills. He was cleaning his shop and all his projects were complete, so he felt the freedom to join her.

She took the carpenter first around the Royal Porch surrounding the temple, then out through the Huldah Gates to gaze over the Kidron Valley. They watched children playing in the snow on the Mount of Olives.

Unexpectedly, Suzanna grabbed Caleb's hand and squealed in delight.

Caleb clenched his fist as shivers raced up his spine, not knowing what to do. *Why is she doing this here? All I need now is for some Pharisee to see me.*

He pulled his hand away.

"Do you find me repulsive?" Suzanna asked, turning her back to Caleb and facing the valley.

"What kind of question is that?" Caleb asked, raising his hands. "Does every girl I meet have to ask that question just because I'm trying to be careful?"

Suzanna nudged a rock with the toe of her sandal. "Have you no more room in your heart for anyone apart from your angel?"

Caleb stepped around her. "If you're talking about Rebekah, she's only a shadow in a corner."

Suzanna lifted her face toward him. "What do I have to do for you to notice me? Do you know my past so well that you can't give me a future?"

"It isn't you," Caleb said. "You're as beautiful as the mountains with their snow. Your voice is as musical as any flute I've ever made. Your smile is like sunshine on my darkest days. Your past belongs to a woman in a story far away. It's not your past; it's mine that shackles me."

Suzanna stepped closer. "What secret can be so great that it would overpower the secrets of my past?"

Caleb walked down the steep grade of the valley toward the pool of Siloam. He led Suzanna out the Water Gate and down onto the floor of the Hinnom

Valley. They stood looking up at the massive walls of the city and the majestic glimmer of the temple.

"When the centurion was training me to be more than a carpenter, he taught me to hate the Parthians who killed my father," Caleb said. "He taught me to make crosses and to uncover those who were the enemy of Rome. One day he forced me to nail a woman to a cross, and I did it."

Suzanna gasped as she raised her hands over her mouth. She turned and paced for a minute. "Did she die?"

"Not right away," Caleb admitted. "She screamed for days."

He turned his back on Suzanna and on the Temple.

"I hear those screams in my dreams. Most days I tell myself that it was her life or mine." He took several steps from Suzanna and dropped his chin to his chest. "I tell myself that she was working to kill the people I loved. I tell myself she was getting what she deserved." Caleb looked up toward the temple again. "But I can't escape her screams."

Suzanna moved close and embraced him, her head on his chest. The carpenter's shoulders tightened and he held his arms firmly by his sides.

"Our father David once wrote a psalm in this very place," she began, speaking from the heart. "The words he wrote have been healing for me, and they can be healing for you: 'Yahweh is gracious and compassionate. He is slow to anger and rich in love. Yahweh is good to all; he has compassion on all he has made.'"[1]

A sob emerged from deep within Caleb's chest. Suzanna reached up and pulled his head down on her shoulder. He shook and wept as she softly sang the psalm in the darkness.

"The Son of David, Yeshua Ha Meshiach, your friend and brother, has told us how to pray," she continued once her song had ended. "He said, 'Forgive us our sins as we forgive those who sin against us. Lead us not into temptation but deliver us from the evil one.'[2] If you forgive others who sin against you, the Father of heaven will forgive you."

Caleb relaxed in the warmth of Suzanna's embrace and the words of life she spoke.

"Today is a day to be forgiven," she said, "to take the love of the Almighty and to live again."

He stilled himself, then lifted his head and watched the flickering torches lighting the snow-covered temple. It all seemed glorious again.

---

[1] Psalm 145:9–10.
[2] Luke 11:4.

"You too are an angel." He turned back to her and took her hand. "My sin is too dark and I'm cold. But let's get back and find a fire."

Suzanna rested her head against Caleb's shoulder, gave his hand a squeeze, and started the uphill climb toward home.

Caleb walked her through the streets until they reached the door of a stately home near the eastern wall.

"It's my uncle's home," Suzanna said. "I've moved here to start a new life. I cannot show you where I used to live."

Caleb released her hand. "May the Almighty bless you with a sleep of peace."

"And may he do the same for you." Suzanna turned and followed a servant through the iron gates.

For Caleb, it was a lonely walk back to his cold, barren room. Sleep did not come easily.

The next morning, while it was still dark, Caleb felt an unnatural presence in the room with him. He opened his eyes and looked up into the face of Sestus, standing over him. A distant flickering torch gave faint illumination.

"Rise up, carpenter," the centurion said. "Your skills are required. Put on your mantle. Take your sword and dagger. All our needs will be provided for along the way."

Caleb sprang to his feet, pulled on a fresh tunic and outer wrap, then raced out into the cold pre-dawn air.

An Ethiopian slave had already saddled Caleb's black Arabian, and as the first tinges of light crested the horizon the carpenter and the centurion emerged from the city's Fish Gate and joined the thirty mounted legionnaires who were waiting for them. At the bottom of the hill, they turned onto the road toward Jericho.

Among the riders were young warriors from Gaul, Spain, and Persia. They were broad-chested in full battle gear with strips of iron and leather forming armor over their torsos. They carried short swords, javelins, and bows, and four-foot rectangular shields of wood and leather provided further protection.

A mile from the city, another two dozen riders joined the force. Caleb sensed immediately from Sestus's urging of his mount that the centurion was determined to get somewhere quick. The group forded the Jordan River at a narrow crossing and turned south. Their speed increased and Caleb did all he could to keep up with the more experienced riders.

By noon, the group had passed Mount Nebo, the spot where Moses had taken his only glimpse of the Promised Land before he died.

A large hill rose in the distance, and upon it sat the black, impregnable fortress of Machareus, Herod's castle. This was where Yeshua's cousin, John the Baptizer, had been held and beheaded. The newly rebuilt fortress, originally built by the Macabees, provided a frontline outlook on the Arab peoples who wandered the wilderness.

From the deepest crevices of the Salt Sea, the ragtag cavalry pushed up the hill toward the citadel. Its steep rocky sides challenged the horses. Caleb's mount heaved and the carpenter fought his own weariness. When they approached the top, he slowed his ride.

At that moment, the horse stumbled and Caleb was pitched onto the ground. His shoulder stung with fire as he hit the hard, rocky clay and rolled away from the falling horse. His headpiece fell off and floated down a ten-foot drop.

He was about to call for help when he heard the shouts of battle just ahead. As he limped forward, he hid behind a boulder and saw that the cavalry of Romans had been attacked by a large gang of zealots. Twenty archers stood at the entrance to a cave above them, launching their death sticks down on the tired Romans from an eastern position. The sun was directly in the eyes of the Romans trying to see where the archers hid.

A band of fifty zealots, directly to the south of the Romans, drew attention to themselves by throwing rocks and shouting. Sestus was compacting the group as they raised their shields to block both arrows and rocks.

A charging force of fifty horsemen emerged from the west. As the Romans turned to meet the charge, the archers unleashed more arrows into the soldiers and their horses. The cacophony of horses screaming in pain and bandits screaming to terrorize and confuse the Romans was mind-numbing.

Roman after Roman fell under the fusillade of arrows. Horsemen with javelins rode over the fallen and pinned them to the ground, expertly circumventing their victims' protective armor. When the imperial soldiers reformed as a unit to divert the next charge, zealot swordsmen rushed into the fray and delivered fatal blows to the neck. Weapons lay abandoned where they fell as one man after another was eliminated from the battle.

Caleb was paralyzed for a moment, but in a fit of insane rage he worked his way along the rocky ledge toward the battle and snatched up a discarded javelin. He charged one of the swordsmen from behind, skewered the surprised zealot, and with a single chop beheaded him with his short sword.

Two swordsmen broke away from the battle and moved toward him. Caleb pulled out his javelin and prepared to defend himself.

Sestus, Titius, my life depends on what you taught me. I hope it's enough.

With a two-hundred-foot ledge to his left and a steep, rocky rise to his right, he moved past a small cavern and set himself up on a flat ledge where he could see the action below. The Roman forces were dwindling quickly.

The two swordsmen reached him, and one moved to the right while the other went left.

Almighty God, if I meet you now, have mercy on my soul. But in this moment, make me like David.

Suddenly, a horseman broke from the Roman ranks and charged in his direction. The hoofbeats echoed off the mountainside and momentarily distracted the zealots. Before they could react, a carefully aimed javelin pierced the back of the zealot on Caleb's right. The charging horse then flattened the zealot on his left. The two men crumpled and rolled. Caleb ran toward them and tossed them over the cliff's edge.

"Get up, quick!" called Sestus, the rider who had come to his rescue. "We're going to run."

As Caleb hoisted himself up and sprinted, a fiery pain ran up his leg and exploded into his brain. An arrow had lodged itself deep in his calf. He screamed in pain.

Sestus reached back and pulled the arrow out.

"Tear your tunic," yelled the centurion. "Stuff it in the wound."

Caleb fought to remain conscious. With his teeth, he bit down on the sleeve of his tunic and ripped a strip from it. Twice he almost slipped off the bouncing saddle as Sestus's horse hurdled down the rocky face of Machareus. Sestus held the shield over them and blocked several arrows.

The next twenty minutes were filled with moments of choking dust and terrifying screams as zealots tried to gain ground against the warhorse. But Sestus was skilled in evasion and eventually the zealots dropped out of the chase.

Caleb felt the strength draining from him as the small piece of tunic he had stuffed into his wound barely staunched the flow of blood.

"We got away," Caleb slurred, feeling his grip loosen.

"I lost my men! The zealots should be fastened to a cross by now. I need to go back for reinforcements. This battle cannot be lost."

When they reached the desert floor, Sestus stopped the horse and tied Caleb's hands to the saddle. He poured water into Caleb's mouth, then took a rag from his saddle bag and tied it around Caleb's head. He took another and tightened it over the wound.

"You saved my life," Caleb said.

The horizon grew hazy and Caleb's grip on Sestus loosened.

Caleb awoke in a shelter meant for legionnaires recovering from battlefield injuries. His head felt like it was burning up, but he still shivered. An Ephesian physician, with the healing medallion from the Temple of Diana, hovered over him and gave him potions to drink.

In Caleb's lucid moments he noticed supplies on shelves around the room: herbs and medications, amulets, balances, scales and weights, bottles, amphoras, clay jars, glass vials, pestle, and mortar.

A miracle would be so much easier, he thought. *Where is Yeshi when I need him?*

Caleb propped himself up on his elbows and felt the world swirl around him. He tried to focus on another set of shelves. Scoops, spoons, forceps, and scalpels were set in place.

An Egyptian slave held medicated wine to Caleb's lips and urged him to drink. The potion tasted bitter at the back of his tongue and throat.

The Ephesian picked up a saw and laid it beside Caleb's leg. Caleb shivered as the physician poked, prodded, and poured powders into the wound.

"What shall we do with you?" the doctor mused aloud, picking up the saw again. "Do you pray to a god who can heal you, or do we save everyone the trouble, cut this off, and give your leg to the fire?"

Caleb found himself praying out to the Almighty, even calling out to Yeshi to help him in his distress. Psalms he hadn't considered since childhood came to mind and directed the words of his prayers.

Two legionnaires stopped by and spoke with the physician while looking in Caleb's direction. Ignoring his cries of pain, they lifted him onto a stretcher as if he was a sack of grain.

Caleb fought for consciousness as he noticed the physician reach for his saw again. He realized too late that the wine he'd been given was for more than just pleasure.

Chapter Twenty

Jerusalem, Palestine 30 A.D.

The months of Tebeth, Shebet, and Adar came and went. Although Sestus came to ask Caleb to ride again, the carpenter couldn't ride even if he was tied to the saddle. His recovery was slow and painful during the months before he was released from care.

News from the fortress was sparse, although casualties seemed to be mounting on both sides according to the few reports Caleb overheard.

He thanked the Almighty daily that his leg had been spared. Someone, and he didn't know who, had intervened at the last moment. The physician described an old bony Roman doctor with a beard like a goat. Had it been Titius? The old man had stopped the saw-cutting and taken responsibility for Caleb during that first critical week of his treatment.

Even Caleb's limp couldn't dampen his pleasure at being able to maneuver around his shop.

Three days after his return, Suzanna rushed into his space.

"Caleb, you're alive!" She knelt down by his side. "Don't move. I'll get you some tea and another blanket. Tell me what happened."

Caleb watched Suzanna rummage in the cupboard and then set up the fire and pot to boil tea. The scent of wildflowers slowly filled the room.

When Suzanna paused and looked his way, Caleb began to explain. "I was riding with Sestus and some legionnaires to Machareus." He sat up on his mat and adjusted the blanket around him. "We were ambushed by zealots. I didn't see Barabbas, but they must have been his men. Sestus saved my life."

Caleb lifted up his blanket and showed her the ugly scar from where the arrow had hit him and from where the physician had begun to cut.

He knew things were changing between them when Suzanna noticed a bowl of grapes that had been untouched all day. She used the sarcastic twang of a Galilean grandmother to make light of it.

"So are you wanting me to feed you these things like a king, or are you waiting until they turn into raisins?"

He smiled for the first time in years.

She kept it up. "So did that crack in your face come from too much tension or does it mean you're maybe thinking about living?"

Suzanna took one of Caleb's flutes and began to play the love song he had taught her. It was a haunting song of tenderness and hope. The melody tugged at his heart like a robin pulling a reluctant worm from the earth.

When the song was joined with a dance around the shop, the shadows in his mind seem to slip out the door. Healing seemed to come easier after that day.

Caleb was pleased with Suzanna's progress on the flute and the two of them could even play some simple songs together. Small groups of people would stop by to listen in on the music. The sale of flutes became so brisk that he could hardly keep up with demand.

The Feast of Purim soon brought more celebration to Jerusalem, and Caleb and Suzanna walked among the blossoming almond trees in the valley. The citrus fruit was being harvested and the markets were full of special treats to encourage the palate and the soul.

Caleb stopped by the Antonia Fortress and asked for Cato, who told him that Sestus had been in Sepphoris, Caesarea, Tiberius, and Jericho over the past months. Although Sestus was commander of Jerusalem, his reputation and responsibility as legate of Judea meant he had to assist the senior centurions in other cities. Zealots and bandits had intensified their activity throughout the realm and Herod Antipas was encouraging Sestus to work harder to eliminate them.

Sestus had been away so much that things were quiet in the shop. Only once did Sestus stop by for a few moments to look at Caleb's work.

"Secure a larger facility," the centurion commanded. "One day zealots will strike again in this place and we will be ready."

Caleb understood. Reports had to be written. New tactics had to be learned against those like the zealots and bandits who fought in ways outside the recognized order of warfare.

Passover was coming again and perhaps Sestus suspected the holiday would be a time for more unrest. He also knew that news of Yeshua Ha Meshiach was creating great emotion in debates between the city leaders. The soldiers were monitoring the crowds carefully.

Two days after Suzanna's last visit, Caleb disguised himself as a beggar and sat on a stone near the bakery. A merchant leading an oxcart filled with caged pigeons stopped by long enough to leave one cage with the weaver. The transaction was done quickly and quietly and the pigeons were moved out of sight.

Caleb was sure this was a zealot stop, and he decided to let Sestus know about it.

There were days when Caleb felt guilt over how he was taking advantage of Suzanna. He knew he could move around freely, but when she was in the room he acted as though he were helpless.

One day, Caleb watched as she stacked a pile of wood that had been delivered by a merchant. She turned and saw him watching her.

"How does a man control his eyes?" she asked.

Caleb felt the heat rise in his cheeks again. What was he supposed to do? And what could he say?

"I have given my care freely. You have never asked me for anything I wasn't willing to share." She knelt by his side. "But, Caleb, the baker is threatening that I'll lose my work with him if I can't make my deliveries. I still work early in the morning and I finish his deliveries in the evening." She put her hand on his shoulder. "I'm missing out on the teachings of Eli and I feel distant from the group that meets there. I either need to see you less or you need to join me when I go."

Caleb forced himself to his feet and extended his hand. "You are very important to me. I love my time with you, but of course you must go. If I cannot come, you can teach me what you learn."

"Caleb, I think it's time that you forgive Barabbas." Suzanna turned away and moved toward the door. "You must learn to love instead of hate."

Then she was gone.

Caleb had taken in her words on God's compassion and forgiveness, but he had also taken in the words she had quoted from Yeshua: *"Unless you forgive, you cannot be forgiven."*

But what was he to do about the oath he'd taken to avenge his father? He had forgiven Sestus, and he had forgiven his father, but Barabbas? What kind of man would he be if he forgave someone who had killed his own father?

Caleb paced the streets, evaluating the depths of his own heart. He hadn't yet reached the point of forgiving God for allowing the Sicarii to kill his father and the disease that killed his mother. Although he could act outwardly as if he was free, he knew that his heart remained firmly in shackles.

Two weeks before Passover, Caleb took Suzanna for a walk in the Kidron Valley. The steep valley ran north and south between the Mount of Olives and the Temple Mount.

"I've walked all twenty miles of this road with Sestus," he said, looking to see if she was impressed. She wasn't. "It slopes four thousand feet toward the Dead Sea. The Gihon springs would have filled the whole depression, but Jerusalem's residents have diverted the water into pools for their own needs."

Caleb pointed out the diversions that had been cut to channel the water.

Suzanna nodded and stated the obvious. "We need the water, so it's only right that we should use it. It is a gift to us from the Almighty."

He worked harder to impress and filled Suzanna in on the history of the place. "King David travelled this very path and up the slopes of the Mount of Olives to escape Absalom. This was once a place of pagan altars and idols where kings like Asa worshipped and defied the living God. You see now those monstrous tombs being built by peoples of all nations to honor their dead. This is a place of death."

Suzanna looked up at the edge of the temple wall. "One of Yeshua's followers told me that the devil himself told Yeshua to jump from that place to here." She pointed to the southeast corner of the temple. "He told the evil one that we shouldn't test the Almighty."

Caleb looked up at the dizzying height. "Yeshua was wise that day."

They continued to walk down the incline upon a well-traveled path. Caleb admired the cartloads of barley and flax being hauled to market in Jerusalem after the recent harvest.

As the two walked side by side and spoke of the beauty around them, the first of the spring rains began to fall. Suzanna danced for joy with her arms upraised, and Caleb took a small flute from a pocket in his tunic and played for her. A group of children nearby ran over and joined in the merriment.

This is the way life was meant to be. Finally, all is right in my world.

Caleb watched six ladies hugging and kissing each other in greeting. Four of the women wore the simple garb of villagers, with dull fabrics and simple head coverings. Two wore the tunics of nobility, with rich embroidered purple sashes. The tallest of the simple four had long dark hair cascading all the way to her lower back. The rest wore their hair in braids or twisted up on their heads, hidden under their scarves.

The group walked slowly up to the twirling band of dancers and joined in the clapping of onlookers.

Finally, the taller one called out. "Suzanna! What is the celebration?"

Caleb stopped his playing and Suzanna danced her way to the group. He heard her clearly.

"Mary, Martha," she said. "The news of your brother Lazarus took my breath away. The whole city is talking about what Yeshua Ha Meshiach has done. It's unheard of to raise someone after four days of death."

Caleb stepped closer to the group. Had he heard right? Had Yeshua raised someone from the dead after four days? Impossible! If the whole city was talking about it, why hadn't he heard?

"You must be careful," one of the women cautioned. "The chief priest and the Pharisees are watching for him this upcoming Passover. Everyone is being told to report when he comes. I was even warned that plans are being made to kill both Yeshua and Lazarus."

Suzanna took a step toward Caleb, then turned back to the huddle of ladies and spoke earnestly. "Someone must warn him to stay away. The zealots are active again and the Romans are nervous. This isn't a good time to make the religious leaders angry."

"We'll talk to him when we see him next week," the other woman promised, "but he already seems to know everything that is happening. Yeshua always does what he says the Father is telling him to do. We cannot guarantee anything. Herod Antipas and Pilate are arriving in the city, so there is a lot of security."

Caleb approached the group and was welcomed by the ladies. Mary, Martha, Joanna, Phoebe, and Ana introduced themselves and Suzanna introduced him.

"This is Caleb," she said. "He's the carpenter I told you about from Nazareth. He's known Yeshua since he was a boy."

"We will tell him that you're here," Martha said. "He will be delighted to meet you again. Perhaps after Passover is done, we can have you to our home to talk together. I can't wait to hear all the stories of those days." Her eyes danced at the thought. "It must have been so wonderful to be part of the world where Yeshua grew up. My sister Mary bought a liter of pure nard for this festival. This will be a very special year in Jerusalem."

The woman named Mary tugged at her sister's mantle. "Leave them be," she said. "Lazarus is probably hungry by now. We need to get home and feed the poor man."

When the group had wandered off, Caleb lowered his hand gently onto Suzanna's elbow. "And here I thought you danced for joy because of being with me. Now I know it's because of my friend, Yeshi. No matter what I do, it's never enough for you women."

"If I didn't know you were joking, I would be offended. If you really want to know what's happening in our city, all you need to do is ask. Maybe if you got away from that shop of yours, you could learn a little more about life, and maybe you'd even see who Yeshua is now instead of just talking about how he used to be."

Caleb fixated on Suzanna's smiling face. "Okay, tell me about what I should know."

Suzanna filled Caleb in on the incredible miracle that had taken place in Bethany. "Yeshua came to the home of his friends after Lazarus had been dead four days. He wept deeply, and everyone could see how much Yeshua had loved his friend."

"I wish he had wept for my mother," Caleb said.

Suzanna took his hand and began walking back up the hill toward the city gate. "We don't always know God's plan. Yeshua could have healed Lazarus before he died." She pointed toward Bethany, where Mary and Martha and their group were just cresting the Mount of Olives. "With one command, Yeshua told Lazarus to come out of the tomb—and he did. You can see why the sisters are so excited to have him back again."

Caleb had to stop several times up the steep climb to give his throbbing leg a rest. He was perspiring heavily. Whatever had happened to his youth?

When Caleb and Suzanna reached the gates of the fortress, after a final rest, they noticed a large group of legionnaires dressed for battle standing in formation.

Caleb asked a bystander what was happening.

"The zealots ambushed a group of Roman cavalry near Emmaus, and this group is going after them," the man said. "It looks like the zealots may have inflicted some major casualties."

Caleb abandoned Suzanna at the gate and rushed around the perimeter of the formation until he saw Cato conversing with a small group of other centurions. Without thought, Caleb rushed toward them. Two legionnaires stepped in front of him and smashed him to the ground with their shields.

Although he was dazed from the blows, he recognized Cato's voice: "Carpenter, what is in your mind rushing in here like this?"

Caleb looked up and noticed the man extending a hand. He grasped it and allowed Cato to pull him back to his feet. Strong arms held him in place.

"What are you doing here?" Cato asked.

"I heard about the attack," Caleb replied. "I wondered about Sestus. Was he with the cavalry? Is he still alive?"

Almighty God, protect this protector of your people, he prayed.

Cato looked at the centurions standing nearby. "Sestus was there," he said grimly. "We're waiting to hear the news. Right now, we must hunt for zealots. It would be best that you prepare your crosses."

Caleb was left to stumble his way out of the gate and back into the arms of Suzanna. She had clearly been crying.

"I thought they were going to kill you," she said with tears still streaming down her face. "Why did you have to run in there like that? What is so important that you have to risk your life?"

Caleb looked back at the gathering of centurions. "My friend Sestus was in the Roman cavalry just attacked. I have to go and make more crosses. The trouble has come to Jerusalem."

Suzanna covered her mouth with one hand and held onto Caleb's wrist with the other.

"Please, Caleb, don't let fear and hatred steal your soul. Pray to the Almighty for his peace."

Caleb pulled away from Suzanna. "There will never be peace until Barabbas is hanging on a cross."

He hurried back to his shop and began preparing for the work ahead.

Caleb knew from the approaching sound of hobnailed sandals that someone from the Roman military was coming his way, but he kept working. The steps stopped outside his door, as he had known they would. The chatter of neighborhood children and passing vendors seemed to fade away.

Silence descended on him as the messenger waited for his attention. He waited for a familiar voice to call to him, but it never came. He finally stopped working and straightened up.

When Caleb turned, he saw Cato watching him intently.

"Sestus is dead."

Caleb's lungs momentarily stopped working. The air seemed to be gone from the room. Caleb reached for his throat.

"The zealots overpowered him," Cato continued. "It won't be long until we find those responsible. Justice will be needed."

The centurion left and the carpenter sank to his knees, retching.

He heard the renewed chatter of the early Passover pilgrims, but he couldn't arise above the dark cloud that swallowed his thoughts. He didn't even respond to customers as they came to inquire about his products. When he heard Suzanna arrive for her flute lessons, Caleb didn't even acknowledge her. He kept working.

When the olive oil lamp went dark one day, Caleb stumbled around until he found new oil. He relit it and kept working. There was justice to pay and there were crosses to make. Demons lunged into the shadows of his mind.

I should have been there with Sestus, instead of caring for my own desires with Suzanna, he thought. *When I needed him, he saved me. When he needed me, I was nowhere. I really am a worthless apprentice. What good is all that training if all I do is sit in a shop all day? I should have been out there.*

At the first light of dawn, Caleb remained crouched beside the dying embers of his fire. He bowed under the weight of his interlocked hands and heard the slither of sandals entering, but he couldn't look up.

"I brought you something to eat," Suzanna said, moving toward his table. "You have to gain your strength. I'll leave the tray here and pick it up later. Do you want me to make you some tea?"

Caleb didn't respond and her sandals eventually slithered away again. Even the aroma of fresh bread and oranges couldn't move him past the chains that bound his will.

Shadows moved across the floor as the hours of the day passed, and Suzanna's sandals sounded again toward evening. He heard her sigh of disappointment.

"Caleb, I brought you fresh dates, figs, cheese, oranges, and bread. You've let it get stale. I have more. Please eat."

Caleb stepped away from the fire as if in a trance. His mutterings made no sense, even to him.

I must be a madman.

Suzanna grabbed his shoulders and shook him. "Caleb, I don't understand what you're trying to say. Please, eat."

When Caleb refused to respond, Suzanna left and returned with Cato. Caleb heard her speaking as if he wasn't even in the room.

"I'm so worried," she said. "He's losing his mind. He won't eat or speak."

Cato grabbed Caleb by the shoulder and forced him to sit on a stool. The centurion raised a wineskin and poured some of the contents down Caleb's throat.

"This is not how Sestus trained you, carpenter," Cato said. "Drink up. Live. There is work to do."

Cato gripped the carpenter's hand and gently pried the plane out of it. Caleb's fingers were so clenched that he couldn't even hold the skin of wine being offered. Cato pushed him back against the table and lifted the wine to his lips again.

Someone else stepped in and held the flask for Cato until the drink was done. The newcomer tried to feed Caleb from off the trays brought earlier by Suzanna, but Caleb clamped his teeth shut.

"Master," said an old familiar voice. "I'm back. Don't let that ol' devil Barabbas win. Sestus freed me to serve you again. I know he's gone now, but I am here. Master, you have work to do. But eat first."

Caleb opened his eyes and saw the dark jowls of Nabonidus. The Persian's round face held compassionate eyes under drooping eyelids. There were ugly scars across the man's bald head, but he was alive.

Caleb accepted a piece of bread, but he couldn't stop staring at Nabonidus. The slave began to smile as Caleb consumed a date, a fig, and finally an apricot.

"That there is zealot food," Nabonidus said. "It is good even for carpenters."

When Caleb had eaten enough, he held up his hand to stop Nabonidus from giving him more.

Afterward, Cato took hold of the carpenter and walked him back to the Antonia Fortress. In silence.

When morning came, Caleb heard faraway voices lapping over him like crashing waves.

A legionnaire entered the room and stared at him a moment. "The city has gone mad. The Jewish Messiah has come to town and there are a million people chanting. Go up on the roof and see for yourself. It's a sight you may never see again. Centurion Cato is calling for reinforcements. Both Herod and Pilate are in residence, so this is a serious threat."

Caleb shook off the grogginess and pushed himself to his knees and then onto his feet. He stumbled to the stairs and stepped his way up to the rooftop.

The sight was breathtaking—humanity stretched as far as he could see on the road from the Mount of Olives. More people were flowing out of the temple grounds to join the group working their way up the hill toward the city. The trees had nearly been stripped bare of branches along the route as the people lay down a mat of greenery for a lone figure on a donkey.

Yeshi.

Caleb could hear the chants clearly from his perch: "Blessed is the king who comes in the name of the Lord! Blessed is the coming kingdom of our father David! Hosanna in the highest! Peace in heaven and glory in the highest!"[3]

Several young women were dancing out in front of the procession, and for a moment he thought one of them might be Suzanna. The women looked as free as the birds circling above the procession. The entire scene seemed ethereal, as if heaven and earth had somehow orchestrated something too magical for either to appreciate alone.

Caleb kept his eye on the stream of Pharisees, religious leaders coming together and then separating only to reform into new clusters. He knew with certainty that these men wouldn't be pleased. Out-of-control messianic fever could undermine all the stability the Pharisees had worked for. Every time a new Messiah rose in this land, the oppressor came down on the people harder, especially on the leaders.

Dozens of the Pharisees' disciples moved near the lone figure on the donkey. They seemed to be trying to wave off the celebrants.

Caleb turned to survey the Roman military on the rooftop of the Antonia fortress and saw a dozen centurions stationed there, watching closely.

Cato broke off the discussion he was having and started to move in his direction. "Carpenter! This Nazarene, the one you grew up with… what are the chances he may be connected with the zealots?"

"None," Caleb said.

"Why does he have zealots among his followers then?"

Caleb waved his hand over the swelling masses below. "He attracts all people, as you can see."

"Does the crowd intend to make him their king, to overthrow Herod and Rome?"

"The crowd is chanting the psalms of David, which they chant at every festival," Caleb replied. "They're simply fueled by the excitement of the Feast."

"We've gotten requests from their religious leaders to end this celebration."

---

[3] Matthew 21, Mark 11, Luke 19, and John 12.

Caleb turned to watch Yeshi dismount and walk into the temple's Courtyard of the Gentiles. "I have only known him as a man of peace," Caleb countered.

"We cannot violate the sanctuary of the temple. They'll have to watch over their own Messiah while we watch over the city."

The crowd was filling the courtyard and dispersing to change money, purchase sacrificial animals, and listen to the various teachers. Apart from a long strip of greenery stretching from the Mount of Olives to the temple, not much evidence of the celebration remained.

As Caleb descended the stairs behind a few of the centurions, a messenger came running up to them.

"We have the zealot leaders," he announced. "We have Barabbas. The rebellion is crushed."

One of the centurions turned to Caleb. "Barabbas deserves a special cross. See to it, carpenter."

Chapter Twenty-One

Jerusalem, 30 A.D., Passover Week, Monday

The next morning, Caleb decided he would have to fashion a special crossbeam for Barabbas. It would have to be heavy enough to make the man's knees buckle in humiliation, but not so heavy as to crush him under its weight. And it would be kept rough to create maximum discomfort and irritation.

As he stuffed handfuls of parched grain into a fold of cloth for his journey out to the forests, he felt his hands wanting to clench. He spilled kernels onto the floor. In frustration, he tossed a hammer against the wall of his shop, breaking off the handle. His heart raced and his head ached. He felt the same level of explosive anger he had experienced with Deborah before he'd driven the nails into her hands.

Why do I have to care for people so much when all they do is leave me?

His rage was flowing now, and he decided to go to the temple. He needed to clear his mind and set his heart right. The anger made him feel so impure, so hypocritical after all he'd done over the years.

He changed, washed, and walked out of the Antonia fortress into the mayhem and marketplace madness in the Court of the Gentiles. Moneychangers argued with pilgrims about the right price of exchange. Men argued with sellers of doves about the purity and quality of the birds. Animals bleated and bawled and squawked. A few weary pilgrims attempted vainly to find a quiet place to focus their thoughts on God.

Caleb felt sorry for the strangers and wondered what had attracted them to such a religion.

He made his way through the melee and stood at the entrance to the Court of the Men. On the wall, etched in Greek and Latin, were ominous words:

No foreigner is to go beyond the balustrade and the plaza of the temple. Whoever is caught doing so will have himself to blame for his death.

He shook his head and passed into the courtyard. What had possessed people to come so far for such little access to the architectural masterpiece?

Caleb completed his purification and found his place for prayer.

A short time later, a loud clamor floated over from the Court of the Gentiles. At first he ignored the shouting and protests, but as several others rose up and worked their way out to satisfy their curiosity, he too walked toward the exit.

The way was blocked by hundreds of men.

"What's happening?" he asked.

A man standing on a small table turned to him. "The Nazarene threw over the tables of the moneychangers. He let the birds free and scattered the sheep and cattle penned up for sacrifice. He was whipping the merchants and yelling that his house should be a house of prayer for all nations."

It didn't make sense! The carpenter from Nazareth he knew had always been in control and focused on peace. Granted, there were times when Yeshi had gotten riled up at an injustice in the village, such as the poor treatment of orphans and widows. But nothing like this.

By the time Caleb worked his way through the dispersing crowd, the messianic action in the Court of the Gentiles was finished. He couldn't find Yeshua and no one seemed to know where he had gone.

As Caleb walked by a cloistered group of priests and teachers of the Torah, he overheard one of the men declare, "We must destroy the Nazarene before he destroys us."

Others in the group nodded their heads in agreement. "Yes, this time he's gone too far."

The carpenter felt a familiar clutching sensation in his throat. He'd already lost Sestus, and now another of his friends was under attack—from the very people who should be protecting him. Jewish leaders should be protecting Jews, not planning their destruction!

Caleb was torn. His task for the day was to get the right tree to prepare a cross for Barabbas. Justice had to be served soon or other zealots might be tempted to try to free the murderer. More trouble would come.

But he also had to warn Yeshua about the plans being made to destroy him.

Caleb weighed his options. There had been a citywide parade of support for the Messiah just one day before. Certainly, his friend would be okay during the Feast.

His decision made, Caleb made preparations to go down to the forests at the base of the Mount of Olives.

The natural flow of the land led him into the Tyropoean Valley in the middle of the city and then out into the Kidron Valley. Gethsemane was the perfect place for what he needed. A grove of solid olive trees were clustered there. He didn't usually use olive for his crosses, but the wood was heavier and he could rough it up for his purposes.

It took two hours of scouting and examining, for the olive trees were ancient and almost sacred to his people. Some were massive and would be wasted. Others were preparing to yield their first crops. Finally, he found his tree. He marked it by nailing a small banner of authority onto the trunk. The banner still bore the name of Sestus.

His work for the day was done. The next day, he would return with a horse and cart and the tools to do his job. Within three hours of returning to the city, he had all he needed: the permit, the tools, and a place to store the excess wood from his tree.

Suzanna came by the shop with a bowl of lentil stew and more bread. His life had become a strange mix of light and darkness, with Suzanna bringing light and the death of Sestus bringing darkness. Suzanna tried to soothe his spirit by playing the psalms she had learned. Occasionally, he would stop what he was doing and join her.

Pounding rain beat down on the roof of the shop. While getting tea for himself and Suzanna, he heard the familiar sound of hobnailed sandals echoing off the paving stones outside. Cato stepped through the doorway, shook the rain off his cape, and studied Caleb's work on a cedar crossbeam.

"Carpenter, how long until you're ready?"

Caleb set down his tea and moved to a pile of finished crossbeams at the back of the shop. "Seven are finished. The special one for Barabbas will take a little longer. I will be cutting a beautiful olive tomorrow."

Cato ran his hand along the rough surface of the crossbeam on the carpenter's table. "Such a waste to use good trees on worthless men."

The centurion shook out his cape, put it back in place on his shoulders, turned, and left.

In the morning, the rains continued bouncing several inches off the paving stones outside his shop. Caleb delayed his task once again. He had only secured the horse and cart for the day, however, so by early afternoon he defied the slippery cobblestones and muddy trails to slog down to the olive trees of Gethsemane.

A fruity scent arose with each measured, confident swing. The sturdy specimen he chopped stood more than thirty feet tall and was a good four feet in diameter. It would produce several good crossbeams.

The crimson stains of blood would be clearly seen by onlookers against the wood's creamy inset tones. It would represent beauty in the midst of ugliness. This would be the ultimate work of art, the one he'd been striving for ever since his start in carpentry.

By the time he had sliced the tree into manageable pieces, discarded the branches, and loaded the prime lumber into a cart, the day was done. The horse struggled to pull the weight of the wood up the steep incline toward his workshop, but it failed to gain enough traction on the slippery pathway.

The carpenter finally abandoned the effort and trudged his way up the hill alone. He would need a donkey, one that could pull heavy loads uphill.

He was halfway up the slope when he saw a pair of familiar faces.

"James! John!" he called. "What are you doing here?"

The brothers looked back at him for a few moments before recognition dawned on them.

"The carpenter from Sepphoris!" John exclaimed. "You look like you've been bathing in mud. And you are alive."

They shook hands, careful to keep from getting the muck on their fisher capes.

"There were rumors you were killed by the Sicarii," James said. "We're here for Passover with our Teacher. What brings you here?"

Caleb smiled. "A special project. I've just now retrieved a good old olive from Gethsemane. The horse can't pull the weight, so I'm going back to the fortress to get a pair of donkeys."

"Go no farther," James said. "Our hosts own several fine strong beasts. I'm sure they won't hesitate to loan them to a brother of the Master. We'll ask about the donkeys."

"I would be grateful," Caleb said. "Please, let me walk with you while we get them. How do you come to be so generous with the possessions of your host?"

"We only try to live as our Master would expect," John replied.

"Who is your Master?" Caleb inquired. "I thought you were fishers from Galilee. Free to sail the sea. Have you become slaves to someone?"

"In a way," James said. "We follow Yeshua Ha Meshiach as his disciples. We've come with him for Passover. He speaks of dark days, but we saw the people and we think that perhaps he will become a king."

Caleb removed his sandals and washed off his feet in a puddle at the side of the road. "You left the sea to walk in dust and mud? Yeshua must have spoken powerful words to change your lives that way."

"He only told us to come and follow him and he would make us fishers of men," John replied. "We are simply obedient to what he tells us. He's showing us so much about the God of Abraham, Isaac, and Jacob. The things we heard in synagogue seem empty compared to what he teaches us."

Caleb saw the shadows dissipating and sought to bring the conversation to a close.

"I think I'll have to get those donkeys tomorrow," he said, his thoughts filled with remorse at the loss of Sestus. "It has been quite a day for me."

"And for us," John agreed. "The Master cursed a fig tree yesterday, and today it withered to the ground. Then he debated with the religious leaders and I was afraid they would wither like the tree. Then he faced down some Pharisees and Herodians who tried to trick him with questions about taxes. Then the Sadducees tried to catch him on questions about marriage and resurrection. Even a teacher of the law asked him about the greatest of the commandments. It was like a battlefield of tongues and minds."

Caleb nodded. "I'm sure Yeshua held his own. What did he answer about the greatest commandment?"

"He said there were two," James replied. "The first is to love the Lord our God with all our heart, with all our soul, with all our mind, and with all our strength. The second is to love our neighbor as ourselves."

"Good answer!" Caleb said. "I'll see you tomorrow morning for those donkeys. I have to tell the two of you, though, that I've heard the religious leaders plotting to kill Yeshua. With you around, and with the crowds hanging on his every word, it seems my concerns may be nothing but empty clouds."

John looked around. "Actually, there are many who utter threats against the Master. Yeshua tells us strange things about death, but we know God is able to deliver him. He is the promised Messiah Israel has been waiting for. We know it won't be long until we see his glory."

"Ah, look," James said. "Andrew comes with the donkeys. The Master knew you needed them."

Caleb looked ahead and, sure enough, two donkeys followed a well-built fisherman who was marching toward them. How could anyone have known he needed a donkey before he did?

He thought of his boyhood days with Yeshua and a shiver ran down his back.

Maybe Yeshua did know about my times with the winemaker and Sophia, he thought. *Maybe he did know about the revenge I planned against my father. I wonder if he knows this wood is for a cross for Barabbas?*

"Andrew," John called. "How did you know we needed donkeys?"

Andrew laughed. "It wasn't me. The Master just turned to me and told me that someone needed the donkeys at the foot of the hill going up to Jerusalem. He didn't tell me it was you."

James grabbed hold of the reins and pulled them toward Gethsemane. "If we all work together, we can get this load up before morning. The gates may be closing soon."

The donkeys finally finished hauling up the wood by torchlight. John, James, and Andrew helped unload the rough-cut logs and branches into the back of Caleb's shop. They refused his offer of fruit, figs, and salted Nile perch since they wanted to get back for the evening teaching session with Yeshua.

Caleb was almost convinced to go along, but he knew he had a cross to finish and he reasoned there would be plenty of time to talk with Yeshua after the Passover. Tomorrow he would choose a lamb for his Passover meal and try to find another nine people to join him in the age-old tradition of celebrating the salvation bought by the blood of the lamb.

He wished Suzanna's uncle had invited him to spend the celebration with their family, but perhaps Suzanna hadn't mentioned him.

Perhaps she's ashamed for them to meet someone like me.

He worked late into the night and eventually fell asleep in his shop with his head resting on the olive crossbeam he had hacked into shape.

The carpenter felt a tickle on his face, and as he moved his head back and forth to escape the irritation he heard laughter he hadn't heard in years. Was that Rebekah?

He raised his arm to swipe away the intrusion and opened his eyes to find Suzanna smiling down at him. He had never seen a smile like that before.

Caleb shook his head and wiped his eyes. *Thank you, Almighty, that I didn't call out Rebekah's name.*

"Caleb!" Suzanna whispered. "He's even more amazing than they say."

"Who is amazing?" Caleb asked as he sat up and looked into her dark, dancing eyes.

"The Master, of course," she said. "You should have seen him riding into Jerusalem on a donkey. We all waved palm branches, then lay them down as we sang to him. It seemed like the whole world was there. I danced and he smiled and now I know for sure. He's the Son of David, the Messiah, the King for us all." She tossed her cape onto the table, set down a bowl of soup, and took a cup out of the cupboard. She stirred the bubbling pot sitting on the fire and ladled out hot tea. "Caleb, you should have been there."

He got to his feet and put his hands gently on her shoulders. "Suzanna, I was there. I was up on top of the Antonia tower, looking down and watching it all. It was even more amazing from up high with all the Romans looking down on you."

Suzanna relaxed against Caleb's chest. "You were watching me?"

"I was watching everything. Yeshua is taking many risks during this Passover, though. The religious leaders are jealous and angry. The merchants are upset at his attack on their temple profits. The Romans are nervous about whether he's working to lead a revolution against Herod and Pilate."

"Why would the Romans be tense?" Suzanna asked. "We have these feasts three times a year without major troubles."

"The zealot leaders who murdered my centurion are scheduled for crucifixion in two days. Everyone is tense." Caleb rearranged his tools to focus on the cutting he had to do. "Anyway, thanks for the soup. I need to finish this crossbeam."

Suzanna ran her hands over the wavy patterns in the rough-cut log. "I've never seen a crossbeam made of olive wood like that. The grain looks so beautiful. It's hideous to think about its purpose." She tried to push it across the table. "Don't you think it'll be too heavy?"

"This one is specially designed," he said. "It will send a message that people won't soon forget. We must show them the terror of the cross."

Suzanna put her hand on his. "Caleb, promise me that soon you'll leave this crossmaking."

Caleb nodded. "This is the one cross I've been waiting to make. After this, I have no need to make anymore."

Suzanna stayed for a while and filled the room with her chatter about what the Messiah was teaching here. What more could a man want? Good work and a good woman. Not just a good woman, but a beautiful woman. A wise woman.

The Almighty is good, he thought.

His attention wavered in and out of her chatter, and throughout it all he heard words about being poor in spirit, mourning, meekness, righteousness, mercy, and peace. They were the words of Yeshua.

"Smell this," the girl said as she placed a heavily scented cloth under his nose.

"Woman!" Caleb uttered as he jerked back his head. "What is that?"

"Pure nard. Last night I was at a dinner with the Master and Mary broke an alabaster jar of this and poured it all over Yeshua's head and feet. The whole room was filled with the aroma of heaven. I could have danced all night except his own disciples were complaining about such a waste."

"Where did you get the perfume if it's so expensive?"

"I helped wipe it up off the floor. It's my reminder of the one I've given my life to."

Caleb looked her in the eye. "I thought that maybe you would give your life to me."

Suzanna took a step back. "Are you trying to distract me, or are you trying to say something more?"

Caleb hesitated. He was in unfamiliar territory and needed to weigh his words carefully, but his tongue felt twisted.

The silence stretched out so long that he had to turn away from Suzanna.

"When you know what you're thinking, let me know," she said.

She tilted her head back, shook her hair loose, reached for her cape, and raised her eyebrows.

The carpenter turned away and reached for his plane. When he turned around again, Suzanna was gone.

Chapter Twenty-Two

Jerusalem, 30 A.D., Passover Week, Thursday

Despite being a follower of Israel's God, Caleb hadn't made the effort to come to Jerusalem on pilgrimage for many years. Only Jewish men living within a day's journey of the capital were mandated to bring a sacrificial lamb, and to be there every time. Having lived in Galilee, the passion fires had never been lit in him.

As a result, the morning before Passover proved confusing. This was to be the first lamb he would choose as a sacrifice for himself. He still hadn't found nine others to share it with, as he knew he was supposed to do, but he knew there would always be a group of recent arrivals looking for hospitality. It would have been nice to eat with Suzanna and her family, but he'd never met the uncle she now lived with and he didn't want to improperly impose himself on this family event.

Since Yeshua's diatribe in the Court of the Gentiles, the sheep pens had been relocated near the Sheep Gate. The crush ahead of him meant it would take some time to get there, but lambs were moving quickly out of their pens and into people's arms as the shepherds completed their transactions. When his turn arrived, he held out his money bag and it was snatched from his hand. A lamb was in his arms before he even understood what was happening. He had always envisioned that perhaps he would get to look over the year-old male lambs available and choose one he thought especially suited for his Passover.

He knew the Almighty required a spotless lamb for a perfect sacrifice, but everyone knew that shepherds were lying, thieving scoundrels. Risking that their choice would be enough for the Almighty left him feeling tense. He tried to turn back, but the crowd caught him like driftwood in a rushing river and pulled him away toward the place of sacrifice.

When he made it into the temple courtyard with his bleating bundle, he endured the ritual questioning as to whether he was circumcised, clean before the Law, and without leaven in his possession. The midafternoon Tamid sacrifice had just been completed and there was a crush of sacrificers eager to have their lambs slain.

His turn eventually came some forty minutes later and the lamb was taken from his arms, held over a row of priests with their rounded gold cups, and the neck was sliced with precision. The blood poured into a cup, and when it was full it was passed onto the next priest, who handed over an empty bowl and kept passing the full one down the line until the last priest dumped the contents on the altar.

The body of the lamb was hung up, skinned, and disemboweled, its fat removed, salted, and placed on the altar by another priest. The rest of the innards were cleaned while the Levites on a raised platform sang the Hallel psalms of David. He had held his lamb less than an hour, yet a grief still filled him. When the carcass was placed back in his arms, he wrapped it in silence.

He wondered if there were any poor people who couldn't afford a lamb.

Caleb tried hard to remember all the details of the next ceremony, which he had heard about long ago from Yeshua in Nazareth. He knew he was supposed to roast his lamb on a spit of pomegranate wood and that no bones could be broken. He wondered why there were so many details for such an action.

The entire lamb had to be eaten this very night, and no one could leave until it was gone. He tried to remember the prayer he had to say: "Blessed are you, eternal God, King of the world, who made us holy by your command and told us that we should eat the Passover."

Or something similar.

The Passover story had to be shared and the history of his people remembered. He had heard the story many times without clearly understanding it. He just knew that this was a huge declaration to the world that his people were free and that his God knew how to save his own.

As he faced the prospect of finding the right people to share his lamb, he watched a strange transaction taking place between a small group of priests and a follower who he was certain he had seen with Yeshua during his friend's triumphal entry into the city. The man took a pouch of coins and stuffed it quickly under his tunic, then made a gesture toward the Kidron Valley. The man slipped into the crowd, leaving the priests hugging, shaking hands, and offering themselves exclamations of praise.

It didn't take long to find a group of paupers in the courtyard outside the temple. Caleb first called a pair of mud-covered orphans to his side and received their enthusiastic agreement to join him in the seder meal. A young woman with a small child also agreed to accompany him. Next he found an old man with a cane leading a woman who appeared to be blind.

Lastly, Caleb found a band of six, led by a man named Barnabas, trying to collect their ten. He invited them to join his band and to celebrate the Passover as a special community of the freed. After some haggling over who would be master of the Feast, Caleb gladly released the ownership of the meal to Barnabas in exchange for hosting them in his carpenter's shop.

The group gathered to show what they'd brought for the seder, and everything was present except the apples. One of the men was given instructions and then dispatched to find this last ingredient. The rest of the group began their trudging march down the hill toward the shop.

By nightfall, the lamb was roasting on a pomegranate spit, the rest of the meal was prepared by eager hands, and introductions and stories were exchanged. Barnabas took the lead and explained the story of the ten plagues of Egypt and of God's great release of his people by the blood of his lamb. A vacant chair was set aside for Elijah, as tradition demanded.

Caleb carved the lamb with his cleaned carpenter's knife. In the flickering lamplight, they chanted psalms, questioned the children about why each food item was part of the Feast, and exchanged the familiar responses as Barnabas laid out the history of his people in Egypt. It was all mesmerizing.

I think I know why Yeshi used to love coming here, he thought. *This is powerful. Jerusalem seems so much closer to where the Almighty worked to save his people. Next time I see Yeshi, I'll tell him that I understand why this place is so special. He'll be glad to know I finally understand.*

Caleb dipped his parsley in the bitter herbs and remembered the sorrow of his people. He nibbled the apple in its sauce and remembered the slavery of the Jews making bricks for the Egyptians. He ate the egg and lamb and bread and remembered the provisions of the Almighty. He drank the cups of wine and remembered that his redemption was near.

Caleb cut off a piece of lamb and held it out. "Barnabas, we need to finish this all. You know the Law of Moses says we can't leave any of it until morning. Take one more piece."

Barnabas patted his significant girth and untied the sash around his tunic. "Carpenter, I am about to burst. I'm already fatter than Pharaoh ever was. Are you sure you didn't buy two lambs in your enthusiasm?"

Caleb scanned the room. "I think I needed to invite another six of your friends, Barnabas. These seem hardly able to open their mouths anymore."

The cleaned-up orphans drooped, bent over, heads resting on their arms. The old man continued to feed small tidbits of bread to his sightless wife. The small child suckled at her mother's breast in a corner. Only two of Barnabas's six, Saul and Joshua, continued to pick away at the plate of meat, doing their duty.

Joshua drained his final cup of wine and stood to stretch. "This lamb reminds me of the time Yeshua Ha Meshiach multiplied the fish and loaves for us. No matter how much we ate, there was more."

"Tell me more, Joshua." Caleb lowered the plate of carved meat to the table. "How did Yeshua feed so many? Did he encourage you to be generous with each other?"

"We were foolish," he said, reclining. "We heard his words and they were life to us. Yeshua left by boat and we chased him along the shore. We didn't even think of finding provisions. The day passed so quickly that we didn't even think of our stomachs. A boy brought him a few loaves and fishes, he prayed, and then he gave baskets to his followers to give to us. All of us had enough."

Caleb shook his head. "You know that what you are saying is impossible?"

Joshua smiled and pointed at the plate of lamb. "Impossible is eating all this lamb. With the Messiah, nothing is impossible."

"You can all get your rest for a few hours, but this lamb must be gone by morning." Caleb stood. "I'll wake you before the sun rises."

The old couple and the young mother were given spots closest to the fireplace. The boys also had good places, away from the breeze, by the carpenter's bench. The young men settled down near the walls.

One of them lay out on the olive wood crossbeam and called across the room to Caleb.

"This olive smells special on a Passover night," he said. "Where did you find it? What are you going to use it for?"

Caleb walked over to the young man. "It's a crossbeam and I'm going to crucify someone on it tomorrow. The Romans will be here at first light to pick it up."

The young man sat up quickly and stood to his feet. The other young men broke out in raucous laughter at their companion.

"You should have seen the look on your face, Nathaniel," one of the men called. "You looked like that was a crossbeam meant for you."

Two of the young men lay out four crossbeams side by side in the middle of the shop.

"Think, man. This is the Passover. Who are they going to crucify on the Passover? And besides, if what you're sleeping on is a crossbeam, then we're all sleeping on crossbeams. Why would a cross maker be here in Jerusalem inviting guys like us to eat his lamb?"

The last of Caleb's guests were just leaving after dawn when Suzanna came running into the carpenter shop.

"They've arrested Yeshua!"

Caleb dropped the shank bone he was cleaning.

Suzanna grabbed his arm. "Caleb, come quick. Call your centurions. You've got to save him."

Caleb pulled his arm away and grabbed Suzanna by the shoulders. "Who has arrested Yeshua?"

"Last night, the chief priest had him arrested," she said. "They're taking him to Pilate. I heard it from John Mark. We've got to stop them!"

He walked to the doorway just as two legionnaires with a donkey and cart arrived.

"Run back and find out what else is happening," he said to Suzanna. "I'll talk to the centurion and see what he says. Maybe it's some kind of misunderstanding."

Suzanna ran out as the legionnaires entered, looking at him with a knowing smile. He ignored the look.

"We're here to pick up the crossbeams for the zealots," one soldier said. "We need three today, including the special one. Centurion Cato says we can wait until next week for the rest."

Caleb helped load the first crossbeam in place. The olive grain on his special cross looked especially beautiful in the morning light.

"Kind of heavy, isn't it?" the first soldier asked. "What are you trying to do, crush a man before he even gets nailed down?"

"It's almost the same weight as Sestus," Caleb said. "The man who carries this crossbeam will feel like he's carrying the weight of the world on his shoulders. He won't soon forget the choices he made to get to this point. So a dead man will be carrying the weight of the dead man he killed. Is there not power in that? Is that not justice?"

The second legionnaire shook his head. "You are more Roman than we," he said. "Maybe we should beat this murderer up a bit to make it even more powerful."

Caleb finished adjusting the beams on the cart and then gave the donkey a pat to get it moving. "Tell Cato I want the nails from the olive beam."

Once the legionnaires had left, Caleb rearranged his room and tidied up the remnants of the seder meal from the night before.

Why would they arrest Yeshi? he asked himself. *Barabbas and the zealots are the problem. I'm sure this is all a misunderstanding. Maybe he knows something about the zealots.*

Caleb extinguished the wick on the lamp and headed toward the Antonia fortress. Somehow he had to find out what was happening with Yeshua.

When he arrived at the fortress, Cato wasn't available for him. Instead Caleb took an escort up to the tower roof to see if he could get a better view of any problems brewing in the city. There he saw a large mob moving toward the palace of Herod Antipas. Out in front of the crowd marched two dozen temple guards, and they seemed to be dragging someone behind them.

"What's happening down there?" Caleb asked.

"Probably one of those zealots," his escort said. "The sooner we get justice done, the better."

The carpenter hurried down the stairs and returned to Cato's office, but the centurion still wasn't available. Caleb reasoned that he was probably tied up with the final trial of the zealots.

I need a rest. Suzanna's probably overreacting. Caleb settled down in the courtyard of the fortress and waited.

An hour later, caught up in a game of knucklebones with a legionnaire, he became even more convinced that this was all a misunderstanding. A mob of irate Jews were screaming from Pilate's judgment seat: "Barabbas! Barabbas! Give us Barabbas! Crucify him! Crucify him!" The sound of the mob echoed across the plaza. Jerusalem was being Jerusalem.

Although he could hear none of Pilate's words, he knew how Roman justice worked. An accusation would be made, a decision reached, and the sentence carried out.

I need to see what's going on, Caleb realized. *I need to see the man who murdered my father finally receive justice.*

Caleb wished he could mete out justice himself, but Roman justice was better than no justice at all. He just wanted to see Barabbas carrying that crossbeam to the hill outside the Esquiline Gate where the crucifixions were to take place.

Rushing to get ahead of the crowds, he climbed up onto a fence fastened to a tailor's shop to get a better view of the criminals leaving the fortress. An advance wave of legionnaires on security detail walked through the growing crowd, checking for weapons. When two of the soldiers reached Caleb, they searched him and removed his carpenter's knife.

He shifted in place for half an hour before the first sounds of the moving mob washed over him. Roman justice didn't take long once it was unleashed.

He looked toward the site where the crucifixions would happen. Twelve soldiers were already securing the three cross stipes in place. The posts were each dropped into a hole and then rocks were jammed in around the base. Caleb shuddered as he imagined which cross would serve as Barabbas's final resting place.

The empty posts pointed toward the heavens and reminded everyone that the Almighty was a deity of law and order. They reminded observers that the governing authorities were his hands of justice. And they reminded everyone that this place of judgment would soon be busy with guilty men bearing their own crossbeams on their shoulders. For the walk of shame, the arms of the criminals would be tied to their crossbeams. Once they arrived at the site, the nails would be hammered in.

I've never taken the nails after a criminal's crucifixion, Caleb thought as Deborah's defiant face flashed in his memory. *Not even Deborah's. I hope Cato remembers that I want the nails this time. The nails from the olive beam. I won't forget that Sestus has been avenged. And my father.*

When the first cross-bearer came into sight, it was clear that he was still arrogant and defiant. He seemed to know of a few supporters in the crowd and acknowledged them. He was playing the martyr, but Caleb knew that his spirit would soon change once the nails and hours took their toll.

His was not the olive crossbeam, however.

The second cross-bearer walked a slower pace and kept his face pointed toward the ground. For this one, the shame was already at work. He knew justice was being served and he felt regret. Caleb had seen enough condemned men take their final walk that he knew the signs of internal struggle.

His was not the olive crossbeam, either.

The third cross-bearer was even slower, and great wailing accompanied his walk. Caleb smiled to himself as he pictured Barabbas stumbling under the weight of it.

When the cross-bearer finally stumbled into sight, the man slumped and fell to the ground.

At last! This is for my father. This is for Sestus. And this is for the scar your men gave me around my neck.

But as Caleb looked on, he saw that the olive crossbeam was on the shoulders of a man whose face was flattened into the cobblestones. That wasn't unusual, although the weight was obviously heavy.

Something wasn't right.

Caleb had seen only a glimpse before the man fell, but there was evidence of unusual torture and humiliation. His loose tunic was soaked in blood. A woven crown of inch-long thorns had been jammed into his skull.

When two legionnaires grabbed the ends of the crossbeam and hoisted the criminal to his feet, Caleb almost gasped out loud. The man's face had been beaten beyond recognition and his beard had been half-pulled from his face. Caleb knew that the cat o' nine tails had been liberally applied to this man's back to rip apart whatever dignity and resistance might still be left. Caleb remembered a few men whose backs had been shredded into pulp by the vicious leather thongs embedded with bits of bone and metal.

Who was this man? It wasn't Barabbas.

A woman stepped out of the crowd and offered the criminal a sip of water. To his shock, he recognized her face. Was it one of the ladies whose brother had been raised from the dead? Mary? Martha? He then scanned the group behind her and recognized even more faces.

Even Suzanna's.

His horror grew. Could it possibly be? The body size and shape would be right… the hair would be right… the face…

No, no, no…

It was his boyhood friend, Yeshi.

Caleb's gut knotted as hard as a rock. His legs petrified under him and he fought to breathe. It was supposed to be Barabbas carrying this special cross. Yeshi was the Messiah. The healer. The teacher.

When Yeshua stumbled and fell flat again, the soldiers moved quickly. They untied the crossbeam, grabbed a huge mountain of a man from the crowd, and compelled him to carry the heavy piece of wood.

Shame washed over Caleb as he clung to his perch on the fence. He fought to keep his legs from buckling under him. This was not how it was supposed to be. Carpenters in Nazareth didn't make crosses so other carpenters from

Nazareth could be nailed to them. Especially when the other carpenter was like a brother.

Not Yeshi.

Caleb dug deep to find the adrenaline surge he needed. He left his perch by the tailor's wall and worked his way through the crowd to get closer to the roadway. Surely he could talk to someone. Surely he could stop this travesty before it went any further. This was a horrible mistake. Where was Barabbas?

He had finally taken a significant Passover in Jerusalem. He had chosen his first lamb. Its blood had been shed. All was forgiven. All was made right. Surely this was not the time of year for injustice.

Caleb saw Cato walking down toward the group, and determined to speak to him. Cato would stop this!

As the centurion reached Yeshi, he did not intervene. Instead Cato grabbed Yeshua's elbow and pulled him up the hill with the new cross-bearer walking behind.

"Centurion! Cato!" Caleb yelled. "You've got the wrong man. This isn't right."

Cato didn't even look his way, but Yeshua did. When Caleb felt the eyes of his friend penetrating him, he felt himself break. Memories of their shared childhood flooded over him. Memories of carpentry projects, of laughter, of exploring ravines and caves and forests filled his heart. The memory of a healing touch on a broken hand, the hand that had shaped the olive crossbeam…

Yeshua hesitated a moment, but then he was yanked forward beyond eye contact.

A line of legionnaires standing shoulder to shoulder blocked the crowd from interfering, and with the thousands of bodies crushing up between the walls and the soldiers Caleb was unable to follow the procession. Thousands more were pushing up the street behind the cohort of soldiers, however, and finally Caleb managed to join this group on their way up the hill.

By the time he had fought and elbowed his way to the site of the crucifixions, it was too late. The gibbets already hoisted their bloodied trophies. The nails had already been driven into the men's wrists. A group of bystanders screamed obscenities at the trio.

The olive crossbeam was wet with the blood of Yeshua, the cream tones marred by streaks of crimson. The crossbeam was no longer a beautiful thing.

Caleb's right hand clenched. *I need my knife. I can take out the legionnaires and get him down. Maybe I can talk sense into them. They have the wrong man. I need to get him down from there. Where is Cato? He's got to listen.*

A huddle of Pharisees and priests focused their venom on Yeshi.

"So!" a man yelled. "You said you were going to tear down the temple and build it in three days? Why don't you try saving yourself first? If you're the Son of God, do something."

One of the religious teachers called out to another nearby. "Ha, he saved others, but he can't save himself. If this is the Messiah, the King of Israel, then let him at least come down from the cross so we can see for ourselves and believe. He said he was the Son of God. Now let God try to save him."[4]

Caleb pictured the sword Sestus had given him for hand-to-hand combat and decided he needed it to stop the words of these so-called leaders. Perhaps he could grab a sword from one of the soldiers.

Even as he thought this, however, he realized the act wouldn't save anyone.

Cato emerged from the crowd and moved close to the center cross where Yeshua fought for breath. Caleb shouted for him, but his voice was swallowed in the din of a mob gone hysterical.

He worked his way closer and saw John standing near the cross alongside Yeshua's mother and several other women. Yeshua's bloodied head and naked vulnerability forced Caleb to look away. He swallowed the bile rising in his throat.

When Caleb regained his strength, he looked up to see Yeshua talking with his own mother and John. Then he turned his head and spoke with the thief crucified next to him. Caleb couldn't hear the words, but he saw the facial expression of the thief change to one that almost looked hopeful.

As Caleb wondered if there might still be some way to save his friend, he heard Yeshua called out, "Forgive them for they know not what they do."

A weight like a millstone slammed against Caleb's chest and then evaporated into nothingness. Darkness dropped around the city like a curtain, the sun obliterated. People screamed in terror and the ground began to shake.

Another cry sounded from the cross: "My God, my God, why have you forsaken me?"

Terrifying silence fell on the crowd.

Caleb heard one of the men nearby crawl toward the cross. The man seemed possessed.

"He thirsts, he thirsts…" the man muttered. "Wine vinegar… a spear, a sponge, and wine vinegar…"

Somehow the man managed to find what he wanted and lift it high enough for Jesus to moisten his mouth.

---

[4] Matthew 27, Mark 15, Luke 23, and John 19.

"Now, let's see if Elijah saves him," the man said to whoever still listened. "Maybe he'll take away the night."

Caleb stood in expectation. Nothing changed except for the deep moaning that rose from the people trapped in the darkness.

Yeshua seemed to lift himself up for one final effort and thundered defiantly, "It is finished!"

The shaking of the ground intensified and the carpenter on the cross died. Caleb felt it as powerfully as if the breath had gone out of his own lungs.

Caleb fell back to his knees, sobbing. *Almighty God, no! Why did he heal my hand? If I had my knife, I would cut it off. Why have you forsaken Yeshua? Why have you forsaken me? Almighty God, what have I done? Forgive me... I didn't know what I was doing. I only wanted Barabbas.*

Caleb remained on his hands and knees as a major tremor struck

"Surely this was the Son of God," he heard Cato murmur.

He found himself crawling forward as the crowd evaporated back into the city. With the ground shaking, no place seemed safe. He heard screams of agony as soldiers broke the legs of the thieves. He didn't even look up to see what would happen to Yeshua, but he knew the hammer wouldn't be needed to speed up his friend's death.

Caleb's head felt feverish and he shivered. More memories of life in Nazareth flooded over him. Miriam feeding him. Yuseph teaching him. Rebekah singing over him while he healed. And Yeshi himself, walking with Caleb, laughing with him, encouraging him to trust in the Almighty even if Caleb's mother had leprosy.

The sunlight came back as quickly as it had gone. The hill emptied as people scrambled away.

Caleb curled up on the ground, terrified to leave. Yeshi's words through the years poured into his spirit. It was his last connection to the friend hanging dead above him.

As the sun descended toward the horizon, two religious leaders shuffled up to the soldiers.

"Centurion Cato," one of them said. "I bring authorization from Pilate to release the body into my custody for burial before the Sabbath begins."

"It is done," Cato said. "I have verified the death of your Messiah. A spear into his heart proves it. I will get the legionnaires to take him down for you."

A few minutes later, Caleb looked up to see the body of Yeshua being lowered and wrapped up in a shroud. Cato then deliberately picked up the nails and walked in Caleb's direction.

Cato held out the bloodied nails. "Here are the nails you claimed," Cato said. "The nails from the olive crossbeam."

Caleb looked at the crimson-tipped spikes. Horror gripped his heart and he pulled back, putting up his hands to block the sight of the nails. Cato simply lay them on the rocks in front of Caleb and walked away.

Caleb fell flat to the ground and buried his face in his forearms, wailing with grief like he had never wailed before.

He was still prone on the ground when a gentle hand began to stroke his back. He raised his head and looked into the face of Suzanna.

"It is over. What he promised has happened. The Sabbath is here." She took hold of his elbow and tried to pull him up. "Come, I will take you home. It is time you met the others."

Chapter Twenty-Three

Jerusalem, 30 A.D., Passover Week, Friday

Caleb felt himself floating through the alleys and pathways as Suzanna pulled him forward. The hypnotic swish of her simple tan tunic and blue mantle mesmerized him into submission.

The streets were almost empty as dusk arrived to mark the start of Sabbath. Caleb had never been one to worry about the exact moment Sabbath began, but he knew that the time was important to Suzanna. He began to move in rhythm with the hurried steps of his guide.

Suzanna finally stopped and knocked on a door. She waited a minute, then knocked again—three times again. What was this? A secret code? What was he getting involved in?

At last the door was opened and Caleb was ushered into a room filled with a handful of men and women preparing the Sabbath meal. Twenty or thirty people were sitting on the floor, and most of them appeared to be in a daze. Expressions of grief and pain sucked the life out of the room

A group of ten lay prostrate in the middle of the floor. Some wept and others prayed out loud to the Almighty. They called on the Almighty for mercy and understanding.

Caleb stood with his back against the wall and surveyed the scene as a deep agony welled up from within. How could this be happening?

A woman's voice whispered to Suzanna, but it was loud enough that Caleb heard it clearly. "Why did you bring him here?"

"He has no one else," Suzanna whispered back.

"But he's the cross maker!"

"He is as forgiven as the rest of us. You heard the Master: 'Forgive them for they don't know what they're doing.'"

"You can feed him then."

Caleb lowered himself to the ground and hung his head. A platter of food was set on the mat before him, but he had no appetite. In arrogance he had built a heavy crossbeam to serve as a lesson for Barabbas. Instead his pride had resulted in extra torture for his childhood friend.

Words of forgiveness cannot apply to me, he thought dully. *No matter what the Master said.*

Some time in the coming hours the lights were dimmed and a single torch flickered to guide those who couldn't sleep. Moans and prayers of anguish continued to float through the room. Caleb drank in the pain and added it to his own.

In the first wisps of dawn, someone slouched down next to him.

"Brother Caleb!" a familiar voice said. "It's Simon of Capernaum, if you remember. The fisherman, son of Isaac. May God give you peace."

Caleb stretched open his heavy eyelids and aroused himself from the field of despair. He turned his head and looked at the distraught face of the fisherman.

"I know you," Caleb said, "but I can't know peace. The Almighty has brought his destruction on me."

"On all of us. I despair to live."

"Why you? I'm the one who carved the cross to add to his torture. I thought I was making a trophy for Barabbas to hang on. Instead my own brother, my friend, is killed. What happened?"

"Yeshua was betrayed by one of our own," Simon replied. "He was arrested as he prayed in Gethsemane and taken to trial before the Sanhedrin. He was rushed through trials with the religious leaders and with Pilate and with Herod Antipas. It was a mockery of justice."

"Why didn't you all stop it?" Caleb asked. "You have stopped them all before."

"We were afraid. I tried to swing a sword and I cut off a man's ear. The Master stopped me and healed the man." Simon pushed away a tray of food and stretched out his legs. "He let them take him. What could we do? We ran."

"But surely you could be his witnesses at trial."

"No one came to his defense," Simon moaned. "What's worse, I denied even knowing him. He looked at me and I wept bitterly. I've spent this whole night in remorse and repentance."

Caleb raised his hand and placed it on Simon's shoulder. "Can there ever be forgiveness for ones like us?"

"I can only pray so. I must go see the others. May God be merciful to us all."

After Simon left, Suzanna returned and knelt before Caleb. She set a single torch in the wall above him and returned with a basin. She slowly washed his feet in soothing water. Her own mantel was used as a drying cloth, and Caleb felt shame that such a beautiful girl would be reduced to washing his hands and feet. This was the work of a slave, not a friend.

"Suzanna," he whispered. "Please don't humiliate yourself before me. You are a noble woman of worth. I am a wretched man."

Suzanna looked up and it was clear there were tears in her eyes. "If I could only be worthy of your love. But even now I understand that can never be."

"But why? Why is it that a cross maker couldn't love an angel?"

"Because the 'angel' is a zealot's daughter," she said. "I may be the cousin of Barabbas. A child of rape. A child left to the streets. A woman who has been humiliated more than you could ever imagine."

Caleb instinctively pulled his feet away from her touch. A spawn of the devil? How could he fall for this again?

Her head drooped lower. She gathered the bowl and backed away without a word.

How can I treat her like this? he asked himself. *What fault has she ever committed against me?*

As morning light filtered into the inner recesses of the room, others stirred and received their washing. Food was delivered on trays as on the night before. It was placed on mats where people could sit cross-legged and eat with their hands. Large sections of barley bread, yogurt, dates, pomegranates, figs, parched wheat, an egg, a glass of cool water… Caleb ate and felt strengthened.

As he stretched, Caleb noticed Suzanna slouched in a corner, her arms wrapped around her shins. Her head rested on her knees and he could see her shoulders convulse.

Why do I do this with every woman I know? I refused to take her seriously when she told me Yeshi was arrested. I prepared the cross for Barabbas, and I couldn't even stop the Romans from murdering my friend. She came to bring me to safety. She washed my feet. And now I can't even move to comfort her.

Caleb rested his own head on his knees and allowed dark thoughts to swallow his mind.

Several hours later, John stepped into the middle of the room and read the words of a psalm. Andrew then read the words of the prophet Isaiah and Matthew led in a simple prayer of peace. John recounted what had happened with him at the cross, where he had been charged with the care of Yeshua's mother.

A knock sounded at the door and many of the women instinctively scrambled toward an inner room. The knock sounded again and several of the men moved toward the entrance.

"It's the Sabbath," said the man seated on the floor next to Caleb. "There should be no one knocking on this door. It must be Romans, and they're your friends. You should answer it."

Caleb stood up and the others made way for him without question.

As the knock sounded longer and louder, Caleb removed the restraining bar and opened the door a few inches to look out. It was indeed a pair of legionnaires.

"We seek Caleb the carpenter at the request of Cato the centurion," one of the legionnaires barked.

"I am Caleb. I will come."

The weary carpenter slipped out the door and closed it behind him. He heard the latch slide back into place.

His time for the cross had come. Aligning himself with the Messiah's people would have been seen as an act of treason against Rome. There was no place left for him to run.

When the pair of legionnaires finally marched Caleb into the Antonia fortress, he found Cato waiting for him. Caleb bowed his head and waited.

The centurion walked up to him. "You forgot the nails. You claimed them, and now you must take them."

Caleb could only stare at the stained iron nails being held out to him.

"I claimed the nails of Barabbas," he said. "I claimed the nails of the one who murdered Sestus. I did not claim the nails of an innocent man."

Cato stepped closer and spoke in a low, firm voice. "This one took the nails for us all. Someone needs to keep them. You claimed the nails of the one crucified on the olive beam. You knew him. You keep them."

"But I heard the crowd," Caleb said. "They were yelling, 'Barabbas, crucify him.' How could this have happened?"

"Where were you standing?"

"I was at the edge of the plaza."

"It is the custom to release one prisoner at Passover," Cato informed him. "Pilate gave the crowd an option: choose the killer Barabbas or choose the king Yeshua Ha Meshiach. He asked them which they wanted, and you heard them yelling for the release of Barabbas. When Pilate asked what he should do with the king, they shouted that he should be crucified."

"How is it possible to sing the praise of a Messiah one week and call for his crucifixion the next?" Caleb asked. "I don't understand."

Cato turned and motioned for Caleb to walk with him. "Even a centurion like me knows he was a righteous man. Sometimes one takes the nails for everyone so everyone can have peace."

Caleb's legs were heavy as he tried to keep pace with the quick-stepping centurion. "This is a mockery if I ever heard it. My life's ambition was to build a trophy of wood to serve as a symbol of peace for everyone… and this is what I end up with? A crossbeam that held the Messiah, the hope of Israel, the King of the Jews?"

"All of us must carry the weight of our profession. Your Messiah could have stayed a carpenter in Nazareth and found his own peace. He chose a greater path."

"His path was always chosen for him," Caleb said. "He was always more than a carpenter from Nazareth."

"I only wish he were alive. I would willingly follow a teacher of courage who led his followers into peace."

"So would I." Caleb stopped walking as they exited the fortress and scanned the busy square. "How did you find me?"

Cato chuckled. "We have eyes and ears everywhere, Caleb. Without eyes and ears, we would be blind and deaf. Our power would be useless."

"Please do not harm the followers of Yeshua," Caleb pleaded, reaching into a public fountain and scooping up a drink of water. "They are people of peace."

The centurion placed his hand on Caleb's shoulder. "Go take your rest. The city is still restless and we need to keep you safe until the pilgrims return home. People of peace face no harm from Rome. I bid you farewell, friend of Sestus. I will go to Rome today to give my report on these events."

For the rest of the day and through the night, Caleb remained in his room at the fortress. Suzanna's tear-filled eyes, glistening in the torchlight, filled his mind.

A zealot's daughter! How could he have given his heart to the offspring of a zealot? And one related to Barabbas? And how could Yeshua have accepted a zealot as one of his followers? Could the homage of so many have blinded him to who his followers really were?

There was no way he could love a zealot, yet there seemed to be no way he could avoid what was happening in his heart toward Suzanna. It was true that she wasn't a zealot by choice, but how far could love stretch? A zealot's daughter! A cousin of Barabbas! A child of rape! A woman of the street! How much forgiveness could the Almighty expect?

The sun rose up over the hills on the first day of the week. The carpenter took his breakfast and then fished out a flute from his travelling bag. The slow haunting melody rose into the space around him.

The scurry of feet caught his attention and Caleb laid the flute down. He stepped into the shadowed doorway of his room and watched. Four legionnaires stood at attention before the new commanding centurion, wearing grim expressions. The commander paced quickly in front of the small group. The others all stood as stiff as statues.

"What say you about this?" the centurion barked at his soldiers.

"The official report is that the followers of Yeshua stole his body while we were sleeping," one of the legionnaires said. "The chief priests have given a large donation toward this story. Here is your share."

A large bag of coinage was offered to the new commander. He stood still for a moment, his eye on the prize.

"Were you sleeping?" the man asked, finally turning to another legionnaire.

"No, commander!" the legionnaire replied. "The stone was rolled back by powerful beings who shone like lightning. The gods came to claim their own. We were like the dead ourselves, although we were wide awake through it all. Hebrew women had come to anoint the body. We then went straight to the high priest to tell him of this."

"What does the high priest want from us?" the centurion asked.

"To claim that we were asleep and that the followers stole the body."

"What about the governor? It is death to be asleep on your watch."

"They will satisfy the governor with his own gift if he hears of it," the legionnaire said.

The centurion held out his hand and took the coins. "Who am I to refuse the gift of my hosts, to be above the sacred priests and governor in my sense of right and wrong? Let no word of this be shared with anyone."

Caleb withdrew back into his room and waited until the final echoes of the soldiers' footsteps were gone. He then slid to the floor and slowly inched out through the doorway. Seeing that no one was in sight, he slipped out of the Fortress and headed toward the meeting place where he had first met the other believers.

Something terrible had happened to Yeshua. Someone had to tell those who had given their lives to him.

Caleb eventually found the doorway after getting disoriented a few times. Somehow, standing in this place, he realized that something dramatic had happened inside his own heart.

He hammered on the heavy wooden planks, but no one answered. It occurred to him that only a Roman would knock so loudly, so this time he knocked lightly—three times.

The door opened a few inches. "Who goes there?" a woman's timid voice called.

"Caleb, the carpenter from Nazareth, friend of Yeshua."

"One minute please." The door shut in his face.

While he stood, a burly man darted across the street from a nearby alley. His arms were loaded with bread and bundles of fruit. He rushed up to the door and knocked three times with his elbow.

"Who are you?" he asked Caleb.

"Caleb, the carpenter from Nazareth, friend of Yeshua."

"He never mentioned you. Why didn't you follow him if you were such a friend?"

Caleb didn't have to answer, as the door opened and Suzanna and Miriam stood at the entrance.

"Caleb! Thomas!" Miriam exclaimed. "Come in quickly. You must hear the news."

The door was shut behind the newcomers and Simon stepped forward to address them.

"He is risen!" the fisherman shouted with his arms raised. "The angels have released him and declared him risen. Mary of Magdala has seen him with her own eyes and spoken to him. Our friends from Emmaus have broken bread with him. And now he has just been here to prove himself and to eat with us."

An ecstatic shiver raced up Caleb's spine and he felt himself shudder.

The man next to Caleb, the one Miriam had called Thomas, seemed unconvinced. "Unless I put my hand in that wound in his side and put my finger in the nail punctures on his hands, I cannot believe."

"But you know him," Suzanna said. "He was here, and he explained to us from the Scriptures how this must be. We can tell you as he told us. He told us that we are his witnesses."

Thomas shrugged. "Perhaps it was his ghost."

"Not at all," Suzanna declared. "He told us that a ghost doesn't have flesh and bones like he does. We even gave him broiled fish to eat and he ate it."[5]

"But how?" Caleb stuttered.

Simon stepped away from a small group of disciples in the middle of the room. He hugged Thomas and Caleb.

"Is it really true?" Caleb asked. A whirlwind of thoughts threatened to consume him.

"It was Yeshua in the flesh. He showed us from the Scriptures how the holy one had to suffer, die, and rise again." Simon kept a firm grip on Caleb's shoulder and urged him toward the group still gathered. "He told us to wait in the city until he clothed us with power from above."

"What did he mean by that?" Caleb asked.

"We believe it is the prophecy of Joel and the promise of John the Baptizer," Simon said. "He breathed on us and instructed us to receive his Holy Spirit. He is alive!"

"When will we see him?" Caleb persisted.

Simon motioned for Suzanna, who was distributing a basket of bread to a group of women, to come forward. "Some are going to meet him in Galilee,

---

[5] Luke 24:39–43.

but others will wait here," he said. "You must decide if you are truly one of his followers."

Simon pulled Thomas to the huddled group in the center of the room, but Suzanna took Caleb by the elbow and pulled him aside.

"I'm one of the ones wanting to go to Galilee," she said. "I want to meet him there, and I want you to take me." She looked into Caleb's eyes and released her grip on his arm. "I want to see where he lived. I want to see where you lived. Please say you'll go."

She bowed her head and pulled her shawl back in place over her hair.

"I will not beg for your love again. I only ask for your mercy."

Caleb fell to his knees and looked up into her face. "It is I who needs your mercy. I'm only beginning to realize just how wide and deep and high is the love of Yeshua for his own."

Suzanna lifted her head. "I must go to where he will be."

"But what about waiting in the city?" Caleb asked. "What about the power from above?"

Suzanna shook her head. "That is a promise for others. We can return soon for Pentecost. All I know is that I must go to Galilee."

"I will take you. Let me get my things and return. Who else is coming?"

"I will ask and meet you at the gate in two hours."

A few minutes later, Caleb was hurrying through the streets toward the woodshop where he stored his extra clothing. He got ready and reached the gate long before Suzanna. When she finally showed up, seven others were straggling behind her.

Six of the seven were grey-haired women who used canes to steady themselves on the uneven cobblestones. The seventh was a grinning middle-aged man who led a donkey packed with all the belongings of the group.

"I am Eliab," the middle-aged man said. "I am a follower of Yeshua Ha Meshiach, Lord of Lords and King of Kings."

Caleb studied his piercing eyes. "I knew Yeshua and his family from his early years. I am only now learning that he is far more than he appeared to be."

"I am at your service," Eliab stopped to adjust part of the load on the donkey. "Others are coming soon, but we wanted to get ahead since the journey is long for these few."

Caleb watched Suzanna coax the shuffling women.

Oh no, he lamented. *If they're going to walk all the way to Nazareth, it'll take us a month.*

Chapter Twenty-Four

Jerusalem to Jericho, Palestine 30 A.D.

At the city gate, Caleb bartered with a merchant who was returning to Jericho with an empty donkey cart. He urged the elderly travelers to crawl up onto their rides. The women welcomed the assistance, although their quick complaints at the jarring bumps within the first several hundred yards made Caleb regret paying the merchant in advance.

"Young man," said one woman with a high-pitched voice, "this thing will break my bones and put me into the arms of the Almighty. Why don't you ride and we'll push the donkey?"

Caleb asked the merchant to wait a few minutes and rushed back into the market to purchase pillows. When he returned, his arms filled with the feather-stuffed cushions, the resounding cheer made him feel like a hero.

Suzanna joined him for most of the walk as they trailed the donkey cart and watched the chatter of their charges. Eliab walked for a few miles, then tied his donkey to the cart and sat up with the driver. The two men chatted like long-lost friends.

Within an hour, the twenty-three other followers of Yeshua caught up, passed on their encouragements, and then moved on. There were two horses and three donkeys and the young travelers took turns walking and riding.

Caleb fought the bitterness rising up inside him. How was it that these believers, showing the care of Yeshua, could leave these old people at the mercy of bandits?

At the next bend, his questions were answered. Two sword-carrying men, who had been with the group ahead, stepped out of the shade of a pomegranate on the side of the road and took their places at the side of the cart. Now guarded, the ladies chattered at the men like schoolgirls. Suzanna giggled and moved a little closer to Caleb.

Whenever a traveler passed on the way to Jerusalem, a cacophony of cheers rose from the donkey cart. "The Messiah lives again! Yeshua has arisen to be the savior of the world! We have seen Yeshua Ha Meshiach risen! We are going to meet the Messiah!"

Several convoys slowed to hear the testimonies of the group and then hurried their pace toward Jerusalem to find out more. Some people shook their heads and scoffed.

"The sun has given you delusions, old woman."

"You've had too much to drink, old man. Let someone else drive that donkey."

"I've lived long enough to know that a dead man is a dead man, no matter who he thinks he is."

Caleb battled a confusing stream of excitement and unease. Excitement arose when he thought about his hometown and Yeshi again. Unease grew when he wondered how he should respond to Suzanna, walking beside him.

The blood of Barabbas runs through her veins, he reminded himself. *She is a woman of the streets.*

On the way down the hill, the group passed the site where Caleb and Sestus had rescued the merchants. His stomach twisted as he noticed that a few trees had been cut back from the edge of the road. The steep banks on either side aroused his anxiety and he repeatedly scanned the path for suspicious activity.

Suzanna nudged him as they walked. "How sincere was your plea for mercy?"

Caleb stopped in his tracks. "What do you mean?"

"I promised you that I would no longer plea for your love, but only for your mercy." She looked ahead at the group. "We need to keep walking. I can see that you're nervous."

Caleb reached out and touched her elbow. "I can see that you want to speak about something which you are also trying to avoid."

"I'm concerned about the hatred that has hardened your heart." She held out her hand to keep him from speaking. "Let me finish. I may not be the woman who will share your love, but no woman should have to share your hatred for another. Embrace the love of Yeshua and release these chains on you."

Caleb waited until he was sure Suzanna had finished. "Hatred fuels the anger which allows me to seek vengeance for my father." He increased his walking speed and Suzanna grabbed onto his arm to keep up. "It's Barabbas who stands in the way of everything I love. He has stolen my life, and even my chance for justice."

"Barabbas is only a man," Suzanna said, breathing heavily. "He's a man who set out to avenge his family, killed by the Romans. He chased his hatred, and he chased his revenge." She hurried in front of Caleb and stood her ground. "Do you want to become like Barabbas? Haunted by the faces you kill, trapped by your reputation, forced to live through your shame?"

Caleb stopped. "The man is a hero to the people. Perhaps his blood in your veins compromises your mind and your heart."

"He's just a man, Caleb. A man who lost the ones he loved. A man looking for answers in a world that seems to have no answers. He's a man confused by how the Almighty has freed him from certain death. He's just a man, like you."

"Don't you dare compare me to Barabbas," Caleb snarled. "I don't know what kind of man he is, and now I'm not sure what kind of woman you are."

Suzanna held out her arms to block Caleb as he tried to walk around her. "Hear this now, Caleb. I may have been a child of zealot rape. I may have given my body to men in order to survive. I may have done many things for which I bear shame." She let down her arms and looked up into his eyes. "But I have the blood of Yeshua running through my veins. I'm a new woman, ready for a new life. I see love in a clear way. If you don't forgive, you'll die a bitter old man."

"I don't want to die bitter."

The group made Jericho at nightfall and stayed in an inn, which had been arranged by the other disciples who had arrived several hours earlier. Caleb settled in with the men around the fire and listened as they shared more stories of Yeshua.

Early the next morning, Caleb found a caravan of merchants heading up to Tiberias and Sepphoris. He connected his small group with the larger one, then stocked up on provisions for the rest of the journey, including a handful of Jericho's special dates. It would be two days of steady travel up to Galilee.

The merchants kept their carts rumbling along on the roadways within sight of the Jordan. They made frequent stops for shade and water, as there were many elderly and young in the caravan.

Just after midday, the six elderly women chose to leave the group while the merchants pressed on. Caleb made sure the older women were settled in the shade of a palm before rejoining the caravan.

Suzanna tugged at his mantle as they walked. "We can't go on and leave these old women alone. There's still the danger of bandits."

Caleb scanned the road both ways. Small convoys had appeared in both directions, the Jordan was close enough for water, and frequent groves of palm trees provided shade. He also knew that the women would encounter towns and merchants at regular intervals along this route.

"The Romans have cleared the roads," Caleb said. "The bandits are afraid of the crosses now that Barabbas has been captured."

"But Barabbas is free. Pilate freed him when the people chose him over Yeshua. And the bandits grow bolder than ever. Didn't you hear the talk at Jericho?" She tilted her head, coaxing him. "The Romans have a new centurion who isn't yet prepared for this region. This is the perfect time for them to strike."

"Then why would we stay? Surely they would attack the merchants rather than a few elderly pilgrims."

Suzanna put her hands on her hips and furrowed her eyebrows. "Then let us remain out of compassion."

"The sons and daughters of these women should be here to guard them," Caleb said, shrugging.

Suzanna lowered her arms and backed away, eyeing him.

Caleb finally surrendered. "Okay, we can walk them to the next village. They can rest there until the next caravan comes."

Suzanna smiled, twirled around, and skipped back toward the elderly ladies resting in the shade.

The rest of Suzanna's group chose to go on with the merchants. Caleb assured the two sword-carrying guardians that they would be fine on their own. He then ensured that Eliab and his donkey carried the bulk of the women's belongings to make the journey easier.

They all made farewells and promises to meet at the next town.

As the group sipped water and nibbled on dates, Caleb took time to get to know the ladies.

Sarah, the matriarch of the group, was originally from Cana and she had a tongue as sharp as any Roman sword. She laughed from her belly. Leah, tall and slender, fought to hide her age. Only tinges of grey showed beneath her bright crimson scarf. She was passionate about the Messiah, and she was apparently the best cook among the women. Miriam was hefty and short, puffing at every step along the way. She was the best storyteller. Naomi held her head high, betraying some relation with nobility, and dressed in fine fashion compared to the others; she rarely spoke unless directly questioned. Elizabeth had been healed of leprosy by Yeshua and she was still self-conscious about being too close to others. She frequently examined her hands and turned them from back to front. Lastly, there was Bathsheba, self-conscious about her name. She had once been a slave, sold young to please the lusts of Roman soldiers. Abandoned when she'd crippled her ankle, she too was grateful to Yeshua for his healing touch on her body and mind.

An hour later, Caleb came to believe that Suzanna was a prophetess for having warned him about bandits. A cloud of dust from a group of charging horsemen formed on the road behind them and Caleb prayed that it was Roman legionnaires, but he feared the worst. These horsemen didn't ride in formation like the Romans, and he didn't even have a carpenter's knife to defend them.

He instructed the elderly group to join him and Suzanna in a grove of trees off to the side of the road. They were too slow, though, and Caleb urged them to circle up. Miriam was huffing behind as Suzanna supported her by the elbow. Bathsheba and Elizabeth attempted to hide behind the others, but Sarah stood out front with Caleb as if she believed she could protect her troop.

The bandits charged off the road and formed a circle of sweating mounts all around them. Their spiked metal helmets and thick vests added to the intimidation of their drawn swords.

"Lay down your jewelry and your coins," the leader shouted, his weapon swinging menacingly. "Or today you have made your last pilgrimage."

Sarah raised her fist. "Look at us, you scoundrel. Do you think we have what it takes to go on another pilgrimage?" She waved her arms over the group. "Do we look like we're loaded with jewelry and coins? Does your mother know what you do?"

Caleb stepped forward. "I alone have any possession of value. These pilgrims are elderly and poor. They've spent all they had for sacrifices in Jerusalem."

"And what possessions do you carry?" the swordsmen asked. "Show me!"

Caleb reached into his bag, pulled out the crimson-tipped nails, and held them up above his head.

"Iron spikes?" the bandit mocked. "What value is there in iron spikes?"

"These are the spikes designed for Barabbas and taken by the Messiah of Israel," he said. "We are witnesses that this Messiah died, was buried, and rose again on the third day. The blood on these nails was shed so that the life of Barabbas could be spared. It is reason enough to spare ours as well."

"What is the name of this Messiah?" demanded the leader. "This country spawns them."

"We follow Yeshua Ha Meshiach of Nazareth," Suzanna spoke up. "We have watched him die and seen him risen again."

"I know the man," the bandit leader said. "He healed my sister. His words are mysteries, but he does many good things."

Caleb watched three of the bandits dismount.

"We are going to him now," Caleb said. "In Galilee."

"Barabbas is a patriot and you speak with courage," the leader acknowledged. "If this Messiah truly lives again, perhaps he will yet rid us of these Romans. If he can show that their crosses are powerless, we shall never fear again."

"Change your ways," Caleb said. "Rome is more powerful than you can imagine."

The horseman moved his mount directly toward Caleb. "Are you not afraid to die?"

Caleb turned when he heard shrieks behind him. Two of the bandits had taken hold of Bathsheba. Naomi was pulling at one of the men and Miriam was lying on the ground holding onto one of her legs.

"I am more afraid not to live," Caleb replied.

Suzanna picked up a rock and hit one of the aggressors on the side of his helmet. The man released his hold on Bathsheba and reached for his sword. Caleb kicked him in the side of the knee and pounced on him. He grabbed the sword and held it to the bandit's neck.

Caleb looked up at the leader, still mounted. "I believe we have nothing more to offer you."

"Well said," the leader agreed, sheathing his sword. He looked down at the bandit with the sword at his throat. "We can't waste our time here. The merchants ahead may reach the village before we catch them." He turned back to Caleb. "Guard carefully the nails of Barabbas. They have let you live another day."

Caleb stepped back from the fallen bandit and returned his sword. In his other hand, he raised the iron spikes.

"These are the nails of life for me," Caleb said.

"Indeed they are," the leader agreed as he pulled his horse back toward the road.

The band of bandits raced off in a cloud of dust.

Chapter Twenty-Five

Jericho to Galilee, 30 A.D.

The upcoming phase of the journey was peaceful, although each of the elderly women had plenty to say. Caleb shouted "Hosanna" and hugged each of the women when the group reached the next village.

Eliab met them near the town well and shared the news that the larger caravan had safely made the protection of the village only moments before a band of raiders had ridden by on the road. He let the women tell about their encounter with the bandits.

Eliab showed the ladies the inn he had reserved for them. Caleb was left to find his own place in the hay, with the livestock.

That night, a group of travelers sang and danced around the fire. Caleb watched the festivities, reviewed his conversations with Suzanna, and drifted off to sleep.

During the night, a dark dream haunted him. Barabbas hung on the cross Caleb had made, screaming for mercy. Yeshua was there, too, wanting to give forgiveness, but Caleb stood in the way, demanding that justice be paid. In the vision, Caleb had felt his heart shrinking, hardening, until his own life began to fade away. He woke up sweating.

He felt the urge to get up, so he took a walk through the village. Caleb saw a few Roman sentries and a caravan driver standing at their posts, after which he stopped by the well and used the bucket to get a drink. Finally, he walked the edges of the fading fire next to the inn. The night was silent apart from the heavy breathing of tired travelers and the occasional snores of the donkey.

While rounding the fire, Caleb noticed a man huddled against a tree, his head resting on his own knees. Caleb heard the man groan and moved to see if he needed help. When Caleb was within three steps of the hunched figure, the man picked up his head, saw Caleb, and sprang to his feet with a knife drawn.

Barabbas!

Caleb backed away and looked around quickly for a weapon with which to defend himself. Anything would do… maybe a rock or stick from the fire…

Barabbas took a step forward, staring. "Is that you, carpenter?"

"Which carpenter do you mean?"

Only five more steps to the fire…

Barabbas took another step forward, holding his knife out to the side. "The carpenter of Nazareth who carries my mark. The one who fights like a lion. The friend of the Messiah."

"I am Caleb of Nazareth, friend of Yeshua Ha Meshiach."

Three more steps.

Barabbas's eyes looked haunted in the flickering firelight. "He died for me, you know."

As the zealot lowered his knife, Caleb took another step toward the fire. But he stopped.

"What do you mean?" Caleb asked.

Barabbas dropped the knife. "The people chose him to die instead of me. I'm a dead man. I cannot live." The zealot took a step back. "Take the knife. Do what you must. I cannot run any longer."

Caleb looked around for an ambush, but nothing moved in the darkness.

Almighty God, is this what you are calling me to do? he prayed.

Barabbas fell to his knees and waited.

A deep anguish came over Caleb, and he too sank to his knees. "The Messiah has died for both of us. He has forgiven you for killing my father and Sestus. He has forgiven me for killing Deborah and your child."

Barabbas furrowed his eyebrows and then lowered his head to the ground, weeping.

Now what do I do?

Caleb crawled the few steps between them and laid his hand on the zealot's back. Nearby, the knife glistened in the firelight.

No further words were said. When their grief was fully expressed, Barabbas rose up and walked away into the darkness. Caleb returned to sit in the hay with the animals.

The group stayed the night and then paid a cavalry of six Romans to escort them, along with another caravan, the rest of the way to Nazareth. When they reached the familiar hills, Sarah ordered the cart to stop and called for Eliab to lead them in prayers of thanksgiving. Bathsheba, Elizabeth, and Leah stepped off the cart and tested their legs. Suzanna helped them and then joined in an impromptu dance with Sarah.

"May the Almighty bless you with his peace," Eliab declared. "I will escort these women to their homes nearby and we will meet the Messiah soon near Capernaum on the lake, where he told us to meet him."

"Suzanna and I will stay in Nazareth for a few days and join you later if we can," Caleb said.

"May the Almighty bless you with his peace," Eliab said.

Sarah smiled at him. "May he prosper you and keep you strong and courageous."

Caleb paid off the caravan leader for his protection and helped the women back into the cart to resume their journey.

Once they were alone, Caleb led Suzanna to the road running toward the village where he had grown up. The forests stretched out their welcoming limbs and he felt again the freshness of the Galilean air. He took in the familiarity of the birdsong and smiled as a young fawn twisted amidst wildflowers in a meadow. He looked across the hills toward Sepphoris, an odd ache gripping his chest. Never again would he hear the voices of Sestus or Yeshi in this place.

Suzanna rested her hand on his back, breaking him out of his trance. "Caleb, what do I say to Yeshua's family?"

Caleb took her hand and squeezed it. "They may not even be in Nazareth anymore. So much has changed over the years." He pointed out a swarm of bees buzzing around a hive in an olive tree. "Life continues as it always has. I have much to learn, and so do you."

"And how will I learn everything?"

He swung their arms as they walked. "I will tell you one story of Yeshua when he was young with me, and you will tell me one teaching you learned from Yeshua when he was older with you."

"Okay. Start with any easy one."

Caleb smiled. "Let me tell you Yeshua's story from the beginning…"

The miles passed and several times Caleb and Suzanna simply stood in the shade of a tree and lost themselves in the life of the Messiah who had pulled them both together.

When Caleb began to tell the story of the day the zealots had killed his father, he sobbed. Suzanna held onto his arm and did her best to comfort him.

"What a terrible day," she said. "The Almighty knows your pain. He cares for your soul, Caleb."

A layer of numbness fell away from his heart. "Suzanna, please, have mercy. I don't know if my heart can hold this pain. I'm not sure whether I'm beginning to live or beginning to die."

"Caleb," she whispered, "I have two more things I must tell you before all your mercy for me has gone."

He held out his hand to stop her, then bent over and secured his hands on his knees. He took several deep breaths.

"Speak freely," he said.

Suzanna stepped off the road and backed up against an ancient olive tree. She patted the place beside her and sank down to the ground. When Caleb was seated beside her, she looked away into the forest.

"My mother was stoned to death by the religious leaders as an immoral woman. My father…" She paused. "…was crucified by the centurion you obeyed. When I first saw you, I knew I could never soften my heart toward a cross maker. But Yeshua taught me many things about love. The feelings I have toward you are a testimony that our Creator can still do the impossible."

Caleb pushed himself up off the ground and stood over her. "Are you telling me that you didn't come for flute lessons?" He walked away a few steps, looking up to the heavens and raising his arms. "Almighty God, what other surprises do you have for me?"

"I took those flute lessons to test my heart," Suzanna admitted. "I knew if I could be in the same space as the one responsible for leaving me an orphan, surely Yeshua had kept his promise to change my heart."

"Are you here now to test my heart?" he asked. "You're the child of an immoral woman who was stoned to death. Your father was crucified by Sestus on a cross which I made. You're a cousin of Barabbas, and you only came near me to test your heart. Is that right?"

Suzanna's face turned red, but she gritted her teeth and shook her head slowly. "My mother was raped by a zealot, an uncle to Barabbas. She had been betrothed to a Pharisee in a very powerful family. Yes, my father was a childhood friend of hers who rescued her from her fate and secretly took her away from her village. They raised me until my mother was discovered. The religious leaders tore her from my arms and stoned her right in front of me. I tried to protect her, but they held me until she died."

She stood up and began to sob.

Caleb held her, comforting her, whispering the same words of comfort she had spoken to him.

When Suzanna settled, she eased herself out of his arms and began to walk again. "My father was a good man. He was falsely accused of being a zealot because he grew apricots and gave them freely to the men who stopped by our home." She bent down and picked up a stone, tossing it at a tree. She hit it squarely.

"Remind me never to get you angry at me," Caleb said. "Your aim is better than King David's."

Suzanna smiled. "If you had the heart, there's much you could learn about me." She turned, hesitating. "But there's one more hard thing to tell you. I was taken by the soldiers for their own pleasures. I was sold in a market in Caesarea and used for the pleasures of men until I ran away."

Caleb reached out for her. "None of that is your fault."

Suzanna nodded. "I went to Jerusalem to hide, but the only life I knew was with men. I gave myself freely so that I could live. For this, I cannot beg your mercy or forgiveness. I only ask you to believe that Yeshua has changed my heart, and he is still changing it."

Caleb felt helpless. Suzanna stood limply before him, having poured out her life. It was as if Barabbas was handing him his knife again.

He filled his lungs with a big breath of fresh Galilean air. "Perhaps he can yet change mine," Caleb mused. "Let's finish this walk to Nazareth."

The familiar sound of barking dogs greeted the pair and Caleb found himself smiling at the old man who hobbled to the gates of Nazareth with his cane.

"Samuel, I'm Caleb ben Samson, returned home again."

The aging gatekeeper's poor hearing allowed him to understand just enough to get his messages mixed up. "The Samsons? No. They've all gone away."

Caleb tried introducing himself again, after which Samuel smiled and invited them to his house for tea.

"Yes, bring your lovely wife and we'll catch up on old times," Samuel said.

Samuel was completely confused when Caleb told him that Suzanna wasn't his wife.

After tea, Samuel took them on a tour of the neighborhood. Yuseph and Miriam's home had deteriorated in the past year, since there was no one taking care of it. The roof had a sizeable hole in it above the kitchen and a few boards had come loose. Weeds had grown in through the doorways and up through the floor. Nonetheless, Suzanna was fascinated to see where Yeshi had slept.

Caleb's former home was now nothing more than a fenced-off yard for goats and sheep.

As the group walked through the village, more children, dogs, and even adults joined their little entourage.

"Is it true?" Samuel asked. "Yeshua ben Yuseph was crucified by the Romans for blasphemy? He was always one who honored the Almighty. How could this have happened?"

Caleb wrestled to answer as best he could. "It's true… it's true that he was crucified, but he did not blaspheme. And he did not stay dead. He's alive!"

Samuel stopped midstride and leaned harder on his cane. "How is such a thing possible? A dead man is a dead man."

For the next few hours, Caleb and Suzanna took turns telling their personal experiences and memories of the Messiah. Caleb even pulled out the old iron nails as evidence, and this drew horror and fascination from the listeners.

"I still remember the year Yeshi and I were preparing to be men," Caleb said. "A week before my twelfth birthday, I walked into Yuseph's carpenter shop." He pointed to the place. "I slammed the door behind me. Shavings jumped and skittered and scattered. The smell of freshly planed wood hung in the air."

One of the young girls ran to Caleb and extended her arms for him to pick her up. Caleb hoisted her onto his hip.

"What did you make?" she asked.

"I'll tell you if you let me finish my story," Caleb said, tweaking her nose. She giggled. "I perched like a stork against the wall and shook out the gritty gravel that had gotten lodged between my sandal and my sole. The gurgle in my gut reminded me that the urgency of my search had already come at some sacrifice—"

"I don't know what you're talking about," a small boy interrupted.

"Let me finish. My eyes quickly adjusted to the dim interior and focused in on my target. A hooded figure. Kneeling. Head bowed. A young man preparing for his first pilgrimage."

"Who was it?" the boy asked.

"Shhh!" the girl in Caleb's arms urged. "Let him finish!"

Caleb smiled and nodded at the boy. "I said, 'Yeshi! Forget Jerusalem. Passover can wait another year. The walls of Sepphoris need builders now. The Parthians have started their spring raids.'"

"How did the Messiah respond?" Suzanna asked.

"Already he was focused on the Almighty and I was blind to it. He could never forget Jerusalem. To me, he was just another carpenter in training."

Caleb set the little girl down and turned to follow Samuel along another path. The others followed.

"When I interrupted Yeshi, he hesitated a moment, removed his prayer shawl, and bounced to his feet. 'So are we now reduced to these choices?' he asked. 'Chisel or sword? Caleb, what about prayer? Has the Almighty abandoned us?'"

Several of the elderly residents who knew Caleb's family surged in to welcome Caleb and listen to his tale. Caleb hugged an old woman he hadn't seen in a long time.

"Before Yeshua's first pilgrimage, he was already looking to the Almighty," a neighbor confirmed. "How did you respond?"

"I said, 'We need all the tools we can get. Look at our shops. I'm reduced to whittling flutes. I haven't made a yoke or a plow in a year. The Romans have stripped the cedars of Lebanon for their forts. The Parthians leave us guarding our wild olives for food to keep us alive. The wood is gone. Building Sepphoris is our only hope to feed our families.'"

"So it was," another neighbor chimed in. "What did the Messiah do next?"

"Yeshi reached for a folded cloth on the carpenter's bench and opened it up. Inside were two barley loaves, a few chunks of goat cheese, some dates, and a handful of green olives. 'My mother said you would probably be hungry,' he said. 'If we're going to hike over to Sepphoris, we'll need some strength. The hand of the Almighty is open. Blessed be our God, King of the universe, who causes bread to come out of the earth.'"

One of neighbors nodded. "He did love to bless the Almighty."

"I spoke to him about being an orphan because my father was never home and my mother was dying of leprosy," Caleb said. "He always spoke kindly of others. Even my father. I still remember his words: 'Your father tries his best, Caleb.' He knew that my mother's leprosy was hard on my father."

"It was a hard time for your father," Samuel said.

Caleb took hold of the old man's cane and tugged at it playfully. "That's when I grabbed him and told him that unless I worked and provided soon, I would be nothing more than a goatherder. 'Let's go,' I urged him. 'Sepphoris awaits.'"

"We have survived because of Sepphoris," another neighbor declared. "You're welcome in this place as long as you need."

"I have two rooms in my home," a widow offered. "My Zacharia was one of the carpenters killed by the zealots. I remember how you went out to bring us justice. Whatever happened to that murderer?"

"Allow us to settle into your home," Caleb said. "We will pay for our food and lodging. I'm still an able carpenter and I'll help you with any projects that remain undone. We await the Messiah's return, but tonight I will tell you about Barabbas."

Weeks later, after making or repairing tables, chairs, cribs, animal troughs, and roofs for dozens of the residents in Nazareth, Caleb and Suzanna went for a walk through an olive grove. As they chatted, a young man came running out to them.

"He was here!" the man shouted. "He was here! The Messiah came and showed himself to hundreds of us. The fishermen were down on the lake and he appeared to them as well. It's true. He's alive!"

"Where is he now?" Caleb called as the young man turned away to run up the road. "Where can we meet him?"

"He's gone. He vanished before our eyes, but he is alive."

Caleb ran after the young man. "He can't be gone. He promised to meet us here."

The young man kept running, yelling his news to anyone who would listen, so Caleb stopped and returned to Suzanna.

"Maybe we'll see Yeshi if we wait in Nazareth a little longer," Caleb mused. "He's already been in Capernaum. Why wouldn't he come home?"

"Caleb, I don't think Yeshi will be back here," Suzanna said.

"Why not?"

She smiled and pointed up. "Yeshi told us that his home was not in this world. He told us that we weren't to let our hearts feel troubled, because he was going home to make room for us."

Caleb sat down on a rock by the roadside. "But I brought you all the way here to meet with him. I came here to meet with him!"

Suzanna draped her hands around his shoulders. "I think the Almighty knew exactly what needed to happen on this trip."

"I'm sorry you missed your Messiah."

She took Caleb's hand and laid it against her cheek. "I didn't miss my Messiah. I walked with him and talked with him." She stood up and pulled Caleb to his feet. "He healed me of my past and taught me how to live. He gave me the freedom and peace to dare to love again."

"What are you saying?"

"Only that you and I have no one else in the world who belongs to us. If you can agree, then I believe the Almighty has brought us together as witnesses of something special."

Caleb squeezed Suzanna's hand and followed as she quickened her pace on the way back to the village.

"Tell me," Caleb said, "what do you and I have that is so special compared to everyone else in the world? How can we be witnesses?"

She pulled Caleb to a stop and touched his beard where it covered the scar around his neck. "You and I have faced death and life. Our hardened hearts have been changed. We've learned to love instead of to hate. We 've learned to forgive and to be forgiven."

Caleb placed his hand over Suzanna's hand, still resting against his cheek. "How do you know I no longer hate? How do you know I have learned to forgive?"

"I saw you with Barabbas by the fire. He tested you. You didn't reach for the knife."

"I couldn't find the hate to do what I wanted. When I saw him on his knees, he was just a man. A man whom Yeshi had forgiven."

"And in seeing that Barabbas was just a man, you saw that you were just a man."

Caleb cupped Suzanna's chin. "You saw me and yet said nothing until now?"

Suzanna pushed away from, laughing. "If you can dare to love again, I would want to grow together in that love with you. Perhaps the Messiah needs witnesses in other places where we can travel and share our stories."

Caleb took five quick steps to Suzanna, caught her by the wrist, and pulled her back toward him. He adjusted Suzanna's head covering. "I don't want to talk any longer about the crosses I made for Rome and the nails I carry as a debt for my arrogance and pride."

"Then bury the nails here in a place where they will never be found," Suzanna challenged him. "The shame is gone. The terror of the cross is gone. Those who believe without seeing will gain the blessing of the life we offer."

Caleb took out the pouch and unrolled the cloth covering the crimson-tipped spikes. He used two of the spikes to dig a hole under the surface root of a pistachio tree. When the hole was deep enough, he rolled the nails up in the cloth and laid them in the hole. He then reached up and ran his fingers along a deep scar in the trunk—a scar made by his own axe, when he had still been young. When his father had died nearby.

He turned to Suzanna. "Can you respect a man who helped kill your Messiah?"

"My Messiah is alive," she said. "I can respect a man who knows that the Messiah is alive, who lives like he's alive, and who's not afraid to tell others."

Caleb looked down at the spikes in the hole. "I know he's alive. He took the hate out of my heart." He pushed dirt over the nails. "This is the place where my hatred for Barabbas began, and this is where it will stay buried."

Suzanna stood back as Caleb stepped on the soft ground covering the nails, making it firm. He then covered it with stones and leaves.

Caleb looked long at the sun glistening off Suzanna's long dark hair.

"I can respect you, but can you love a woman with my past?" she asked.

"Only the Almighty truly knows our past. I believe he's calling us to grow into our future." He reached up and brushed a tear from her cheek. "It will take time, but I believe in a God who can even change the heart of a cross maker."

"We have no parents and no families to arrange things for us."

Caleb took her hand and walked out into a clearing. "I'm sure if the Almighty has worked out everything else, he can fix that, too." Caleb looked toward the towering gates of Sepphoris rising on the hill above them. "All I wanted so long ago was to build a trophy of wood to be a source of peace for the world. That's all I wanted."

"Perhaps your cross will be that source of peace in ways we still don't understand," said Suzanna. "Come and show me this famous city of Sepphoris. Show me the tile mosaics built by your friend and his father. Show me the place where you built your first crosses. Show me your life."

"I will show you," Caleb agreed. "On one condition."

"What's that?"

"As soon as we're done looking at the city, we must walk immediately to meet a rabbi I know in Cana. He'll know how to help us become one together."

"Yeshua will make us one," Suzanna said.

"I'm sure he will. If Yeshua can change me to forgive Barabbas, then helping me to love you like you deserve will be no challenge for him at all." He paused, smiling. "There's one great gift the Almighty has given me besides you."

"And what gift is that?"

"That the one person I never got to see on my cross is Barabbas."

Other Books In This Series

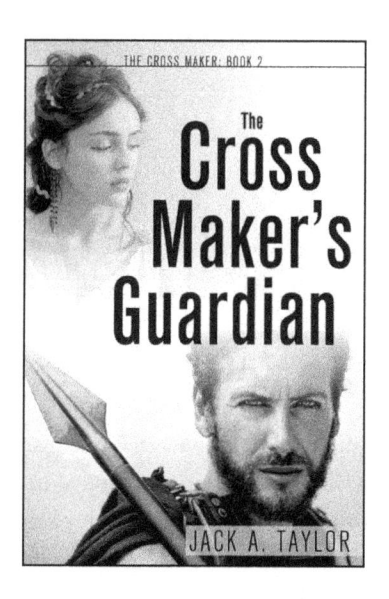

The Cross Maker's Guardian
ISBN: 978-1-4866-1858-3

Roman legions thunder across first-century Palestine, seeking to use the power of the cross to crush the lightning strikes of the zealots led by Barabbas. Behind the scenes, a secret squad of thespian assassins are being trained—and Titius Marcus Julianus is caught up in this silent whirlwind, conscripted to be the new guardian of the crossmaker, Caleb ben Samson.

Titius is fuelled by vengeance and love as he seeks to regain his stolen Roman estate and the young Jewish slave who once captured his heart. Meanwhile, voices from his past and present wrestle for control of his heart and mind.

In *The Cross Maker's Guardian*, Jack Taylor unveils the clash between the Roman and Jewish civilizations as they battle for life in a world suffused with international intrigue. Descriptive narrative, biblical history, and powerful characters all come alive in this thrilling read where death and love are only a blink away.

The Cross Maker's Champion
ISBN: 978-1-4866-1860-6

Persian slaves who fight for their lives in gladiator arenas rarely rise to be anyone's champion. But the wounded Nabonidus is soon wooed by two women—a priestess at the Temple of Diana and a humble follower of Yeshua, Daphne. Soon he must learn the truth about himself—is he a missing Persian prince or simply an unwanted orphan?

The arena claims whatever soul may venture there, and Alexander, a silversmith, joins forces with a giant German gladiator, Selsus, to confront the followers of The Way.

Meanwhile, Caleb, Suzanna, Titius, and Abigail fight through their own life-threatening challenges to join the Apostle John and Nabonidus in time. Soon the arena will be packed with chanting patrons. Who will still remain standing when the final blood is spilt?

Jack Taylor weaves his readers through a maze of Ephesian mysticism and terror as Roman and pagan powers combine to destroy the infant movement of The Way before it takes its first steps out of its birthplace.

Other Books by Jack A. Taylor

One Last Wave
ISBN: 978-1-7706-9261-9

Katrina [Katie] Joy Delancey has staked her life on keeping the past and future away from her heart. But she is no master of fate or captain of her own journey. *One Last Wave* is a story about being discovered by faith and love no matter where you are, no matter where you've been, and no matter what you think may lie ahead.

No Place to Run
ISBN: 978-1-7706-9786-7

No *Place to Run* continues the adventures of Katie Delancey, begun in *One Last Wave*. It's a story of rediscovering faith, hope, and love when the maze of life seems to close in around you… about realizing that the whispers of the past can be keys to your future.

Streching for Home
ISBN: 978-1-4866-0996-3

A blissful love nest amidst a brutal Minnesota winter turns into a fiery ordeal of grief and terror as Katie is caught up in the never-ending pursuit of human traffickers who want to eliminate her from their deadly game. *Stretching for Home* is an education into the heart of missionary kids searching for healing as life tumbles in around them. Their quest for home can be as elusive as a rainbow's pot of gold. Finding old roots and spreading new wings can be a challenge.

CPSIA information can be obtained
at www.ICGtesting.com
Printed in the USA
BVHW032125261119
564929BV00001B/21/P

9 781486 618569